Lincoln~~shire~~

KT-475-941

discover libraries

This book should be retur~~ned~~
the due d~~ate~~

DELI 2/20

09.

DIRTY
DOZEN

Lynda La Plante was born in Liverpool. She trained for the stage at RADA and worked with the National Theatre and RDC before becoming a television actress. She then turned to writing – and made her breakthrough with the phenomenally successful TV series *Widows*. Her novels have all been international bestsellers.

Her original script for the much-acclaimed *Prime Suspect* won awards from BAFTA, Emmy, British Broadcasting and Royal Television Society, as well as the 1993 Edgar Allan Poe Award. Lynda has written and produced over 170 hours of international television.

Lynda is one of only three screenwriters to have been made an honorary fellow of the British Film Institute and was awarded the BAFTA Dennis Potter Best Writer Award in 2000. In 2008, she was awarded a CBE in the Queen's Birthday Honours List for services to Literature, Drama and Charity.

If you would like to hear from Lynda, please sign up at www.bit.ly/ LyndaLaPlanteClub or you can visit www.lyndalaplante.com for further information. You can also follow Lynda on Facebook and Twitter @LaPlanteLynda.

Lynda La Plante

THE DIRTY DOZEN

ZAFFRE

First published in Great Britain in 2019
This paperback edition published in 2020 by
ZAFFRE
80–81 Wimpole St, London W1G 9RE

A CIP catalogue record for this book is
available from the British Library.

Hardback ISBN: 978–1–78576–850–7
Export ISBN: 978–1–78576–851–4
Paperback ISBN: 978–1–78576–852–1

Also available as an ebook

1 3 5 7 9 10 8 6 4 2

Typeset by IDSUK (Data Connection) Ltd
Printed and bound in Great Britain by Clays Ltd, Elcograf S.p.A.

Zaffre is an imprint of Bonnier Books UK
www.bonnierbooks.co.uk

*To celebrate the centenary of female officers
in the Metropolitan Police Service*

CHAPTER ONE

It was a rainy and overcast April morning as the brown 1976 Mark 4 Ford Cortina saloon parked up on the offside of Aylmer Road, a few metres down from the junction with Leytonstone High Road. The four men in the vehicle sat in silence as the engine slowly ticked over and the windscreen wipers swept away the rain. The men were dressed in blue boiler suits, heavy black donkey jackets and leather driving gloves. The heat from their bodies was making the windows mist up and the musty odour of sweat filled the car. The man in the back opened his window a couple of inches and the two men in the front used their jacket sleeves to wipe the condensation off the windscreen, so they could get a better view of Barclays Bank on the far side of the High Road. The bank manager was holding an umbrella as he opened the large wooden front doors for business at 9.30. Smartly dressed in a three-piece grey pinstripe suit, white shirt and tie, he stood to one side to let two customers in, and looked up the High Road, which was quieter than usual for a Thursday morning, due to the bad weather.

As the manager turned and walked back inside, the driver of the Cortina put a cap on and opened the car door. He hadn't seen the elderly lady pulling a canvas shopping trolley along the pavement, and narrowly missed hitting her with the door. The lady swore at him, but the driver ignored her and pulled the peak of his cap down, before walking towards the bank.

As the old lady moved off, one of the men in the back of the Cortina reached under the driver's seat and pulled out a twelve-bore, double-barrelled, sawn-off shotgun. He pushed the unlocking lever to one side to 'break' the gun, then placed a cartridge in each chamber. Holding the wooden stock of the gun with one hand, he snapped the barrel closed with a well-practised upward flick of his wrist, then slid the shotgun into a home-made pocket inside his jacket.

*   *   *

Jane drove up and down Rigg Approach twice, but couldn't see a police station or blue lamp anywhere. She was becoming frustrated and beginning to wonder if she'd got the right place, as she appeared to be in an industrial estate with a variety of different businesses. She parked her yellow Volkswagen Golf opposite a mobile burger van, and got out to speak to the owner. Pulling her coat up over her head, to protect her hair from the rain, she ran across the road.

'Excuse me, is there a police station near here?' she asked.

'There's no nick around here, luv . . . the nearest are Stoke Newington or Hackney – a couple of miles away, but in opposite directions.'

'I know where they are, but I'm looking for the Flying Squad offices, which I was told were in Rigg Approach.'

'The Sweeney work out of that place over there, not a nick,' he said, pointing to a two-storey, grey brick office building with a flat roof. 'I know most of the lads, as they're regulars at my van. Anyone in particular you're looking for?'

'The DCI. I've got an appointment with him.'

'Bill Murphy? That's his office on the top floor – far right. I don't think he's in yet, as he hasn't been down for his usual bacon and egg roll.'

'Thanks for your help.'

Jane crossed the road and on closer inspection thought the building looked run-down. Although there were large windows on both floors, the ground floor ones all had faded white metal Venetian blinds, which were closed. The metal front door had a numbered push-button entry pad above the handle, and an intercom on the wall beside it. As Jane pressed the button on the intercom, she wondered what the building would be like on the inside.

'How can I help you?' a female voice asked over the intercom.

'I'm WDS Tennison. I'm here to see DCI Murphy.'

'Is he expecting you?' the woman asked, in a haughty manner.

'Yes, he is. I start on the Flying Squad today and was told to report to his office for ten a.m.'

'It's only 9.30, and he didn't mention you to me – new officers generally start on Mondays.'

'I've been in court all week and . . . Look, I'm getting soaked out here. Can you please open the door or tell me the number for the entry pad?'

The woman sighed. 'I suppose so . . . The squad office is on the first floor.'

Jane thought the woman was rude and wondered if she was a detective on the squad or clerical staff. As she waited for the electronic lock to be released, she flapped her coat to remove some of the rain. As it was her first day on the Flying Squad, Jane wanted to look good and had worn a blue two-piece skirt suit, white blouse, stockings and black high-heeled shoes. She heard the electric lock on the door buzz, and leant forward to open it. Her hand was on the round knob when the door was pulled open with force from the inside, causing Jane to stumble forward. She felt a hand grab her arm tightly, stopping her from falling over.

'You all right, luv?' a deep male voice asked, as the man helped her straighten up.

Jane was dwarfed by the man. She noticed he had a pickaxe handle in his left hand. He was about six foot seven, with wide shoulders and a muscular frame. He had blond hair, blue eyes and boyish looks. He was dressed in a white England rugby shirt with the red rose emblem on the left breast.

'Come on, Bax, I need to get the motor fired up,' the man behind him said in a broad Scottish accent, as he used a pickaxe handle to usher Jane and Bax to one side. He looked to be in his late thirties, and although slightly smaller, at about six foot two, he had a large beer belly.

Bax frowned. 'All right, Cam, less haste more speed.'

Jane heard footsteps running down the metal stairs.

A male voice called out, 'Right, I'm tooled up, so we're good to go, Bax. The Guv and the Colonel are booking out their guns and will go in Cam's car. Teflon is on his way round the front with Dabs in the Triumph for us.'

Jane instantly recognised the voice of Detective Sergeant Stanley, who she had worked with on the 'Dip Squad' a few years ago. They had also been involved in the hunt for an active IRA unit that had bombed Covent Garden Tube Station. Stanley had helped to disarm a car bomb and been awarded the Queen's Police Medal for his bravery.

Jane looked up and saw the short, slim frame of Stanley tucking a police issue .38 revolver into a shoulder holster under his brown leather jacket. He still had his long, dark, straggly hair, but had grown a 'Jason King' style moustache, which on first sight didn't suit him.

'Hi, Stanley.' Jane waved. She still didn't know what his Christian name was, as everyone just called him 'Stanley'.

'Tennison, what are you doing here?'

'I've been transferred to the Flying Squad.'

'Have you? That's news to me.'

'And me,' Bax said.

Jane thought it strange that no one seemed to know about her transfer, and began to wonder if she'd got the right starting day.

'Are you off on a shout?' she asked.

'Yeah, we just got a call from Information Room. There might be a blagging about to go down in Leytonstone. Gotta go, so I'll catch up with you later.'

Stanley hurried out of the building with Bax.

Jane started to walk up the stairs when two more men appeared, armed with .38 revolvers carried in belt holsters around their waists. The man in front was wearing a blue baseball cap and tight white T-shirt, which accentuated his muscular frame and large biceps. As he hurried down the stairs two at a time, Jane moved quickly to one side to let him pass.

The man behind wasn't rushing and stopped in front of Jane. He had a chiselled jawline, defined cheekbones and a slightly misshapen nose, which looked like it had been broken in a fight. He wasn't dressed casually like the others, and wore a tailored slim-fit grey suit and white open-neck shirt. He sniffed and stared at Jane with narrow eyes.

'You Tennison?'

'Yes, sir,' she replied, sensing his air of authority.

'I'm DI Kingston. We're short on the ground today as some of the team are out with the surveillance squad on another job, so you may as well come with us.'

'What, to Leytonstone?'

'No, to a tea party,' he replied, drily.

'DCI Murphy was expecting—'

'He's not back from Scotland Yard yet, so come on, shift your backside.'

Kingston had the swagger of a confident man and Jane followed him out to the street, where she saw Stanley sitting in the front of a dark green four-door Triumph 2500S, which had a blue magnetic flashing light on top of it. A black man was driving and Bax was in the back, with a diminutive-looking man wearing dark glasses next to him. Behind the Triumph, Cam was in the driver's seat of a four-door black BMW 525i, again with a flashing light on the roof and its engine running.

'We're in the Beamer,' Kingston told her.

'Come on, Guv!' the man in the white T-shirt shouted from the back seat of the BMW.

Kingston got in the front passenger seat as Jane ran around the back of the car and got in behind Cam, but there was little room for her legs as the driver's seat was almost as far back as it would go. No sooner was she in the car than Cam pulled the automatic gearstick to Drive, and pushed the accelerator pedal to the floor. The car took off at high speed, causing Jane to jolt backwards, and it felt like someone had pushed her hard in the chest as her back slammed against the seat. As Cam braked at the T-junction, she felt her body lurch forward, but just managed to get her hands on the back of his seat to brace herself before her head hit it. The Colonel had his feet firmly propped up against the front passenger seat and a large London *A-Z* open on his lap.

'Fastest route is left onto Lea Bridge Road, then right—'

'I've worked this manor for years, so I know how to get there, Colonel,' Cam said calmly, and turned the siren on.

Kingston opened the glove box and picked up the radio mike.

'MP from Central 888, receiving, over?'

'Yes, go ahead, Central 888, MP, over,' a male voice replied.

'We are en route with Central 887 to Aylmer Road and the men acting suspiciously near Barclays Bank. Any updates?'

'The vehicle is still in situ. It's a brown Mark 4 Ford Cortina, 1.6 litre saloon, index Sierra Lima Mike 273 Romeo. The vehicle is not reported stolen and may have false plates as the PNC shows a blue Mark 4, 1.6 GL saloon with a registered keeper in Sussex.'

'Can you give me the informant's details, please?' Kingston got out his pocket notebook and pen.

'Fiona Simpson. She's the landlady of the Crown public house on the High Road and corner of Aylmer. She lives on the premises and noticed the suspect vehicle parked up with its engine running and wipers on. The driver has left the vehicle and turned right into the High Road, out of sight of the informant. He's wearing a grey cap, black donkey jacket and blue overalls.'

'Number of other occupants in the Cortina?' Kingston asked.

'The informant can only see the nearside of the vehicle. One male in the front passenger seat and another male behind him, both wearing dark clothing.'

Kingston ran his hand through his hair.

'There could be a robbery about to take place, MP. We and Central 887 are armed gunships. Our ETA is about four minutes, so tell uniform to hold back until we get there.'

'Received and understood . . . we will advise you of any developments . . . MP, over.'

Jane felt uneasy. As it was her first day on the infamous 'Sweeney', she wasn't sure what was expected of her, especially if DI Kingston was right in thinking an armed robbery was about to take place.

* * *

The driver of the Cortina returned to the car.

'She's coming,' he said, as he got in the car and put on a full-face balaclava, which had a mouth and eye holes cut out.

The two men in the back also put on balaclavas, but the man in the front passenger seat pulled a light brown stocking over his head, which distorted the features of his face. Having adjusted the stocking so it was comfortable, he reached into his jacket pocket and took out a Second World War 9mm German Luger, then pulled back the toggle, which loaded a bullet from the magazine into the chamber.

The four men sat and watched as the blue Ford Transit Securicor van pulled up outside the bank. The driver remained in the van while his colleague went to the rear and looked up and down the High Road, before knocking three times, pausing and then knocking twice.

The passenger from the front of the Cortina and the two men from the back got out of the car and strode with purpose towards the bank. The men knew exactly what they had to do, as everything had been well planned thanks to the information they had received about the cash-in-transit delivery. They knew from experience that robbing the Securicor van should take no more than a minute. As the cash box appeared in the chute at the rear of the van, the three men pounced with military precision.

* * *

Jane was beginning to feel nauseous due to the speed Cam was driving and the way he was skidding the car around corners and roundabouts in the rain. She'd been in police pursuits before, but never encountered high-speed driving as dangerous as this.

'This is our new WDS, Jane Tennison,' Kingston told the others, as he lit a cigarette and handed one to the Colonel.

The rim of the Colonel's cap cast a shadow over his steely eyes and accentuated his high cheekbones and dimpled chin.

'Hello,' Jane said.

'You really been posted to the squad?' the Colonel asked as he lit his cigarette.

'Yes, sir.' She put her hand out to shake his.

He didn't reciprocate. 'Well, you've got a bit more essence than most plonks.'

Jane didn't have a clue what he meant by 'essence' and wasn't sure she should ask.

Kingston laughed. 'Gorman's not an officer – he's an ex-corporal and just a lowly DC, who thinks you're better looking than most female officers.'

Jane blushed, embarrassed that the Colonel thought she had 'essence'.

'My father was a soldier and served in the Second World War.'

He glared at her as he pulled up the sleeve of his T-shirt, revealing a globe with a laurel wreath on either side and an anchor at the bottom, with the Latin words *Per Mare, Per Terram* underneath.

'I'm a Bootneck not a Pongo! I was a Marine Commando in the Royal Navy before I joined the Met. My name's Ken, but this bunch of knobheads decided to call me the Colonel. The tattoo is the Marines' insignia and the Latin means "By Sea, By Land".'

'Ironic really as he can't swim,' Cam laughed.

'Shut up, OFD,' the Colonel said, and looked at Jane. 'In case you're wondering, OFD means "only the fucking driver", and he's only a temporary DC.'

'I like to think of myself as a shit-hot taxi driver without whom they'd get nowhere,' Cam replied, as he went the wrong way around a roundabout to turn right.

Kingston smiled. 'As much as we all hate to admit it, Constable Cameron Murray is the best Class 1 driver in the Met. He even souped up this car's engine himself so it outperforms every other Flying Squad vehicle.'

Jane could sense the mutual bond of respect and camaraderie among the officers and felt a bit of an outsider. She instinctively knew that she would have to prove herself a capable detective if she wanted to become part of the team.

'What should I do when we get there?' she asked, wanting to show her enthusiasm.

'Stay in the car with Cam,' Kingston and the Colonel said in unison.

'Central 888 from MP, receiving, over?' the same male voice from the Met's control room asked over the radio.

'888 receiving,' Kingston replied.

'A Securicor van has pulled up at the bank and three men dressed in blue boiler suits, donkey jackets and head masks have just left the vehicle.'

'They're going to rob the van, not the bank,' Kingston said calmly. 'We're about two minutes away and approaching silent,' he replied.

Cam switched off the car's siren.

* * *

The man with the sawn-off shotgun tapped the Securicor driver's window with the barrel and rotated his finger, indicating to him to wind it down, which the driver quickly did. The man leant into the van and pulled the key from the ignition, then spoke in a deep tone to disguise his natural voice.

'Keep your hands on the steering wheel. You so much as twitch towards the horn or alarm and I'll blow your fucking head off.'

The Securicor driver shook with fear as he nodded, and gripped the steering wheel so hard his knuckles turned white.

The man with the Luger was at the back of the van, pushing the barrel of the gun into the neck of the other Securicor guard, who was frozen to the spot. The unarmed robber grabbed the metal case with the money in it from the guard's hand and pushed him down onto his knees. He leant forward and whispered, so as not to alert the security guard in the back of the van.

'Tell him to put the other case in the chute.'

The guard's voice trembled as he said, 'There's only the one.'

The robber shook his head. 'Don't lie, son . . . I don't want to hurt you, but I will if you don't do exactly what I tell you.'

'Frank, George . . . What's happening out there? Is everything all right?' the third guard shouted from inside the van.

The man with the Luger moved around and put the gun to the forehead of the kneeling guard.

'Last chance, son . . . Tell him to put the fucking case in the chute.'

The guard was unable to stop shaking and the fear in his voice was evident.

'Everything's fine. You can send out the other case.'

Suddenly the van's alarm went off, closely followed by the sound of a shotgun being fired once. The two robbers at the back of the van ran to the front and saw their colleague standing over a young man lying on the ground, clutching his stomach and crying out in pain. The robber with the shotgun was breathing heavily, causing a white foam of spittle to build up around the mouth hole of his balaclava.

'The fucking idiot tried to get the shotgun off me.'

The unarmed man raised his hand to shut his colleague up. The man with the Luger turned and headed back to the rear of the van, intent on getting the second cash box. The unarmed robber grabbed him by the arm, shook his head and pulled him towards the Cortina, which skidded to a halt beside the Securicor van.

* * *

'Central 888 from MP, receiving, over?'

'Go ahead 888, over,' Kingston replied.

'Sounds of gunshots heard outside the bank. Local uniform units requesting permission to move in.'

'ETA, Cam?' a concerned-looking Kingston asked.

Cam hit the accelerator. 'A minute, tops, Guv.'

'MP from 888, local units can move in. Is India 99 in the air?' Kingston asked, referring to the police helicopter's call sign.

'No, at present 99 is refuelling, but should be airborne shortly.'

Kingston threw the radio mike against the dashboard.

'Fuck it. They'll be well on their toes before we get there!'

'Central 888, update from MP. Call received for an ambulance to Barclays Bank, Leytonstone . . . One man shot in stomach by an armed suspect.'

The Colonel punched the roof of the car.

'Bastards. If I get my hands on 'em I'll fuckin' kill 'em!'

* * *

As the two armed robbers jumped into the Cortina, the unarmed man put the Securicor cash box in a travel bag in the back of the vehicle and got in. The driver knew from experience the 'Old Bill' would use the main streets, so he decided to take the back roads and drive within the speed limit. As he indicated right, to turn into Grove Road from the High Road, two uniformed officers in a marked Rover 3500 V8 police car came flying past in the opposite direction, sirens blaring and blue lights flashing. The unarmed man looked over his shoulder, out of the rear window, and saw the brake lights of the police car come on as it skidded to a sudden halt and started to do a U-turn.

'They've seen us – put your foot down and get us out of here,' he said calmly.

The driver pressed the accelerator hard and turned right across the path of an oncoming car, which swerved across the road and hit another vehicle head-on in the inside lane.

'This car's not as powerful as theirs. Maybe we should take a side street down here and bale out while they can't see us,' the man with the shotgun suggested.

As the driver approached the junction with Mornington Road, he looked in his rear-view mirror and saw the police car in the distance.

'That ain't an option, they're closing on us.'

He drove straight across the junction into Woodville Road without stopping. An oncoming car clipped the rear of the Cortina, knocking the bumper off and causing the car to judder and swerve erratically. The driver gripped the steering wheel hard to maintain control, but the Cortina sideswiped a parked car and careered across the road. Left with no alternative, the driver hit the brakes hard and skidded across the road, towards a parked car. The four men lurched forward as the car came to an abrupt halt inches from another vehicle. The man with the Luger smashed his head on the front windscreen, causing a deep cut to his forehead, which began to bleed heavily through his stocking mask.

'Fuck dis for a game of soldiers,' he said in a broad Irish accent, and got out of the car.

'Get back in or I'll go without you!' the driver shouted.

He was ignored, so he leant over and pulled the front passenger door closed, then reversed to straighten the car up and drive off.

'Stop!' the unarmed man snarled.

He grabbed the shotgun from his colleague's lap and opened the car door.

* * *

'Central 888 from MP, receiving, over?'

Kingston picked up the radio mike. 'We're a mile away at the Langthorne Park end of the High Road and nearly on scene, MP.'

'Received . . . I'm linking you up with Juliet 1, who are in pursuit of suspect vehicle Sierra Lima Mike 273 Romeo,' the radio operator replied.

'Listen up for their location, Colonel, and find it in the *A–Z*,' said Cam.

The calm voice of the PC in Juliet 1 came over the radio. 'Suspect vehicle has turned right into Grove Road . . . heading towards junction with Mornington Road.'

'Got it. Cam,' the Colonel said, 'Grove Road is the next right after Aylmer Road. Your best bet to catch up is a right into Lister Road, which leads into Mornington Road. I'll tell you when Lister is coming up.

'Thanks, mate.'

Cam was now swerving in and out of the inside lane to the offside lane to overtake other vehicles. Jane was clutching the back of the driver's seat with one hand and the door pull with the other, to stop herself from being flung about the back seat. Although the speed and manner of Cam's driving scared her, the adrenaline rush to her body was strangely stimulating. She felt excited to be involved in the apprehension of four armed robbers on her first day with the Flying Squad.

The radio operator on Juliet 1 came back on the radio, the pitch of his voice becoming slightly higher as the pursuit progressed.

'Suspect vehicle accelerating. Forty . . . forty-five . . . fifty miles per hour. Jesus Christ, he's gone straight across the junction without stopping.' There was a brief pause before the officer continued, 'Suspect vehicle has been hit by another car and now stopped in Woodville Road.'

'We're gonna get the bastards. Next right, Cam,' the Colonel said, and Cam turned into Lister Road.

'They're probably about to bale out and do a runner,' Kingston surmised.

'They won't get far if Teflon's after them – he's quicker than Allan Wells,' Cam replied, referring to the British and Commonwealth sprint champion.

'All units from Juliet 1 . . . a suspect is decamping from the front passenger seat towards the rear of the vehicle. Lima 1 under attack: suspect armed and firing at us!'

The distress in his voice was obvious to everyone listening in. The sound of gunfire could be heard over the radio, as well as the impact thud of the bullet.

'I've been hit! I've been hit!' the radio operator cried out.

Next there was the sound of a loud bang, followed by screeching tyres, then a sickening crunch of metal and breaking glass before the radio went dead. It was clear the police vehicle had come to an abrupt halt after a serious crash.

'That sounded like a shotgun going off,' Cam remarked, and the Colonel nodded.

'Let's hope they're both alive.' Kingston replied, but he feared the worst.

CHAPTER TWO

Jane and her colleagues sat in silence as they waited anxiously to hear from the crew of Juliet 1.

'MP to Juliet 1, receiving, over?' the operator asked repeatedly, but there was no reply.

'Central 888 from 887, receiving . . . ?'

Stanley's voice came over the radio from the squad car behind them.

'Go ahead, Stanley,' Kingston replied.

'We're going to head off to Bushwood Road, which runs along Wanstead Flats. All the back streets around Woodville Road lead to Bushwood so we might pick them up if they're on foot or still in the Cortina.'

'Good thinking, Stanley. We'll go to Woodville to see what's happened to Juliet 1 and let you know if the suspect car's been abandoned.'

'Central 888 and 887 from MP . . . Uniform patrol vehicles are also searching the area. Foot patrol officers are holding the scene at Barclays Bank and identifying witnesses. Two ambulances have been called there – one for an off-duty officer who was shot in the stomach and the other for three members of the public involved in a two-vehicle RTA during the incident.'

'How bad is the officer's injury?' a concerned Kingston asked MP.

'We don't have any current information on his condition. An ambulance has also been called to Woodville Road for the Juliet 1 officers as they're not responding.'

'We're nearly on scene, MP, and will give you a situation update on arrival,' Kingston said as Cam stopped the car just short of Woodville Road.

'Lie flat on the back seat, Tennison,' Kingston said as he and the Colonel withdrew their revolvers and got out of the vehicle.

'Are you going with them, Cam?' she asked, wondering if she was going to be left on her own.

'Like they said, I'm only the fucking driver – and apart from that I'm not firearms trained, so I'm happy to let them do the cops and robbers stuff.'

Jane couldn't resist sitting up a bit to look out of the front windscreen. The rain had stopped, and she watched as the two officers crouched down behind a parked car at the corner of Woodville Road. The Colonel stood up, his gun raised, and, using the parked cars as cover, started to move down the road in a crouched position. Jane lost sight of them but was relieved there was no sound of gunfire. Cam picked up the radio and informed MP that two armed officers from Central 888 were now on foot in Woodville Road.

Within a few seconds the Colonel reappeared, took off his cap and waved it to signal the area was safe. As Cam drove into Woodville Road Jane noticed that the Colonel was totally bald, which surprised her for his age.

Cam pointed down the left side of the street.

'Bloody hell, Juliet 1 has crashed into the front of that house.'

Jane could see a plume of steam rising from the badly damaged police vehicle. Its sirens had stopped, but the blue light on top was still flashing and the front half of the vehicle was covered in brick and rubble from the bay window of the Victorian terraced house it had crashed into. A small elderly man was attempting to lift the unconscious driver out of the car but having difficulty. Kingston was by the front passenger door, trying to pull it open and get to the injured officer.

'Bring the jemmy from the motor, Cam!' he shouted.

Cam jumped out of the car. 'I'm on it, Guv!' he shouted back, and ran to the boot of the car.

It was the first time Jane had got a proper look at Cam, who had a badly pockmarked face and receding dark brown hair. As he ran across the road to Kingston with the jemmy and a first aid box, the Colonel opened the passenger door and picked up the radio mike.

'Central 888 to MP. We are on scene in Woodville. Suspects have left in the Cortina and Juliet 1 has crashed into a house – the crew are injured and we're attempting to extract them from the vehicle. Do you have an ETA for the ambulance?'

'About two minutes,' MP replied.

Jane got out of the car and surveyed the scene.

'Juliet 1 must have hit the bay window at high speed to cause that much damage.'

'No shit, Treacle,' the Colonel replied.

'I'd prefer "no shit, Sergeant", Detective Constable Gorman,' Jane said lightly, to remind him of her rank and knowing 'treacle tart' was cockney rhyming slang for 'sweetheart'.

'There's a woman with a baby sitting on a wall over there.' He pointed across the road near the crash site, but Jane couldn't see her due to a parked car. 'She looks pretty distressed and might have seen what happened. It would be helpful if you could have a chat with her . . . Sergeant,' he said pointedly, then ran across the road to assist Kingston and Cam.

Jane was frustrated by the fact that even seven years on from integration, many male officers still thought their female colleagues should only deal with women and children. She didn't like the Colonel's attitude but didn't feel it was the time or place to challenge him about it. She was glad that DS Stanley was an old acquaintance as he would be able to tell her more about the officers on the squad, especially as the few she'd met so far seemed rude and intimidating.

By now uniformed assistance had arrived. Jane instructed some officers to tape off both ends of Woodville Road and ask the people, who had come out of their houses and gathered on the street, if they had seen the incident and to obtain their names and addresses if they had. One resident, whose car was hit by the speeding Cortina, was arguing about who was going to pay for the damage and insisting the police should. A uniformed officer told him politely that he'd have to claim on his own insurance, which upset the man even more.

The uniformed driver was out of the crashed vehicle and being given first aid by the small elderly man, who it transpired was the owner of the damaged house. The officer had a bad cut to his head and scratches to his face caused by flying brickwork and glass that had smashed through part of the windscreen when the car crashed. His injury was bleeding heavily, but he was conscious and reasonably coherent. The Colonel introduced himself to the officer and told him an ambulance was on its way.

The PC looked worried. 'My operator Gary was shot – is he OK?'

'I'll be straight with you, mate, I don't know yet. My governor and driver are trying to get him out of the car. As soon as I know, I'll let you know, OK?'

The driver nodded. 'Did the bastards get away?'

'Don't worry about them – they won't get far.'

The officer looked upset. 'I tried to run the gunman down, but I missed.'

'You did a good job. Your motor's a write-off so the Commissioner might be pissed off with you,' the Colonel joked.

The officer smiled. 'You Sweeney lot are full of bullshit.'

The Colonel patted the officer's shoulder. 'That's what I like to hear – a woodentop who respects us detectives. If you don't mind, I think your mate needs me more than you do.'

Kingston and Cam tried in vain to jemmy open the front passenger door of the police car, but it was badly buckled from the crash and wouldn't budge. There was structural damage to the building, and bricks and debris were still falling, so they had to get the officer out quickly rather than call the fire brigade to cut him out. Cam went inside the vehicle and held his jacket up against the passenger door window while Kingston smashed and cleared the glass away with the

jemmy. They were then able to lift the officer, who was still unconscious, through the window, away from the car and damaged house.

'How is he?' the Colonel asked Kingston.

'His breathing is shallow and rasping – he might have damaged
his ribs when the crash occurred. I can't see any bullet holes in him,
but he's got a deep narrow wound to the right side of his head,
which could be from a bullet.'

'The ambulance should be here soon.'

'Where's Tennison?'

'Speaking to a woman who might be a witness. She got the right
hump when I just called her "treacle".'

Kingston laughed. 'Well, that's her nickname sorted then.'

*　*　*

The driver of the Cortina approached the estate within the speed
limit and pulled up at the far end of a row of garages, where they
couldn't be seen through any residents' windows. The man who'd
fired the shotgun at the bank was looking over his shoulder out of
the rear window.

'No sign of the rozzers.'

He then put the shotgun under a towel in the travel bag, which
also covered the cash box. The Irishman got out and opened the
end garage for the Cortina to drive in. Once the vehicle was inside
he closed the garage door and all four men quickly removed their
donkey jackets and blue boiler suits, under which they were wearing casual clothes. The driver opened the boot and removed a petrol can, then he and the others threw their robbery outfits into
the boot. The man who had led the robbery got the travel bag
containing the cash box from the rear seat. He opened it and the
Irishman placed his Luger under the towel.

The Irishman opened the garage door and the leader, along with
the man who had fired the shotgun, walked slowly off the estate and

down the street. When they were out of sight, the driver waited for a minute before pouring petrol over the discarded clothes and the interior of the Cortina. He then removed a Zippo lighter from his pocket, opened it and flicked the spark wheel to ignite the wick. He threw the lighter into the boot of the car, causing a loud *woomph* as the boiler suits and donkey jackets caught light, then shut the boot lid and closed the garage door. He and the Irishman left the estate on foot and, once in Blake Hall Road, walked off in the opposite direction to the other two men.

* * *

Jane approached the young white girl, who was in floods of tears and clutching a mixed-race baby to her chest. Her face was pale from shock, she looked about seventeen and her blond hair was tied in a side ponytail. She was wearing a black Puffa jacket, white T-shirt, bell-bottomed jeans and brown boots.

'Hi, I'm Detective Sergeant Tennison. Are you OK?'

'The police car nearly hit me and my baby.'

She wiped her nose with the sleeve of her jacket. Jane sat beside her on the wall, got a tissue out of her pocket and handed it to the girl.

'What's your name – and your baby's?'

'Mine's Abby Jones, and he's Daniel. He's only eight months old and got a rash, so I was taking him to the doctor's in the High Road.'

Jane got her pocket notebook and pen out of her jacket pocket and started asking questions. Abby said she'd just turned seventeen and lived with her parents at 6 Leybourne Road, which was off the bottom end of Woodville Road. She explained to Abby that the men in the car the police were chasing had just committed an armed robbery at Barclays Bank in the High Road.

'Did you see what happened here before the police car crashed?' Jane asked.

'Yeah, some of it.'

'I don't want to keep you too long if your baby's not well, but it would be helpful if you could tell me what you saw.'

Abby explained she was walking up Woodville Road to the doctor's surgery when she heard a car crash and tyres screeching. She'd looked up and saw a brown car coming towards her, which was swerving from side to side down the road.

'Did you see how many people were in the car?'

'Three, maybe four people, I think, but I don't know for sure – they passed me so quickly. The car hit that parked car over there, then skidded to a halt. A big tall man got out of the front passenger side, then I heard the police siren and saw the police car coming down the road—'

'Sorry to interrupt you, but can you describe the man who got out of the car?'

'Not really. He had a mask on his face.'

'When you say a mask, do you mean a balaclava?'

'Yeah, that's right.'

'Did this man have a gun?'

Abby nodded and trembled as she clutched Daniel to her chest.

'When I was looking at the police car I heard some bangs and looked back down the road. I could see the man in the mask holding up a gun and shooting at the police car . . . I was terrified I might be shot and screamed, which made Daniel start to cry, then I heard a loud bang like a firework going off and saw the police car skid across the road towards me . . . I just managed to pull Daniel's pram out of the way in time – the police car was inches from hitting him.'

'Can you describe the gun, and which hand the man held it in?'

'Only that it was black, and I think in his right hand.'

'Do you know how many shots he fired?'

Abby thought about it before answering.

'Three, I think, but maybe four. It all happened so quickly I can't be sure.'

'Did you see anyone else with a gun?'

'Yes, there was another person who got out of the car – his gun was longer, with two holes at the end.'

Jane knew from the description that this man must have been holding a sawn-off shotgun, and what Abby thought was a firework going off was the shotgun being fired.

'Can you describe him?'

'No, he had a black mask on as well, but he was shorter than the man who shot at the police car.'

'An officer in the crashed police car was on the radio at the time the shotgun was fired, and I heard the bang on our radio. It must have been terrifying for you to be in the middle of it all,' Jane said to console Abby.

'It was, but I don't think the man in the balaclava fired his gun.'

'Are you sure?'

Jane wondered if Abby was so frightened she'd become confused about what had happened.

'I didn't see him until after the police car crashed – so he must have got out of the car after that happened.'

'What did the man with the shotgun do?'

'He followed behind the man with the small gun, who was walking towards the crashed police car with the gun raised towards the policemen.'

'Then what happened?'

'The smaller man held his bigger gun towards the big man's back. I think he said something as the mouth hole on his mask moved, but I couldn't hear what it was . . . Then they got in the car and it drove off.'

'What do you think made the loud bang you heard?'

Abby shrugged and put Daniel in the pram.

'I don't know . . . Can I go now?'

'I'll need to speak to you again to take a more detailed statement, which you'll need to sign. Can you give me your home phone number, please, then I can call you to arrange an appointment time?'

Abby looked apprehensive. 'Will I have to go to court and give evidence.'

'Possibly, if we catch the men responsible for the robbery.'

'No, I'm sorry, no way, I'm not giving evidence against people like that. My life and Daniel's would never be safe.'

'There's ways we can protect you and make sure your details are not revealed. I'll come and see you tomorrow, but in the meantime would you like me to get someone to contact your parents?'

'No, I need to take Daniel to the doctor's now.'

'Are you sure you'll be all right on your own?'

'Yeah . . . I hope those two policemen that were in the police car are all right.'

'I'm sure they will be, Abby. You can call me at work any time if you want to talk.'

Abby frowned. 'I won't change my mind about making a statement.'

'If you did, would you contact me if I give you my office number?'

'I'll think about it,' she replied with a big sigh.

Jane was about to write it down on a bit of paper when she realised she didn't know her new office number.

'Can you hang on a minute and I'll just get the number from one of my colleagues . . . ?'

'No, I gotta go to the doctor's now,' Abby said as she walked off without looking back.

CHAPTER THREE

As Jane watched the ambulance leave with the injured officers, she thought about the loud bang Abby had heard; if it wasn't the sound of a shotgun, it had to be something else near the scene of the incident. As she walked towards the damaged house she noticed skid marks and bits of shredded car tyre on the road. It reminded her of the time she was driving on the motorway and a tyre on the car in front of her burst, leaving shredded bits all over the road. It struck her as unlikely that a tyre on a police car would suddenly blow out, especially as the vehicles were checked daily by a civilian 'garage hand', but she suspected a bullet penetrating a tyre could cause a blowout.

About eight metres past the crash site Jane saw a distinct skid mark veering from right to left across the road, which stopped just short of a parked car. She realised, from what Abby had told her, that the skid mark might have been caused when the getaway driver braked hard and came to an abrupt halt. She decided to inspect the area more closely and was walking towards it when she heard Kingston's voice.

'What are you doing, Tennison?'

She turned around. 'I was just following up on something a witness to the incident told me.'

'As the DI in charge of this case I'd prefer it if you consulted me first, then I'll decide what action should or should not be taken by my officers.'

'Sorry, sir. I thought I might find some evidence for the investigation.'

'Are you a forensics expert?'

'No, but I've dealt with a number of murders and rapes during my service and have a good knowledge of major crime scenes—'

'But no real experience with armed robbery scenes, firearms or GSR.'

'No, sir.'

She didn't know what GSR was but didn't want to appear uninformed by asking.

'What did the woman you spoke to have to say?'

Jane told him the woman was a young mother called Abby who had just turned seventeen. She got out her pocket notebook and started to brief Kingston on what Abby had told her, but he interrupted her again.

'Did the girl see their faces?'

'No, she saw two armed men get out of the car, but both were wearing masks. She's a bright young girl and saw everything—'

He interrupted again. 'Is she willing to make a statement and give evidence in court.'

'Not at the moment, but—'

'Then she's not a lot of use to us, is she?'

'I think I could persuade her to make a statement, and we could always consider witness protection.'

Kingston shook his head. 'I'm not gonna waste time wet-nursing some kid with a baby. Move on and see if you can find an adult who saw what happened.' He started to walk off.

'Something she said about the two men with guns was interesting . . .'

Kingston spun around. 'What part of move on don't you understand, Tennison?'

'Sorry, sir, I'll see if there are any *adults* who got a closer look than Abby did.'

'Don't be flippant, Tennison. I've heard a few stories about you – some good, some not so good. I don't doubt your enthusiasm, or abilities as a divisional detective investigating murders – but when it comes to the Flying Squad you've a lot to learn. We're a specialised close-knit unit, not just because of the work we do, but also the dangers we face together. As you can see from the carnage of this morning's events . . . The villains we deal with don't play games and they hate the police with a vengeance – to them the only good cop is a dead cop.'

'I'm a quick learner and I believe I can be a positive addition to the squad, sir,' she said in her defence.

'That remains to be seen. Everyone of sergeant rank and above served on the Flying Squad as a DC prior to promotion . . . unlike you. Right now, you're the rookie, not to mention the first female officer we've ever had.'

'I appreciate that, sir, but I don't see my gender as a hindrance—'

'Take my advice – if you want to fit in and get on, then best to just look, listen and learn for now.'

Jane suspected he was being polite, and what he really wanted to say was to keep her eyes and ears open and her mouth shut.

'Yes, sir, and thank you for the advice.'

He forced a smile. 'Good, and cut the "sir" crap, please. It's "guv" or "guvnor" when we're on duty and "Stu" in the pub.'

The Colonel came over and spoke to Kingston.

'Stanley just radioed in – no one's been able to find the Cortina. Looks like the robbers have gone to ground.'

Kingston sighed. 'Any of the Woodville residents see anything?'

'Uniform lads have knocked on all the doors and spoken to the people who gathered in the street. No one saw what happened here, though some heard the crash and bangs before it, which was probably the guns going off.'

Jane wanted to say that Abby was the only witness, so trying to get her to make a statement would be beneficial, but she didn't want to incur Kingston's displeasure again. Kingston looked frustrated.

'They probably had a changeover vehicle nearby. Get on the radio and instruct the uniform cars and foot patrol officers to check the local estates and back roads for the Cortina. Call Stanley as well and tell him to drop Dabs off here to deal with this scene.'

'Shall I call a SOCO out to the bank scene if Dabs is coming here?'

Kingston nodded and told the Colonel to make sure it was a senior SOCO who had experience of examining armed robbery scenes. Jane assumed the nickname 'Dabs' must have originated from the police slang for fingerprints. She asked Kingston if she would be going to the bank with him and the Colonel to take statements, but he said no as he wanted her to help Dabs.

'I take it you know how to fill in an exhibits book?' Kingston asked her.

'I've done it a few times, but on big cases like murders the lab liaison sergeant did everything.'

'Well, we work differently on the Flying Squad, as time is of the essence at a crime scene. Dabs, our SOCO, is permanently attached to the team and one of our DCs always works alongside him at a robbery scene, helping to gather evidence and listing the exhibits. Even though you're a DS it would be beneficial for you to assist Dabs on this case.'

Jane said she'd be happy to assist Dabs and Kingston walked off towards the squad car.

'Would you like me to brief Stanley when he gets here, guv?' she asked the Colonel.

'No, he and his crew will be joining me at the bank to interview the Securicor guards and other witnesses there,' he said without looking back.

She waited for him to leave and went to have a look at the area where the skid mark stopped just short of the parked car. As the sun broke through the clouds she noticed something glint by the side of the road next to the pavement. On closer inspection she could see it was a brass cartridge case, which must have come from the handgun the tall man had fired at the police car. Looking around she could see another cartridge case a couple of feet away, by the rear nearside tyre of a parked car. Crouching down, she tilted her head to one side. Looking under the car, she could see two more cartridge cases. As she stood up and looked around she noticed two trails of blood drops, running between the skid mark and the middle of the road, where there were a number of drops confined to a small area, which meant the bleeding man had stood there.

'This is a crime scene, ma'am, you shouldn't be this side of the tape,' a male voice said.

Jane saw a small man wearing glasses, whom she recognised as one of the passengers in the other Flying Squad car with Stanley. She knew he must be Dabs, as he was wearing latex gloves and carrying a scene of crime case and a camera over his shoulder. He was about five feet six inches tall, early thirties, with dark brown collar-length hair and long sideburns. He was dressed casually in a white shirt, blue jumper, grey trousers and black windcheater.

Jane held out her hand. 'I'm WDS Jane Tennison. I've just started on the Flying Squad today.'

He shook her hand. 'Pleased to meet you, Sarge. I'm Dave Morgan. DS Stanley mentioned you in the car earlier. We were all a bit surprised as no one knew you were joining the team – especially as you're a woman.'

'Well, speaking as a woman, the day's been quite a surprise for me too,' she said, forcing a smile and wondering if his 'woman' remark was intentionally derogatory.

'Have you found something?'

She pointed to the two visible cartridge cases and told him there were another two under the car and blood drops on the road.

'From what a witness told me, the skid mark there is where the Cortina stopped sharply, then a man with a handgun got out and shot at the police car. If he was injured the blood trails might have come from him getting out and returning to the car.'

'Good spot, Sarge.' He got a swab out of his pocket and dabbed it in one of the blood spots and the end turned red. 'And they're fresh. I'll take some photos and swabs of the blood . . . From the nearby position of the cartridges to the blood drops I'd say the gun was a semi-automatic. Do you know much about firearms forensics, Sarge?' he asked politely as he put his case down.

Jane knew a semi-automatic pistol ejected cartridges each time it was fired, but six-chamber Smith & Wesson revolvers, which the Flying Squad used, didn't.

'A bit. I've dealt with major crimes involving guns, including a shooting murder scene – and post mortems where I assisted the lab liaison sergeant.'

'Who was the lab sergeant?'

'Detective Sergeant Paul Lawrence.'

Dabs's eyebrows raised. 'He's a legend when it comes to crime scene examination. I met him at a lecture he did at training school, but sadly never had the privilege of working alongside him.'

He bent down and picked up one of the cartridge cases.

'Looks like a nine-millimetre Parabellum,' he observed.

'What's a Parabellum?'

'It's a type of bullet cartridge and Parabellum is Latin, meaning "prepare for war", which is appropriate considering what happened here today.' Dabs showed her the base of the cartridge case. 'See the markings on the bottom – that's what we call the head stamp.'

Jane looked closer and could see the number 43, ST+ and DNH. She asked what the numbers and letters meant.

'The 43 is the year of manufacture, which is 1943. I'm not sure what ST+ means, but DNH is where the bullet was manufactured. However, the firearms section at the lab will be able to tell us more.'

'The cartridge is nearly forty years old – what sort of gun do you think it was fired from?'

'I don't know ... Again, that's a job for the lab to determine. I've seen older ammo and nine-mill is used in different makes of revolvers and semi-automatics.'

'Will you be able to get fingerprints off the cartridge?'

He shook his head. 'Unfortunately, no, when a gun is fired, the heat created has a destructive effect on any fingerprint evidence. Even unfired bullets are almost impossible to get a print off.'

'What's GSR?' she asked, remembering Kingston referring to it.

'Gunshot residue. A plume of gas and GSR particles is ejected from the barrel of a gun when it's fired, and the residue gets deposited on the skin and clothing of the person who fired the gun. It can also be found on the clothing of the victim, but that depends on how close they were to the gun when it was fired.'

'So, the suspect who fired the gun that left these casings will have GSR on them.'

'Yes, on his clothes for sure, but if he washes his hands and body then it's gone from his skin. Whenever we arrest any suspects for armed robbery, we always Sellotape their hands for GSR and the lab examines the tapings under a scanning electron microscope to look for GSR as evidence they have fired, handled or been near a gun.'

'You know a lot about firearms and bullets,' Jane said respectfully.

'Enough to get me by, but the forensic scientists are the experts. If you fancy it, you can come to the lab with me when I submit the cartridge cases and other evidence for examination. I think you'd find the firearms section really interesting and informative.'

'I'd like that, thank you.'

She was warming to Dabs. His helpful, polite manner reminded her of Paul Lawrence.

'I've ordered a tow truck to remove the police car to the lab, then it can be examined for any bullets that may be lodged in it. We need to crack on and photograph the scene, then gather up the cartridge cases before it gets here.'

* * *

Arriving at the bank with the Colonel, Kingston spoke briefly to a uniformed PC and asked where the Securicor guards were. The officer told him they were in the bank manager's office and the off-duty PC who'd got shot was in the ambulance parked next to the Securicor van. The back doors of the ambulance were open, and Kingston could see one of the crew attending to someone on a stretcher. He thought it strange that someone who'd got shot in the stomach wasn't rushed to hospital. The Colonel looked around the area where the Securicor van was parked. He saw a small pool of blood near the front of the van and some droplets leading to the back of the ambulance.

'I'd have expected more blood and guts from a close-range shotgun discharge,' the Colonel said, and noticed something odd. 'If that's your shotgun victim in the ambulance he's a lucky sod.'

'What?' Kingston was bemused by the Colonel's glib remark.

'Look there, by the blood, there are a load of rice grains on the pavement.'

Kingston realised that the shotgun cartridge must have been loaded with rice, as opposed to lead pellets. He stepped up into the ambulance and saw a young man, aged about nineteen, who was clearly still in shock and grimacing with pain while having his stomach and chest wounds cleaned with iodine. Kingston held up his warrant card and introduced himself.

'I take it you're the officer who got shot?'

'Yes, sir.'

'What's your name, son?'

'PC 642 Richard Beadle, sir. I'm a probationer attached to Edmonton Police Station.'

'Well, you're very lucky, Richard. From the looks of it the shotgun cartridges were loaded with rice – which is why you're still alive. Can you tell me exactly what happened?'

'I was going to the bank to collect some drachmas I'd ordered for a holiday in Corfu with my girlfriend. I'd just got off the bus and was crossing the road when I saw a masked man holding a sawn-off shotgun at the Securicor driver. I realised a robbery was happening and I thought he was on his own. He hadn't seen me, so I ran up behind him and tried to get the gun off him.' He paused to take a deep breath as the memory of the moment was making him close to tears. 'The next thing I knew he'd knocked me to the ground and was pointing the gun at me. I closed my eyes and begged him not to shoot . . . Then there was a loud bang and I felt something thump hard into my stomach . . . The pain was unbelievable, and I thought I was going to die.' A few tears rolled down his cheeks.

'Did the man with the shotgun say anything?'

'I don't know, but when I opened my eyes I saw three masked men getting into a car, which drove off. I'm sorry I didn't manage to stop the robbery, sir.'

Kingston put his hand on the officer's shoulder.

'You've nothing to be sorry about, son. What you did was very brave. On the positive side, you're not dead and can still go to Corfu with your girlfriend.'

The officer smiled and wiped the tears from his face. Kingston said he would need him to make a written statement before he went on holiday. The officer said he lived at Lea Bridge Road section house and wasn't going on holiday until Saturday morning. Kingston told him he'd get a Flying Squad officer to take the statement from him on Friday morning at the section house.

'I need to speak to some other witnesses. You take care and have a good holiday,' Kingston said, then he stepped out of the ambulance.

The Colonel stayed behind to speak to the young officer.

'Let me give you a bit of advice, son. While I admire your bravery, what you did was stupid. If that gun had been loaded with lead pellets it could have gone off when you tackled the suspect and members of the public may have been injured or killed. The money they stole is immaterial and not worth dying for – so next time think twice before putting your life and other people's on the line.'

The officer's lower lip trembled as he acknowledged the advice he'd been given. The Colonel got his wallet out and tucked a five-pound note into the officer's trouser pocket.

'That should get you pissed tonight and numb the pain. Make sure you get a doctor's sick certificate, then you won't have to use annual leave for your holiday.' He winked.

The Colonel joined Kingston by the steps of the bank, where he was speaking to the Senior SOCO, who had just arrived. They knew each other of old and Kingston told him about the robbery and what he knew so far. The SOCO said that on the face of it there weren't many forensic opportunities at the bank scene, as the men wore gloves, and would no doubt dispose of their donkey jackets and overalls, but he'd do his best.

'I'll seize the outer clothing from the officer who got shot – there should be a cross-transference of fibres as he struggled with one of the robbers. Have you got someone doing exhibits who I can give the items I seize?' the SOCO asked.

'Yeah, WDS Tennison. She's a bit wet behind the ears when it comes to robbery scenes as she just started with us today,' Kingston told him.

The SOCO was taken aback. 'A woman on the Flying Squad? My God, this integration thing is getting out of hand.'

'Tell me about it,' Kingston said, and he went into the bank.

'Who'd she sleep with to get on the squad?' the SOCO asked when Kingston was out of earshot.

The Colonel shrugged. 'Don't know, but my money's on Kingston shagging her within a week.'

The SOCO laughed. 'He still got a roving eye then?'

'More like a roving dick, which rules his brain when it comes to a bit of skirt with big tits.'

'So where is this Tennison?'

The SOCO looked into the bank, eager to see what she looked like for himself.

'Not here, she's with Dabs Morgan at the crash site.' He stepped towards the bank, then stopped. 'We call her Treacle, and believe it or not she's OK about it.'

'Really?' The SOCO was unsure.

'Yeah, she seems to have a sense of humour, unlike most plonks.'

The Colonel walked off with a sly grin the SOCO didn't see.

CHAPTER FOUR

Dabs photographed the spent cartridge cases where they'd fallen, at a distance and close up, then left Jane to gather and package them while he photographed the skid marks and blood trail before taking some swabs, which he gave to Jane. As instructed by Dabs, she put the four cartridge cases into small individual plastic containers, then separate exhibits bags. She did the same with the four blood swabs and made a detailed entry in the exhibits book of the items seized, writing a description, date, time and place found.

'Will these be your exhibits or mine?' Jane asked Dabs when he returned.

'The squad detective always signs and numbers them as his.' He realised his error. 'Or hers . . . Sorry, I meant you need to do that as the exhibits officer.'

Jane smiled. 'It's all right, I know what you meant.'

She signed the exhibits bags and put JT/1, 2, 3 and 4 on the ones containing the cartridge cases, and JT/5 to JT/7 for the blood swabs, as the reference numbers.

'If anyone gets arrested and goes to court, you'll give evidence about where they were found and what forensics work they were submitted for,' Dabs told her, and he looked back up the road towards the crashed police car. 'We won't know how many bullets are in Juliet 1 until we examine it under cover at the lab.' He moved a few feet into the road. 'The man with the handgun stood and fired about here, as the cartridge cases ejected to the right. We need to examine the parked cars on both sides of the road for any stray bullet holes, and check underneath them, as well as in the road, in case any bullets bounced off the police car.'

'Shall I do one side, while you check the other?' Jane asked.

'It's probably better we do it together – as they say, two heads are better than one.'

Jane appreciated he was politely saying he didn't want to risk her missing a bullet hole or indentation in one of the cars. They started on the left-hand side and found nothing on, or under, the cars they looked at. They were having the same result on the opposite side of the road until they reached a silver two-door Ford Fiesta hatchback parked nearest to the crash site. Dabs pointed to the tarmac by the front of the vehicle.

'See the pool of water there . . . ? You notice anything unusual about it?'

Jane thought his remark odd.

'No. What's unusual about a pool of water after it's been raining?'

'It's a rusty brown colour, like you sometimes get from a leaky car radiator.'

She realised what he was thinking. 'And if something's leaking it must have a hole in it.'

'Exactly, and in this case the hole might have been caused by a bullet.'

He put on some latex gloves, then took a picture of the Fiesta with the camera he was still carrying over his shoulder.

Jane looked closely at the front of the car.

'I can't see a bullet hole anywhere.'

He crouched down and put his right index finger between two of the grille slats.

'That's because these are wide enough apart for a bullet to pass between without hitting the grille.' He crouched further and looked under the car. 'There it is.' He held the camera at ground level and took some photographs.

Jane crouched down and could see a small cylindrical silver object, which she realised must be a bullet.

'Looks like it lost velocity when it passed through the radiator, then it hit the engine block and fell to the floor.'

He got on his hands and knees and started to lower himself to the road to get to the bullet.

'You'll get your clothes dirty – shall I look for a stick or something to get it out with?'

He didn't stop what he was doing as he lay on the road and reached under the car.

'No, we never do that, or use tweezers to pick up bullets. The last thing you want to do is mark or damage them in any way.' He picked up the bullet, then stood up and showed it to her. 'Although it's squashed a bit at the top it's in reasonable condition.' He held the bullet flat in the palm of his hand. 'There's marks on it left by the rifling inside the barrel of the gun.'

He pointed to some tiny linear marks and asked Jane to put on some latex gloves and hold the bullet, so he could take some close-up photographs of it.

Jane thought they looked like scratches and asked him what he meant by rifling.

'A firearms expert would be able to explain it better, but basically every gun barrel is rifled during manufacture. The rifling process creates spiral grooves that run along the barrel and improve a bullet's accuracy as it rotates during flight. A fired bullet goes out through the barrel and ends up with mirrored markings on it, which match the rifling on the inside of the barrel . . . Am I making sense?'

'Yes, I think so. The principle sounds the same as striation marks left on bones when a body is cut up,' she said, remembering a case she had had where a body was dismembered with a hacksaw by a dentist.

'That's right, if somewhat gruesome. There are several methods used in rifling a barrel, which in turn makes a revolver or semi-automatic unique in its own way . . .'

'Like a sort of fingerprint?' she asked.

He nodded, and she continued.

'So, if we recover the gun that fired the bullet, the barrel can be examined to see if the rifling marks on the bullet are the same.'

'Sort of, but not quite like you described. The lab will test fire the suspect gun in water, then compare the test bullet against the ones recovered from the scene of the shooting. If the markings on the test bullet match the suspect ones, then you know you have the gun that was used in the robbery. But even if we don't recover a gun, the marks on this bullet can help identify the type and model of firearm that was used.'

'How do they test fire in water?' she asked, imagining someone in a swimming pool firing a gun at a target.

'You'll see when you come with me to the lab, so I won't spoil it by explaining.'

He reached into his jacket pocket and brought out a small round plastic container in which he placed the damaged bullet. Handing it to Jane, she put it in an exhibits bag, then signed and marked the bag JT/8. She also entered the details in the exhibits book.

'What about the skid marks – will they be of any use for tyre impressions?' she asked.

'I've already photographed them, though they won't be a lot of use unless we find the car the robbers were in – even then it was probably a nicked or ringed motor. Ideally, we'd need evidence like their fingerprints, or fibres from their clothing inside the vehicle, to physically put them in it . . .'

'A young girl I spoke to, who witnessed the incident, said the two men she saw get out of the Cortina wore masks and gloves; they were also dressed the same in donkey jackets and blue overalls.'

'That's your standard outfit for an armed blagger these days. Bank robbers are often forensically aware, having been nicked before, but they're not as bright as they like to think they are and make mistakes. You only have one crack at examining a scene like this as you can't seal the street off for ever. If you miss anything of evidential value, no matter how small, it could hinder the investigation.'

'What about informants? Do you get many cases where someone tells you who's responsible for an armed robbery?'

'Sometimes, but I don't get involved in that side of squad work as I'm just a SOCO. As I see it, criminals grass on each other for a variety of reasons, such as money or to remove a rival. Being a police informant is a highly dangerous occupation, which can get you killed.'

'I've never had a registered informant, but sometimes people I arrested told me, "off the record", who else was involved to get a reduction in their own sentence at court.'

'Well, if you want to get on in the Flying Squad you'll be expected to cultivate informants. A lot of the lads on the squad have them and their information has led to pavement arrests during the commission of armed robberies.'

'How's the team feel about the Operation Countryman investigation?'

Jane knew some Flying Squad officers had been arrested in the investigation into police corruption in London.

'Thankfully no one at Rigg has been arrested or interviewed on suspicion of corruption by the Sweedy—'

'Did you say the Sweedy?'

'Yeah, it's what the squad guys call the officers on Countryman. They're all from Hampshire and Dorset, which are rural forces, and the name "Sweedy" comes from the vegetable swede.'

Jane grinned. 'I've heard county officers referred to as "carrot crunchers", but never "Sweedy".'

'The latest I heard was the officer in charge of Countryman is alleging that the investigation is being wilfully obstructed by Commissioner McNee and the Director of Public Prosecutions. McNee wants all the Countryman evidence to be passed to the Met and dealt with by its own internal investigation unit, A10.'

'I've been interviewed by the "rubber heelers" myself.'

She used a police term that had come about because you can't hear the internal investigation officers coming due to the rubber heels on their shoes.

Dabs looked surprised. 'Have you?'

'Not for corruption, I hasten to add. One was a case when I was a probationer and the other more recent, when a dentist who murdered four people committed suicide. Thankfully I was only given some words of advice and a slap on the wrist in both cases.'

'I remember reading about the murders in Peckham Rye about a year ago and the press kept using the headline "Murder Mile". I couldn't believe a Harley Street dentist was responsible.'

'Believe me, neither could I, and the monster evaded a life sentence by killing himself.'

The tow truck for the police car arrived and Jane watched as Juliet 1 was slowly pulled out of the rubble by a winch cable. The elderly owner of the house stood watching with a solemn expression as more bits of the bay window gave way and fell on the front of the car. Once it was safely extracted, and a safe distance from the house, they cleared the debris from the car. Dabs pointed to a bullet hole in the bonnet. He tried to open it, but was unable due to the damage from the crash.

'From the entry point it's probably lodged in the air filter. Hopefully we'll find it at the lab or in the house rubble when we sift through it.'

Part of the front windscreen, on the passenger side, was still intact but covered with fractures that looked like large spiders' webs. Dabs pointed to a one-centimetre circular hole in the windscreen.

'That's a bullet hole as well.'

He got in the car to look for any bullets.

After a few minutes he came out holding the front passenger headrest and showed it to Jane. She saw some of the white headrest padding protruding from holes on either side of it. As Dabs got the car keys from the ignition, he said a bullet had penetrated the windscreen, then hit the right side of the radio operator's head, before passing through the headrest and into the rear seat, and was probably somewhere in the boot.

'Even though the bullet would have lost velocity when it passed through the windscreen, the officer was lucky it didn't hit him straight in the forehead and kill him.'

He opened the boot of the car and looked inside. He had a big smile as he photographed the bullet, then picked it up and showed it to Jane.

'That one's in even better shape than the bullet we recovered under the car,' she observed.

She took the bullet from him and put it in a plastic container and then an exhibits bag.

* * *

After speaking briefly to the bank manager, who couldn't help much as he didn't see the robbery, Kingston left the Colonel, Stanley and Bax to take the Securicor guards' statements. He crossed over the High Road to the Crown public house to speak to the landlady, Fiona Simpson, who'd initially called the police. He knocked on the pub door and it was opened by a small, slim, buxom woman in her mid-forties, who had shoulder-length, black curly hair. She was dressed casually in a blue velour jumpsuit and slippers, and had an orange dusting cloth in her hand. He held up his warrant card.

'I'm DI Kingston, from the Flying Squad. Is the landlady Mrs Simpson in?' he asked, thinking she was the cleaner.

'The name's Fiona and you're looking at her. You come about the robbery at the bank?'

'Yes, I was told you were a witness. Can I come in and speak to you, please?'

She opened the door to let him in, then closed and bolted it shut.

'Excuse my attire, Inspector, but I haven't had time to shower, change and put on my make-up yet,' she said as she went behind the bar. 'You want something to drink or is that a silly question to ask a detective?'

'You get a few "tecs" in here, then?'

He thought she looked attractive, even without make-up.

'Yeah, CID from Leytonstone drink here, so do the uniform, but only when they've finished a shift, unlike the CID who like a pint at all hours.'

'I'll have a Scotch, thanks. Some publicans think having the police in damages their trade,' he remarked.

She poured a large measure from the optic.

'It also helps to keep the arseholes out. I've run the place on me own for three years since my husband died, and there have been a few occasions where officers have helped me out with drunk or obnoxious punters – and I'm grateful for that . . . Plus I don't get done for serving afters.'

She smiled as she handed him his whisky.

'Cheers.'

Kingston opened a blue folder he'd brought with him and took out some statement forms and a pen from his jacket pocket.

'I was told you saw the face of the driver involved in the robbery.'

'Yes, briefly when he got out of the car and then returned.'

'I'll need to take a detailed statement off you . . .'

She raised her eyebrows. 'Detective inspectors take statements now, do they?'

He grinned. 'When it's in a pub with a generous landlady, yes.'

'You'll need to be quick as I've got to get dressed and open up for eleven.'

'I can make notes for now in my pocket notebook and take the statement later, if that's easier for you.'

'I can do it early morning before I open, or after three as we don't reopen until six. I'm pretty busy with this place and don't get much time for relaxing.'

'Do you never take a day off?'

'Rarely. The last person I had in to look after the pub while I was away had his fingers in the till, which has made me a bit wary of leaving bar staff in charge. Mind you, I could ask one of the girls to do an extra shift this evening and make the statement then – if you're free . . .'

'That would be helpful, thanks, but tomorrow would probably be easier as I'm not sure I'll have time today. I'll take your phone number and ring you later to let you know.'

She borrowed his pen and wrote 'Fiona' and the pub number on a beer mat, which he then put in his pocket.

'I was told you first saw the Cortina in Aylmer Road. Can you tell me what time it was and exactly where it was parked?'

She pointed to the pub's side entrance. 'Opposite the door there, on the far side of the road. It was around 9.20 to 9.25.'

'What drew your attention to the car.'

'I was upstairs in the living room, ironing my dress and blouse for today, when I looked out of the window at the heavy rain and saw the car. Because I was looking down I could only see the nearside and two people in it – one in the front passenger seat and another person sitting behind him. There were fumes coming out of the exhaust, so I knew the engine was running, and the windscreen wipers were on. At first I thought they were maybe just waiting for someone.'

'Can you describe any facial features of the first two men you saw?'

'No, the door windows were covered in rain and misted up on the inside. They were wearing dark clothing and the man in the front must have been tall as I could see his shoulder pressed against the middle of the passenger door window. About ten minutes before the robbery the driver got out of the car and nearly hit Betty with the door as he opened it—'

'Sorry, who's Betty?'

'She lives alone round the back of the pub at Dacre Road. She's been a regular here for years and comes in most days at six on the dot, apart from Sundays. She has two bottles of Mackeson Stout then goes home for her tea.'

'She'd have seen the driver's face close up, then?'

'Yes. She was upset and pointing her finger at him. I didn't hear what she said, but knowing Betty she'd have called him a few choice names – that even I would be too embarrassed to repeat. What made me suspicious was the fact he ignored her, pulled his cap down and walked off up the road. That was when I phoned the police.'

'Do you know Betty's surname?' Kingston asked, ready to write it down, as she'd be a crucial witness.

'Do you have to speak to her? She's just turned eighty and not been well lately – she's very frail and her eyesight's not so good. I doubt she'd even remember the incident.'

Kingston thought for a second. 'I'll leave her be for now, but I'll still need her details.'

Fiona wrote Betty's full name and address down on another beer mat and gave it to Kingston, who slipped it in his pocket.

'Would you recognise the driver if you saw him again?' he asked.

'I think so . . .'

'On a scale of one to ten, what's a "think so"?'

'Six, maybe seven . . . I got a slightly better look at him when he returned to the car, but most of the time his head was down, and the pouring rain didn't help.'

'If we make an arrest would you be willing to attend an identity parade?'

'I'd be willing, but as I said I didn't see his face clearly, so I'm not certain I could pick him out.'

He wondered if Fiona was scared after witnessing the robbery.

'Do you think the driver saw you?'

'No, he never looked up. I know what you're thinking, Inspector, but believe me I'm not afraid of people like him. I got robbed at knifepoint by a spotty-faced kid who forced his way in here on a Friday night. I was on my own closing up and he forced me to open the till. He took his beady eyes off me while he was stuffing the night's takings in his pocket – that's when I hit the thieving little bastard as hard as I could over the head with a brandy bottle. He ran off, but the police saw him staggering up the High Road with blood pouring down his face. At first they thought he was drunk and had fallen over, but I'm pleased to say he got nicked and I got my money back.'

Kingston could hear the anger in her voice as she spoke about being the victim of violent crime, but he wanted to know more about the driver of the Cortina.

'Can you tell me, in as much detail as possible, what the driver looked like?' He held the pen to his pocket notebook.

'About five feet eight to ten inches tall. He might have looked broader than he was because of the donkey jacket, so I'd say he was probably of medium build. He wore a grey cloth cap, with the peak pulled low over his forehead, but I could see he had a round face and ruddy complexion – like some of the heavy drinkers I get in here. I couldn't see much of his hair because of the cap, but the sides were black, and his sideburns came down to just below his earlobes.'

'What about his age?'

'Hard to say, really, but maybe late thirties to mid-forties.'

'What about his eyes and nose?'

'I never saw his eyes, but his nose looked a bit bulbous and red, again like a heavy drinker's.'

'Would you help a police artist create an impression of the driver?'

'Yes, but I can't leave the pub for long—'

'It's OK, I'll get the artist to come here. It should only take about an hour, if that, and I'll make sure it's after three while you're closed.

Can you talk me through the robbery from the moment the three men got out of the car?'

She said the three men who got out from the car and did the robbery wore black balaclavas, except the big man in the front, who had a stocking mask on. The man who was sitting in the rear nearside passenger seat led the other two at a steady pace across the street in an 'A' formation. Kingston asked if she could give an estimate of their heights and any weapons they were carrying now they were out of the car. She thought about it and said the man in the front of the car was about six feet to six feet two inches tall and carrying a gun in his right hand. She thought the man next to him and the leader were both about five feet ten inches, and the one behind the leader had a sawn-off shotgun, which he held with both hands on his right side.

'The man leading them – was he armed?'

'Not that I noticed. The only thing I saw him carrying was the cash box from the Securicor van as they left.' She continued and said that while the tall man and the leader were at the back of the van, the man with the shotgun was at the front, pointing it at the driver. 'A young man suddenly ran across the road and tried to get the shotgun off him, but got knocked to the ground. He was on his back and I could hear him beg for his life, then there was a loud bang and he screamed in agony as he thrashed around on the pavement and clutched his stomach. I couldn't believe what I'd just seen – he was defenceless, there was no need to shoot him. The next thing I saw was the Cortina outside the bank and the three men jump in it with the cash box. I ran downstairs to go and help the man who'd been shot, but when I opened the pub door I could see the two Securicor guards and the bank manager helping him, so I stayed here.'

'The young man who got shot was an off-duty police officer.'

'Is he dead?'

'Thankfully no. He's got cuts and bruises over his chest and stomach, which are no doubt painful. In some ways it's his lucky day as the shotgun cartridge was loaded with rice – lead pellets would have killed him at that range. The next person who crosses their path might not be so lucky,' he said intentionally.

He wanted to gauge Fiona's reaction and see if, after recounting the terrible event, she'd still be willing to assist the investigation.

'Then let's hope you catch the bastards and I can identify the driver before anyone else gets hurt. You want another Scotch?'

'No thanks.' He finished his whisky and handed her the empty glass. 'I'd appreciate it if you kept what you've told me to yourself – the less people that know, the better it is for us, apart from the team, that is.'

She touched the side of her nose and smiled.

'Mum's the word and Fiona's my name, DI Kingston.'

'For future reference, Fiona . . . mine's Stewart.'

He admired her feisty spirit; she was strong-willed and confident, yet courageous and considerate of others. He wondered if she had always been that way, or if being a widow and a pub landlady had moulded her outlook on life. Although it seemed the bank robbers hadn't seen her watching them, he was concerned about her safety if they ever found out she could possibly identify one of them. He thought about warning her, but knew she was the kind of woman who would quickly dismiss his concerns.

CHAPTER FIVE

Cam was outside the bank, speaking to MP on the car radio and making notes, as Kingston returned to the vehicle.

'Can you give me the location again, Central 888, over?'

'It's Edgar House off Blake Hall Road. The garages are at the rear of it.'

'Thanks, MP. DI Kingston is with me now, so I'll update him.'

Cam replaced the radio mike on its clip.

Kingston heard the last bit of the radio conversation and looked pleased.

'Have they found the Cortina?'

Cam handed him the pocket notebook.

'Possibly. The fire brigade got called out to a garage on fire at Edgar House, which they're still dousing down. They found a vehicle inside it on fire, which they think might be a Mark 4 Cortina.'

'Any index?'

'I asked, but apparently the number plates have melted.'

'Do we know who owns the garage?'

'Not yet. The location is just over a mile away and there's a uniform officer on scene who spoke to the fire brigade and radioed it in. Shall I get MP to tell him to start making enquiries re the garage owner?'

Kingston shook his head. 'No, go back to Woodville Road, then take Dabs and Tennison to Edgar House. He can examine the burnt Cortina while she organises the house-to-house enquiries about the garage. Call in uniform assistance and tell Tennison she's in charge. I also want to know if any of the residents saw anyone coming or going from the garage, not just today but in the last two weeks.'

'She's just started on the squad, Guv. I can run the H to H if you—'

'She's a bloody DS and worked on murders, so she should be capable of supervising house-to-house.'

'There are over a hundred flats there, so it might take a few hours to—'

Kingston was becoming irritated. 'You can help Tennison, but I want it done today. Me and the Colonel will get a lift back to the Rigg with Teflon and his crew in 887.' He looked at his watch. 'I'm calling an office meeting for three. Bring Tennison and Dabs back with you, as I want everyone on the team there.'

'We might get a tip-off about who was responsible,' Cam suggested, trying to cheer Kingston up.

'In my opinion these guys are professionals, and from the way they operate, a tip-off seems about as likely as me winning the pools.'

* * *

Two uniformed officers were helping Dabs and Jane search the rubble-strewn ground where the police car had crashed into the house, looking for any bullets that might have become dislodged from the engine block on impact. Jane felt quite nervous as some of the bricks were still hanging precariously from the building and one fell quite close to her. After twenty minutes of searching, Dabs looked up at Jane and the two officers.

'I think that's the best we can do for now. We've recovered two bullets earlier and I'm reasonably sure we'll find a third somewhere in the engine compartment when we examine the car at the lab.'

'Do you want me to check across the junction in Grove Road to see if the bullet hit anything there?' she asked as she brushed the brick dust from her clothes.

'I wouldn't worry – it'll be a bit like looking for a needle in a haystack as it could have gone anywhere.'

As Juliet 1 was taken away on the low-loader, Cam pulled up and told them about the burnt-out Cortina and the house-to-house enquiries Kingston wanted done at Edgar House.

'As a DS I've overseen house-to-house in murder investigations, so I'm happy to organise it.'

Cam smiled. 'It's OK, Kingston asked me to organise it while you and Dabs deal with the Cortina.'

Jane was disappointed. 'Fine. If you need any advice or help, then please just ask.'

'Thanks, but I know how to do house-to-house ... Sarge,' he replied.

Jane thought his attitude was rather surly considering she was just trying to be helpful. She also wondered from the way he addressed her if the Colonel had mentioned her objection to being called "Treacle" instead of Sergeant. As she got in the car with Dabs, Cam turned on the siren and blue light before pulling out at speed. This time she was prepared for the sudden acceleration and braced herself with both hands firmly on the passenger side of the dashboard.

Travelling to the scene, they received a radio call that the garage the Cortina was found in was number 29, but they hadn't yet located the owner. As the car turned into Blake Hall Road they could see a plume of grey smoke rising above the flats and a large LFB engine blocking the entrance route to the garages, so Cam parked as near as he could. Edgar House consisted of 128 maisonette flats in three two-storey blocks that were built, and joined together, in a Y shape. Jane initially thought Edgar House would be council flats, but on seeing the well-maintained communal gardens and how neat and tidy the estate was, she wondered if it was a private estate.

As Jane, Cam and Dabs got out of the squad car, a uniform van pulled up behind them and a sergeant and five PCs got out. The sergeant walked straight up to Cam.

'Are you from the Flying Squad?' he asked, and Cam nodded. 'The duty inspector told us you needed some assistance with house-to-house enquiries regarding the armed robbery at Barclays. Will someone be briefing us on what needs to be done?'

'Yes, I will. DI Kingston asked me to sort it out for him as he's still at the bank.'

Jane was getting fed up with Cam's attitude and thought he should have had the decency to introduce her and Dabs.

'I'm WDS Tennison and this is Dave Morgan, our Senior SOCO on the squad—'

Cam cut in, 'They'll be doing the forensic work on the burnt-out motor. DI Kingston wants enquiries made at all the flats to find out who owns the garage, and to see if the residents noticed any suspicious activity around the garage the car was found in during the last two weeks.'

'No problem, I'll let my team know.' The sergeant started to walk off.

'It might help to see how many garages there are first and if they have corresponding numbers to a flat,' Jane remarked.

Cam looked flustered. 'I was just going to do that '

Jane hadn't finished. 'Have you got any house-to-house forms for the sergeant and his officers to fill in?'

'There should be some in a box in the boot of the car,' Cam muttered.

He went to the boot, opened it and rummaged through the box, which contained plenty of statement forms but no house-to-house ones.

'There don't appear to be any left,' he said, red-faced.

Jane moved over to Cam's side and spoke quietly.

'Have you led a house-to-house enquiry team before?'

'I know what I'm doing – someone obviously forgot to restock the box with them,' he whispered.

'I take it that would normally be the driver of the car's responsibility?' she asked, but he didn't reply. 'I thought as much.' She turned to the sergeant. 'Would you mind contacting your station and asking if someone could kindly drop off some house-to-house forms, as we seem to have used them all in Woodville Road. Can you also ask for some copies of the Edgar House electoral register to be printed off for each officer, then they can check the residents' names against the register.'

The sergeant contacted the station on the radio and the operator told him they'd get the forms and copies of the register sent down right away. When he finished Jane continued.

'If any residents did see anyone acting suspiciously on the estate, or near the garages, today or recently, we will need a detailed description of what they saw and the person or persons they saw. Please notify me right away in case urgent follow-up action is needed – the same goes for the owner of the garage when you identify them. If there are any flats where you get no reply, then you still need to fill in a proforma to that effect and leave a note asking them to contact us at the Flying Squad office – ADC Murray will give you the squad details. When you've finished, give him the completed forms and we'll go through them later.'

The sergeant was confused. 'I thought you were with forensics?'

'No, I'm a WDS on the Flying Squad,' she replied firmly.

'Really?'

The sergeant looked surprised, as did his uniformed colleagues next to him. Jane looked around, then leant closer, as if wanting to speak to him in confidence. The sergeant leant forward, but she spoke loudly enough for everyone to hear.

'Keep it to yourself, but I'm actually making it up about being on the Flying Squad just to shock every male officer I come across – and so far, it's working a treat.'

She turned sharply, stepped over the fire engine hosepipes, and strode off towards the garages, followed by Dabs.

'Is she always so touchy?' the sergeant asked Cam.

'It's her first day on the squad so she likes to think she's "the big cheese".'

'She seems to know how house-to-house should be done,' the sergeant remarked.

Cam shrugged. 'There's nothing difficult about house-to-house. Truth is she hasn't a clue about how we work on the squad.'

'You reckon she'll last long?'

'Doubt it. She's already pissed off the Governor.'

* * *

At the far end of the flats there were thirty numbered brick-built and asbestos-roofed garages in two rows of fifteen facing each other. The burnt-out garage 29 was at the far end of the row, and five fire brigade officers were present. Two firemen were still hosing down the roof and the inside of the garage, while one was working on the Cortina, which had been winched out onto the concrete driveway by a red fire brigade Land Rover. A cloud of steam rose from the car as the cold water hit the hot metal, and the acrid smell of burnt rubber from the tyres filled the air.

Jane approached a young uniformed PC, who was encouraging some residents who had gathered to return to their flats as the smoke and burnt tyre fumes were not good for their lungs. Jane introduced herself and he told her what had happened so far and gave her the details of the occupant who had made the original 999 call to the fire brigade.

'He was going to go out in his car, which is parked in a garage at the opposite end, and said he saw smoke coming out of garage 29, so he ran back to his flat and dialled 999. I spoke to him and asked if he saw anyone in or around any of the garages before the fire, but he said he didn't. A few residents were coming out to see what was going on and I asked them to return to their flats for their own safety. Also, knowing you'd probably want to do house-to-house, I thought it was best they were indoors.'

'You've done a good job. Are the properties council-owned flats?' she asked.

'No, they belong to a housing association who rent them out to the tenants, most of whom are forty-plus. The flats and grounds are well maintained, and the majority of the residents are friendly and pro-police – you always get a cup of tea and a biscuit when you walk round the estate.'

'Sounds like crime is a rare event round here?'

'Pretty much. Problems only occur when the little scrotes from the estate down the road come up here causing trouble. There's the occasional burglary and criminal damage but that's about it.'

'Would you mind manning the scene while myself and SOCO Morgan deal with the forensic examinations?'

'Not at all. If you need a hand I'm more than happy to help out.'

Jane thanked him and walked over to one of the fire brigade officers who, unlike the others, had two black bands on his yellow helmet and was giving orders to his colleagues. She showed him her warrant card.

'I'm WDS Tennison and this is Senior SOCO Morgan. We're investigating a bank robbery and believe the burnt-out Cortina might have been used as a getaway car.'

'I thought the Flying Squad dealt with bank robberies?'

She frowned. 'We do and that's why I'm here. Are you the senior brigade officer in attendance?'

'Yes, I'm the duty crew manager. I'd say the car was deliberately set alight as the smell of petrol was strong when we ripped the garage door off with the winch. It's fortunate the garages are brick-built with asbestos roofs otherwise the fire could have spread quickly along the whole row.'

'I'm surprised the petrol tank didn't explode,' Jane remarked.

The crew manager grinned. 'It's extremely rare for that to happen, other than in the movies. As you can see the petrol cap's still in place, which suggests your bank robbers wanted time to get away without attracting attention from a petrol tank explosion.'

'They probably had a changeover car hidden in the garage,' Dabs added.

The crew manager said the car would need hosing down for a few more minutes, then it should be cool enough for SOCO Morgan to examine. Jane looked inside the garage, but it was now just a wet, sooty shell with nothing in it other than a large pool of black water. The interior of the car was so badly damaged, just the bare metal frames and springs of the seats were left, and both number plates had been destroyed. Dabs took some photographs of the car and pointed to the back footwell.

'From the shape of it and small remnants of red paint, I'd say that burnt metal object is a petrol can.'

'Are you going to get the car towed to the lab for examination?' Jane asked.

'I'd like to do it here, if possible, then have the vehicle taken to one of our car pounds for closer examination if it's needed. They get a bit touchy about burnt-out cars being taken up to the lab as they make such a mess.' He turned to the crew manager. 'Could you open the bonnet and boot for us, please?'

The crew manager used the hooked end of his fireman's axe to force the boot open. Inside they could see the congealed remnants of badly burnt clothing, which they agreed were probably what was left of the outfits the robbers wore.

'They'll sort out what's what and take fibre samples at the lab,' Dabs said as Jane held open an exhibits bag for him to put the bits of burnt clothing in.

The crew manager was having difficulty prising the bonnet open with his axe and asked one of his colleagues to assist him. As Jane watched them, she suspected the car was probably stolen and knew that identifying the owner would be an important part of the investigation. She recalled her attachment to Traffic Division, near the end of her uniformed probation, and learning how a small metal plate riveted to the chassis under the bonnet contained unique details about the car and its origin, which could be used to identify the registration and the owner.

'You know much about chassis plates, Dabs?'

'A bit, but don't ask me what all the numbers and letters on them mean.'

'We could get a traffic officer to examine it here and now,' she suggested.

Dabs nodded. 'Chassis plates are stamped metal and pretty resilient to fire.'

The crew manager and his colleague finally managed to open the bonnet and used the prop to hold it up. The engine compartment was badly burnt, with heat-buckled metal parts, molten plastic and burnt wires. Dabs leant forward and pointed to the fire-damaged chassis plate, which was barely readable.

'On second thoughts, it's probably best I remove the plate and send it to the lab for examination . . .'

Jane knew that would take even more time for a result.

'A traffic officer might be able to give us something positive here and now . . . Nothing ventured, nothing gained.'

Dabs agreed and asked the uniformed PC guarding the scene to contact a traffic vehicle examination unit and ask them to attend Edgar House. Jane thought about the scene at Woodville Road.

'Will the car's door sills have been damaged by the fire?' she asked the crew manager.

'Not if the seal between the sill and the door is tight enough.'

'Will it be all right to open the car doors now?'

He held up his right hand. 'I've got heavy-duty gloves on, so best I do it in case the handle's still a bit hot. I'll retrieve the burnt petrol can for you as well.'

'Thanks. Could you open the front passenger door first, please?'

'What's the interest in the door sills, Sarge?' Dabs asked as the crew manager opened the passenger door.

'It's to do with the blood we found on Woodville Road.'

She stepped forward to get a closer look at the sill, as did Dabs, who now realised what she was hoping to find. Jane smiled as she pointed to two drops of blood on the sill.

'A young witness called Abby said the man who shot at the police car got out of the front passenger seat and back in it when the car left. I think the blood drops on the sill and in Woodville Road might be from an injury he sustained.'

Dabs was impressed with her thought process.

'I'll bet you're right, Jane – to be honest I hadn't thought about checking the sill. Sorry, I meant to say Sarge.'

'It's OK to call me Jane when we're in a one-to-one situation, but obviously not in front of the team.'

'I don't mean to be rude, but you might have a problem there . . . No one calls Stanley "Sarge", and the DI and DCI are both referred to as "Guv". In fact, DI Kingston doesn't mind you calling him Stu or Stewart, off duty.'

'I don't have a problem with Christian names off duty, but I think you should always show respect for rank at work. I've even told DC Gorman I expect to be addressed as Sarge when I'm on duty.'

Dabs winced. 'And how did the Colonel take that?'

'He didn't say anything, but he seemed all right about it.'

Dabs wanted to give Jane some words of advice about how different things were on the Flying Squad compared to a normal CID office, but he decided it was best to let her find out for herself. He changed the subject and said he'd take swabs of the blood on the sill, then get it tested at the lab against the blood at the Woodville Road scene to see if the samples were the same blood group. The crew manager retrieved the burnt can from the back seat, sniffed the inside and said it smelt of petrol, then handed it to Dabs, who put it in a large nylon exhibits bag to prevent the evaporation of any fluid left inside it.

Jane entered the details of the can and burnt clothing in the exhibits book while Dabs photographed the burnt-out garage. She looked up and saw a traffic patrol PC walking towards her.

'I'm PC Turner from the vehicle examination unit. A DS Tennison from the Flying Squad wants us to examine a car. Is he about?'

Jane sighed as she raised her eyebrows.

'You're talking to him,' she replied tersely.

Turner looked embarrassed. 'Sorry, I was expecting—'

'I know – a man. You're not the first to be surprised by me today.'

'How can I help you, Sarge?'

She told him about the bank robbery and the discovery of the burnt-out car.

'It's possible the Cortina is stolen, and the registration plates were copied from a similar make and model. The chassis plate has burn damage, but I'd appreciate it if you'd have a look at it and see if you can glean any info from it.'

'No problem.'

He walked over to the car, followed by Jane, and looked in the engine compartment.

'A bit buckled and charred,' Turner observed, and rubbed his finger on the plate, removing some of the soot. 'I've got chemicals in the car for cleaning off burn damage. If it's all right with you I'd like to remove the plate, because the details are stamped in the underside like a mirror image and often less damaged in arson cases.'

Jane could sense his enthusiasm as he spoke.

'Fine by me, PC Turner. You're the vehicle expert so do whatever you feel will get the best results.'

'I'll go fetch my equipment,' he said and walked off at a brisk pace.

Having finished updating the exhibits book, Jane decided to speak to Cam Murray and ask how the house-to-house enquiries were going. She could see the uniformed sergeant and some of the PCs speaking to people on their doorsteps but there was no sign of Murray. She walked over to the sergeant when he'd finished speaking to the resident.

'How's the house-to-house going?' she asked.

'No reply at a lot of the flats – so they're probably residents who work during the day. I'll arrange for some of the late turn officers to attend the no reply's this evening.'

'Anything of interest so far regarding the owner of garage twenty-nine?' she asked, hoping to hear something positive.

'The garage numbers don't directly relate to a flat number and you pay extra to rent one. My officers have got details of some of the garage owners, but not twenty-nine so far.'

'Is there not a resident caretaker?'

'Yes, but he's on holiday. I spoke to the relief caretaker – he doesn't know who uses what garage. He also said some of them are vacant and left open all the time to avoid break-in damage.'

'When will the regular caretaker be back?'

'Next week. I also spoke to a lady who's sixty-two and lives at flat fourteen Edgar House. She'd been out shopping and got off at the bus stop in Blake Hall Road. From her timing I'd estimate it wasn't long after the bank robbery occurred. She saw two men walking towards Felstead Road and one was carrying a large black holdall in his right hand. They caught her attention because the holdall was like the one she bought her grandson at Christmas.'

'Any description of the men?'

'Not really, she was on the opposite side of the road and only saw them from behind. She thought they were about five feet eight to five feet ten in height, one was dark-haired, the other lighter col-oured. Both were smartly dressed in casual clothes and she thinks one of them was smoking a cigar.'

'Which one?'

'She didn't know.'

'Then what made her think it was a cigar?'

'I didn't ask, but I guess from the smell.'

Jane felt he could have gone into more detail about the clothing and the cigar with the witness, but didn't want to be critical as she knew the woman could be interviewed again.

'She didn't say they were acting suspiciously or looked nervous,' he remarked.

'Where's Felstead Road?' Jane asked, suspecting the men may have been involved and changed clothes.

'Left out of Edgar House, then first left again.'

'When you've finished at Edgar could you make enquiries in Felstead Road to see if anyone saw two men, or one carrying a black holdall?'

The sergeant looked at his watch. 'Well, my lads are all early shift and off duty at two, but if you're prepared to authorise some overtime we could . . .'

'Three hours max, that's all – get what you can done and hand the rest over to the late shift.'

'You've also got Selsdon Road, which is off Blake Hall and directly opposite Felstead. The two men could have crossed the road before they got to Felstead—'

'If you get nothing of use at Felstead then do Selsdon as well. Have you seen ADC Murray?'

'Last time I saw him he went into the ground floor flat at the far end of the block there.'

'Can you ask him to come and see me when he reappears?'

'Will do.'

The sergeant went back to making his enquiries.

Returning to the garages, Jane saw the crew manager helping his colleagues reel in the hoses they had used to put out the fire.

'Are you off now?' she asked him.

'Yes, we're all done here. I'll type up my report when I get back to the station and get it delivered to you . . . Sorry, I forgot your name,' he said, taking out a pocket notebook and pen.

'Detective Sergeant Jane Tennison – two n's and one s.'

'Do I address the envelope "The Sweeney" or "The Flying Squad"?' he asked, trying to be funny.

'Flying Squad, twelve Rigg Approach, which is just off Lea Bridge Road.'

THE DIRTY DOZEN | 64

'I loved that TV series, *The Sweeney*. I don't recall any police-women working on the squad with Regan and Carter – they were right hard nuts who loved giving the villains a slap. Is it like that in real life?'

Jane ignored his remark.

'Can you tell me if the garage door was locked or unlocked when you got here?' she asked, recalling what the uniformed sergeant had told her.

'I don't know, we used some hooks attached to a winch to pull it from the frame. Hang on a minute.'

He walked over to the burnt and buckled garage door, which had been placed up against a high brick wall, and examined the lock.

'I'd say it was locked—'

'Are you sure?' she asked him, realising the investigative impor-tance of his observation.

'Reasonably. Then again, it could have been unlocked and rip-ping it off somehow re-engaged the lock. Either way I can't be certain and I'll have to say the same in my report.'

As the crew manager left, Jane checked the garage door for her-self but couldn't tell if it was locked or unlocked as the metal pulley wire that would have been attached to it had been ripped off. She called out to Dabs, who was examining the interior of the car, to join her.

'Can you remove the lock from the garage door?' she asked as he approached.

He lifted the door from the wall, so he could see the exterior and interior mechanism of the lock.

'It's held in place by rivets that will need to be broken off with a hammer and chisel.'

'Don't damage the lock—'

'I'll get the traffic officer to help me as he's got the right tools for the job, but why do you need it?'

'It might be useful if we arrest a suspect and find a key that fits it.'

Dabs grinned. 'Bit like Cinderella and the shoe . . . I have to say, Jane, you're a good lateral thinker.'

'Like I said before – Paul Lawrence taught me well.'

'I doubt that it's all down to him.'

'Where's PC Turner gone?' she asked, looking around.

'He's on his car radio about the chassis plate. He's really into his work and it's actually quite interesting how much a chassis plate can tell you. He managed to clean a lot of the burn damage off and used . . . Actually, ask him to show you how he got the details from the plate – it's quite simple but ingenious.'

Jane did as Dabs had suggested and Turner held up the chassis plate for her to see.

'A good rub down with a few chemicals allowed me to record some of the details, then to get the rest I used this.' He held up a lump of plasticine. 'Although you can't read some of the numbers and letters on the top side of the burnt plate, the original stamping leaves marks on the underside. I pressed it into this plasticine and got most of the numbers and letters missing from the top – simple but effective, don't you think?'

'And I thought Play-Doh was just for kids.'

'Actually, I made this myself, with flour, water, salt, boric acid and mineral oil.'

'Have you got enough detail from the plate to identify the registration and owner?'

He handed her a bit of paper on which he'd written down the information on the chassis plate.

'The details provide information on things like the manufacturer, country of origin, body style, engine type, model year, assembly plant, and production number.'

'And the owner is . . . ?' Jane asked, wanting him to get to the point.

'I'm waiting for Traffic Control to radio me back with that. There are eleven figures in the code, and the last six are a number unique to that vehicle, which control are checking out.' He pointed to the Cortina, then the chassis plate he was holding. 'The first five figures break down like this. B is the country of origin, obviously Britain in this case. The second letter A is the assembly plant and the code for Dagenham. The next two numbers are for body and gear change type, then the following two are the year and month of manufacture, which is February 1976.'

'Oscar November two, from control, receiving . . . over?' a voice said over the traffic car radio.

PC Turner picked up the radio. 'Oscar November two, receiving. Go ahead . . . over.'

'We've got a match to the chassis plate number. It comes back to a brown 1976 Mark 4 Ford Cortina saloon reported lost or stolen two weeks ago by a Mr Frank Braun of nineteen Mount Pleasant Road, Tottenham N17. He's owned the vehicle from new.'

'Did you get all that?' the PC asked Jane, who nodded as she jotted down the details in her pocket notebook. 'All received, control, out.'

She flicked back a page in her pocket notebook.

'The index of the car seen outside the bank was SLM 273R, with a registered keeper in Sussex.'

'If, as it would seem, the burnt-out car is the one they used during the robbery, then they must have changed the plates to a matching Cortina just after the car was stolen. That way it wouldn't come up as LOS if you did a check on it.'

She had already considered the possibility but didn't say so.

'Thanks for your help, PC Turner. Identifying the owner of the Cortina so quickly is a step forward for the investigation.'

'There is something else of interest I noticed about the car I'd like to show you.'

'Certainly.' Jane followed him to the driver's side of the vehicle.

'I examined what's left of the car's steering column and couldn't see any signs that the ignition system was bypassed to steal it.'

'Do you mean like 'hot-wired?' she asked.

'Yes. The plastic covering around the ignition barrel has melted in situ and that means it wasn't removed, which you'd need to do to get access to the wires. To be sure, I cut away what was left of it and there were no signs that any of the wires connected to the ignition barrel had been cut or tampered with.'

'Are you saying the Cortina wasn't actually stolen?'

'It's possible, but you can easily start these types of cars by pushing a screwdriver into the ignition keyhole and turning it.'

'Has that been done in this case?'

'Because of the fire damage it's hard to say without physically removing the ignition barrel.'

'You have my permission to do that.'

'Thanks, but I'll need to take it back to the station where I can clean it up and take it to bits, so I can examine it under a microscope for any damage or screwdriver marks. Then I can give you a definitive answer.'

'That would be great, thanks. If it turns out the ignition is undamaged, then whoever was driving the Cortina must have had a key, which also suggests the owner of the car may have made a false report about it being lost or stolen.'

CHAPTER SIX

Jane helped Dabs hold the garage door while PC Turner removed the rivets from the front of the lock.

'You should button up your coat. Your clothes are getting soot on them from the garage door,' Dabs told her.

She looked down and saw black streaks on her white blouse, blue jacket and skirt. She knew there was no point in trying to brush them off as it would only make the marks worse. She'd have to wait until she got back to the station to try and clean them off.

'It's about time the job issued some sort of protective clothing for this type of work,' she remarked.

'As Scene of Crime Officers, we're issued with waterproof leggings and a coat, but they make you sweat so much it's not worth the bother of wearing them. I always keep a change of clothes at work in case I get dirty at a crime scene.'

'As this is my first day on the squad I didn't think to bring in any casual clothes.'

'I wouldn't worry about it too much. Apart from the governors, no one dresses smart on the squad – it's not the type of work where you want to stand out as a detective.'

'Do they have a woman's locker room at Rigg?'

Dabs laughed. 'There's a locker room, men's toilets and a shower in the basement, as well as a small gym area with some weights, a punchbag and boxing gloves. Some of the lads like to keep fit with an early morning workout, especially the Colonel, as you probably noticed from his physique. Personally, I'm not into all that keep fit stuff. Snooker's my sport and I play for the Met team.'

'No ladies' toilets then?' she asked, not relishing the thought of sharing with the men.

'There's a loo on the top floor that KP has labelled "ladies only".'

'Who's KP?'

'Katie Powell, the office clerk, also known as "Nuts". She thinks it's because her initials are the same as the peanut brand, but some of the lads think she is nuts.'

'Why's that?' she asked, deducing KP was the woman she'd spoken to over the intercom when she first arrived at the squad office that morning.

'KP's pedantic about the office being neat and tidy, she checks every bit of paperwork to make sure it's written up, filed and labelled correctly. If you're one penny out on your weekly expenses claim, she'll make you type the whole form out again instead of just using Tipp-Ex to correct the error. You'd think the money was coming out of her own bank account, not the Commissioner's.'

'A good filing system isn't a bad thing if you've got a big investigation running; it makes the paperwork easier to find.'

'Don't get me wrong, she's good at her job but likes to think she knows best all the time – and she's a bit of an arse-licker around the governors.'

'How do you mean?'

'Yes, sir, no, sir, three bags full, sir – especially with Kingston, who she worked for as the CID clerk when he was at Tottenham nick.'

'How long's Kingston been on the squad?'

'Since he was promoted to DI, which was just over a year ago, but he was also a DC and DS on the squad before that. He's as hard as nails, knows his stuff and is well respected. He was a good boxer in his day and won the Met's Lafone Cup.'

'To be honest, I'm not into boxing. I don't see the point in two men trying to knock each other out.'

'Are you the first woman to be attached to the Flying Squad?' PC Turner interjected.

'Yes, and no doubt you are amazed as everyone else seems to be – but please, I'm not in the mood for any more wisecracks about it.'

'Actually, I was going to say you've done well for yourself.'

Jane was surprised. 'Oh, thank you . . .'

'My wife's a WPC in the job at Plaistow on K division. She was in the Women's Police before it became integrated with the men in 1973, so I know first-hand how hard it is for women to get on in the police force. She's applied three times for the Advanced Driver Course and been turned down. I'm an advanced driver myself and given her lessons, so I know for a fact she's up to it, and as capable as any male drivers – it's just prejudice because she's a woman.'

Jane smiled. 'I've no doubt you're right, PC Turner.'

'Well, for what it's worth, I say give as good as you get. My wife does – even at home!' He laughed as he prised the garage door lock off and handed it to Jane. 'Good luck with your investigation and I'll ring your office in the morning with the result of my examination on the Cortina's ignition barrel.'

She and Dabs thanked PC Turner for his help. As he left, the low-loader turned up to take the burnt-out Cortina to the car pound. While Dabs spoke to the truck driver, Jane decided to have a look in Selsdon and Felstead Road, to see if there were any parking restrictions and if the robbers could have parked a changeover car there.

As she walked off the estate into Blake Hall Road she noticed a block of four-storey flats opposite, called the Mallards, of which at least forty overlooked the entrance to Edgar House. Similarly, there was also Harley Court, next to the Mallards, which was a three-storey block of about forty flats on the corner of Blake Hall Road and Selsdon Road. She could see that some of the flats also overlooked part of Felstead Road and realised that the house-to-house enquiries would have to be widened, in case anyone in the other flats had seen the two men with a holdall or anything suspicious that might help the investigation. She made some notes in her pocket notebook to give PC Murray, beginning to wonder why he had been told by Kingston to organise the house-to-house enquiries.

Jane crossed over into Selsdon Road and saw there were fourteen garages at the rear of Harley Court, and none of them were numbered. She spoke to a middle-aged male resident she saw coming out of the rear of the flats, who said the council owned the garages and rented them out, some to people who didn't even live in Harley Court. Jane made another note in her pocket notebook that this would also need to be followed up with the council, as any change-over car could have been left in one of these garages.

As Jane crossed Blake Hall Road towards Felstead Road she noticed the position of the bus stop, and an island in the middle of the road. She thought to herself that if the two men had parked a changeover car at the rear of Harley Court, they would have crossed the road before passing the bus stop and not been in the position they were when the elderly lady saw them. The first five metres on either side of Felstead Road had double yellow lines and then the parking was unrestricted. The sides and back garden fences of numbers 21 and 23 Blake Hall Road ran along Felstead Road for about thirty metres on either side, which meant that stretch of the road was not really overlooked, other than through a couple of side windows at 21 and 23 Blake Hall Road. Jane thought it seemed a likely place to leave a changeover car inconspicuously parked, as a short distance up the road there were rows of large semi-detached Edwardian style houses with driveways and street parking that was overlooked by the residents.

She remembered the sergeant mentioning the witness thought one of the men was smoking a cigar, and looked around for any recently discarded cigar and cigarette butts. There was no sign of any cigars, only a few butts from different cigarette brands that looked quite old.

'I thought you wanted me and my officers to do the house-to-house in Felstead Road.'

Jane looked up and saw the sullen-faced uniformed sergeant and three of his officers standing behind him.

'I do – I was just checking out the street to see what it was like for parking access as it's possible the robbers had a changeover car.'

'Some of my lads needed to get off home, so there are just the four of us left to do the house-to-house until the late turn lads show up. It might take a bit longer than three hours' overtime . . .'

She knew what he was after.

'All right, make it four hours, but just do as much as you can at Edgar House and the houses on this side of Blake Hall Road for now. I'll need to speak to DI Kingston about extending the house-to-house to cover the flats at the Mallards and Harley Court. I take it you've finished at Edgar?'

'Not yet, and there has been no reply at quite a few flats.'

'Did anyone say anything of interest or that's worth following up?' she asked, wondering if the sergeant was being intentionally difficult.

'Nope – except for an old woman who saw the two men in Blake Hall Road . . .'

'I know, you already told me about her. Did no one you spoke to know who owned garage twenty-nine?'

'Yeah, a lady one of the lads spoke to said she thought the man at number forty owned it, but she hadn't seen him about for a while.'

'Did anyone knock on his door?'

'I don't know—'

Jane was amazed at the sergeant's incompetence.

'You don't know? Did you even bother to get a description of the man at number forty?'

'If you'd let me finish, I was going to say I told ADC Murray about him—'

'It's *PC* Murray. Where is he now?'

He held up a blue folder. 'I don't know. If I did I'd have given him these completed house-to-house forms.' He handed Jane the folder. 'I'm not responsible for Murray. He's on your squad – so *you* are . . . Unless there's anything else I can help you with, I've work to do.'

Jane was getting frustrated by his nonchalant attitude. She looked at her watch and saw it was nearly two o'clock.

'Seeing as the late shift officers should be here soon, we'll make that two hours' overtime, Sergeant. Just do the houses in Blake Hall Road – late shift can do Felstead and Selsdon.'

As she walked off towards Edgar House, a disgruntled PC shook his head.

'Well done, Sarge. A poxy two hours' overtime is hardly worth the effort.'

* * *

Approaching Edgar House, Jane could see Murray sitting in the squad car. She tapped on the window, but he wafted the radio mike in his hand at her to indicate he was talking to someone. She went around to the passenger side, and as she got in the car she recognised DI Kingston's voice over the radio.

'Well done, Cam – the lads have finished taking the statements from the Securicor crew, so we'll head back to Rigg. Tell Tennison to get the uniform lads to continue with the house-to-house for now and I'll decide what more needs to be done down there after the office meeting.'

'Will do, Guv . . . out.'

'What was that about?' she asked, wondering why Kingston said she was to speak to the uniformed officers.

'The woodentop sergeant was getting a bit stroppy with me giving him orders, so the Guv thought it'd be better if you spoke to him.'

'I just did that, and he said he hasn't seen you since you went into one of the ground floor flats.'

Cam looked flustered. 'I spoke to him before that . . . Anyway, I've updated the Guv about the owner of garage twenty-nine—'

'Who said . . . ?' She was eager to hear what Cam had found out.

'He was pleased I'd traced the owner and wants us to return to Rigg for an office meeting,' he said with a smug grin.

'I meant what did the owner of the garage say.'

'He wasn't there – he's in hospital recovering from a cataract operation. I spoke to his wife, Mrs Helen Clarke, who's in her late sixties. She said they've lived at the flats for six months, but since his eyesight problems Mr Clarke couldn't drive and she hasn't got a licence. They stopped using the garage just after they moved in.'

'Are they renting it out?'

'No, they've given the car to the daughter and son-in-law to use for now. His wife said if the cataract operation is successful he hopes to start driving again and then they'll carry on using the garage.'

'Did they keep it locked when they weren't using it?'

'I don't know – I didn't ask.'

'Did you ask who owned it before them?'

'No – I was told to find out who owned garage twenty-nine and that's what I did.'

'Sometimes you have to look beyond the end of your nose, Cam. I'll speak to the wife myself.'

She opened the passenger door to get out.

'She's gone to the hospital to see her husband.'

'Did she say when she'd be back?'

'No. I've got their details recorded on a house-to-house form – there's a phone number as well.'

'Put it in here with the others you've done,' she said, opening the folder the uniformed sergeant had given her.

Cam handed her four completed forms.

'Is that it? You've only visited four flats since we've been here?'

'A couple of them were elderly residents who needed reassuring that everything was fine, so I had a cup of tea and a chat with them.'

She couldn't help noticing the crumbs around his mouth.

'And a few chocolate digestives by the looks of it. I'll go and get Dabs – then I'd like to go back via Barclays Bank in the High Road.'

'Why? The team and scene of crime are all finished there and gone back to Rigg, so there's nothing to do—'

'Well, there's something I want to check out – so just do as I ask, please, and don't question my decisions.'

Cam gave a grunt of disapproval, making it clear he didn't think she'd last long on the squad if she started throwing her weight about like that.

*   *   *

He pulled up outside the Crown public house, where Jane got out of the car and crossed over the road to the bank. The Securicor van had returned to its depot and life had returned to normal in the street, with several people out shopping. Jane stood on the steps and looked around, surveying the scene of the robbery and the short distance to Aylmer Road, where the four robbers in the Cortina had parked.

'Can I help you, madam?' a well-spoken male voice asked.

She got out her warrant card as she turned around and saw a man in his forties, smartly dressed in a three-piece grey pinstripe suit, white shirt and tie. She suspected he was something to do with the bank and introduced herself as WDS Tennison from the Flying Squad.

'Ah, I'm the manager of this branch. Is there something I can help you with? I've already been interviewed by a DI Kingston and I also made a statement to a DC, whose name I can't remember, but everyone else referred to him as the Colonel.'

'That'll be DC Gorman,' Jane told him.

'Would you like to come in and have a coffee or tea?' he asked with a polite smile.

'Thank you, but I'm a bit pressed for time as I have to get back to the office for a meeting.'

'It was a relief to hear that the officers in the police car and the off-duty one who got shot here are all all right. The men who did this are the dregs of the earth. I suspect if they knew it was an off-duty officer who tried to stop them they would have shot him with a real bullet as well.'

'You're probably right, sir, but thankfully they didn't and he's alive . . .'

'If somewhat shaken, no doubt. You can still see the rice that was in the shotgun cartridges on the pavement.'

Jane asked the bank manager if he knew exactly where the men had parked up in the Cortina before the robbery. He pointed across the road.

'I believe it was on the left side of Aylmer Road as we look at it – about where that white builder's van is now parked. I didn't see the car, other than from behind when they made their getaway. I was in the bank during the robbery and set the alarm off when I heard the sound of a shotgun.'

'Do you know if the area where the Cortina was parked was searched by the scene-of-crime officers?'

'I would have thought so. I know they fingerprinted the Securi-cor van, even though the robbers wore gloves, as there was loads of fingerprint dust over the front and back of it.'

Jane knew the initial 999 call, about the suspects in a Cortina, had been made by the landlady of the Crown, but she couldn't remember her name. The bank manager told her it was Fiona Simpson, and he thought DI Kingston had spoken to her as he saw him going in the pub just after he arrived at the scene.

Jane nodded. 'Thanks for your help.'

She carefully scanned the street as she crossed slowly over to Aylmer Road where the white van was parked. She checked the pavement and road beside the van but didn't see anything that caught her eye. She went into the pub; the premises had a large horseshoe bar, wooden floor and a snug area around the other side. Although the decor looked faded the premises had a clean, well-run look about it and an old but pristine Wurlitzer jukebox stood out in the corner of the bar. There were also several framed posters and pictures from Alfred Hitchcock films hanging on the walls, prompting Jane to recall reading somewhere that Hitchcock had been born in Leytonstone High Road, above his father's grocery shop.

'What can I get you, luv?' the woman behind the bar asked as Jane approached.

'I was looking for Fiona, the landlady.'

She frowned. 'Are you from the press? Because if you are I can't help you about the robbery.'

'No, I'm WDS Tennison,' Jane replied, showing her warrant card.

Fiona sighed. 'DI Kingston said he'd ring me first, and I did tell him I wasn't available until after three. You'll have to wait until I close the pub to do the artist's impression.'

'I'm not a police artist, I'm one of the Flying Squad officers investigating the robbery.'

'What? You're Flying Squad? Do me a favour! I've met a few in my time and none of them look like you, darling. You're a reporter and that's a fake police card you just showed me, ain't it?'

'Two of my colleagues are parked up outside your pub in an unmarked BMW – you can ask them if you don't believe me.'

'I will.'

Fiona lifted the bar counter flap and exited the pub into the High Road. It wasn't long before she returned and spoke to Jane.

'The Cortina was parked up opposite the Aylmer Road entrance to the pub, on the far side of the road – just about where Pete the plumber's white van is now.'

'Do you know where I can find Pete? I need him to move his van so I can look under it.'

'Yeah, he's in the snug bar playing pool with his apprentice. Look, I'm sorry if I doubted you. I just needed to be sure about who you were, especially as you didn't look like a detective with black marks all over your coat.'

'It's soot from a burnt-out car, and you're not the first to doubt who I am today. I'm beginning to wonder if I should have come to work in jeans and a T-shirt with a false moustache and a deep voice.'

'Slip your coat and jacket off and I'll give them a quick dab down with a sponge and water.'

'Thanks, but I'm pressed for time, so I'll do it when I get back to the station. Would you mind asking Pete to move his van for me?'

Jane noticed a sullen-looking Cam entering through the High Road entrance of the pub.

'The DI's been on the radio again wanting to know where we are.'

'What did you tell him?'

'That you were in the Crown talking to the landlady and I didn't have a clue what it was about.'

'And what was his reply?'

'That he'd already spoken to her and to get our arses back to Rigg right away – and that's putting it politely.'

'I'll be a minute or two yet—'

'What exactly are you doing?'

'Looking for something.'

'Looking for what?'

'I'll know if I find it.'

She walked off, leaving Cam shaking his head in frustration.

As Jane waited in Aylmer Road, Fiona came out of the pub.

'Pete's just finishing his game of pool and said he'll be two minutes . . . Hello, Betty, you all right?'

Jane turned to see who Fiona was speaking to and saw a frail elderly woman with a hunched back walking slowly and pulling a canvas shopping trolley.

'No, I bloody ain't, Fi,' Betty replied in a strong cockney accent. 'I couldn't get me shoppin' done what with all that 'oo-'a goin' on outside the bank this mornin'. If I was forty years younger, I'd 'ave 'ad a go at them bleedin' robbers.'

'It was terrible, Betty, but thankfully no one got badly hurt—'

'Oh, I'm glad to 'ear that. The sound of that gun goin' off was deafenin', and I honestly thought the young man who was lyin' on the pavement screamin' was a goner.'

Jane turned to Fiona. 'It sounds like she witnessed the robbery – I'd better have a word with her.'

'It's OK, your DI Kingston's dealing with her. Do you fancy a bottle of stout on the house, Betty?'

'I gotta get this shoppin' in the fridge, but I'll 'ave it when I come in later.'

She shuffled off.

As Fiona returned to the pub, a man dressed in blue overalls came out and held out a set of car keys to Jane.

'I'd better not drive the van as I've had three pints, officer. I was going to leave it here and pick it up in the morning.'

'I won't tell anyone if you don't.' She smiled.

As Pete got in his van, Jane asked him to reverse back about ten feet as the area behind him was clear. He started the engine, disengaged the handbrake and moved slowly backwards. As Jane watched the front nearside wheel rotating, she saw a squashed two-inch-long soggy-looking brown object stuck to the wheel.

'Stop!' she shouted, banging her fist on the side of the van.

Pete hit the brake pedal.

'Christ, have I run over another cat? That'll be the second one this week!' he said, ashen-faced.

'No, there's something stuck to the front wheel that I need to remove and have a closer look at. Stay where you are, it'll only take me a second to get it off.'

Jane removed a small exhibits bag from her coat pocket and, using her pen, slowly prised the brown object from the wheel and it dropped into the bag. Looking closely at it, she was reasonably sure it was what she'd hoped to find. To be certain she opened the bag and took a deep sniff. Not only did the object look like a squashed cigar butt – it also smelt like one.

CHAPTER SEVEN

It was raining again as Dabs opened the security gate to the rear of the building so Cam could drive in and park up.

'It would make it a damn sight easier if they left the bloody gate open while the office is manned,' Cam moaned.

Jane said nothing as she handed Cam the house-to-house folder, then got the bag of exhibits from the boot of the car and ran across the yard to join Dabs. He was entering the number code on the rear entrance keypad. She put the bag down, got out her pocket notebook and pen and asked him what the code was.

'They're easy to remember. It's 1066 for the front door and gate and 1812 for the back – Battle of Hastings and the Battle of Waterloo,' Dabs told her, entering the numbers.

But when he turned the handle nothing happened.

'Waterloo was 1815, you dunce,' said Cam, as he pushed past Dabs and Jane to enter the right code.

'Sorry, I was listening to Tchaikovsky's *1812 Overture* while I was driving to work this morning.'

'You like classical music then?' Jane asked.

'Yes, very much. I quite often go to concerts at the Royal Albert Hall.'

'It soothes the savage beast in him.'

Cam smirked as he shoved the door open and entered the building. He made no effort to hold the door open, and as it was on a hinged spring, it would have hit Jane if Dabs hadn't put his hand out just in time.

'Where's your manners, Cam?' Dabs said, as he held the door open for her.

Cam mumbled an apology, said he needed a 'Jimmy Riddle' and turned left to go down the concrete and worn green lino-covered stairs to the basement toilets.

The hallway and stairwell walls were painted a puke green, which couldn't disguise the patches of mould, and a damp smell filled the air. Jane was a bit surprised to find the interior of the building was in a worse condition than any police station she'd worked in before.

'Sorry about Cam – he can be a right surly git at times. He gets frustrated at not being involved in the investigative side of things. Mind you, he is a good driver.'

'You don't need to apologise for Cam's behaviour. If he wants to be an investigator he should apply to become a detective and stop moaning.'

Dabs put his hand on Jane's arm.

'Mind you don't slip on that wet patch. We've got a leaky roof, which was supposed to have been repaired weeks ago, and some of the stairs to the top floor are a bit wet as well. The cleaner does her best to keep on top of it, but she can't predict the rain unfortunately.'

'Was this building ever a working police station?'

'No, it used to be an office block with a woodwork factory on this floor where they made doors. The company went bust and the building lay empty until the Met bought it specifically for the Flying Squad a few years ago. As you can see, it needs some repair work and a lick of paint, but it's much better upstairs in the squad office.'

'Who uses the downstairs?'

'The surveillance team – though one section of it is used as a lock-up for the exhibits we seize during our investigations.'

'What – like guns and ammunition?'

'Yes, among other things. They go up to the firearms unit lab first for examination and when they've finished with them we store them here.'

'The building doesn't look very secure,' Jane said, having seen the outside in the morning.

'Believe me, it is, especially the exhibits room, which has an alarm linked to central control at the Yard. We had a case a year ago where a criminal did try and break in. He wanted to get the gun he used in a robbery so there was no evidence against him, but he was caught in the act and got an extra three years on his sentence when he was found guilty.'

Jane followed Dabs up the flight of stairs to the top floor landing, which was decorated similarly to the ground floor, though the mould on the walls and smell of damp were not so pronounced.

'Through the first door on the right there's a small kitchen area with a fridge, electric cooker and a kettle. Would you like a coffee?'

Jane said she was fine and Dabs continued.

'Next to it is the ladies' toilet.' Dabs pointed to a door that had an A4 sheet of paper Sellotaped to it and KP's TOILET written in large black letters. 'She'll have to add JT to that notice now,' he joked, and Jane smiled. 'The squad office is down the end on the left and opposite is my office with all my equipment and a forensic examination area. Though I do go into the main office quite a bit for a chat and office meetings.'

'How many are on the team?'

'Not including the surveillance team, there are twelve in total. Ten detectives – that's including the two Governors and you, PC Murray the driver and myself as the SOCO.'

As Jane followed Dabs she saw a wooden plaque screwed to a door and knew it was the squad room. On the plaque was a golden eagle, with its talons outstretched as if about to grab its prey. Above the eagle were the words THE FLYING SQUAD and below it NEW SCOTLAND YARD written in gold lettering. She knew the swooping eagle was the emblem of an elite unit, which had gained a reputation for courage and determination in opposing the most violent of London's armed robbers and hardened criminals. She touched the plaque with her hand, not for luck, but because she felt immense pride in being the first woman detective posted to the Flying Squad in its sixty-year history.

Standing in the corridor Jane could hear male voices chatting and laughing on the other side of the door, as well as the click-clack of typewriters and the ding of the bell as the carriage reached the end of the page. She straightened her coat and swept her hands through her hair. She didn't know why, but for the first time in ages she felt nervous about walking into an office full of male detectives, as Dabs opened the door for her. But her anxiety eased as she recognised the hearty laugh of DS Stanley. Being the first female member of the Flying Squad probably wasn't going to be a bed of roses, but it felt like it was the beginning of an exciting new chapter in her life. She walked into the room and saw the Colonel and Stanley standing together, with their backs to her, looking at something on the wall. Before she could speak, the Colonel nudged Stanley with his elbow.

'Get me Tennison's joining photo out of her job file on KP's desk – I'll stick it on the poster under her nickname.'

The Colonel sniggered, still with his back to Jane.

Stanley turned around and took a few steps towards the desk before he saw Jane and grimaced. She glared at him and held her finger to her mouth, making it clear she wanted him to keep quiet. She could see her police file, with her CID photograph clipped to it, on a neat and tidy desk near the door, which had a 'Katie Powell' name plaque on it.

The Colonel continued to look at the poster, admiring his handiwork.

'Get a move on, Stanley, Tennison will be here soon.'

Jane handed Dabs the bag of exhibits, then removed her photo from the file. As she crept up behind the Colonel she could see a 40in. by 30in. film poster for the 1967 movie, *The Dirty Dozen*. The poster depicted twelve men in army fatigues charging forward in a V formation, with machine guns blazing. Jane knew the film was considered a classic, full of Hollywood stars of the day like Lee Marvin and Charles Bronson. In the top left corner of the poster, in capital letters, were the words DAMN THEM OR PRAISE THEM . . . YOU'LL NEVER FORGET THE DIRTY DOZEN and added on a bit of paper underneath was OR TREACLE TENNISON.

'There you go,' Jane said and stuck the photograph under her name. The Colonel was visibly startled.

'Where'd you come from?' he asked, red-faced, and some of the detectives couldn't help laughing at his embarrassment.

'And there was us thinking you were a rough, tough marine,' DC Baxter said.

'You must have shit yourself when the enemy crept up on you.' Teflon grinned.

The Colonel glared at Teflon as everyone laughed, then turned to Jane with a smirk.

'It's just me and the lads having a bit of fun—'

'To be honest, DC Gorman, I was expecting a more traditional initiation ceremony, like cling film or fingerprint ink on the ladies' toilet seat. But this poster is so much more revealing . . .' She paused.

'What do you mean?' he asked.

'It shows you think you're a big Hollywood movie star, not a lowly copper working in a dingy office in Leytonstone.'

Some of the detectives chuckled.

'I'll take the photo down if you're that bothered about it,' he snapped, reaching to remove it.

Jane put a hand on his arm.

'If it makes you happy, leave it there. Now let me try and guess which one of the Dirty Dozen you are.' She deliberately paused to make out she was studying the poster and thinking about it. 'I'm leaning towards the character Charles Bronson played – but I can't remember his name . . .'

She paused again, knowing the Colonel would answer.

'Wladislaw,' he said smugly, clearly pleased she thought he was like Bronson.

'No, not him, it's another character I was thinking of.'

'Who?'

'Wasn't one of them a bigot nicknamed Maggott?'

Teflon laughed. 'Right on, Sarge, he was played by Telly Savalas. Ya man was bald like de Colonel,' he said in a comic Caribbean accent.

'Shut up, Teflon – no one asked for your opinion.' The Colonel scowled.

Teflon shook his head and tutted. 'You like to dish it out, Colonel, but you can't take it, can you?'

'Not when it's you,' the Colonel said coldly.

'What do you mean by that?' Teflon said, taking a step towards the Colonel to front him out.

The animosity between the two detectives was palpable, and Jane was about to step between them, but Stanley beat her to it and held his hands up to keep them apart.

'Right, fun's over. We've got a fucking robbery to investigate, where some of our own were nearly killed – so stop pissing about and get on with your work,' he said in a firm voice.

As the detectives returned to their desks, Stanley took Jane to one side.

'It was only a bit of fun, the Colonel didn't mean anything by it. Besides, we all have nicknames and take the piss out of each other, it helps relieve the pressure.'

'I don't mind a bit of fun or banter, but if I'm honest it felt a bit demeaning, especially as I've already told the Colonel I don't like being called Treacle.'

'I didn't know that—'

'And if you did would you have stopped him?'

'Treacle's not a demeaning term, Jane, it's just cockney rhyming slang – "treacle tart" . . . sweetheart.'

'I know where it comes from, Stanley, but I'd expect to hear my mother or father use it – not a junior officer in what was clearly a derogatory manner. I don't think it's too much to ask to be called Sarge or Sergeant when I'm on duty – do you?'

'Well, I've always accepted being called Stanley—'

'That's your choice – besides, I heard people call you Sarge when we worked on the Covent Garden bombing.'

'That was different from working on this squad—'

'So, it's all right to refer to the DI and DCI by their Christian or nicknames, then?' Jane asked, with a touch of sarcasm.

'You know that's not what I'm saying.'

'Well, what are you saying?'

'That you might want to calm down a bit. I don't mind if you give as good as you get, but that's because I've worked with you before. For now just soak up the mickey-taking and ease yourself in gently.'

'Oh, I see, because I'm a female I'm the one who should be submissive. I thought this was the Flying Squad – not a gentlemen's club.'

'I've given you my advice, Jane, so take it or—'

'I'll leave it, Stanley, and make my own decisions, thank you.'

As Stanley returned to his desk, a woman came out of one of the offices at the far end of the room carrying some case folders. She was in her mid-thirties, five feet seven inches tall, with a slim waist and good-sized bust, and walked with an air of authority. Her long dark shiny hair hung down her back and she was smartly dressed in a white blouse, black pencil skirt and high heels. She put the folder on the desk next to Jane's police file.

'Hi, you must be Katie. I'm Jane Tennison.' She smiled as she raised her hand to greet her.

She looked Jane up and down condescendingly.

'Yes, I know, I've seen your police file,' she replied, without a smile.

Jane wasn't going to put up with Katie looking down her nose at her.

'So have the rest of the office by the looks of it,' she retorted, glancing towards her file on Katie's desk.

'DCI Murphy gave me your file earlier to enter your personal details in our squad address book. I'm not responsible for the behaviour of the rest of the team.'

Jane sensed Katie knew about the addition of 'Treacle Tennison' to *The Dirty Dozen* poster but decided not to pursue it.

'Is DCI Murphy in his office?' she asked, changing the subject.

'Yes, it's the one on the left I just came out of. DI Kingston's is next to it.'

'I'll just nip to the ladies' and freshen up. I've been helping Dabs and got a bit dirty.'

'Yes, I did notice,' Katie said with a frown. 'DCI Murphy doesn't like to be kept waiting, so I wouldn't take too long if I were you.'

'Which desk is mine?' Jane asked, wondering why Katie was being so cold and unfriendly.

'That one over there.'

She pointed to a single desk in the corner of the room, next to another one on which there was a large police radio, a teleprinter and a computer for doing vehicle and name checks.

Although the squad room wasn't as large as the CID offices Jane had worked in before, she noticed that all the other desks, apart from Katie's, were organised in two groups of four and abutted each other. Stanley was seated in one group, with DC Baxter, DC Gorman and ADC Murray, and in the other group there was only Teflon and three empty desks, which were clearly in use as they had filing trays full of paperwork and case files on them. She knew that some of the team were out on another case but thought, as the only other DS on the team, she would have been given a desk with the others. She wondered if she had deliberately been put on her own to ostracise her.

She put her coat on the rack by the door and looked around the room. The large wall behind Katie's desk was covered with artists' impressions of robbery suspects, wanted posters and mugshots, as well as an array of surveillance and robbery crime scene photographs. There was also a large wallchart of the date, time and venue of all the cases they were currently investigating, and in the corner next to it there was a flip chart easel.

On the left-hand wall there was a large map of the north-east London area that the Rigg Approach Flying Squad team covered; it ran from Tower Hamlets in the East End to Enfield, Chigwell in Essex and Upminster, which was an area of nearly a hundred square miles. The map was covered with red, yellow and green pins, which, according to the handwritten guide beside it, signified where armed robberies on banks, building societies, betting shops and cash-in-transit vehicles had taken place. Jane was struck by the fact that the clear majority were red pins, which signified that firearms had been discharged, as opposed to yellow pins, which meant they hadn't. Green pins, of which there were about half a dozen, meant someone had been shot. On the right side of the room there were several filing cabinets for case files and bookshelves with box files and clip folders relating to ongoing investigations. Jane recalled Dabs saying that Katie was fussy when it came to office tidiness, and could see that everything was laid out neatly and well labelled, making it clear what was contained in everything on display.

The squad room, like the rest of the building, was painted a bland green and the carpet was cheap, thin and worn, but there was plenty of natural light entering through a row of large windows that looked out on to the front and rear of the building. The desks were old wooden ones with a locking drawer and side lockers, and each officer had some filing trays full of folders and paperwork.

She went to the ladies' toilet, brushed her hair and tied it back, then using some damp tissues she managed to get some of the soot streaks off her jacket and skirt. She tried to get one of the marks off her white blouse, but it smudged and ended up looking worse, so she buttoned up her jacket to hide them. Her mouth felt dry and she went to the small kitchen area to get a glass of water, where she found Teflon making some toast and coffee. He was a handsome man in his early thirties, five feet ten inches tall, with short Afro hair and a smooth complexion. Although dressed casually in dark grey Farah slacks and a blue and white striped shirt, his clothes accentuated his slim body and he looked smart.

'Would you like a coffee?' he asked, with a friendly smile that was very welcome.

She smiled back. 'No thanks, a glass of water's fine, please. I'm Jane Tennison, we actually haven't met yet.'

She put her hand out and he shook it with a firm grip.

He poured her a glass of water.

'Pleased to meet you. I'm DC Lloyd Johnson, or Teflon as the team like to call me.'

'Do you mind being called Teflon?' she asked cautiously, unsure if "Teflon" was a reference to the colour of his skin. She knew that life as a black police officer could be tough, and sometimes it was easier to just deny the existence of racism if you wanted to be accepted by your white colleagues.

He looked surprised. 'You think they call me Teflon 'cause I'm black?'

She blushed. 'Sorry, I didn't mean any offence . . .'

He laughed. 'None taken. It's because I was chasing a robbery suspect with a pickaxe handle and it slipped out of me hands when I swung it at him.'

'Sorry, but I don't get the analogy—'

'It's not that complicated. Teflon is non-stick, you see?'

'OK, so nothing to do with your colour.'

He grinned. 'If it was about me colour I'd hit them with a bloody pickaxe handle.'

The kitchen door opened, and Katie looked in.

'DCI Murphy is wondering where you are. Get a move on as he wants to speak to you right now.'

Jane knew she was going to have to do something about Katie's manner, but it wasn't the time or place.

And besides, Katie had walked off before Jane could think of a suitable retort.

'Is Katie like that with everyone?'

Lloyd nodded. 'Pretty much, unless you're inspector rank or above. She's probably jealous of you,' he said, pouring hot water into his cup.

'Jealous of me – what on earth for?'

'KP likes attention, and being the only woman in the office, apart from the cleaner, she gets plenty of it – especially from DI Kingston. Now you're on the scene she's got some competition.'

'I can assure you I'm not an attention-seeker. I've also learnt from experience not to mix business with pleasure,' she added wryly. She finished her water, swilled the glass under the tap and put it on the draining board. 'I'd better get a move on, then, before Katie gives me a detention.'

Lloyd chuckled as he put some sugar in his coffee.

'Just be careful what you say around her as it will get straight back to Kingston and Murphy. And don't let the Colonel niggle you. He likes a bit of confrontation and winding people up – but he doesn't like it when he's the butt of the joke.'

'There was certainly a bit of tension between the two of you earlier,' she remarked.

'I got a lot of stick when I first came on the squad a year ago, especially as I was the first black officer to join the team, but I treated it as banter and gave back as good as I got – that way it didn't bother me. The Colonel and me don't always see eye to eye, but he knows not to push things too far – and he's a good man to have on your side in a dodgy situation.'

'From the size of him and his marines background I don't doubt that,' she said as she opened the kitchen door.

'Nice to meet you, Sarge. Now you're on the squad I won't be the odd one out any more,' he said with a cheeky grin and a wink.

Jane knew there were not enough black and ethnic minority officers in the force. She had certainly never worked in uniform or the CID alongside a black officer. She was also aware that despite efforts to encourage black people to join the police force, the response had been poor. Many in the Afro-Caribbean community believed, with reason, that if they joined the police they would be subjected to racism within the force as well as opposition and hostility from friends, relatives and members of the community.

She would like to have chatted more with Lloyd and wondered when he said Katie liked attention, 'especially from Kingston', if he was implying that something was going on between the two of them. She'd noticed that Kingston wore a wedding ring and Katie didn't have any rings on her left hand, but realised it was none of her business if they were in a relationship. She'd made a big mistake as a probationer when she'd had an affair with a married DCI, followed by a disastrous relationship with a self-centred bomb squad officer. Since then she'd vowed not to get involved with another police officer ever again.

*　*　*

Jane knocked on DCI Murphy's office door and a gruff voice shouted, 'Come in!'

She quickly brushed herself down and entered the room. DCI Murphy was sitting behind a wooden desk, which had a green leather inlay and was twice the size of any in the squad room. The walls were covered with green and white damask-style flock paper and lined with photographs relating to Murphy's police career, from his joining class at training school, CID and senior officer's courses, as well as some from the three times he had served on the Flying Squad. Several framed Commissioner's commendations he had received for bravery and detective ability were also on the wall. A picture of his wife and teenage twin daughters took pride of place on his desk, next to several different types of ball-shaped paperweights, which he liked to collect. Like the squad room, his office was bathed in daylight streaming through the large windows.

DI Kingston was sitting opposite Murphy, and both men were smoking and sipping on whisky from crystal tumblers. Murphy was a burly-looking man with a mop of swept-back ginger hair and a neatly trimmed beard. He was smartly dressed in a dark blue three-piece pinstripe suit, white shirt and dark blue tie with the Flying Squad eagle printed on it. Although Jane had never met DCI Murphy before she had gleaned a little about him from her former boss at Peckham, DCI Nick Moran, who was a pal of Murphy's and had approved her application for the Flying Squad. According to Moran, Murphy was a man 'married to the job', who didn't suffer fools gladly and, having served on the Flying Squad at all ranks, was respected by his colleagues and feared by many in the criminal underworld.

'I was about to send out a search party for you!' He frowned as he sipped his whisky.

'Sorry I'm late, sir.'

Kingston finished his drink, said, 'Thanks, Bill' and left the room, without acknowledging Jane's presence, let alone introducing her to Murphy. It left her with an uneasy feeling.

Murphy looked at his watch. 'It's half past three and I've had to delay the office meeting because you're late – five and a half hours late, to be precise.'

'You weren't here when I first arrived, sir, and DI Kingston told me to go with him to the robbery in Leytonstone. Then I was dealing with the scene where the police car crashed and the burnt-out car—'

'That's obvious from the soot on your blouse. I'll let it go this time, but in future if you have a meeting with me I expect you to be there on the dot – or waiting for me if I'm running late. Take a seat.'

She sat down opposite him while he topped up his glass from the whisky bottle, then screwed the cap back on and put the bottle in his desk drawer.

'Do you know much about the Flying Squad?'

He took a sip of his drink and leant back in his chair.

Jane thought for a moment. 'It was formed in 1919 in response to growing concern about organised crime in London and the unit's original twelve detectives could pursue criminals into any police division area, hence the nickname "the Flying Squad". Over the years, the unit became primarily involved in preventing and investigating armed robbery and organised crime. Currently there are four squad offices in London, based here, Barnes, Finchley and Tower Bridge.'

Murphy yawned. 'Ten out of ten if you were writing a history essay, Tennison, but what I meant was do you know what we do on a daily basis?'

Jane wondered if Murphy was deliberately trying to catch her out by not making his question very specific. She tried again, being as precise as she could.

'From what I was told, the Flying Squad carries out surveillance on criminals it suspects may be about to commit armed robbery on business premises, banks and betting shops, then arrests the suspects before the commission of the crime. The squad also investigates offences already committed by armed robbers on the aforementioned premises.'

Murphy frowned. 'Basically correct. Flying Squad operations generally start with lengthy surveillance, followed by armed intervention and an arrest for conspiracy to rob prior to the offence being committed. That way Joe Public is safe from flying bullets and no one gets shot – not even the bloody suspects . . . unfortunately.'

'Isn't that a good thing, sir?' she asked, remembering the first thing she'd had drummed into her at Hendon training college, that the primary object of the police was the prevention of crime and the protection of life.

Murphy sighed and shook his head, as if she'd said something stupid.

'The professional armed robbers of today are wily, hardened criminals, Tennison. They know the law inside out, and pay through the nose for corrupt lawyers to represent them. If we arrest suspects before an actual robbery is committed, a shrewd brief can tear most conspiracy charges to shreds in court. Even if we make arrests after the fact it's rare that any evidence is left behind. Unless your armed blagger sticks his hands up and says, "Fair cop, guv, you got me bang to rights", you're often left with nothing but egg on your face. Do you understand what I'm trying to tell you about how we need to carry out our work to be successful?'

'That it's preferable to arrest the criminal when they're actually committing the crime.'

'Exactly – my Flying Squad officers are specialists in the "pavement ambush". Sheer speed usually wins the day and arresting a piece of shit with a gun in one hand and a bag of cash or jewellery in the other is not only exhilarating but it also means the villain is, as we like to say on the squad, "well and truly fucked".'

Jane felt relieved she'd finally said something he agreed with. She could sense his loathing of criminals went deep.

'My officers inevitably face considerable dangers on armed operations. Our methods are a high-risk form of policing and not for the faint-hearted – how strong is your nerve, Tennison?'

Jane was quick to answer. 'I received a Commissioner's commendation for bravery when I was a decoy and attacked by a man with a knife. I also received a commendation for detective ability and devotion to duty during an IRA bombing investigation. The details are in my case file, as I'm sure you know. Also I—'

He held his hand up, cutting her short.

'I didn't know because I haven't read your file,' he said bluntly.

Jane was surprised. 'May I ask why not, sir, as I'm now one of your officers?'

Murphy ignored the question. 'Tell me, Tennison – why do you think you're here?'

'Because of my proven abilities in a number of murder investigations and the IRA case. I was recommended by DCI Moran after I uncovered a dentist who was a serial killer in Peckham.'

He looked surprised. 'That was your arrest? I remember the case in the papers. He murdered three women and a young man in Rye Lane, which the press started calling "The Murder Mile", as I recall.'

'That's correct, sir, and—'

'Didn't the dentist kill himself before he stood trial?'

'Unfortunately, yes.'

'So technically he was never proven guilty of any crimes.'

'Correct, but it was definitely him and there were certainly no more murders after his death.'

Murphy looked sceptical. 'You may be a competent murder investigator – but have you ever arrested anyone for robbery?'

'Yes, a few times when I worked at Peckham and Hackney.'

'Street muggers, no doubt?' He smirked.

'Yes, but some of them used knives in the commission of the crimes.'

'Were they pavement arrests or a result of your investigations?'

'One was pavement during a team operation and the others were through good detective work.'

'Flying Squad officers are renowned for their knowledge of the underworld and cultivating informants within it. "Snouts" are the jewel in the crown of our intelligence operations. Do you have any registered informants?'

'No, sir, but I have been given information by people I have arrested, which has led to further arrests, convictions and the recovery of stolen property.'

'How many years' service have you got?'

'Just over six and a half.'

'And as a DS?'

'Just over a year.'

Murphy toyed with his glass for a moment.

'Apart from DC Baxter, who was also a police cadet, there are none of my team with less than ten years in the job. On top of that, Stanley has six years as a DS and the sergeant you replaced had been a DS for fifteen years. All of them are seasoned detectives . . . unlike you.' He said the last word as if it left a nasty taste in his mouth.

Jane felt she was standing up for herself well but couldn't help being a bit intimidated by his dismissal of her police record. Even though Murphy would have had to agree to her joining the Rigg Approach team, it was abundantly clear he thought she shouldn't be on the Flying Squad and she wanted to know why.

'I went through the selection process like everyone else who applied for the squad. There were many officers with more service than me who didn't get selected. I was successful because of my abilities as a detective – not my length of service.'

He laughed dismissively, shaking his head.

Jane fought to control her anger.

'If you don't want me here, sir, why did you allow me to join your team?'

'I don't think you'd like the answer. Besides, you're on the squad now so it doesn't matter anyway.'

He took a sip of his whisky and a long drag on his cigarette.

But Jane was determined to get a straight answer.

'Being frank and honest matters to me, sir. As a female officer I've put up with more than my fair share of insults and male chauvinism during my *six years'* police service, so let me assure you, I'm not easily offended.'

He leant forward and looked her in the eye.

'I don't doubt that, but do I have your word that what I say goes no further than this room?'

'I'm not one to complain about fellow officers, so if that's what you want, then yes, I won't say a word to anyone.'

'I don't have anything against you as a person, Tennison, and from what I was told you are a very competent divisional detective, but the truth is your appointment to the Flying Squad is nothing more than an experiment, which I personally disagreed with, but to no avail.'

He leant back in his chair to let her digest what he'd said.

She was surprised. 'What do you mean, I'm an experiment?'

'Have you heard of Commander Kenneth Drury?'

'Yes, he was a former head of the Flying Squad, who was found guilty of corruption a few years ago.'

She wondered what on earth that had to do with her.

'Several other officers were also arrested and convicted for taking bribes – a couple were from the Flying Squad, but the majority were from Obscene Publications and the Porn Squad. Have you heard of Operation Countryman?'

Jane nodded. 'Yes, it's an investigation by two county forces into police corruption in London. They recently arrested and interviewed some Flying Squad officers—'

He looked annoyed. 'None of them were on my squad, and not one of the officers arrested has been charged with any offences. The fact is the whole Countryman investigation is a bloody farce, based on the uncorroborated word of a career criminal who has it in for the Flying Squad because he was caught committing armed robbery. The two county forces investigating are on a fucking crusade to find some dirt on the squad – and it's pissing me off.'

He paused to light a cigarette.

Jane could understand Murphy not being happy about Countryman, but he seemed to be protesting a bit too much. It made her wonder if he knew, or suspected, Countryman were investigating members of his team.

'I'm sorry, sir, but I don't see what Operation Countryman has to do with me being an experiment.'

He inhaled deeply and blew the smoke out in Jane's direction.

'Some idiot in the Commissioner's inner circle persuaded him having a woman on the squad might be a calming influence and make the men think twice before giving a suspect a slap, fitting them up or taking a bribe. The Commissioner decided a sergeant would be better as they have the authority of rank as well. Out of the sixteen WDS's in the Met, you were the only one who applied to join the squad when my DS got a promotion.'

Jane tried to hide her shock. For a moment she wondered if he was making it up just to belittle her, but from the way he spoke it sounded true. She presumed Murphy had goaded her into demanding the truth, so she'd know the 'experiment' was not his idea.

'Have you told me this in the hope that I'll resign from the squad?'

He shrugged. 'No, not at all. You asked me to tell you the truth, so I did. Personally I don't think it's fair on you to be put in a position where you will be out of your depth – but as I said, my hands were tied by the top brass.'

'Is that why no one on the team knew I was starting today?'

'Partly, but I can assure you none of them know the real reason you're here. If I'd told them before you started there would have been uproar and I'd have had a barrage of questions wanting to know why . . . I probably still will, especially from the Colonel.'

Jane remembered Kingston asking her if she was Tennison when she first met him on the stairs that morning.

'Does DI Kingston know about me being an experiment?'

'Yes, but he's the only one besides me. He believes what's done is done, therefore we should accept it and move on.'

'What will you tell the rest of the team if they ask why I was accepted for the squad?'

'I know you'd like me to say it was on merit, but they'll smell a rat as soon as they find out your length of service. They've got women

THE DIRTY DOZEN | 102

in traffic patrol now, mounted branch also and in the dog section as handlers, so I'll say the Metropolitan Women Police Association made a complaint to the Commissioner that none of the central squads had any females on it and—'

She shook her head in disbelief. 'Thinking they have a token female in the office should fill them with bags of confidence about my detective abilities and leadership skills. It's not much better than telling them I'm an experiment!'

'Don't get me wrong, Tennison. I don't have a problem with woman police officers in the CID, and I appreciate they can often resolve a difficult situation with the least possible upset or confrontation – but that's not a lot of use when a violent criminal is pointing a gun at you, is it?'

'I won't know until it happens – will I?' she said, making it clear that she was staying put.

'It won't happen, because you won't be on the front line during a pavement ambush.'

'I want to be treated the same as my male counterparts—'

'You're not firearms trained—'

'Then maybe you could send me on a firearms course . . . as another experiment,' she added with deliberate sarcasm.

Murphy shook his head. 'I don't want my men worrying about your safety in an armed situation as it will reduce their effectiveness and put their lives at even greater risk. Even if the suspects weren't armed, you're not as strong as a man and could be badly injured in a one-on-one arrest situation.'

'You should ask the rape suspect I put down with a kick to the groin if I can handle myself.'

'That's different – you were a decoy and no doubt had male backup close at hand. It's true that when we carry out static observations on premises we think are about to be robbed, we can't be sure the robbery will take place. But when it does, speed and surprise is of the essence on a pavement ambush – if you don't want to get shot.'

'I hear what you say, sir, but I won't be going back to Division to appease you or anyone else on this squad. If you won't let me be involved in arrests, can I be part of the surveillance team?'

'The mobile surveillance team often find themselves in a position where they have to react quickly and some of them are armed. Have you done static observations before?'

She nodded, determined to persuade him she could be a useful asset to the squad.

'Yes, both in premises and an observation van. Some of them were with DS Stanley, who, as you no doubt know, is an experienced and highly respected surveillance officer from whom I learnt a lot.'

Murphy paused, and Jane could feel her heart beating as the silence lengthened.

'You've got balls, Tennison, I'll give you that . . . I'm OK with you being a silent observer to start with, so you can see how we work – but if you fuck up, the experiment is over, and I will be the first to recommend your return to Division.'

CHAPTER EIGHT

Jane felt a mixture of dismay and anger as she left Murphy's office, but she was determined to show him, and the other squad officers, that she was a good detective and not just a token female. She didn't doubt what Murphy said about getting rid of her if she messed up and knew he would be watching everything she did closely and going over her paperwork with a fine-toothed comb. She also realised that being accepted by the team was going to be hard work, especially if Murphy and Kingston told them she was nothing more than an 'experiment', but even if they did, she'd make sure they got the message that she was staying put and they could like it or lump it.

At the back of her mind, though, was another thought that had come from Murphy's mention of Countryman. What if the real reason he didn't want her on the squad was because they had something to hide? She hoped it wasn't the case, but if she did stumble across any evidence of corruption, that would put her in an even more difficult position.

She saw Dabs sitting at her desk and looking through the open exhibits book as he tapped away at her typewriter.

'What's the problem?' she snapped, still angry with Murphy and suspecting Dabs was scrutinising her entries in the book.

Dabs looked up in surprise. 'Nothing – I was just looking through everything we collected today and typing up the lab form for the priority exhibits for submission and forensic examination.'

Jane took a deep breath. 'Sorry, Dabs, I didn't mean to be rude and snap at you. Are the entries in the exhibits book OK?'

'They're excellent. I wish the rest of the team were as thorough when listing and describing exhibits. I'd like to use this book as an example to the others, then they can see how it should be done.'

'Thanks, but I'm not sure they'd appreciate that.'

Dabs looked at Jane more closely. 'Are you all right, Sarge?'

'I've got a bit of a headache from dealing with all that burnt material.'

He stood up to let her sit down.

'So did I earlier. The smell of burning rubber from that car was really nauseous. I've got some strong aspirin in my office if you want a couple.'

She thanked him but said she'd already taken some. As she was a supervising officer, he asked if she'd sign the lab form when he'd completed it. Jane knew a DS's or DI's signature was required before the lab would start any forensic examination.

'I think it's best you ask DI Kingston since he's running the investigation.'

'OK, but as the exhibits officer you should be present when we discuss the submissions. I think he'll be quite impressed when he sees the exhibits book and hears about your idea to seize the garage lock in case we find a key that fits. I'd appreciate your input regarding the forensic strategy as well.'

She shrugged. 'If DI Kingston wants me to be present, I'm sure he'll ask.'

Murphy had put her in a position where she was nervous about any form of confrontation with her superiors, and it really annoyed her.

Dabs leant forward and spoke quietly. 'Don't let it get to you, it's just—'

'Let what get to me?' she interjected, worried he knew the real reason she'd been posted to the squad.

'The Colonel's childish behaviour with the poster. Everyone gets a bit of stick when they start here. God knows I did – they kept calling me NickNack. At first I thought it was something to do with the fact I was a civvy and couldn't arrest anyone, but then I found out it was because of my height.'

'Your height?' She was confused.

'Yeah, Nick Nack's a dwarf villain in a James Bond film.'

She remembered the film and had to stop herself smiling at the comparison as she didn't want to offend Dabs.

'Thanks for your concern, but I'm fine with a bit of banter. Besides, I didn't expect to be welcomed with open arms by everyone.'

'From what I've seen so far you'll soon settle in; you're a thinker and a grafter – and that's what counts most.'

He picked up the typewriter and said he'd use one of the empty desks next to Teflon to complete the lab form. The way Dabs treated her with respect made Jane feel even worse about the way she'd snapped at him, and now she could feel a real headache coming on. As she took out her pocket notebook and pen she noticed a blue folder in one of her filing trays. She supposed Katie must have put it there. She looked inside and saw that it contained the completed house-to-house forms, none of which had been signed or marked up for further, or no further, action. She assumed Cam would have been checking and supervising the forms as he'd told her DI Kingston wanted him to organise the house-to-house enquiries. Jane glanced up and saw Cam watching her out of the corner of his eye, then say something to the Colonel, which made him grin. She walked over to his desk and put the folder down in front of him.

'I thought you were dealing with the house-to-house forms.'

'I spoke to DI Kingston and he wants you, as a DS, to check them and raise any further action if it's needed,' he said with a self-satisfied smile.

She wondered if he was lying because he was too lazy to check them himself.

'Then why didn't Kingston tell me personally?'

Cam shrugged. 'Probably because you were with DCI Murphy when I spoke to him. I expect he'll want to go over the results of the house-to-house during the meeting.'

'Right, we can get the meeting started now WDS Tennison has honoured us with her presence.' Murphy's voice boomed out as he strode into the squad room, followed by DI Kingston.

Cam had a smug look as he spoke to Jane. 'Don't panic, I've looked through the forms and there's nothing that needs an urgent follow-up and I've told Kingston about the owner of garage twenty-nine.'

'Can someone grab the flip chart and felt pens?' Murphy asked.

Seeing she was nearest, Jane went to get it but, as she picked up the two pens, Katie suddenly snatched them out of her hand.

'DCI Murphy likes me to write the salient points on the flip chart at office meetings since I'm the only one with legible handwriting.'

Jane was taken aback by her petulance.

'I was only going to carry it over, not write—'

'That's kind of you,' Katie said, scampering off to position herself next to Murphy.

'Stupid bloody woman!' Jane muttered, shaking her head in disbelief.

Murphy coughed to clear his throat.

'Right, I'd like to go through this morning's robbery step by step. I don't normally have to remind you of this, but for the benefit of our new arrival, DS Tennison – what is said within these four walls remains within these four walls.' He looked at Jane, who nodded.

Murphy continued, 'DI Kingston has already briefed me on what the landlady of the Crown told him. It would seem she's our best witness as she at least got a look at the driver of the Cortina. Anyway, Stewart, can you tell us what she saw and give us the description of the driver?'

Kingston got out his pocket notebook but said he'd yet to take a full statement from Fiona. The artist's impression of the driver was being done at 5 p.m., so it should be with them in the morning for circulation. He went over what Fiona had told him and when he gave the description of the driver he spoke slowly, so Katie could write it on the flip chart. As Kingston was about to continue the Colonel spoke up.

'You might like to add "shit-hot driver" to that description—'

'Why would that be, Colonel?' Murphy asked.

'I spoke to the driver of Juliet 1 before he was carted off in the ambulance. He's an experienced Class 1 driver himself and said the driver of the Cortina knew how to handle the car at high speeds.'

Katie wrote 'shit-hot driver' on the flip chart, which made the Colonel chuckle.

'"Good driving skills" would have been fine,' Kingston told her with a smile.

Katie looked flustered. 'I assumed those were the exact words the police driver used.'

Kingston continued, 'The landlady said the driver was late thirties to mid-forties. The collar on his donkey jacket was pulled up and he wore a grey cloth cap, pulled forward as if trying to conceal his face. When the three men got out of the car they walked in an "A" formation. She thought the man at the front was about five foot ten, and the one behind on his right was about the same – he carried the sawn-off in his right hand. The third man, who got out of the front passenger seat, was about six foot two, wearing a light-coloured stocking mask and had some sort of gun in his right hand.'

Jane flicked through her pocket notebook. Abby had said the tall man was wearing a mask over his face, but when Jane asked if it was a balaclava she said yes. Of course, being distressed at the time, she might have been mistaken.

'Can any of the guards help us with a detailed description of the handgun?' Murphy asked, but there was no immediate reply.

Dabs raised his hand. 'DS Tennison found some spent nine-mill cartridge cases before I got to the Woodville Road scene. The stamp on the cases revealed they were made in 1943.'

'So, we're maybe looking for a World War Two semi-automatic?' DC Baxter asked.

'Not necessarily – the bullets may be old, but the gun could be newish and capable of firing old nine-mill bullets. Tennison and I also recovered two bullets that were in reasonable shape and had rifling marks for comparison testing against any guns we recover. Once the firearms section at the lab have done their forensic examinations, I should be able to tell you more.'

'What else was on the cartridge case, Dabs?' the Colonel asked.

'ST+ and DNH.'

'ST+ is for improved steel cases and DNH means the casings were made in Germany – but don't ask me what part,' the Colonel added.

Dabs looked impressed. 'I don't doubt your knowledge as an ex-soldier, Colonel, but I'll get the lab to double-check.'

The Colonel frowned. 'Ex-Marine, thank you, Dabs.'

'Good job, Dabs, and it's something for the lab to work on,' Murphy said.

It was considerate of Dabs to mention her work at the scene but Jane felt Murphy had deliberately avoided acknowledging her part in assisting him. Murphy asked the three detectives who had taken statements from the security guards to read out the salient points.

The Colonel, who had interviewed the van driver, spoke first. Jane found it chilling to hear how the robber with a sawn-off shotgun said, 'You so much as twitch and I'll blow your fucking head off.'

'How did the driver describe his voice?' Murphy asked the Colonel.

'He thought it was a London accent and at first the voice was deep, but high-pitched after he shot the off-duty officer and said, "The fucking idiot tried to get the gun off me". He said the robber's eyes were dark coloured and the bits of eyebrow he could see were light brown. He was about the same height as the off-duty PC who got shot, which according to his police file is five foot ten—'

'Good, that's two people putting him at the same height,' Murphy said.

'Anything about the way the robber walked?' Kingston asked.

'No, Guv, the driver didn't see him approaching and when the robber shot the PC he wound up the window and lay across the front seats shitting himself that he was next.'

Kingston went over what the off-duty PC had told him about tackling the man with the sawn-off shotgun: how the officer thought he was going to die when he heard the gun go off and felt what he thought were lead pellets hit his stomach.

'Poor lad's lucky to be alive, but at least he'll think twice before doing something like that again,' Kingston said.

'I expect he won't be having the egg fried rice next time he has a Chinky takeaway,' the Colonel added, raising a few chuckles.

Murphy asked who'd dealt with the guard in the back of the van and DC Baxter raised his hand.

'There was nothing of real value from him as he didn't look out of his viewing window while the robbery was going down. He put the first box in the chute and thought it was being delivered to the bank. He was reading a paper while waiting for the second coded knock on the van, which means it's safe to send out the next cash box. When he heard his colleague say, "You can send out the other case" without knocking, he knew something was wrong and set off the van's alarm. He then heard the shotgun go off and stayed where he was until the lids arrived.'

Baxter used a CID term to refer to the uniformed officers who were first on scene.

'Well, you've had an easy day, Bax,' Murphy joked.

'I tried to string his statement out to three pages, Guv, but I didn't think you'd want to know about him spewing his breakfast up all over the back of the van.'

Murphy laughed. 'Who interviewed the guard that was carrying the cash box?'

Stanley raised his hand and waved a lengthy statement he was holding.

'This poor guy literally shit himself when the barrel of the gun was put against his forehead—'

'Just take us through what he saw and heard, Stanley, not his bowel movements, thank you,' Murphy said, to general laughter.

'Couldn't he give a good description of the gun?' the Colonel asked.

'Not really, other than the barrel was round, black and had what he described as a fin on the tip of it – understandably he closed his eyes when it was first put to his forehead . . .'

'That might be a Luger,' the Colonel commented. 'A Luger barrel is round and has a sight tip on the end, whereas with many semi-automatics the barrel is an oblong shape. Dabs also mentioned the 43 and DNH stamps on the cartridge case, meaning the ammunition was German. A Luger can also fire nine-mill ammo. Don't take my word for it, though, Dabs.'

'Good point,' Murphy said. 'Dabs, make sure the firearms section at the lab are aware of the Luger idea and keep me and DI Kingston updated with the results.'

Dabs nodded, and Murphy asked Stanley to continue.

'The guard was still on his knees with the gun to his forehead when the unarmed man said, "Last chance, son. Tell him to put the other fucking cases in the chute." The voice was calm, but gravelly, as if he maybe had a sore throat. His eyes were brown, and his stare was "pure evil", he reckoned. The next thing he heard was the van's alarm going off, followed by the shotgun blast – then when he saw the two robbers run to the front of the van he legged it into the bank.'

Jane put her hand up.

'Yes, Tennison?' Murphy sighed.

'I just wondered if the guard said anything about smelling smoke on the unarmed man?'

LYNDA LA PLANTE | 113

'They didn't set light to the car until after the robbery, Tennison,' Murphy shot back.

'I meant tobacco smoke—'

'No, he didn't,' Stanley put in.

'Did you ask?' Jane enquired.

Stanley showed his annoyance. 'I know how to take a victim statement, Jane. I asked the guard if the robber had bad breath and he said no, so for me that means it didn't smell of smoke.'

Murphy sighed. 'Whether or not this person is a smoker doesn't really help the investigation at this stage.'

Jane was determined to make her point.

'A witness who lives at Edgar House saw two men walking towards Felstead Road not long after the robbery and thought she smelt cigar smoke. They caught her eye because one of them was carrying a holdall like one she bought her grandson for Christmas.'

'Any description of the men?' Murphy asked.

Jane got out her pocket notebook to check what the uniform sergeant had said.

'I didn't speak to her personally, but she thought the men were about five feet nine, one was dark-haired and the other lighter coloured. She thinks the one carrying the bag had a blue jacket on—'

'The blaggers were all dressed in dark boiler suits and donkey jackets,' the Colonel said bluntly.

'Actually, we found evidence of burnt clothing in the boot of the Cortina,' Dabs said, 'which suggests they may have changed clothes in the garage—'

Murphy interrupted. 'Is there a description for these two men?'

'She only saw them from behind, but if they were involved in the robbery, they may have had a second getaway car parked nearby.'

Murphy looked unimpressed.

'We could always do an ID parade where the witness looks at the back of the suspects' heads.' The Colonel laughed, and some of the others joined in.

'Thank you for your input, Tennison, but I'd like to move on to the three crime scene examinations.'

'I found a cigar butt in Felstead Road and there was one—'

Murphy interrupted her. 'The fact one of our suspects may smoke cigars is not incriminating evidence, Tennison, so move on to the scene examinations.'

'SOCO Morgan and I examined the crash site and the burnt-out car—'

Murphy held up his hand again. 'I am aware of that, but I'd like Dabs to take me through it.'

Jane could feel herself getting worked up, but bit her lip, knowing that standing up to Murphy would only make him come down even harder on her.

Dabs opened the exhibits book to use as a reference.

'DS Tennison also found two fresh blood drop trails in Woodville Road running from a car's skid mark, which we believe was left by the Cortina.'

'How do you think they got there?' Kingston asked.

'Sergeant Tennison has a theory on that,' Dabs said, looking over at Jane.

She checked her notes. 'A young girl was in Woodville Road when she saw the Cortina hit a parked car at speed then skid to an abrupt halt. A tall man wearing a balaclava got out of the front passenger side, then walked into the middle of the road and started shooting at Juliet 1. Having fired four times he returned to the Cortina, which then left the scene. It's possible that this man was injured at some point during the car chase and left the blood trails.'

Dabs spoke up. 'I took swabs and will get them tested for blood grouping. Thanks to Sergeant Tennison's perceptive thinking we also recovered some blood on the front passenger door sill of the burnt-out Cortina.'

'Can I see the exhibits book?' Murphy asked, and Dabs handed it to him.

'There's more,' Dabs said, getting their attention again. 'She also thought to call out a traffic officer to examine the car's chassis plate in situ, and as a result we now know it was reported stolen and who the owner is.'

There was silence in the room as Murphy looked through the book.

'I see the traffic officer took the ignition barrel out of the Cortina – why was that?' he asked Dabs, who again looked at Jane.

'I asked him if there was any sign that the Cortina had been hot-wired or if a screwdriver had been used to start the ignition,' Jane explained. 'He was positive it hadn't been hot-wired and took the barrel for microscopic examination to see if the inside had signs of screwdriver damage.'

Dabs smiled, realising that she'd twisted things slightly to make herself look good.

'If we know the car was nicked how does damage to the ignition barrel help us?' Cam asked dismissively.

'It's the opposite—' Dabs said.

'What do you mean the opposite?'

'Sometimes it's obvious why you're OFD,' the Colonel said. 'If it wasn't hot-wired and there's no damage to the barrel then a key must have been used to start it – which would suggest . . .' He paused, waiting for Cam to answer.

'That maybe the car wasn't stolen, and the owner's lied for some reason.'

'Finally, you're thinking like a detective,' the Colonel said, and Cam gave him a 'piss off' look.

Jane held up a bit of paper. 'The owner reported his Cortina stolen two weeks ago.'

She handed it to Kingston, who said he knew where Mount Pleasant Road was as he'd worked at Tottenham as a DI, but didn't recognise the name of the owner.

'This Frank Braun needs to be spoken to asap,' Kingston said.

Stanley volunteered to visit the address with the Colonel after the meeting. Murphy said it was best to wait until they had the result of the examination of the car's ignition barrel and handed Kingston the exhibits book.

'I see you also seized the burnt-out garage door lock.'

'I thought that if we arrested any suspects with garage keys, we could test them against the lock,' she explained.

Kingston nodded his approval. 'Seems you have a good working knowledge of forensics.'

'I've had the privilege of working alongside an experienced lab liaison sergeant at several murder scenes – DS Paul Lawrence.'

'He's regarded as the best in the Met,' Dabs chipped in.

Kingston looked at Murphy. 'I think it might be a good idea if DS Tennison continues to work alongside Dabs on this investigation.'

Murphy reluctantly agreed, but Jane wasn't sure whether they were trying to help her fit in or put her in a role where she would be distanced from the team's outside enquiries and surveillance duties. Again, the thought crossed her mind that there might be things about their working methods they didn't want her to see or hear.

'Can you continue supervising the house-to-house enquiries as well?' Kingston asked.

Jane was quick to say, 'Yes, sir', making it hard for Murphy to object to his second in command. She suspected Cam had lied to her about Kingston saying he was to run the house-to-house.

'Good, and if you need any assistance, let me know.' Kingston smiled.

'After I briefed the uniform sergeant, ADC Murray offered to oversee the house-to-house for me,' she informed him.

Kingston looked surprised. 'Did he now?'

Jane nodded. 'I haven't had a chance to check the completed house-to-house for further actions yet, but I believe Cam can bring you up to speed.' She gave Cam a sideways look.

Kingston knew something was up. 'In that case he can continue helping you . . . when we don't need him to drive us somewhere.'

'Anything of interest come up during the house-to-house, Cam?' Murphy asked.

'Er, yes,' Cam began nervously. 'The owners of garage twenty-nine are in their late sixties, living at flat forty Edgar House, and the male occupant was in hospital recovering from a cataract operation and hadn't used the garage for some time. He'd loaned the car to his daughter.'

'How many of the flats still need to be visited?' Kingston asked.

'Er . . . quite a few. A lot of the occupants were presumably at work.'

Jane knew Cam was waffling as he hadn't checked the forms, and decided to interject.

'Enquiries are still being made by the late-shift uniform officers. However, there are two blocks of flats opposite Edgar House where I feel it might be worth making—'

Murphy held his hand up. 'You can discuss the house-to-house with DI Kingston after the meeting. Right, do we know how much they got away with?'

Baxter held up the statement he'd taken.

'According to the guard inside the van, the stolen cash box contained two grand in one-pound notes.'

'Two fucking grand. They shot an off-duty PC and nearly killed the crew of Juliet 1 for five hundred quid each!' the Colonel exclaimed.

'The other cash box contained six grand in fives, tens and twenties. We should release that to the press to really piss the bad guys off,' Baxter suggested.

'Up till now I thought we might be dealing with professional criminals – not a bunch of amateur desperados,' Teflon said.

'Actually, I think these guys knew exactly what they were doing,' Kingston said.

'Look, the robbery went pear-shaped when the off-duty PC decided to have a go and got a stomach full of rice for his troubles,' said the colonel.

'The other barrel of the sawn-off was probably loaded with a real cartridge, ready to be used if needed,' Murphy added.

Kingston nodded in agreement. 'Although the guy with the handgun popped off a few shots at the crew of Juliet 1, he seemed calm and precise in his actions during the robbery.'

'The torching of the Cortina and clothing suggests planning from experience as well,' Stanley said.

Jane raised her hand and Murphy pretended not to notice, but she kept it raised until he acknowledged her.

'What now, Tennison?'

'I spoke to a young witness called Abby Jones. After the police car crashed, the man with the handgun walked towards the officers, but a man with a shotgun said something and the two of them got back in the Cortina.'

'Why didn't you tell us this earlier?' Murphy asked, clearly annoyed.

'She didn't see their faces because of the masks and refused to make a statement.'

Murphy sighed. 'Did you try and persuade her?'

She looked to Kingston.

'Tennison did mention it to me, but the girl was only seventeen, in shock and had a baby with her, so I said to let her go for now and speak to her again in a day or two.'

It wasn't quite the truth, but Jane appreciated that Kingston was at least backing her up.

'Is there anything else you've overlooked, which you'd like to now share with the team?' Murphy asked.

Jane ignored his sarcastic tone. 'The bank manager told me he'd recently had CCTV installed on the inside of the premises, but none outside where the crime took place. I wondered if it was possible the robbers had been tipped off about this and that's why they decided to rob the security van in the street.'

She realised that everyone was staring at her.

'It's a valid question,' Kingston remarked, attracting a few funny looks.

Jane assumed he was defending her because she hadn't embarrassed him about Abby.

Kingston continued, 'Thursday is a regular cash delivery day at many banks as companies need to withdraw money to make up their employees' Friday wage packets – and criminals are just as aware of that fact.'

'Thank you, sir,' she said, acknowledging his support.

Murphy looked quizzically at Kingston. 'Moving forward, we need to be aware that these four men will undoubtedly strike again, especially as they didn't get away with much this time. It's also highly likely they've robbed other cash in transit vans, banks, jewellers, et cetera, et cetera, so, Katie, I want you—'

Kate jumped in, eager to be centre-stage.

'I'm already on it, sir. I checked with the Tower Bridge and Barnes squads before the meeting and they've nothing on file for any robberies that match the MO or description of the men. I will of course make further enquiries after the meeting,' she added, looking pleased with herself.

'Good work, KP – as reliable as ever,' Murphy said with a smile.

Dabs nudged Jane and whispered, 'See what I mean about her being a teacher's pet?'

Jane looked at Teflon, who blew out his cheeks to show Katie's ingratiating behaviour made him want to throw up.

'Is there anything else you or DI Kingston would like me to attend to?' Katie asked Murphy.

'Not that I can think of for now, but I'd like DS Tennison to spend some time with you. That way she can see how we handle investigations and paperwork within the office.'

Katie didn't look pleased, and Jane knew Murphy was deliberately burdening her with office work, but she could always use the house-to-house as an excuse to get out of Katie's clutches for a while.

'Right, is there anything else anyone wants to raise?' Murphy asked.

Everyone shook their heads apart from Baxter.

'What about "keep 'em peeled"?' He touched his eye with his index finger, then pointed into the room and winked. Everyone recognised the impersonation of Shaw Taylor, the presenter of the *Police 5* TV programme. 'He could appeal to the public for information.'

'Actually, that's not a bad idea.' Murphy looked at Jane. 'Give them a ring and ask if they could fit our case in. Also contact the bank and see if they're prepared to offer up a reward for information leading to an arrest and charge. If you get a result with *Police 5* or the bank, discuss it with DI Kingston.'

Jane nodded to herself. Murphy obviously wanted as little to do with her as possible.

Murphy closed his pocket notebook.

'I know we've other unsolved investigations ongoing, but this case is our number one priority. Once you've finished your reports, I want you out on the streets talking to your informants and hassling any other lowlife on our patch for information. If it means visiting any dodgy pubs, you go in pairs, and I don't want any of you coming back here shit-faced. We'll regroup here at ten tomorrow morning. I want results, lads, and I want them quickly before someone does get killed by this gang.'

CHAPTER NINE

When the meeting finished, Murphy told Kingston he wanted a chat with him in his office.

'How did Tennison take being told she was an experiment?' Kingston asked as he pulled up a chair and sat down.

'Not as badly as I hoped she would,' Murphy replied as he opened his desk drawer, then got out the bottle of whisky and two glasses.

'Just a small one for me,' Kingston said.

Murphy poured him a large measure.

'I was hoping she'd tell me to stick the Flying Squad up my arse and piss off back to divisional CID. She's thicker skinned than I thought she'd be . . .'

'As a female officer she's probably used to being put down all the time—'

'Why are you defending her?'

'I'm not – I just reckon she'll do her best to show us we're all wrong about her abilities, that's all.'

Murphy gave him an inquisitive look. 'You don't think she'll be an easy ride then?'

Kingston pretended to look offended. 'What do you mean by that?'

'I know you too well, Stu. Your dick has always ruled your brain and you're only being nice to Tennison so you can get in her knickers.'

Kingston laughed. 'No way! She's not my type – far too po-faced for me.'

'Bollocks! She's reasonably attractive, got big tits and a nice arse—'

'Sounds like you fancy her, Bill.'

'Don't try and turn it around, Stu, we both know she ticks all the boxes in your quick leg-over book. I'd rather you steered well clear of her. She'll screw up soon enough and then we can get rid of her.'

'I don't fancy Tennison – but as I see it we're stuck with her for now so there's no harm in giving her the menial stuff to do to keep her out of harm's way.'

'Most of the bloody office reckons KP's got the hots for you and some even think she's your bit on the side. If you start making a play for Tennison it could cause you all sorts of bother. The last thing I want is two women in the office fighting like tarts over you!'

'For Christ's sake, Bill, I flirt with KP, that's all. She likes attention and it keeps her on her toes.'

'Well, for everyone's sake keep it that way, Stu.'

Kingston downed his whisky. 'Is there anything else you wanted to talk about?'

'Yes, this landlady, Fiona Simpson – is she a good witness?'

'Yeah. She's feisty, that's for sure, and she seemed willing to go the whole way – as a witness, that is,' he added quickly.

'Stop being so bloody defensive. Get a statement off her, then take her up the Yard to look through the Flying Squad mugshot albums.'

'I've already arranged for an artist's impression to be taken from her at five today, then she has to open the pub at six. But I'll give her a ring and see if she can do a statement tonight.'

'Get Tennison or one of the others to take the statement off Simpson.'

'The rest of the team are all busy and I don't think Tennison is experienced enough to do it—'

'Ten minutes ago, you were telling us what a good job she's doing.'

'What I meant is she's inexperienced when it comes to armed robbery investigations. Simpson is our only witness who might be able to identify one of the blaggers and needs to be handled carefully.'

'Point taken. Try and get the statement tonight if you can, if not, tomorrow morning at the latest. I need you to hold the fort here this evening as I've got a seven o'clock meeting at the Yard re this Operation Countryman fiasco.'

'Are they looking at us for anything? Or the rubber heelers?' Kingston asked.

'I don't know for certain . . . but it's only a matter of time before they decide to stick their noses into our business.'

'I don't think we've got anything to worry about—'

'Come on, Stewart, we both know some of us have sailed close to the wind evidence wise – especially the Colonel.'

'To be fair,' Kingston insisted, 'he's never put a man in prison who didn't deserve it—'

Murphy slapped his hand down on the desk. 'A disgruntled man in prison turned supergrass and started bloody Countryman!'

Kingston shrugged. 'But we wouldn't get convictions if we didn't use the occasional verbal.'

Murphy shook his head. 'The ends don't justify the means as far as Countryman's concerned. To them bending the rules is corruption even if it means putting villains away.' He leant forward across the desk. 'I don't want any fit-ups on the Leytonstone job, Stu – especially with Miss Goody Two Shoes on the team.'

'Don't worry about her. Tennison doesn't need to be involved in any arrests. You could stick her in the office to man the radio.'

Murphy nodded. 'You know I'm not averse to putting words into the mouths of suspects when it's necessary, but I prefer to nick them red-handed on the plot, that way the evidence is watertight.'

Kingston smiled. 'I'll make sure the lads are aware of your feelings and everything is above board – as far as possible.'

'OK, I'll leave a number with KP so she can call me at the Yard if anything urgent comes up.'

'Have you heard back from the rest of the team on the surveillance operation?' Kingston asked.

'They think the gang they're following is going to hit a jeweller's in Chingford next week, so we'll all be needed if that's a goer. I'll let you know when I hear more, but they've got enough to be getting on with.'

* * *

Waiting for Kingston to finish his meeting with Murphy, Jane phoned Barclays Bank to speak to the manager, but there was no answer. It was nearly 4.30 p.m. and she suspected the bank must have closed and the staff had gone home. Next, she contacted ITV and asked to be put through to the office that produced Shaw Taylor's *Police 5*. They were very helpful and said the best they could do was to give the robbery a voice-over mention at the end of the show next week, as they had other cases that had been filmed and were ready to go on air. Jane thanked them and said she would speak to her DCI and get back to them.

She then phoned Leytonstone Police Station and spoke to the duty sergeant. He said that the house-to-house enquiries at Edgar House were still ongoing; there was no important information to relay to her and they hoped to be finished by 6 p.m. Jane said she would try and collect the completed forms later in the evening, or the following morning.

She sat at her desk checking the completed house-to-house forms and signing off those that needed no further action. A lot of the residents were elderly people and she made some notes about the couple at number 40 Edgar House, where ADC Murray had spoken with Mrs Helen Clarke about garage 29. She wanted to speak to Mrs Clarke as there were some important questions Cam had failed to ask her. She read through the form the uniformed sergeant had completed regarding the woman who'd seen two men walking towards Felstead Road, and felt it was lacking in detail. Jane decided she should also visit this woman, who was called Rita Brown and lived at flat 14 Edgar House.

Katie walked up and dropped some statements on Jane's desk.

'When you've finished what you're doing, would you check these for any further action or enquiries that need to be made and type them up,' she said, before starting to walk off.

Jane called after her. 'When I've finished what I'm doing I will be going over the house-to-house enquiries with DI Kingston and then revisiting some of the residents at Edgar House. I might have time to check the statements for further action, but I'm not an office typist.'

Katie started to say something, then, spotting DI Kingston coming out of Murphy's office, she picked up the statements and called out to him.

'Excuse me, sir, could I have a word with you?'

'Not just now, Katie.' He looked across the room. 'Colonel, I need a word with you.'

The two men went into his office.

'What's up, Guv?' the Colonel asked as he closed the door.

'Murphy thinks I fancy Tennison,' Kingston whispered, worried that Katie might be waiting outside his office close enough to hear what was being said.

'I'm not surprised, the way you were buttering her up in the meeting.'

'You mentioned our little bet to anyone in the office?'

'Don't tell me you're welshing on it – because if you are, you'll still owe me twenty quid.'

'The bet's still on . . . but I don't want Murphy, or anyone else on the team, getting wind of it.'

The Colonel double-tapped the side of his nose with his finger.

'Trust me, Guv, I won't tell a soul.'

'You'd better not or I'll make sure you're the one that gets screwed. Tell Tennison I want to see her.'

'Making your play already?' He winked.

'About the bloody house-to-house. Now get out on the streets and start hassling your informants for information about the robbery.'

'I was going to speak to Gentleman Jim. He's always had his ear to the ground when it comes to armed robberies, especially among the old-style blaggers – having been one himself, of course.'

'Bloody hell, is he still about?'

'Yeah, he's sixty now and set up a Sunday antiques stall in Brick Lane flea market—'

'Antiques! What the fuck does he know about antiques apart from stealing them?'

'He does a nice line in watches, if you're interested.' The Colonel pulled up his jacket sleeve. 'I got this Omega Seamaster from him – apparently Jacques Cousteau used to wear one like this.'

Kingston laughed. 'That watch is either a fake or knocked off – you tried it out in anything deeper than a bathtub?'

'It worked fine in me local swimming pool. Anyway, Gentleman Jim always likes a few quid up front first before he starts digging around, so I'll need at least a score out of the squad informants' fund.'

'Twenty quid's a bit steep to start with – sweeten him up with a tenner and see what he comes up with first.'

'He generally turns up trumps, so he'll be expecting a twenty.'

'All right, but it'd better be worth it. Knock out a request then. I'll get Murphy's approval. He wants this case done by the book so don't let Jim participate in any way or get into agent provocateur territory—'

'He said he's too old for robbing banks and reckons he's going straight.'

'We both know that's bollocks!'

As the Colonel left Kingston's office, Katie walked in, holding the statements up.

'I asked Tennison to check these statements and help me type them up, but she refused . . .'

Kingston sighed. 'Not now, Katie. I've got other things to sort out first, then I'll have a chat with you.'

As Jane walked into the room Katie gave her a scowl and stomped out.

'What's bothering her?' Jane asked with a knowing smile.

'You are. She said something about refusing to help her type up the statements.'

'That's not quite true.'

'Well, I'll have a word with Katie and remind her you're a DS, not a typist.'

'Thank you, sir, I'd appreciate that.'

She handed him the house-to-house folder.

'I'd like to revisit Mrs Clarke and Mrs Brown personally and go into a bit more detail about garage twenty-nine and the two men seen walking away from Edgar House,' she told him.

'Seems strange they should choose that particular garage to dump the getaway car, so further enquiries are fine by me,' he said without looking up.

'Is this evening OK, or would you like me to stay in the office and help Katie?'

'She's got by on her own many times before and right now the investigation is more important than typing up statements. You mentioned about extending the house-to-house at the office meeting?'

Jane told him about the two other blocks of flats in Blake Hall Road, but Kingston said that for the moment she should just get the enquiries at Edgar House and Felstead Road completed. As he checked the rest of the house-to-house forms, Jane looked around his office. It was much smaller than Murphy's but had the same style desk and chairs and a large locked filing cabinet; the grey carpet was stained and worn, and the walls were painted the same puke green as the squad office. She noticed a couple of Flying Squad team photographs on the wall behind the desk, and some taken at boxing matches. There was also a large black and white group photograph with about thirty teenagers dressed in sleeveless vests, shorts and boxing boots, with CHINGFORD AMATEUR BOXING CLUB 1958 at the bottom. Lined up on the ground in front of them was an array of silver cups and shields. Jane squinted to see if she could recognise Kingston in the photo.

'I'm third in from the left on the back row,' he said without looking up.

'How old were you then?'

'Sixteen. The club was at the old Territorial Army drill hall back then, but it's moved since and now called the Waltham Forest Amateur Boxing Club. The photo to the left was when I won the Lafone police middleweight boxing championships. I was nineteen then and just joined the job.' He was clearly proud of his achievements. 'Do you like boxing?'

'I've only ever seen it on TV when I lived at home as my dad sometimes watched it, though he was more into wrestling.'

'That's all fake, boxing is the real thing. You get hit hard sometimes – as you can see from the shape of this. It's been broken a few times,' he said, tapping a finger to his nose.

Although his nose was slightly crooked, Jane thought it gave him a rugged appearance and didn't spoil his good looks at all.

'Do you still box?'

'Not in proper bouts, but I occasionally pop down to the Waltham Forest club to help out with the kids and do a bit of sparring.'

'You live over that way then?'

'Born and raised in Chingford, but I live in Woodford now. What about you, Jane?'

'I've got a flat in Marylebone.'

'Marylebone, very posh,' he said with a grin.

'It's just a small one-bedroom flat, but I'm looking to move somewhere slightly bigger with a garden.'

'Anywhere in particular?'

'Not really.'

'Well, as long it's within twenty-five miles of Charing Cross you're entitled to the police housing allowance.'

'I wouldn't be able to afford a place of my own if it wasn't for the housing allowance,' Jane remarked as she sat down.

'Crack on with the house-to-house for now. I was a bit hasty this morning about that seventeen-year-old girl who witnessed the shooting of the police car – what was her name again?'

'Abby Jones. I've got a gut feeling she may have seen a bit more than she said.'

'I know she's an adult as far as the law's concerned, but when you speak to her again I'd suggest you have her mother or father present to avoid any allegations that we tried to force her to be a witness or put words in her mouth.'

'I was going to see her over the weekend, like you suggested in the office meeting, probably Sunday if that's OK.' She smiled, recalling his change of tune when Murphy said Abby needed to be seen again.

'If you want to work Sunday it can't be for overtime – only a day off in lieu. You can do a couple of hours overtime this evening on the house-to-house, then head off home.'

'Should I not come back to the office?'

'No, it's OK. I've told the others there's no need to but ring the office just in case anything important has come up that needs to be dealt with tonight. Other than that, it's a nine o'clock start tomorrow.'

'I could get the statement from the landlady, Fiona Simpson, if you like. I met her earlier when—'

'I heard you were at the pub,' he interrupted. 'I'd already spoken to Mrs Simpson, so what were you doing there?'

'I hadn't seen the scene of the robbery and wanted to familiar-ise myself with it. I spoke to Mrs Simpson as I knew she'd seen where the stolen Cortina had parked up just before the robbery and I wanted to check the vicinity for any dropped bullets or—'

He frowned. 'The Senior SOCO who attended the bank scene did all that and nothing of interest was found. Next time speak to me first. Mrs Simpson is our best chance of identifying the geta-way driver – if we can identify him that might then lead us to the rest of the team. These men are dangerous and Mrs Simpson's safety is crucial to the investigation. I've told her to tell no one that she saw the driver. I don't want her getting cold feet by put-ting her under any more police pressure right now, so I'll deal with her statement.'

'I understand, sir. Will you be getting a statement from the old lady as well?' Jane asked, as he had mentioned having spoken to Betty in the office meeting.

Kingston looked puzzled. 'Who are you talking about?'

'Betty, the old lady with the hunched shoulders who witnessed the robbery. Fiona Simpson implied you'd spoken to her.'

'Unfortunately she's a bit senile and not very reliable, so I decided it wasn't worth getting a statement off her. Considering it's your first day and you were shoved in at the deep end, you've done well,' he said, changing the subject.

'Thanks, but I don't think DCI Murphy and the rest of the team share your viewpoint.'

'My advice is to carry on as you've started and don't let them get to you.'

Jane felt she could be open with him and part of her wanted to gauge his opinion further.

'That's not so easy when you've been told you're nothing more than an experiment—'

'Look, if you're worried about the team finding out, don't be. I for one won't say anything and I can assure you neither will DCI

Murphy, otherwise he'd have everyone on his back wanting to know what's going on. The Flying Squad has always been a male bastion, but sooner or later that was going to change and some feathers were going to get ruffled. There's guys on the team who will test your mettle, the same as they would with a new male officer on the squad, and the banter can be pretty full on at times – but like I just said, don't let them get to you and if you're not sure about something, just ask.'

Jane knew that what he was saying made sense and it made her feel more relaxed about being the 'treacle' on the Flying Squad.

Kingston handed her the house-to-house folder.

'I've got a shedload of paperwork and reports to do, so unless there's something you want to ask about the investigation, I need to crack on.'

Returning to her desk, Jane noticed a typewriter on it along with some handwritten statements and officers' reports. She picked up the reports, which were written by the Colonel, DS Stanley and DC Baxter. The office was empty apart from Katie, who was updating the incident board with the information gleaned from the earlier meeting. Jane put the reports back in each of the officers' in trays on their desks and the statements on Katie's.

Katie turned around. 'What are you doing?'

Jane walked back to her desk. 'DI Kingston told me that squad officers are expected to type up their own reports. Unfortunately I can't help you with the statements as I've got to go out and make some important house-to-house enquiries.'

'Well, you could do them when you get back.'

Jane jotted down the office phone number on the back of the house-to-house folder, then picked up her raincoat and small shoulder bag.

'I won't be coming back to the office tonight. I'll be heading straight home when I've finished with the house-to-house.'

'You have to come back here to book off duty.'

'DI Kingston said it would be fine to ring in before I go home. Have a nice evening and I'll see you in the morning.'

As Jane left the office, an irate Katie stormed into Kingston's office.

'Tennison has just dumped all the typing back on my desk and walked out of the door – she had the cheek to say you said she didn't have to do it!'

Kingston stood up and gently held her by both arms.

'I did, but—'

'Why are you being so nice and obliging to her?'

'Just calm down and let me explain. I told her to continue the house-to-house this evening for a reason—'

'Well, it'd better be a good one.'

'Everyone's out of the office on enquiries and Murphy will be leaving at six for a commendation ceremony at the Yard, which means we'll be alone.'

He slid his hands onto her backside and pulled her tight against his body.

'That is a good reason.'

She smiled, stretching up to kiss him.

CHAPTER TEN

Jane knocked on the door of flat 40 Edgar House and looked at her pocket notebook to check the name of the owner. The door was opened by a woman in her late sixties, wearing a floral kitchen apron over a white blouse and grey skirt with slippers on her feet.

'Helen Clarke?'

'Blimey, you're quick off the mark – I only rang you a few hours ago,' she said, looking pleased.

'We haven't spoken before, Mrs Clarke,' Jane said, confused.

'Haven't we? Who are you then?'

'I'm Detective Sergeant Jane Tennison,' she replied, holding up her warrant card.

Helen looked embarrassed. 'Silly me, I thought you were from the insurance company about the fire in our garage.'

Jane smiled. 'As it happens I would like to speak to you about the garage fire—'

'An officer whose name I can't remember already spoke to me earlier about it, dear.'

'That was ADC Murray.'

Helen looked confused. 'He told me he was a detective.'

'He works with me – he's a driver on the Flying Squad and helps us with our enquiries.'

'What's the Flying Squad?'

'We investigate bank robberies. I'm here in connection with one that occurred at Barclays Bank in Leytonstone this morning.'

'I don't know anything about any bank robberies, dear,' she said, looking worried.

'Did ADC Murray not tell you why he was asking about your garage?'

'He said the garages had been set alight and ours had been badly damaged and the police were investigating it as a possible arson. He wondered if our car was in the garage and I told him my daughter has it. When I left the flat to go and see my husband in hospital I saw the fire brigade and police next to a burnt-out car. I thought it might be some of them hooligan kids from the estate down the road who'd done it – they come up here breaking into the flats and stealing stuff from cars.'

Jane realised that Murray probably hadn't wanted to unduly overstress Helen, so he didn't mention the possible connection to the armed robbery, but she decided it was time to be honest with her.

'It wasn't kids who did this, Mrs Clarke. We have reason to believe a getaway car used in the bank robbery was dumped in your garage and set alight with petrol.'

'I honestly don't know anything about a bank robbery or the fire,' Helen said, looking more distressed.

'I don't think for one minute that you do, Mrs Clarke, but knowing a bit more about your garage, and anyone who used it, might help the investigation.'

Helen opened the door. 'You'd better come in then. I just boiled the kettle – would you like some tea?'

Jane said she would and followed Helen into the kitchen, which was the first room to the left on the ground floor two-bedroom maisonette. The small kitchen was spotless, and three silver containers marked coffee, tea and sugar were neatly laid out next to a round Swan electric kettle. Helen made a pot of tea and used a small strainer to catch the leaves as she poured the tea into two bone china cups. She let Jane pour her own milk while she got some custard cream and Bourbon biscuits out of a round floral decorated tin and placed them neatly on a side plate.

'Your officer Murray likes his biscuits and ate a plateful himself,' Helen remarked with a smile.

Jane carried the two teas as she followed Helen through to the living room at the end of the short hallway.

'Excuse the mess, I haven't had a chance to hoover and dust in here today.'

Helen opened the door to the living room, which in fact was just as neat and tidy as the kitchen. The room was bright, with white painted Anaglypta wallpaper, a light brown carpet and a cream-coloured three-seater settee with matching armchair. The electric fire was on and the room was warm and cosy. On the mantelpiece above the fire there were pictures of Helen with a man, whom Jane assumed to be her husband. There was a family picture next to it with a couple in their thirties and a young boy and girl, as well as individual pictures of the children and a man in his early twenties.

'What lovely pictures,' Jane commented as she looked at them.

'That's my husband Ronald with me. The picture next to it is our daughter June, her husband and their eight-year-old twins.' She picked up the picture of the young man. 'This is our son Robert – he died some years ago after a motorcycle accident.'

'I'm sorry for your loss.'

Helen took a moment to compose herself.

'Me and Ronald didn't like him riding motorbikes, but he was headstrong and loved biking. He used to go out for long day trips with his friends – they were all safety conscious and wore the proper leather clothes and crash helmets, even though you didn't have to back then. He was going to Brighton for the day when someone pulled out in front of him and he came off his bike. There was hardly a mark on him, but he suffered a bad brain injury and died two days later in the hospital.'

Jane could see how upset Helen was getting and tried to move the conversation forward.

'Do you know if your husband kept the garage locked?'

'I'm sorry, I don't, but I can ask him tomorrow morning when I visit him at the hospital.'

'It would be helpful if you could, then I can ring you in the afternoon.'

'I don't have a phone, but my neighbours do and I'm sure they'd let me call you, or there's a phone box down the road I can use.'

'Whatever's easiest for you.'

Jane wrote down the office number on a back page of her pocket notebook and handed it to Helen, who put it in her apron pocket. Jane looked at the house-to-house form for number 40.

'My uniform colleague noted that you have lived here for six months and haven't been using the garage as your husband can't drive due to his eyesight problems.'

'That's right, Ronald suffers from cataracts, so he gave the car to our daughter to use until his eyesight's better.'

'Do you know who used the garage before you?'

'I assume it was the lady who owned the flat before us. When we were buying the place the estate agent said there was a garage with it.'

'Do you know her name or have a forwarding address for her?'

'We never met her. As I recall, the estate agent said her name was Mrs Smith. She'd been terminally ill in a hospice and after her death the flat was sold by one of her relatives.'

'Do you know the name or address of the relative?'

'No, but after we moved in we had some mail delivered for a Mrs Elizabeth Smith. We didn't have a forwarding address for any relatives and the neighbours couldn't help, so I gave it to the postman and told him the previous resident had died. I doubt Mrs Smith had much use for a garage if she was terminally ill . . . Do help yourself to a biscuit, dear.'

'That's a good point, though she might have rented it out. Do you know the details of the estate agents who dealt with the sale of the flat?' Jane picked up a Bourbon and took a bite.

'I think it was Petty something . . . I can't remember the full details as my husband always dealt with them. Mind you, I'm sure he kept the sales brochure.' Helen got up and rummaged around in the side cabinet drawer. 'Ah, here it is,' she said, waving it in the air.

She handed it to Jane, who noted that Petty, Son and Prestwich had their offices in Woodbine Place, Wanstead.

'I was told the flats were owned by a housing association and most of the residents were tenants.'

'Most of them are, but I expect Mrs Smith bought hers under a "Right to Buy" scheme. We were very lucky that it was up for sale – but for her illness I doubt we'd be here now.'

Jane nodded. 'How many keys for the garage did your husband have?'

Helen got up and walked over to the side cabinet, where she picked up a Winston Churchill Toby jug and tipped out two small keys onto the palm of her hand.

'Just the two.'

She held them up for Jane to see.

'May I have a quick look?'

Helen handed Jane the keys and she could see that although they were both silver, one looked more tarnished than the other.

'Did the estate agents give you both these keys when you moved in?'

'No, just one of them. Ronald said it's always best to have a spare key and asked me to take it down the hardware shop and get a spare one cut – the shiny one's the new one.'

Jane wondered if the previous owner of the flat had also had two garage keys and had given one to someone else.

'Do you know if your neighbours were friendly with Mrs Smith?'

'I've never really spoken to them about her, but I got the impression she was quite frail and kept herself to herself.'

'OK, that's all for now, Mrs Clarke. Thanks for your assistance and I hope your husband has a speedy recovery.'

Jane finished her biscuit and took a last sip of her tea.

'Thank you, dear. I'll remember to ask Ronald your questions, and like I said I'll ring you after I've visited him in hospital.'

After leaving Helen Clarke's flat, Jane spoke briefly to both neighbours. One couple said they had moved in just after Mrs Smith was admitted to the hospice, just over a year ago, and had never met her. The other couple said they had lived next to Elizabeth Smith for five years, had never been in her flat, and only occasionally spoke to her by way of saying hello, and she often ignored them or just nodded. As far as they knew Mrs Smith was in her mid-seventies, a widow, though there was a man in his mid-to late forties who sometimes visited her, and it could well have been her son or other close relation. The neighbours didn't even realise she had owned garage 29.

It seemed to Jane that Elizabeth Smith had been a bit of a loner and not very sociable. She hoped contacting the estate agents who dealt with the sale of her flat might reveal more about who she left the property to in her will and thereby help to trace her extended family. It was also possible they might know more about the garage, and if anyone was using it prior to the sale of the property.

Jane then went to 14 Edgar House to speak to Rita Brown, who shortly after the robbery had seen two men walking along Blake Hall Road towards Felstead Road, carrying a large black holdall. The door was opened by a short rotund man who must have been in the middle of his dinner, as he had traces of food in his grey beard. He looked to be in his early to mid-sixties and was dressed casually in a blue shirt, black trousers and white socks. Jane showed him her warrant card and explained why she wanted to talk to Mrs Brown.

'I'm Peter, her husband. Rita's in the living room watching *Nationwide*.'

'I'm on the team investigating the robbery in Leytonstone—'

'Funnily enough, we've just been watching the news and the robbery was mentioned. Reporter said they shot an off-duty officer and at a police car, causing it to crash. Scum of the earth, these bank robbers!'

Jane nodded. 'I'd like to speak to your wife about the two men she saw in Blake Hall Road just after the robbery.'

'We were discussing the two men she saw and I went over everything with her in detail – as a result she's remembered something else that caught her eye.'

'What was it?'

'Best Rita tells you herself, Sergeant Tennison. It would only be hearsay evidence coming from me.' He stood back to let her in. 'I used to be in the police myself, you know,' he added proudly.

'In the Met?'

'No, the Royal Parks Keepers, which became known as the Royal Parks Constabulary in 1974. We trained alongside regular police officers, though, and wore a uniform. We had full powers of arrest and could instigate criminal proceedings for offences committed in the Royal Parks.'

He helped Jane out of her raincoat and hung it up on the hallway coat rack.

'Are you still serving?' she asked.

'I did twenty years, then had to retire after a serious injury on duty. I'm a security guard manager on a big building site now.'

Jane noticed his limp as she followed him to the living room.

'How did you injure yourself?'

He stopped and turned around before they reached the living room, then started speaking in a formal tone, almost as if he was giving evidence in court.

'I was night patrol in St James's Park when I heard a load of quacking at two a.m. I instinctively knew the ducks were distressed and went to investigate, only to discover a man thieving the ducks.

'On seeing me he started to run, carrying a sack full of ducks in his right hand and one by the neck in his left. I had a torch, but it died on me and there was no moon or park lights, so it was really hard to see. The next thing I knew I ran into a low metal fence, fell over and smashed my right knee to bits on the pavement – it left me with a gammy leg ever since.'

'Unfortunate way to end your career.' Jane was trying not to laugh.

'I got an ill-health pension and a commendation certificate for the suspect's arrest and saving the ducks,' he said, beaming.

'You did well to arrest him with a smashed kneecap.'

'Thank you, but as luck would have it he fell over the same fence and knocked himself out. He was a little Chinaman and wanted to sell the ducks to a Chinky restaurant in Soho for crispy duck pancakes.'

He sighed, and Jane found it even harder to keep a straight face.

The living room was the same shape and size as the Clarkes', with similar decor, but not as bright. Rita Brown was sitting on a brown sofa eating a plate of ham, egg and chips covered in HP Sauce. Peter explained the purpose of Jane's visit and offered her a seat. His own half-eaten tea was on a tray resting precariously on the edge of the armchair. A small Yorkshire terrier was standing on its hind legs with its paws on the armchair, sniffing at the food.

'Get away, Spud!' Peter ordered, and the terrier instantly lay down in front of the electric fire.

'I'm sorry, I didn't mean to interrupt your meal. I can come back a bit later if you like,' Jane offered.

Rita patted the sofa. 'No, we've nearly finished – and there's some ham left if you'd like a sandwich.'

'I'm fine, thanks.'

Jane sat on the sofa, opened the house-to-house folder and got out the form.

'Do you think the two men I saw were involved in the robbery?'

Rita handed her plate to her husband, who used his fork to push what was left onto his plate.

'We don't know for certain yet, but it's possible. Your husband just mentioned you saw something else of interest.'

She nodded. 'When I spoke to the sergeant, he told me about the armed robbery in Leytonstone and that a possible getaway car had been set alight in one of the garages, which I didn't know about at the time I saw the two men in Blake Hall Road.'

Jane instantly realised the significance of the timing between her seeing the two men and the fire.

'Did you see or smell any smoke when you returned to your flat after your shopping trip?'

'No, not a thing, until I heard the fire engines. I went outside, and the firemen were putting out the garage fire. I asked a PC who was with them what was happening, and he advised it was best I return to my flat as inhaling the smoke wouldn't be good for me.'

'How long after you got home was it you heard the fire engines?'

'A matter of minutes, but it wasn't until I was discussing what happened with my husband that I remembered about the other two men I saw. Being a former Royal Parks Keeper, he went over everything with me in detail and he thinks these men might be involved as well.'

'I was going to phone the station after tea, but now you're here you can hear it from the horse's mouth . . . so to speak.'

Peter put his food tray on the floor next to his armchair. Spud jumped up and started licking up the scraps of food. Jane knew there were four men who robbed the bank, but there was a strong possibility that after dumping the car they'd split up. She got out her pocket notebook and pen.

'Can you tell me about these other two men, please? Firstly when and where you saw them.'

'Well, I'd just got back to the flat and put the shopping in the kitchen when Spud started scratching at the door, so I knew he was bursting for a tinkle. I took him out on the lawn at the front of the flats. He was lifting his leg when I heard something behind me. I turned around and saw two men walking and talking quietly together.'

'Rita told me she couldn't make out what they were saying,' Peter added. 'But they stopped talking when she turned around, which is rather suspicious.'

'Did you see where they came from?'

Rita shook her head. 'No, but they were walking away from the estate towards Blake Hall Road.'

Peter sat up. 'They could have come out of the flats at the far end of the estate if they'd been visiting someone, I suppose, but remember the garages are at the back of those end flats.'

Jane knew perfectly where the garages were and wished he'd shut up and let his wife speak, but managed to hide her irritation.

'She didn't get a good look at them, did you, luv?' Peter prompted.

'Not really – it was only a quick glimpse as Spud started yapping and chasing a squirrel, so I had to go after him and didn't see them again.'

'I need as much detail as you can recall about them, please, starting with their height?' Jane asked, eager to get the details down in her pocket notebook. 'Sometimes it helps to close your eyes, take your time and think about the moment you saw them.'

As Rita closed her eyes Jane could see her husband was about to say something. She politely put a finger to her lips and he reluctantly sat back in his chair.

Rita opened her eyes. 'The man nearest me was just a bit taller than my husband and the other one was about this much taller.' She held up two fingers, about eight inches apart.

Peter couldn't help himself. 'I'm five foot eight, which would make the taller man Rita saw six foot two or so.'

Jane smiled tightly as she wrote the men's heights in her pocket notebook.

'How old do you think they were?'

'The shorter man was maybe in his mid-forties and the taller one quite a bit younger.'

Peter sat up and leant towards his wife. 'How much younger, luv?'

'Eight, ten years, maybe.'

'What about their clothing?' Jane asked quickly, to stop Peter calculating their likely ages.

'The tall man had on a dark blue waist-length jacket and the smaller one was wearing a long black raincoat. I'm sorry, but I can't remember much about their trousers or shoes other than they were a dark colour as well.'

'Don't worry, Mrs Brown, you're doing really well. This is all very helpful for the investigation.'

'You forgot to tell her about the newsboy!'

Peter stood up and limped off into the hallway.

'Was someone delivering papers at the time?' Jane asked, wondering if there was another potential witness she could speak to.

Rita laughed. 'No, it's what the smaller man was wearing. Peter's got one just like it.'

Peter quickly returned with a black cloth cap, which he handed to Jane. Jane remembered that Kingston had spoken to Fiona Simpson, who'd said the driver of the getaway car was wearing a grey cloth cap.

'Was it black like this one?'

Rita shook her head. 'No, it was grey.'

Peter took the cap from Jane.

'This isn't a flat cap, it's called a newsboy cap. They both have the same overall shape and stiff peak in front, but the newsboy is rounder and made up of six or eight triangle-style panels with a cloth button on top.'

He pointed out the differences to Jane as he spoke.

'And you're sure it was a cap like this?' she asked Rita.

'Yes, Peter's got some other style flat caps as well, that's how I know the difference.'

'This is really helpful, Mrs Brown. Is there anything you can remember about the smaller man's facial features?'

'No, like I said I only got a quick look at them, but I think the taller man had dark blond or brown hair.'

'How long was it?'

'Above his jacket collar, I think.'

Jane told Rita she'd like to go over the details of the men she saw in Blake Hall Road when she got off the bus, then read out what the uniformed sergeant had written on the house-to-house form.

'You were on the opposite side of the road and only saw them from behind. They were both white men, about five foot eight to five foot ten in height, one had dark hair and the other lighter col-oured hair. Both were smartly dressed in casual clothes and the one who had a green jacket was carrying a black holdall.'

Rita agreed that what the sergeant had written was correct.

'The one with the holdall, can you describe his clothing in any more detail?'

Rita thought about it before answering. 'His jacket was thigh-length and dark green, like the ones posh people wear, and his trousers were grey.'

'When you say like posh people wear – what do you mean, exactly?'

'Like the ones that Audrey fforbes-Hamilton and Richard DeVere wear in that TV show.'

Peter sighed. 'She's talking about *To the Manor Born* with Penelope Keith and Peter Bowles.'

Jane had watched the comedy show a couple of times.

'Do you mean a green waxed Barbour jacket?'

'Yes, that's what they call them – Prince Philip and Charles wear them as well.'

'You also told the sergeant that you thought one of them was smoking a cigar – how sure are you of that?'

'It was definitely a cigar,' she replied without hesitation. 'I saw the thick smoke and could smell it when I crossed the road from the bus stop.'

'Did you actually see either of them holding a cigar?'

'No, but when I worked as a secretary my boss smoked cigars, so I know the smell.'

'Can you describe the other man's clothing?'

'His jacket was black and waist-length, and his trousers were the same colour. You certainly ask a lot more questions than your uniform colleague,' she remarked.

'That's why she's a detective, dear,' Peter said, nodding sagely.

'Did you tell the uniform sergeant what you've just told me?' Jane asked, wondering why he hadn't written it down on the form.

'He never asked and said he had a lot of flats to visit, then left.'

Jane wasn't surprised about the sergeant's behaviour, having experienced his lousy attitude for herself.

'Did you happen to notice if there was anyone else in Blake Hall Road at the time?'

'I know the postman was. I saw him come from Felstead Road and walk past the two men towards the estate. I stopped to wait for him and asked if he had anything for number fourteen, but he didn't.'

'Did you see where the two men went while you were waiting for the postman?'

'Into Felstead Road, but since you've made me think about everything in detail, I've a feeling I might have seen them again.'

'Where and when was that?'

'While I was talking to the postman.'

She wondered if Rita was getting confused.

'You saw them twice in Blake Hall Road?'

'Well, I think it was them.'

'Did they still have the black holdall?'

'I don't know, but it might have been in the car.'

'So, you saw them in a car?'

'Yes, but only briefly. It was a fancy sports car – it caught my eye as it came up the street and went past me.'

'What makes you think the two men were in it?'

'The man driving was wearing the same green butcher jacket and there was a man in the passenger seat.'

Peter sighed. 'Sergeant Tennison already told you it's a Barbour jacket.'

'Did you get a better look at their faces this time?'

'No, they went past quite quickly, and it was the car that caught my eye, not them.'

'Can you describe the make and colour of the car?'

'I don't know much about cars, but it only had one door on the driver's side and was gold.'

'Close your eyes again and think hard, Mrs Brown,' Jane encouraged her.

She opened her eyes after a few seconds. 'It had one of them black cloth roofs that you can put down in the summer and a big upside-down silver Y in a circle on the front grille bit.'

'Sounds like a Mercedes 450SL convertible,' Peter said.

Jane didn't know much about cars herself, though having heard Peter suggest it was a Mercedes, the 'upside down silver Y' now made sense. To be sure she asked Rita to draw the emblem exactly as she remembered.

'What about the registration plate on the car? Can you recall any of the letters or numbers?'

'I'm sorry, I can't.'

'There's no need to apologise, you've given us a lot of information already. Do you know if the postman saw the car?'

'He might have done when it went past, but he had his back to it as it came up the road.'

Jane asked Rita if there was anything else she could remember, but Rita was certain she'd told her everything.

'Will you be getting Rita to help with an artist's impression of the men?' Peter asked.

'I'd have to ask my DI first. Mrs Brown didn't get a good look at their faces, so an artist's impression may not help much.' She looked at Rita. 'What you have told me could be crucial to the investigation. The men you saw may, or may not, have been involved in the robbery, but either way we need to trace and interview them. If you think you see them again, on or off the estate, don't approach them. Just dial 999, say it's about the bank robbery, and uniform officers will attend and deal with them.'

Peter accompanied Jane to the front door and held her coat open while she put it on.

'Rita did well, didn't she?'

'Yes, she did, and you going over everything with her again before I got here certainly helped.'

'I like to think I can still do my bit for Queen and country. You know, I'd love to have been a detective like you – it must be so much more interesting than pounding the beat.'

'Well, it's each to their own, and uniform work is very rewarding as well. Do the Parks Police have a central CID?'

'We didn't have a CID at all. If anything major happened the local Met detectives dealt with it.'

Jane wondered if Peter regretted not applying for the Met, but thought it was probably just as well he hadn't. She thanked him again for his help and left.

Walking to her car she mulled over the information she had gathered. Surely it was more than just coincidence that four men, all with similar builds to the robbers, should be seen on or near the estate shortly after the robbery and close to the time the fire was discovered. Most striking for her was the fact that one of the men was wearing a newsboy cap like the one described by Fiona Simpson, who had seen the driver of the Ford Cortina.

CHAPTER ELEVEN

Jane decided to return to the office and tell Kingston what she'd learnt from Rita Brown. En route she dropped in to Leytonstone Police Station to collect the house-to-house folder and spoke to the duty sergeant. He informed her that all the flats in Edgar House had been visited, as well as the houses in Blake Hall Road and the first six houses on either side of Felstead Road. He had also debriefed the officers who made the enquiries, and no one reported seeing anything of interest to the investigation.

It was 7 p.m. when Jane got back to Rigg Approach and parked her VW in the street outside the squad offices. She couldn't remember the key code, and was flustered for a moment, until she remembered to look in the back of her pocket notebook and quickly entered 1066 to open the door. Upstairs the squad room was empty. She knocked on Kingston's office door, but there was no reply. She knocked again, but still there was no answer, so she opened the door and peeked in, but he wasn't there, though his jacket was over the back of his chair. She then tried DCI Murphy's office, only to find it empty as well.

Having seen Kingston's jacket on the chair, Jane wondered if he might be in the gym working out and decided to go down to the basement to see. As she got near the locker room she could hear a male voice grunting and the rhythmic sound of squeaking metal from gym equipment being used. She entered the locker room and was about to say, 'Excuse me, Guv', when the sight that greeted her froze her to the spot.

Kingston was standing with his back to the door and his trousers down by his ankles, while Katie knelt in front of him on a weightlifting bench that rocked and squeaked in time to Kingston's thrusts.

Jane was no prude, but this was a situation she didn't want to get caught up in. She'd never in her life seen another couple having sex, apart from a brief glimpse of a porn movie she'd caught her male colleagues watching in the snooker room on night duty when she was a probationer at Hackney. Thankful she hadn't disturbed them, Jane crept back up the stairs as quickly as she could and grabbed her coat and shoulder bag, but as she went out of the office onto the landing she could hear Kingston and Katie talking as they walked back up the stairs. She darted into the ladies' toilet across the hallway and sat down to wait for their voices to subside so she could sneak out to her car. She recalled DC Lloyd Johnson saying Katie liked attention and got plenty of it from Kingston, but she'd never imagined they were in a relationship. She heard Katie's voice just outside the toilet.

'I just need to freshen up after that workout.' She giggled.

Jane slowly pushed the slide catch on the door to lock it.

'Fancy a glass of Scotch?' Kingston asked as he opened the squad room door.

'No thanks, I'm warm enough already,' Katie said, trying to open the toilet door. 'Is someone in there? It better not be you, Stanley, or so help me God I'll rub your nose in anything you've left on the seat!'

Jane was in two minds about keeping quiet, hoping Katie might think the door was jammed and give up, but then decided she shouldn't have to skulk about because of their outrageous behaviour.

'It's me, Jane Tennison – is there a problem?'

'Oh, right, I thought it was Stanley. How long have you been in there?' Katie asked sheepishly.

'I just got back and was desperate for the loo. I'll be finished in a minute if you're waiting.'

'It's all right, take your time.'

She grabbed her hairbrush and went into Kingston's office.

'Tennison's in the loo.'

'What's she doing back here?'

Katie started brushing her hair. 'I don't know . . . I think she may have heard what I just said to you about being warm already.'

'So what? She doesn't know what we were up to, but she will if she sees you all flustered. Just calm down and act as if nothing's happened.'

Katie returned to her desk, sat down and started typing.

'Toilet's free now, Katie.' Jane walked into the office but Katie didn't seem to hear her. 'Are you all right, Katie?'

'What makes you ask that?'

'You seemed to be in another world, that's all.'

'The heating's playing up again – it's so stuffy in here it's making me feel nauseous.'

'Is DI Kingston in?'

'Yes, he's been in his office all evening doing paperwork,' Katie replied as she hurried off to the toilet.

Jane thought that even if she hadn't seen Katie in the gym with Kingston, she'd have guessed something was up. Guilt was written all over Katie's face. She might be good at filing, but she was a lousy liar. Jane would have loved to have made a sarcastic comment but bit her lip, knowing it could backfire on her if Katie said anything to Kingston. When she entered his office, he was sitting at his desk writing, with a glass of whisky next to him.

'I didn't expect to see you back here tonight, Tennison. Something of interest come up?'

'You could say that, sir,' she said, reflecting wryly on what she'd witnessed a few minutes ago. She suppressed a smile. 'Mrs Brown saw another two men leaving the Edgar House estate just before the fire, and one was wearing a cap similar to the one Fiona Simpson saw the driver of the getaway car wearing. Also, Mrs Brown thinks she saw the man carrying the holdall in a gold Mercedes sports car, possibly a 450SL convertible.'

Kingston put his pen down and stopped writing.

'Take a seat and tell me exactly what she said. You want a Scotch?'

This time she couldn't help herself.

'Thanks, sir, it's cold out so that should warm me up.'

As he poured the drink she got out her pocket notebook and went over her meeting with Rita Brown, and what Mrs Clarke had said about the garage keys and the purchase of their flat.

'Bloody hell, you've had quite a productive evening, Tennison.'

'Would you like me to make follow-up enquiries with the estate agents who dealt with the sale of fourteen Edgar House?'

'Yes. Do it tomorrow morning after the office meeting and speak to the housing association about Mrs Smith. They may have some useful information we can work on. Get a photo of a Merc 450SL convertible and show it to Mrs Brown. If she says it's the same type of car she saw, stick it on the office wall. Also buy a newsboy cap of the same colour and claim the cost back on an expenses chitty.'

'Is it worth speaking to Fiona Simpson again to get a more detailed description of the cap the driver of the getaway car was wearing?'

Kingston reached into his desk in tray and pulled out two pieces of A4 paper with drawings on them.

'This was dropped off earlier by the police artist.'

He stood beside Jane and put the drawings down in front of her; one was a profile and the other full face. Jane could smell Katie's perfume on him as he leant over and pointed to the profile.

'There's no triangular panels on the cap Fiona Simpson described to the artist, but there is a button on top.' He tapped his finger on it.

He went over to his jacket, which was still on the chair, reached in the side pocket and pulled out a beer mat. Jane wondered what he was doing until he picked up his desk phone and started to dial a number which was written on the mat.

'Hi, Fiona, it's DI Kingston from the Flying Squad. I was wondering if I could come and take a statement from you this evening.

I appreciate you're busy, but I wouldn't ask unless it was important. It'll be easier if I explain when I get there. I'll be about half an hour. Thanks, I really appreciate it. See you in a bit then.' He put the phone down. 'That was—'

'Fiona Simpson. If it will speed things up I don't mind writing the statement while you get the details from her.'

'Thanks for the offer, but Simpson's pub is on my route home, whereas you live in the opposite direction. You've done well today, so go home and put your feet up.'

She finished her Scotch and stood up.

'I'll see you in the morning then.'

'Could you grab me some statement forms from the documents tray in the squad room, please, while I sort myself out?'

He picked up his jacket and put his pen in the inside pocket. Jane nodded and went to get the forms.

'Everything all right?' Katie asked, as Jane opened the statement form tray and got a handful out.

'Yes, DI Kingston needs to get an urgent statement regarding some information I got earlier this evening.' She put the forms in a folder.

'You got the statement forms, Jane?' Kingston asked as he came out of his office.

'Yes, Guv.' She smiled.

He handed a copy of the artist's impressions to Katie.

'Stick them up on the wall for me. I've got to shoot out on an urgent enquiry. Man the phones for another hour then you can go home.'

'Will you be coming back to the office tonight?' Katie asked.

'No,' Kingston said as he and Jane left the room together.

'Bitch!' Katie muttered to herself, wondering exactly what sort of 'urgent' enquiry they were really on.

* * *

Jane's journey home to her flat in Melcombe Place took her forty-five minutes – a lot quicker than her morning trip in rush hour. After parking her car, she walked to a nearby fish and chip shop. It had been open for about a year and served the best cod and chips she had ever tasted. It was owned by a Greek immigrant called Filippos, affectionately known to his customers as 'Fil the Greek', who had sensed a business opportunity as soon as he saw the popularity of fish and chips. Some local residents objected when it first opened, worried he would start selling kebabs as well and lower the tone of the area, but Fil was savvy enough to offer the locals a free first meal. Once they had tasted his fish and chips they soon came back for more. In the far corner of the shop there were three small tables where people could sit and wait for their food to be prepared or eat in if they wanted.

'Long time no see, Sergeant Jane. How you doin'?' he asked in a strong Greek accent

'Fine thanks, Fil.'

She'd become a valued customer after threatening to arrest a couple of drunken 'Sloanes' who were calling him 'greaseball' one night.

'What do ya fancy from the menu tonight?'

'Small cod and chips, please.'

He picked up a large piece of skinned and boned cod by the tail and quickly dipped it in batter before dropping it into the bubbling hot oil, where it sizzled furiously.

'Take a with you wrapped . . . or eat in open?'

'I'll have it wrapped to take away, thanks.'

'So, where you a working now?' he asked as he turned the fish in the oil.

'I'm on the Flying Squad at Rigg Approach in Leyton.'

'You work on de helicopters now?'

Jane laughed. 'No, we deal with armed robberies in London. We're also known as the Sweeney – have you never seen the TV show?'

'I never get a chance to watch a TV as I work most evenings, but I have a Sunday off. My a wife, she a says I should get one of them Betamax things that records what's on TV to tape, then I can watch what I miss in da evening.'

'My dad just got a VHS recorder.'

'I look at one of dem, but the cassette tape is too big. I don't reckon VHS will last as Betamax tapes are much smaller and better quality. You gonna get one?'

'I don't watch much TV myself, I prefer a good book.'

'I like a book as well. I bet you like Sherlock Holmes – he lives near here, in Baker Street,' he said, proud of his local knowledge.

She didn't have the heart to tell him Holmes was a fictional character.

'Conan Doyle's OK. I read a lot of his stuff when I was younger, and I guess in some ways it inspired me to be a detective.'

'Who's your favourite, then?'

She thought for a moment. 'Probably Raymond Chandler. I saw a film called *The Long Goodbye* a few years ago, based on the Chandler book, and it inspired me to start reading his novels. What do you like to read, Phil?'

'Greek history and mythology, like the *Iliad* by Homer and the *Histories* by Herodotus. I think you'd like the tragedy *Medea* by Euripides.'

He scooped up a large portion of chips and placed them on some newspaper.

Jane was surprised by Fil's choice of reading.

'I never studied Greek history – what's *Medea* about?'

'A woman's revenge against her a husband. Have you no a heard of Jason and the Argonauts?'

'I saw the film with my father years ago – I remember it had a lot of special effects and was quite scary.'

'After the Argonauts' quest for the Golden Fleece, Jason he a marry barbarian princess called Medea and they move to Corinth in Greece, where he then a leave Medea for a royal princess, Glauce. Medea, she was a distraught and plotted her revenge . . . You want salt and vinegar, Sergeant?'

'Just on the chips, please. So what did Medea do?'

'She poisons Glauce and her father King Creon, then Jason confronts Medea, only to a discover she had stabbed their sons to death,' he said, shaking salt and vinegar over the chips.

'I can understand revenge against her husband and his mistress – but why did she murder the children?'

He put the fried cod on top of the chips.

'Although Medea loved dem, for her it was the ultimate revenge. She fled a Corinth with the children's corpses, mocking and gloating over Jason's pain, then a leave a him a broken man.'

He wrapped the fish and chips up in the newspaper, put it in a brown paper bag and handed it to Jane.

'Well, there's a saying that "Hell hath no fury like a woman scorned",' Jane remarked, trying to hand him a pound note, which he waved away.

They argued good-naturedly for a minute, and eventually Fil let her pay fifty pence, but only if she let him give her something. He quickly went out the back while she kept an eye on the shop and returned with a book.

'Plays by Euripides. You'll find *Medea* in there.'

'Thanks, Fil. Sounds like the perfect bedtime reading! I'll bring it back when I've finished it.'

* * *

Once inside her flat Jane opened a bottle of white wine and poured herself a large glass, then sat down to eat her fish and chips at her small kitchen table. As she unwrapped the newspaper the aroma of the fish and acidic tang of the vinegar reminded her of days out at the seaside with her parents and sister when she was a girl.

She smiled to herself, remembering sitting in the car at Brighton beach eating fish and chips with her fingers, while watching the waves break on the pebbles. She gently broke off a piece of the golden hot battered cod, blew on it a few times, then popped it in her mouth.

Delicious, she thought, realising for the first time just how hungry she was.

She was halfway through the large portion and beginning to feel full when the phone rang. Grabbing a tea towel, she wiped the grease from her hands and picked up the phone.

'Jane Tennison. Who's calling, please?'

'Da da da . . . Da da da . . . Da da da da da . . . Shut it, son! . . . We're the Sweeney and you're nicked!'

She shook her head with a smile, recognising her sister Pam's voice behind the crude attempt at *The Sweeney* theme tune.

'Just thought I'd ring my favourite sister and see how her first day on the famous Flying Squad went.'

'I'm your only sister, and it was a pretty uneventful day, to be honest.'

She knew Pam would take great delight in passing on to her parents all the gory details of the bank robbery if she told her about it, and her mother would then become distraught about her safety, so she decided to play it down.

'So, you had nothing to do with that bank robbery in Leytonstone on the evening news?'

'No, it's not on our patch,' Jane lied.

'You fibber, Jane. I looked in an *A-Z* to see where you worked, and Rigg Approach is about three miles from where the robbery took place.'

'I didn't get to go out to it as it was my first day. Now, if you don't mind, I'd like to finish my supper—'

'I know better than a judge when you're telling porkies, Jane.' Pam laughed. 'I promise I won't tell Mum if you got shot at.'

'It's no laughing matter, Pam. An officer was shot in the stomach and two others were nearly killed when their car crashed after being shot at.'

Pam's voice became more serious. 'I knew you were involved. Was it scary?'

'I got there after everything had happened. I'm involved in the investigation, that's all – but don't go saying anything to Mum and Dad.'

'I won't. So what happened?'

'I'm really tired, Pam. I want to have a bath and go to bed—'

'Oh, come on, don't leave me in suspense!'

Jane sighed. 'What are you doing this Saturday?'

'In case you'd forgotten I've got an eighteen-month-old toddler, aka your nephew, to look after.'

'How is Nathan?'

'Fine. He's just started walking and causing mayhem in the house. Actually, you could come over here tomorrow night with a bottle of wine and sleep over.'

'I don't think Tony would want me there. I doubt he's forgiven me yet for telling him he should help a bit more and at least try to change Nathan's dirty nappies.'

'I agree with you, but you know how stubborn Tony can be. He's going up the West End to a stag do tomorrow night. I told him I don't want him coming home shit-faced and waking Nathan up, so he's staying at a friend's house and I'll be on my own. We could have a good natter, put the world to rights and keep each other company like we used to when we lived at home,' Pam suggested.

'I don't know what time I'll finish work tomorrow, but I expect it will be late. I was thinking of going shopping in the West End on Saturday if you want to join me,' she said, knowing she had to buy a newsboy cap.

Pam hesitated for a moment. 'That sounds like a plan. I'll ask Mum if she can look after Nathan and let you know what she says.'

'Tell her and Dad I'll come for tea after we've been shopping – that way she won't say no to you.'

'OK . . . Now tell me about the robbery.'

'You'll just have to wait until Saturday, Pam. I'll see you then.'

Jane put the phone down before Pam could argue.

Jane's meal had gone cold and slightly soggy while she was on the phone, so she threw what was left in the bin and poured herself another glass of wine. Although it had been a tiring day, she knew tomorrow Murphy would be on her back, wanting to know if she'd typed her reports and submitted them. Not wanting to give him a reason to find fault, she got her typewriter from her bedroom cupboard and took it into the kitchen.

But before getting down to work, she couldn't help replaying the conversation with Pam in her mind. On the surface, her sister had been breezy and cheerful, cracking jokes about *The Sweeney* and trying to make Jane laugh. But Jane knew Pam's bubbliness was sometimes a mask, hiding deeper anxieties. What could she be concerned about? Jane wondered if it was something to do with their parents. They were getting to that age when serious illnesses seem to lurk just around the corner, and perhaps Pam had noticed something worrying. Was that what she'd wanted to talk to Jane about? Jane sighed, feeling she had quite enough on her plate, and tried to put it out of her mind. She took a sip of wine and started typing from the notes she'd made in her pocket notebook during the day.

After a couple of hours, she felt too tired to continue and decided to leave typing the last of her notes until she got to work. She ran a bath and had a long, relaxing soak, then went to bed, where she read over her report of the day's events. She felt she'd done well, but despite Kingston's praise, she knew she had a long way to go before everyone accepted her as part of the team – especially Katie Powell. Katie's attitude had really got her back up, but she now realised it might be down to the fact she was having an affair with Kingston.

It made sense to try and keep the peace with Katie, and even to be sociable with her, up to a point.

The sight of Kingston's pale white bum cheeks bobbing up and down came unbidden into her mind, and she smiled at how she'd thought she could hear him working out, when he was in fact working on Katie. She liked Kingston, but there was no doubt in her mind that what he was doing was wrong – not just because he was married. She knew from her own past relationships – with a married DCI and a single DI on the Bomb Squad – that mixing business with pleasure could be a recipe for disaster.

At last, feeling her mind beginning to wander, she set her alarm and turned off her bedside light. As she drifted off to sleep, she wondered if her second day with the Flying Squad would be as eventful as her first.

CHAPTER TWELVE

Jane was up at 6.30 the next morning, as she didn't know what the journey to work would be like at that time and didn't want to be late. After a light breakfast of tea and toast with marmalade she got ready for work. Although most of the team dressed in what was commonly referred to in the job as 'scruffs', she decided to dress smart but casual. After a few minutes humming and ha-ing, she put on her blue Wrangler denim jeans, a white T-shirt, blue blazer and white trainers, which she thought would be the most practical if she had to chase anyone. She was out of the door and on her way by seven and was parking her car in one of the spaces in front of the building just before eight, which was quicker than she expected.

There was no one in the office and, looking at her lone desk in the corner of the room, she decided to move it over to Teflon's group of four. She disconnected the phone line, then removed the drawers and tried pulling and pushing the desk, but it was too heavy for her to move on her own. Luckily Dabs then walked in and Jane asked if he'd mind helping her.

'No problem,' he said, taking his coat off.

'It's quite heavy so it's probably best if I push and you pull.'

As they slid the desk across the office, Dabs asked if she'd heard back from the traffic officer about the ignition barrel on the Cortina.

'Not yet. I'll give him a call just before the meeting as DCI Murphy said he wants the owner of the car visited today.'

'How did your further enquiries go last night at Edgar House?'

'Very productive, actually. I found out about another two men who were seen leaving the estate just before the fire was discovered.'

'Well done. Would the witness recognise them again?'

'I doubt it, but she described one of them as wearing a cap like the one the pub landlady said the driver of the Cortina was wearing, and she thinks she saw the two men with the holdall in a Mercedes sports car.'

'Sounds like it's all coming together nicely – the DCI will be pleased.'

'We'll see.' Jane doubted Murphy would be pleased with anything she did at the moment. 'I've got some follow-up work to do on the four men, and the previous ownership of garage twenty-nine. I'm hoping it will give us something positive to work on.'

'Be interesting to hear at the office meeting if anyone else has discovered anything of value. You fancy a bacon sarnie and coffee from the burger van?'

'A bacon roll would be great – I'll put the kettle on and make us a coffee.'

She reached into her handbag and got some money out of her purse.

'I'll get them – your shout next time.'

'OK. Could I have some brown sauce with mine, please?'

While the kettle boiled Jane put the drawers back in her desk, reconnected the phone and went over to Katie's desk to get the typewriter so she could finish typing her report. She noticed that Katie had only started typing one of the handwritten statements taken from the security guards and part of it was still in the typewriter. She sat down at Katie's desk and began to type the rest of the statement.

When Dabs returned with the bacon rolls, Jane made the coffees and sat at her own desk to eat. She could imagine Katie's reaction if she got any crumbs or brown sauce on hers. Dabs said he had a few things to do before the meeting and went to his office. After finishing her roll, she went back to typing up the statement at Katie's desk, and was just about finished when Katie walked in.

Jane smiled brightly. 'Good morning, Katie. I was just—'

'What are you doing at my desk?' she snapped.

'I needed the typewriter for my report and thought I'd finish the security guards' statement for you before I used it.'

'I'm perfectly capable of doing my own typing.'

Jane took a deep breath. 'Sorry. I thought you wanted help typing the statements.'

'I did last night, but I've cleared my desk of other work so I can do them today.'

'Well, if you want me to do some just let me know,' Jane said with a shrug.

Katie pointed to a typewriter on the Colonel's desk.

'There's a spare one there you can use for your reports. Why have you moved your desk?'

Jane thought it was obvious. 'I thought it would be more productive as a DS if I sat with members of the team – like DS Stanley does.'

'You should have asked for permission first.'

'I didn't know I needed it.'

'Well, I suggest you put it back where it was and ask DCI Murphy if you can move it.'

'It's only a desk, Katie.'

'That's not the point. The office is laid out the way it is for a reason.'

'And what reason would that be?' Jane asked, letting her annoyance show.

'How would you like it if I just walked into your house and rearranged the furniture the way I wanted it to be?'

Jane shook her head in disbelief. 'That's a ridiculous comparison, but if it will make you feel better I'll tell DCI Murphy I moved my desk and ask him if he's OK about it.'

'I'd still put it back where it was if I were you.'

'It's that heavy I nearly pulled a muscle moving it in the first place – so it can stay where it is for now.'

At that moment DCI Murphy walked into the office, followed by the Colonel and Teflon.

'Everything all right, ladies?' Murphy asked, sensing an air of hostility between the two women.

Katie was quick to answer before Jane could get a word in.

'As you can see, DS Tennison has moved her desk. I told her she should have asked your permission before doing so.'

'It's fine there by me.' Teflon gave Jane a wink.

Katie glared at him. 'I was speaking to DCI Murphy.'

Murphy sighed. 'It's only a bloody desk, Katie. I couldn't give a toss if Tennison wants to put it in the backyard, as long as she gets on with her work. Who owns that custard tart on wheels that's parked in my space?'

'If you're referring to the yellow VW Golf, that's mine, sir,' Jane said.

'Well, don't park it there again. Someone get me a bacon and egg roll and a cup of tea.'

He slapped a pound note down on the desk and went into his office.

Jane frowned. 'What's the problem? There are plenty of spaces out there.'

Teflon smiled. 'Yeah, but he likes the one nearest the entrance in case it's raining. I'll put the kettle on.'

'Don't move the kettle, Teflon, or all hell could break loose,' the Colonel joked, and Jane smiled.

Katie grabbed the pound note before stomping out of the room to the burger van.

'What's up with her?' Teflon asked.

'Who knows?' The Colonel shrugged. 'Probably the wrong time of the month – either that or she's desperate for a shag.' He draped his jacket over the back of his chair, then threw his cap at the coat rack, where it landed on one of the hooks. 'James Bond or what?' he said with a grin.

'Fiver says you can't do it two out of three,' Teflon challenged.
'That was a bloody fluke, and you know it.'

The Colonel settled himself behind his desk.

'I could do it easy, but I don't want to take your money, so
I won't.'

'You two want a hot drink?' Teflon asked.

Jane said she'd like a coffee and went over to give him a hand,
while the Colonel got a clear plastic sports bottle out of his back-
pack with a thick pale liquid in it and held it up.

'No thanks, I've got me banana, egg and water mix, so I'm fine.'
He shook the bottle then took a swig.

'He thinks it makes him stronger, but all it does is make him
fart a lot,' Teflon whispered to Jane. 'Was Katie really getting upset
about the desk or just having a go at you?'

'I don't know – a bit of both, maybe. I'm doing my best to be
friendly towards her, but I think she's got a bee in her bonnet about
me being on the team.'

'Well, she's going to have to get used to it and stop behaving
like Lady Muck. If she does start on you again just put her in
her place – as a DS she's answerable to you, not the other way
around.'

'Trouble is, I think she'd go running to Murphy and complain.
The last thing I need right now is to give him a reason to reprimand me.'

'As you just saw, Murphy finds her a pain in the arse at times, so
I wouldn't worry about it. If she's going to complain about you it
would probably be to Kingston.'

'Why him?' she asked, trying not to sound too curious.

'Everyone reckons Katie's got the hots for him. She's in and out
of his office like a yo-yo and does whatever he asks at the drop of a
hat – if he said jump, she'd ask how high.'

'Do you think he fancies her?' she asked, wondering if he knew
about their affair.

Teflon laughed. 'Kingston's definitely a ladies' man, but person-ally I think he just likes to flirt with Katie to keep her on her toes. Mind you, some of the lads reckon they're at it.'

'What's DCI Murphy think?'

'Don't know. Although he's pretty close to Kingston, I don't think he'd approve if they were screwing each other.'

Jane realised she was probably the only one on the team who knew for a fact Katie and Kingston were having a sexual relation-ship, and she was going to keep it that way for fear of being called a scandalmonger. The last thing she wanted was to alienate King-ston, one of the few who had so far accepted her on the team. She sat at her desk with her coffee and rang PC Turner, the traffic officer.

'Hi, it's WDS Tennison. I was just calling to ask if there's any news on the burnt-out Cortina's ignition barrel?'

'Did you not get my report?'

'No, but I don't think the morning dispatch has arrived here yet. Your report may still be in transit.'

'I didn't put it in dispatch – I delivered it by hand last night and was told you were out on enquiries.'

'Who did you give it to?'

'I spoke to a lady on the intercom who said she was the office clerk. She came down to the front entrance and I handed it to her. She asked what it was about, and I told her my examination of the burnt-out Cortina and ignition barrel.'

'That would be Katie. It may be on her desk. What was the result with the barrel?'

'I took it to bits and did a microscopic examination. There's no evidence I can find that suggests to me a screwdriver or similar implement was forced into the barrel to start the car.'

'Looks like the owner of the car may be hiding something then,' she remarked.

'Certainly does. My report contains everything I did at Edgar House yesterday. If you need a written statement just let me know and I'll get it typed up here then forward both copies to you.'

'Thanks. Can I ask what time you dropped the report off?'

'About six. Is there a problem?'

'No, not at all. Thanks for everything you've done, it's really useful and I know our DCI will be pleased.'

'It was a pleasure meeting you and I hope you catch the villains.'

Jane put the phone down and looked in her in tray and desk drawers, but there was no sign of the report. She then looked on Katie's desk, but it wasn't there either. She contemplated looking in Katie's desk drawers but didn't want to look as if she was snooping. Looking out of the window she could see Katie walking across the road, carrying Murphy's food in a brown bag, so she went out onto the landing and waited for her.

'Have you got a report that was dropped off for me by a Traffic Division officer last night?' Jane asked as Katie appeared.

'I put it on DCI Murphy's desk,' she said casually, brushing past Jane.

Jane followed her. 'But it was addressed to me.'

'I know, but when the traffic officer said what it was about, and you weren't here, I thought DCI Murphy should see it in case he wanted to action further enquiries right away.'

'Why didn't you tell me about it when I got back to the station last night?'

Katie turned, shrugged her shoulders and looked at Jane nonchalantly.

'I forgot. Now if you don't mind I need to take this to DCI Murphy,' she said, holding up the bag.

'Did he send anyone round to the Cortina owner's house?'

'I don't know, I didn't ask him,' she said, entering Murphy's office.

Jane was certain Katie had given the report to Murphy and not told her about it to deliberately annoy her. As she walked back into the office, she was determined not to let Katie's behaviour get to her, but she knew there might come a point where she would need to heed Teflon's advice and reprimand her.

Katie put Murphy's roll and tea on his desk.

'Just a dab of tomato sauce and lots of pepper, the way you like it, sir.'

Murphy grunted his thanks. 'Is there a problem between you and Tennison?'

'No, sir, I just felt she should have had the decency to ask before she moved her desk, that's all.'

'You don't like Tennison, do you?'

'I don't really know her yet, but I suppose it would be fair to say she's not someone I'd necessarily socialise with.'

Murphy nodded. 'I'd like you to do something for me but keep it between the two of us.'

'Yes, sir, you can trust me to be discreet.'

'While I'm in here, and Tennison's out there, I want you to keep an eye on her for me. When she puts a report in to be indexed, go over it with a fine-toothed comb and let me know if there's anything she hasn't done she should have done.'

'Will DI Kingston still be going over her reports after I've indexed them?'

'Yes, but I don't think he'll be as thorough as he should.'

'Why not?'

'He seems to like Tennison and thinks we should give her a chance to prove herself.'

'He said that?' Katie asked, her brows furrowed.

'Yes, but as far as I'm concerned she should be treated the same as everyone else. If her work's not up to scratch or the standards I expect, I need to know for her first monthly review as a new member of the team.'

Katie smiled. 'Would you like me to eavesdrop on her telephone calls as well?'

Murphy hesitated. 'When you can, but don't make it too obvious. Like I said, this conversation is just between the two of us. It would be good if you were nice to her as well – that way she won't suspect anything untoward.'

Katie sighed. 'I'll do my best.'

He picked up an envelope. 'This is addressed to Tennison; some-one must have put it on my desk by mistake. Can you give it to her?'

'That was me, sir – a Traffic Division officer delivered it late last night.' She explained what the report was about. 'I realised how important the information might be and thought you might like to see it first thing and decide what action needed to be taken before the meeting. I also ran a criminal record check on Mr Braun, who reported the Cortina stolen, but there was no trace of him.'

'Good thinking, Katie. I'll read the report while I have my breakfast – then when everyone's in we'll crack on with the meeting.'

'There was something else that got phoned in last night.'

'Fire away,' he said as he bit into the roll.

'The duty sergeant from Tottenham called last night and said a woman came to the station alleging some men in a local cafe were talking about a robbery.'

'Is that it? No details of what she heard being said?'

'I did ask but the sergeant said he was very busy and had just got her name and address when he had to take an urgent phone call. When he got off the phone the woman had left the station.'

'I doubt the people we're after would be so stupid as to openly talk in a cafe about a blagging they were going to do! Sounds like the woman's a nutter looking for attention to me.'

'I agree it's probably nonsense, but it would be wrong of us to ignore it – so I was thinking WDS Tennison would be the ideal person to follow it up,' she added with a bright smile.

Murphy took a mouthful of tea to wash his food down and grinned.

'Draw up an action to interview the woman and I'll give it to Tennison to deal with at the meeting.'

As she left his office, Murphy opened the envelope containing PC Turner's report, feeling pleased with himself. He knew Katie would do everything she could to find fault in Tennison's work, and that way he couldn't be accused of carrying out a personal vendetta against her.

Katie approached Jane as she was sitting at her desk typing.

'DCI Murphy is reading the traffic officer's report. I explained to him why I put it on his desk and asked if I could give it to you, but he said he'd like to read it first. I'm sorry I forgot to mention it last night, but I wasn't feeling well, and it just slipped my mind. Next time I'll put anything that comes in for you straight on your desk.'

Jane looked up from her typing. She wondered if Murphy had said something to make Katie apologise for her behaviour. Or perhaps she really had just forgotten. After all, she'd just been having sex with Kingston, and was clearly flustered when Jane turned up.

'Forget about it, Katie. Even if I'd known about the report last night no action could be taken until DCI Murphy had read it.'

'Thanks. Would you like a hot drink?'

'No thanks, I've just had one. I've nearly finished my report, then if you like I could type one of the statements on your desk.'

'That would be great, but the office meeting will be starting as soon as everyone's here.'

'Well, I'll do what I can before it starts.'

Katie went to her desk, picked up a handwritten statement and gave it to Jane.

Kingston walked in carrying a coffee and a sausage roll and went straight to his office. Katie quickly followed him, then closed the door behind her and stood by his desk with her arms crossed.

'Where did you go with Tennison last night?'

Kingston put his breakfast down on the desk.

'I didn't go anywhere with her – I went to the Crown to get a statement from the landlady.'

He pulled the statement out of the folder and showed it to her.

'Then why did you leave together?'

'I told her to go home. She got in her car then drove off in the opposite direction to me. For Christ's sake, what's your problem, Katie?'

'I just thought the way you left last night was rather abrupt, especially as we'd just . . . you know. It felt as if you were more interested in her.'

He pointed to himself. 'Me, interested in Tennison? You couldn't be more wrong – I don't even find her attractive.'

'Then why are you being so nice to her?'

'Being nice doesn't mean I fancy her—'

'DCI Murphy doesn't like her.'

'Murphy doesn't like the fact a woman is on the Flying Squad. He sees Tennison as a liability and will do his damnedest to get rid of her.'

'And will you help him?'

'Look, I made a few phone calls before she came here. By all accounts she's not a bad detective, but working on the Flying Squad is a totally different ball game from divisional work and I for one don't think she'll be up to it.'

'Murphy wants me to keep an eye on her and report back to him if she messes up.'

'Then there's no need for me to get involved as well.'

'As her DI you should bring her mistakes to Murphy's attention.'

'I know what my job is, Katie, and I'm not going to put myself on the line with Murphy by not doing it – least of all for Tennison. Now can I please finish my sausage roll in peace before the office meeting?'

'My boyfriend's out with his mates tonight so you could come around to mine if . . .'

Kingston frowned. 'He nearly caught us last time I did that. I ripped my jacket climbing over your garden fence, and my wife started asking me questions about how it happened.'

'Maybe we should tell our other halves that we've met someone else,' Katie suggested. 'Then we can openly be together and stop sneaking around – I'm tired of sex in the gym or a car.'

He obviously wasn't expecting this.

'We both agreed our relationship was just a fling. Besides, you only just got engaged to Brian. You don't really want to break it off, do you?'

'I don't know. I don't think Brian and I are right together. He's not like you – sex with him is like a boring routine.'

This was something new and it was making Kingston anxious. He certainly had no intention of leaving his wife for another woman – least of all Katie.

'Now's not a good time to be having this conversation, Katie.'

'Why not?'

'Because there's a lot to discuss, and it needs to be in private, away from the office.'

'Tonight then, at mine . . . after work.'

She left before he could answer.

Kingston threw what was left of his sausage roll in the bin, his appetite suddenly gone.

* * *

Katie quickly typed up an information sheet concerning the phone call from the Tottenham duty sergeant and took it to Murphy. She told him everyone was in the office ready for the meeting, apart from the officers who were still on surveillance regarding the possible jewellery shop robbery in Chingford. He read the sheet, then wrote 'WDS Tennison to deal' under the 'Further action' box and signed it before going into the office to start the meeting. Katie got the flip chart to write on and stood next to Murphy and Kingston, marker pen in hand.

'Anyone get anything positive from their snouts last night?' Murphy asked loudly to get everyone's attention, but there was no response.

Grim-faced, he went over to Katie's desk to look at the office duty book, in which everyone recorded their times on and off duty along with brief details of what they were doing and why.

'I see you all managed to claim a few hours' overtime for meeting informants – but not one of you has anything constructive to show for it!'

Stanley stuck his hand up. 'I was given a couple of names, Guv. I ran a CRO check on them this morning – they're both known blaggers, but they're in Wormwood Scrubs at present.'

Baxter also spoke up. 'I had a similar result with a suspect, but he popped his clogs from a drugs OD a month ago—'

Murphy raised his hand for Baxter to stop talking.

'What bloody use is that to us? I expect you all to get results – not sit in a pub pissing it up with informants giving you a load of bollocks all night!' He scowled and looked at the Colonel. 'I authorised twenty quid for you out of the informants' fund, so what was the result?'

Kingston spoke up. 'He can't see his snout until Sunday morning.'

'I'm reasonably confident he'll have something for us, Guv – he always proved reliable in the past,' the Colonel added.

'Well, you better put the Commissioner's money where your mouth is. What about the checks on recent armed robberies with the home counties, Katie?'

'I've spoken to Hertfordshire and Kent CID, but they've had nothing similar in the last six months. Essex and Surrey have a possible and I'm waiting for them to fax the details over to me.'

'Why are the carrot cruncher forces always so bloody slow with everything? Let me see it as soon as it arrives. Any update on the forensics, Dabs?'

'I've spoken to the scientist in the gun room. He's aware of the priorities and said he'll start on the exhibits as soon as we submit them, which will be after the meeting. I've prepared the lab form and just need DS Tennison as exhibits officer to check it before you sign it.' He held the lab form up.

'Let me see it.'

Murphy got a pen out, signed the lab form and gave it back to Dabs.

Jane wasn't sure if he'd signed it without reading it to save time, or just to belittle her in front of the team.

'While we're on forensics . . . I've had a result back from the traffic PC who examined the Cortina's ignition barrel. There's no sign that a screwdriver was forced into the barrel, which puts the owner's claim it was stolen in doubt. I'd like the Colonel and Bax to pay Mr Braun a visit after the meeting. If you think he's lying or being evasive then nick him.'

Jane wasn't surprised Murphy hadn't acknowledged it was her idea to call the traffic officer to examine the Cortina, but it was still galling. She raised her hand, but Murphy ignored her and looked instead at Kingston.

'Stewart, did you manage to get a statement from the landlady of the pub?'

'Yes, and the artist's impression, which is up on the wall.'

He took a duplicate out of a folder, which he handed to Murphy.

'That's a good drawing – get some "Appeal for Assistance" posters made up with details of the robbery, then circulate it Met-wide and in the papers. I know it could result in a shedload of dead-end calls, but we might strike lucky. Once it's circulated Tennison can help Katie man the phones and make CRO enquiries with any names we're given. Have you made an appointment for Simpson to view albums at the Yard, Stewart?'

'She's busy all weekend and can't get anyone to manage the pub for her until Monday at the earliest.'

'Tell her it's urgent, see if you can rearrange it for an earlier time, or to speed things up, get an album made up of mugshots that look like the artist's impression and within the same age range. Then Tennison can take it to her to look through.'

Jane knew Murphy was deliberately burdening her with all the menial tasks but knew she couldn't complain about it without angering him further. Teflon nudged her arm.

'I'll give you a hand with the phones and mugshot albums,' he whispered.

'Thanks,' she whispered back.

'Did Simpson remember anything else significant?' Murphy asked.

Kingston nodded. 'Only in relation to the cap the driver of the getaway car was wearing, which, linked with information Tennison obtained, would appear to be a grey "newsboy" style cap.'

'What was the information?' he asked Kingston.

'It might be best if Tennison tells you as she actually spoke to the witness who saw the two men—'

'I'm happy for you to tell us,' Murphy said with an icy smile.

'Er . . .'

Kingston paused to remember the salient parts of what Jane had told him. Jane decided she had to speak up, whatever the consequences.

'There's quite a bit for DI Kingston to remember. Perhaps he might like to read from my report I typed up last night – in my own time.'

She spread the six pages out like a fan and handed them to Kingston.

'Just read out the relevant bits,' Murphy snapped.

Kingston looked at Jane. 'Where does the interview with Mrs Clarke start about the two men she saw leaving the estate before the fire was discovered?'

'It was Rita Brown from flat fourteen Edgar House who saw them. Her account and description starts on page three, second paragraph down,' she replied.

Murphy sighed. 'You told us about them at yesterday's meeting, Tennison, and as I recall Mrs Clarke only saw them from behind, which isn't much use to us.'

'The Clarkes own the garage the burnt-out Cortina was found in, sir. Mrs Brown had returned home after seeing the two men in Blake Hall Road. She immediately took her dog outside for a wee and saw two more men leaving the estate. It was shortly after that the fire brigade were called.'

'Why didn't you get this information from Mrs Brown during the initial house-to-house?' Murphy asked, clearly trying to find fault in her work.

'I was doing the forensics with Dabs. A uniform sergeant initially spoke to Mrs Brown, and having read his report on the house-to-house form I decided a revisit was necessary. When the further information came to light I returned to the station and informed DI Kingston.'

'Which is why I got a statement from Fiona Simpson last night,' Kingston added.

Murphy glared at Kingston, then turned to Jane.

'It would have been helpful to know all this before the meeting. Carry on, Stewart.'

Kingston looked up from the report.

'Mrs Brown's description of the man in the newsboy cap is also very similar to the driver of the car as Simpson described him to me.'

'How can Mrs Brown be so certain it's a newsboy cap?' Stanley asked.

'Because her husband has one,' Jane replied.

'Would Mrs Brown be able to recognise these two men if she saw them again?' Murphy asked.

'I doubt it, she only got a fleeting look at them as her dog ran off after a squirrel.'

'Maybe we could interview her dog and the squirrel for a better description,' Baxter joked, but Murphy wasn't amused.

Kingston held up Jane's report.

'There's some other information Mrs Brown gave Tennison.'

Kingston handed Jane back her typed report.

'I feel like I'm stealing your thunder – and you're also better placed to answer any questions.'

Jane looked at Murphy, who gave her a curt nod to continue. She recounted her meetings at Edgar House with Helen Clarke and Rita Brown, and mentioned the two men in a gold two-door Mercedes 450 SL with a black cloth roof.

'How can she be sure it was them in the Merc?' Stanley asked.

'She can't, but she noticed the driver was wearing a green Barbour jacket and had the same coloured hair as the man she'd just seen.'

'There's no direct evidence to connect any of this to the robbery,' the Colonel remarked.

Jane was determined to make her point.

'Granted it could all be circumstantial, but I think there's more to it when you consider the witness descriptions of the men, especially the newsboy cap, the timing between the robbery, the crash and then the burnt-out Cortina being found nearby.'

There was silence in the room as everyone digested this. Teflon was the first to speak up.

'I'd say it merits further investigation.'

'I'll make that decision, Teflon, not you,' Murphy said.

'I should also add that I found a cigar butt in Aylmer Road where the Cortina was parked just before the robbery,' Jane added.

'When?' Murphy asked.

'Yesterday afternoon on my way back to the office from Edgar House.'

Murphy frowned. 'Why didn't you mention the cigar before now?'

'I tried to at yesterday's meeting, but no one seemed interested. When I revisited Mrs Brown last night she was adamant one of them was smoking a cigar.'

Murphy made a beckoning motion with his fingers.

'I'll have a read of your report then decide what needs to be done.' He looked at the Colonel. 'Have we got a statement from the off-duty PC who was shot?'

'Not yet, Guv. I was going to do it today if I got time.'

'The Cortina owner's your priority. Teflon, you and Cam get the statements from the PC who was shot and the two in the area car that crashed. Did we hear back from the bank about a reward?'

'Not yet – I'll chase him up after the meeting.'

'Right, you all know what you've got to do, so get out there and start grafting.'

He turned and started to walk towards his office.

The Colonel raised his hand. 'Excuse me, Guv, but what's happening regarding the surveillance job the rest of the team are on?'

'It's still ongoing. I spoke to DC Freeman this morning and there's good information that the two men they're watching may hit a jeweller's in Chingford next Wednesday.'

'Will we be involved in any pavement ambush?' Stanley asked.

'Yes, but I'll update you on Monday with the state of play and who'll be doing what.'

There was a buzz of excitement around the room at the thought of arresting armed robbers during the commission of the crime. It was obvious they'd rather be doing that than sitting through another long meeting. Jane doubted if Murphy would let her be involved in the observation or arrests, and resigned herself to being stuck in the office listening to the action on the radio.

'Anything else anyone wants to raise?' Murphy asked.

'Yes, sir,' Katie piped up. 'There was the information sheet I gave you about the woman who attended the front counter at Tottenham Police Station last night, which may be relevant.'

'Thanks for reminding me, Katie.' He got the form out of his folder. 'A Miss Emma Wilson told the duty sergeant at Tottenham she was in a local cafe earlier this week and some men were talking about a robbery. It's information I'd like followed up.'

'Is that it? Nothing about what the woman heard?' Kingston asked.

'The sergeant took the woman's details and rightly passed it on to us to speak directly to her,' Katie said.

'The men we're after don't sound like the sort of blokes who'd blab in a public area,' Baxter remarked.

Murphy said nothing and handed the information report to Jane.

'I want you to deal with it and determine whether or not it's connected to our investigation.'

He walked off into his office and closed the door.

Jane rang Tottenham Police Station and was told that the sergeant who'd spoken to Emma Wilson wasn't on duty until two o'clock. She looked again at the information sheet and was dismayed at the lack of detail. She looked at Miss Wilson's address on the information sheet but couldn't find the estate name in the *A-Z*.

'You know where the Broadwater Farm estate is?' she asked Teflon, who was sitting at the desk abutting hers doing some paperwork.

He stopped and looked at her. 'Why are you interested in the Broadwater?'

'The woman who went into Tottenham Police Station lives there.'

'Ring her and ask her to meet you at Tottenham nick.'

'There's no phone number on the info sheet, just the address.'

Teflon picked up a paper clip and threw it at Cam to get his attention.

'Piss off,' Cam said as the clip bounced off his head.

Teflon gestured with his finger for Cam to join them. Reluctantly he got up and went over to see what he wanted.

'You OK to get the PC's statements on your own?' Teflon asked him.

'The Guv told us both to do it.'

'I know, but Tennison needs to visit the Broadwater and was thinking of going on her own.'

Cam looked at Jane, his eyebrows raised.

'It's a crime-ridden shithole and the last place on earth where you'd want to be on your tod. It's commonly known as "the Farm" – because it's full of animals.'

'Its reputation's so bad that many people who are offered a council flat on the Broadwater refuse it, and there are loads of existing tenants queuing up to get moved off,' Teflon added.

'I'll take a portable radio with me,' Jane said.

Cam shook his head. 'They don't work on the landings or inside flats as the concrete's so thick. Teflon's right, there's no way you can go there on your own. Mind you, he'd be putting his neck on the line more than any of us down there if they knew he was Old Bill.'

She looked at Teflon. 'Why would it be worse for you?'

'There's a lot of black criminals on the estate who see me as a traitor for joining the police.'

'I'm happy to go with Jane,' Cam said.

'No, I'll do it,' Teflon said firmly.

'What are you three planning?' Kingston asked as he approached them.

'Tennison was thinking of going down the Broadwater Farm on her own.'

'Then she needs her head tested.' Kingston looked at Jane. 'Is it something to do with that action DCI Murphy gave you?'

Jane nodded. 'Yes, the informant Miss Wilson lives on the estate.'

Kingston shook his head. 'I was the DI at Tottenham before I came here and believe me it's rare for anyone on the Broadwater to help the police. We tried to arrest a suspect for stabbing a police officer and they threw a full beer barrel down on the car from one of the walkways. We were lucky it landed on the bonnet and not the roof or it could have killed us.'

'Did they get the people responsible?' Jane asked.

'No, the walkways are like rat runs and they all disappeared, and of course no one saw a thing.'

'Murphy's out of order if he knew where he was sending her and didn't say to take backup,' Teflon said darkly.

'He may not have seen the address,' Kingston suggested, but he didn't sound convinced.

'Is it OK if we go with Jane?' Teflon asked Kingston.

'I'm ordering you to go with her.'

CHAPTER THIRTEEN

The Colonel and Baxter parked up outside Frank Braun's address in Tottenham. The large three-bedroom, 1930s-built, semi-detached house was on Mount Pleasant Road, a quiet residential road. The Colonel pointed out to Baxter that the upstairs bedroom curtains were closed, suggesting someone was in, then pressed the doorbell. After nearly a minute there was no reply, so he pressed it again and stepped back to see if the curtains moved.

'They're taking their time. Should I climb over the side fence and cover the back?' Baxter asked.

The Colonel shook his head. 'If this Braun bloke is involved in the robbery and made a false TDA claim he'll front us out . . . Hang on, someone's opening the curtain.'

A bleary-eyed, bare-chested man in his late thirties pulled back the curtain and opened the window.

'If you're selling something I'm not interested!' he shouted.

'You Frank Braun?' the Colonel asked.

'I might be – who are you?'

The Colonel held up his warrant card.

'I'm DC Gorman and this is DC Baxter. We'd like to speak to you about the '76 Mark 4 Cortina you reported stolen.'

'You found it?' Mr Braun asked, looking pleased.

'Yes, but I'd rather we talk about it inside,' the Colonel replied.

Braun put on a dressing gown, went downstairs and let the two detectives in.

'You from Tottenham CID?' Braun asked as they followed him into the living room.

'No, the Flying Squad,' the Colonel replied.

Braun sighed. 'Don't tell me the car was used in a robbery?'

'What made you jump to that conclusion?' the Colonel asked.

'Nothing, it just seems obvious as you lot investigate armed robberies.'

The Colonel nodded. 'Very perceptive – you assumed right, Mr Braun. Have you seen the news about the armed robbery on a security van in Leytonstone yesterday?'

'No, I haven't—'

The Colonel smirked. 'And there was me thinking you might know all about it.'

Braun could tell they were taking the mickey.

'Have you found my Cortina or not?' he asked bluntly.

'Four armed men used *your car* to rob a bank yesterday, then torched it to destroy any forensic evidence.'

'Is the car a write-off?' Braun asked.

'It was totally burnt out, so you won't be driving it again,' the Colonel said.

Braun sighed. 'There goes my no claims bonus.'

'You don't seem very upset that your motor's a write-off,' Baxter remarked.

He shrugged. 'There's not a lot I can do about it now, is there?'

'How many keys do you have for the vehicle?' the Colonel asked.

'Just one . . . and no doubt you'd like to see it.'

He walked over to a side cabinet and, opening a drawer, he removed the key.

'Lose the other one, did you?' the Colonel asked.

Braun frowned as he handed the key to the Colonel.

'As it happens, yes, and I haven't bothered to get a replacement – though it's clearly not worth doing so now, is it?'

'How and where did you lose the key?' Baxter asked.

'I didn't lose it. It was stolen—'

Baxter interrupted. 'Of course it was – no doubt by a pickpocket and you didn't feel a thing.'

Braun opened his eyes wide. 'That's right! Was that a wild guess or can you read minds?'

The Colonel took a step towards him. 'It's not in your interest to be flippant with us, Mr Braun.'

Braun folded his arms. 'Are you threatening to arrest me?'

'We can continue this conversation here or down at the station – the choice is yours,' Baxter said.

Braun glared at him. 'If you'd had the decency to let me finish, I was going to tell you my wife was at the Coolbury nightclub with some friends when her handbag was stolen. And before you ask, she reported it to the police and gave them a list of everything that was in the bag – including the car keys.'

'Where's the Coolbury?' Baxter asked as he got out his pocket notebook to write the location down.

'In Tottenham High Road near the junction with White Hart Lane – a lot of the Spurs players use it.'

'Well, I doubt one of them would nick a handbag.' Baxter smirked.

'I'd like you to tell me exactly why you're both here, because I'm sensing it's not just to tell me my car was found,' Braun demanded.

The Colonel looked him in the eye. 'We had a vehicle examiner go over what was left of your car. In his expert opinion nothing was forced into the ignition barrel to start the vehicle and it wasn't hot-wired either, which means . . .' He paused to let Braun answer.

'A key was used to start it . . . and you think I might be involved in some way.'

'Are you, Mr Braun?' the Colonel asked.

'No, I'm not. The car was stolen from outside my house while I was on holiday in Mauritius with my wife. My neighbour noticed it was gone, but he didn't realise it had been stolen.'

'All sounds a bit fishy to me,' Baxter remarked.

'Do I look like someone who'd be involved in a bank robbery?'

The Colonel grinned. 'Believe me, they come in all shapes and sizes—'

'This is ridiculous, I've got a holiday booking receipt and a dated Mauritian entry stamp in my passport.'

He walked towards the cabinet to get them.

'It's OK, I don't doubt you were on holiday, but who's to say the theft of the key and being on holiday isn't a set up alibi?' the Colonel suggested.

Braun was struggling to remain calm. 'I can put up with you calling me a liar – but don't you dare insinuate my wife is!'

'Where were you yesterday morning?' Baxter asked.

'What time did this robbery occur?'

'About 9.45,' Baxter said.

'I was at work until eleven o'clock Thursday morning, then drove home and didn't get back here until about half past. You can check it out with my work colleagues—'

'You got two cars then?' Baxter asked.

'Yeah, my wife used the Cortina mostly, for shopping and running the kids to and from school.'

'What's your other car?' Baxter asked.

'A BMW 323i, which I now keep in the garage, for obvious reasons.'

'Then what's your wife using now?' the Colonel asked.

'My car if I'm not using it, and public transport if I am.'

'What do you do for a living?' the Colonel asked.

'I'm in the London Fire Brigade, as a senior fire investigator based in the West End. I'm night shift this week and was called out to a residential arson at two o'clock Thursday morning. Someone poured petrol through a letterbox, thankfully no one was hurt, and I worked the scene with a scientist and one of your lab liaison sergeants.'

'Who was the sergeant?' Baxter asked, ready to write the name down.

'Paul Lawrence. I've worked a few arson scenes with him before and socialised with him at forensic conferences.'

'Why didn't you tell us you were a fireman earlier?' the Colonel asked.

'I would have done if you'd asked, but I didn't think it had anything to do with why you came to see me.'

'Well, it certainly puts things in a different light ... Was there anything in your wife's handbag with your address on it?'

'She didn't think so at the time, but it's possible. Our bloody house keys were in her handbag as well, so I had to have the front door locks changed – which wasn't cheap.'

'Can I have a look at the vehicle registration certificate for the previous keeper?'

'I bought it off the station officer on Red Watch at Soho where I work. Mick Goddard – he lives in Romford.'

Braun got the document from a drawer in the kitchen and gave it to Baxter, who wrote down Goddard's details in his pocket notebook.

'Look, my car was obviously started with a key, but from personal experience in dealing with burnt-out cars I have known cases where a different, but similar, key has been used to start a stolen car.'

'It's possible that's what happened, and I'll discuss it with the traffic officer who examined your car,' the Colonel said.

'Can you tell me where the car is now? I'll need to inform the insurance company.'

'It's at the Met lab in Lambeth undergoing examination. You know where that is?' Baxter replied.

'We submit our fire investigation exhibits there for examination, so yes, I know where it is.'

'Give them a ring and they'll let you know when they'll be finished with it,' Baxter suggested.

The Colonel shook Braun's hand. 'Thanks for your assistance. I'm sorry if we got off on the wrong foot, but I'm sure you understand we have a job to do.'

'It's OK, no harm done.'

'Just for our records, what's your wife's name and occupation, please?'

'Elizabeth – she's an assistant teacher at a local school.'

Baxter made a note in his pocket notebook, then tore out a page with his details and the office number on it and handed it to Braun.

'If there's anything else you think of that might be of help to our investigation, then ring us on this number.'

As they got into the unmarked police car, Baxter, who was driving, turned to the Colonel.

'What do you reckon about Braun?'

'He's dodgy. It wasn't that long ago the brigade got pissed off about the Edmund-Davies report recommending a forty-five per cent pay rise for police and they went on strike wanting more money.'

Baxter laughed. 'I remember that. Each nick had to have a dedicated fire patrol car and the army were called in to attend fires in their Green Goddesses – it was a shambles. But what's that got to do with him being dodgy?'

'Yeah, well, they only got a ten per cent rise – their pay and pensions are shit, so a lot of them moonlight to earn more money.'

'You think he's moonlighting as a criminal?'

'The theft of his wife's handbag might be legit, but he could have given his spare key to the robbers and made sure they nicked the car while he was on holiday.'

'You reckon?' Baxter said sceptically.

The Colonel looked at Baxter as if he were a fool. 'Braun's got a nice three-bedroom semi and a BMW 323i, which happens to be the most expensive model in the range – it only came out last year – plus he can afford a holiday in Mauritius. Think about it, Bax. He'd have to do a lot more than a bit of honest moonlighting to afford all that on a fucking fireman's wage.'

'His wife might have a good job.'

'Don't you listen? He said she was an assistant teacher. They get paid a pittance – probably not even half of what he does. For my money, Mr Frank Braun's a wrong 'un and we need to do a bit more digging. Let's go to Tottenham nick and check out the crime report about the theft of Mrs Braun's handbag.'

* * *

The Broadwater Farm estate had 1,063 homes consisting of one-, two- and three-bed flats and maisonettes, in twelve blocks named after Second World War airfields. Aside from Tangmere House, there were eight other six-storey blocks, adjoined by a lower four-storey maisonette block and two nineteen-storey towers. The were 3,400 people from different ethnic backgrounds, with a substantial black population, whose relationship with the police was one of mutual hostility and mistrust.

Cam parked the unmarked squad car by Tangmere House.

'I'll bet you have to use the stairs to get to number sixty-eight.'

'You reckon the lifts will be out of order then?' Jane asked.

'Either that or full of piss and shit – so you'll definitely be using the stairs, but I can guarantee they won't smell much better. If you aren't back here in half an hour, I'm calling in the cavalry.'

'If sixty-eight is on this side facing you, I'll wave out of the window to say we're in the premises and fine,' Teflon said.

Jane and Teflon got out of the car and went through the ground-floor communal door into the lobby, which smelt like a sewer. The walls were covered in abusive graffiti, the lift door was stuck open and inside was a pool of urine. Jane had to put her hand over her mouth and nose to stop herself gagging.

'Looks like it's the stairs. After you, madam.'

Teflon opened the door, and another waft of stale urine assaulted them.

'This place is worse than I imagined. How can people live in this filth?' Jane remarked.

As they trudged up to the fifth floor, two young white men walked past them and Jane heard one say 'white slag' as he passed them on the stairs. She stopped to challenge him, and Teflon nudged her in the back with his hand.

'Ignore them and keep going,' he whispered.

'He just called me a white slag!'

'Only because you're with me and he thinks we're an item. It ain't a good idea to start an argument in here – besides, I've clocked his face and won't forget it next time I see him out on the street.'

'The racist mentality of some people sickens me.'

'Tell me about it,' he said with a shrug. 'If it had been two black guys passing they'd probably have paid me a compliment about you.'

'What would they have said?'

'You don't want to know.'

They reached the fifth-floor landing and Jane knocked on the door of number 68, which was in good condition and had a clean brown coir mat in front of it. They waited, but there was no reply. She knocked again and still there was no answer.

'Looks like there's no one in.'

'Put a note through the letterbox with your details on and ask Miss Wilson to contact you,' Teflon suggested.

'I should have thought to check the electoral register at Totten-ham nick before coming here to see if Emma Wilson is listed as the occupant. Maybe we should knock on the neighbour's door and ask if they know who lives here.'

Teflon agreed, and Jane knocked on the neighbour's door. It had some boot marks on the front and a couple of jemmy marks on the door frame by the Yale lock.

'Who is it?' a female voice asked in a wheezy North London accent, which was overtaken by a bout of coughing.

'It's the police. We just wanted to have a quick word with you about your neighbour—'

'I don't know nothing about any of me neighbours, so clear off and leave me alone,' she demanded.

'We can show you our police warrant cards if you're worried about who we are,' Teflon said.

After a couple of seconds, they heard the Chubb and Yale locks being undone. The door opened a few inches and Jane could see it was on a chain guard. A short, grey-haired white woman in her late fifties, wearing thick-lensed black-framed glasses, peered through the gap with a lit cigarette in her mouth.

'Let me see them cards close up.' She coughed again as Teflon held up his warrant card. 'That ain't close enough.'

He moved his card closer and she peered at it.

'How do I know that's real?'

'I can assure you it is, Mrs . . . ?'

She coughed again and took a deep breath. 'You don't look like police to me.' She glared at Teflon.

It was obvious to Jane that the woman's distrust was based on the colour of Teflon's skin. She stepped forward and held her warrant card by the gap in the door.

'I'm Detective Sergeant Tennison and this is DC Johnson. We were just wondering if a Miss Emma Wilson lives at number sixty-eight.'

'She might do – why ya wanna know?'

'She reported a crime and we're investigating it, but we're not sure if we have the right address for her,' Teflon said.

The woman coughed a few times and looked at Jane. 'He's a bit grumpy, ain't he?'

Jane smiled, saying nothing.

'I don't know her very well, but Emma lives at sixty-eight, and she's probably at work if she ain't in.'

'Do you know when she's likely to be home?' Teflon asked.

'When she gets back from work,' the woman replied, deadpan.

'And what time would that be?'

She ignored him and directed her answer to Jane. 'How should I know . . . ? I don't watch her comings and goings.'

'Do you by any chance know where she works?' Jane asked.

'I seen her at the Co-op department store in the High Street.'

'Thank you,' Jane said.

'You found out who tried to break into my flat yet?'

The old woman pointed to the jemmy marks on the door frame.

Jane shook her head. 'I'm sorry, I don't know anything about that, but—'

'Didn't think so!'

She closed the door smartly and relocked it.

'I thought the way she treated you was obnoxious,' Jane remarked as they walked towards the stairwell.

'She probably thinks it was a black person who tried to break into her flat. She's not going to trust a black policeman to catch him, I guess. You just have to ignore it.'

'But you shouldn't have to ignore it.'

'It depends on the situation – dealing with a witness and making an arrest are very different. If you want to keep a witness on side, you need to be nice to them whether you like it or not. When you're nicking someone you control them – whether they like it or not.' He grinned.

'Well, at least we found out where Emma works and I can go to the Co-op this afternoon.'

He pointed to the damage on the old woman's door.

'Bit strange this flat and most of the others have boot and jemmy marks on them . . . but there's not a mark on number sixty-eight.'

Jane hadn't noticed. 'Maybe it did and it's a replacement door.'

'From the lack of detail in the report the duty sergeant didn't seem that enthusiastic about what Emma Wilson had to say. This whole thing about her hearing men in a cafe talking about a robbery is beginning to sound like a load of crap to me.'

'It could be – but the only way I'm going to find out is by speaking to her face to face today, or Murphy will be on my back again,' said Jane with a sigh.

CHAPTER FOURTEEN

Cam dropped Jane off by her car and left with Teflon to get the PCs' statements. She was looking in her *A-Z* when she saw a woman pushing a pram along the pavement and asked her if she knew whereabouts in the High Road the Co-op department store was. The woman said it was at the north end, near Tottenham Hotspur's football ground, which was about a mile away. Unsure what the parking restrictions in the High Road would be, and as it was a reasonably nice day and not too cold, she decided to walk.

The High Road Co-op was a three-storey art deco-style Edwardian department store with a white rendered facade and a prominent square corner tower with Tuscan-style pillars. On the base of the tower there was a square panel with the Co-op logo of intertwined letters: 'LCS' for the London Co-operative Society and '1930', signifying the year it opened.

Jane asked a female employee where the manager's office was. She said he was on holiday and escorted her to the undermanager's office on the ground floor. He was in his mid-thirties, tall, dark-haired and slim, with a neatly trimmed black moustache, and wore a dark shiny charcoal-coloured two-piece suit, white shirt and black Windsor knot tie. He reminded Jane of someone out of a new wave pop band. He had a pleasant smile, was well spoken and said his name was Jeffery Dobbs. She introduced herself and he shook her hand with a firm grip.

'Does a Miss Emma Wilson work here?'

'Emma's not in trouble, is she?' he asked.

'No, she reported an incident to Tottenham CID that I'm investigating.'

'Is it those kids shouting abuse and throwing food again?' he asked, frowning.

'Yes,' Jane said quickly. She didn't want to reveal she was investigating an armed robbery.

'The youth of today have no respect for anyone, or anything – they make me sick to the stomach, the way they behave. That Broadwater Farm is a terrible place to live. I know Emma regrets ever moving there. When she first told me about the abuse, I helped her draft some letters to the council requesting a move, but to no avail.'

'It's to your credit that you care for your employees' well-being, Mr Dobbs. Can you tell me which department Emma works in, please?' she asked, eager not to waste any more time.

'Drapery. It's like a home from home for Emma – she makes all her own clothes.' He looked at an employee work chart on the wall. 'She will be at lunch just now in the staff canteen.' He opened the door. 'If you'd like to follow me, officer, I'll take you upstairs. Emma's quite reserved and tends not to socialise with the other ladies, but she has a heart of gold. It's unusual for her to complain about anything, and I can only imagine that she reported this latest abuse because she was at breaking point. Actually, come to think of it, now the police are involved I should write another letter to the council. Perhaps they might finally listen and move them off the Broadwater.'

As they climbed the stairs, Jane suspected she might have dug a hole for herself by lying to him about why she'd come to see Emma.

'It's probably best to speak to Emma first and see if that's what she wants you to do.'

'Good point, I'll speak to her later.'

There were several employees in the canteen, chatting and laughing while eating their lunch. The women were all dressed in white frilled blouses and black skirts, and the men wore dark suits, white shirts and ties. Jane noticed a woman in her fifties sitting alone in the corner of the room reading a book.

'Is that Emma over there?' she asked.

'No, that's her over there, putting her dirty plate and cutlery on the trolley.'

He nodded towards a woman with her back to them. She was dressed like the other employees and had shiny black hair neatly tied up in a bun.

He raised his voice. 'Miss Wilson, could I have a word, please?'

Emma turned around and Jane was surprised to see a young woman of about her age, not the middle-aged woman she'd imagined. Although she only wore a little make-up her olive skin had a soft glow, which made her lips stand out. She had a slight Mediterranean appearance, with an hourglass figure, petite nose and brown doe eyes.

'Yes, Mr Dobbs?' she asked with an engaging smile as she walked over.

'Let's go sit over there, shall we . . . ? Away from prying ears.' Dobbs pointed to a table in the far corner.

Jane spoke first in a soft and reassuring manner.

'Hi, Emma, I'm Jane Tennison from the CID. I went to your flat earlier but as there was no one in I spoke to a neighbour who told me you work here. I wanted to speak to you about the crime report you made at Tottenham Police Station.'

'Yes, certainly . . . Pleased to meet you.' Emma put out her hand and Jane shook it.

Dobbs sat back and got a packet of cigarettes out of his jacket pocket, offering one to Jane. She wanted to be alone with Emma and didn't fancy plumes of cigarette smoke billowing around while they spoke.

'No thanks – I would love a cup of coffee though. Would you like one, Emma?'

'A cup of tea would be nice, thank you,' she replied.

Dobbs put the cigarettes back in his pocket as Jane opened her shoulder bag, but Dobbs said he'd get the drinks and asked Jane if she would like anything to eat. She looked over at the counter, saw some teacakes on a plate inside a glass dome cover and asked if she could have one with some butter and jam on it.

As Dobbs got up and left the table, Emma leant towards Jane and whispered, 'Does Mr Dobbs know why I went to the police station the other night?'

'Do you want him to?'

She shook her head. 'No, my sister told me not to tell anyone other than the police for now.'

Jane decided it was best to be honest.

'He was concerned about why I wanted to speak to you and mentioned you'd suffered verbal abuse from some local kids who also threw food at you. I told him a little lie and said it was about that – but he now thinks it's happened again.'

Emma looked concerned. 'Do you think I should tell him the truth?'

'That's up to you, but for now I think it's best we keep it between the two of us and stick to the verbal abuse story.'

Emma nodded. 'I understand, officer.'

'Please, call me Jane. Have you actually reported the abuse incidents to the police?'

'Um, no, we were worried if we did the police would have to speak to the boys and it would only make things worse for us.'

Dobbs returned with the food and drinks.

'I got you a teacake as well, Emma, and I've just arranged for someone to cover for you in drapery, so there's no need to rush.'

He sat down and took a sip of his coffee.

Jane got out her pocket notebook and pen and put them on the table, wondering how best to get rid of Dobbs.

Before she could say anything, Emma gave him a forlorn look, then leant towards him and whispered, 'I don't wish to appear rude, Mr Dobbs, but the officer wants me to tell her about the disgusting language the boys used when they abused us, which as a woman I'd rather not repeat in your presence . . . if you don't mind.'

'I totally understand, Emma. I'll leave you to discuss it with Sergeant Tennison.' He stood up.

She looked up at him and spoke softly. 'Thank you for being so understanding, Mr Dobbs.'

He smiled, put his hand on her shoulder and squeezed it.

'I'll be in my office if you need me, Emma. Perhaps the two of us can draft another letter to the council about the ongoing abuse.'

'Thank you, Mr Dobbs,' she said, and he left.

Jane wondered from their body language if there was more than just a working relationship between them. She was also surprised at how naturally Emma had lied to him.

Jane smiled. 'I don't think Mr Dobbs will be too pleased when he finds out I lied to him – and neither will my boss if he reports me,' she said, and sipped her tea. 'I believe you told the duty sergeant you heard some men in a cafe talking about a robbery.'

Emma dabbed the cake crumbs from her lips with a napkin.

'No, it was my sister Rachel.'

Jane was confused. 'Your sister spoke to the sergeant?'

'No, she didn't want to go into the station, so I spoke to him about what happened in the cafe. I've never been in the cafe – Rachel was, and the men were sat a couple of tables away from her.'

'Then they must have been talking loudly if she heard what they were saying in a busy cafe?'

Jane was beginning to wonder if Emma was confused about what had happened, or even making things up to get some attention.

'Rachel didn't actually hear what was said – she saw what was said.'

Jane put her pen down and sat back in her chair.

'I'm finding this a bit confusing, Emma. Did you tell the duty sergeant you were there on behalf of your sister?'

'In a way, yes, I told him Rachel is deaf and she thought she saw some men talking about a robbery in a cafe. I assumed he'd passed it on, but clearly not.'

Suddenly Jane understood. 'Your sister can lip-read.'

Emma looked around to make sure no one was eavesdropping.

'Yes, but only me and a few close friends know – including you, now.'

Jane was pleased that Emma was confiding in her.

'Thank you for telling me. But I will have to tell my boss if it turns out to be connected to our investigation.'

'That's OK, she'll have no problem with police officers knowing.'

'Why doesn't Rachel like to tell people she can lip-read?'

'She reckons the big advantage of people not knowing is it allows her to judge their personalities when they realise she is deaf.'

'What do you mean?'

'She can lip-read their rude comments about her deafness.'

'I bet she feels like giving them a piece of her mind when that happens.'

Emma frowned. 'She would if she could, but she can't speak.'

'I'm sorry, I didn't realise—'

'It's not your fault. Life would be easier for the deaf if more people learnt to use sign language. That's the way Rachel and I mostly communicate, apart from leaving little notes for each other – especially after we've had an argument.'

'What did you tell the uniform sergeant when you spoke to him yesterday?'

'I spoke to him on Tuesday evening after work.'

'Are you sure about that? The information sheet I was given said you were at the station yesterday evening.'

Emma shook her head. 'I know it was Tuesday evening. Rachel told me about the men in the cafe on Monday evening after I got home from work.'

'What exactly happened at the station?'

'Rachel didn't want to go in and waited outside. The sergeant at the front counter asked how he could help me. I told him my sister was in a cafe on Bruce Grove on Monday morning and saw two men talking and she thought it was about robbing a van. He asked what I meant by "saw" and I told him she was deaf. He gave me a funny look and said there was no CID on duty who dealt with robberies.'

Jane knew there would have been at least two detectives minimum on late turn CID duties, but what annoyed her even more was the fact that the information sheet had nothing on it about Rachel being deaf or a van being robbed.

'Did you tell him Rachel could lip-read?'

'I was about to, but his desk phone rang, and he said he had to answer it. He handed me a police notepad and pen and said to write down my name and address, which I did while he was on the phone.'

'And he didn't speak to you in more detail after he finished his phone call?'

'No, he just picked up the notepad and said he'd pass the information on to CID and they would get in touch with me, and then he just walked off, so I left.'

Jane was infuriated by the duty sergeant's attitude. He could have got someone from the CID office in the station to speak to her, but clearly couldn't be bothered and had just sat on it. She wondered if he'd then heard about the robbery on the security van in Leytonstone on Thursday, and decided to pass Emma's information on to cover his back in case it was connected. He'd either lied about the date Emma attended the station when he spoke to Katie, or deliberately didn't mention it and Katie had just assumed it was the same evening as the robbery.

'Can you tell me the name and address of the cafe and what time Rachel was in on Monday?' Jane asked, ready to write the details down.

'It's called the Bluebird and it's in Bruce Grove, near the Royal Mail sorting office where she works.'

'And what did the men say to each other about robbing a van?'

'Rachel could only lip-read what one of them was saying as the other man was sitting with his back to her. She has a very retentive memory, but I can't remember everything she told me in detail now. When we discussed it that evening, she wrote everything down in a notebook she always carries with her in case she needs to have a conversation with someone who can't sign.'

'Did Rachel write down a description of the men?'

'I don't think so. She said she often sees them in there, but she doesn't like to sit near them.'

'Why is that?'

'Because one of them smokes a big stinky cigar and it puts her off her food.'

Jane tried not to get too excited, knowing that what Emma was saying was merely second-hand information.

'Did Rachel think these men were planning a robbery or had already committed one?'

'From what she told me it sounded like they were planning one.'

'What exactly did Rachel say that made you think that?'

'She said the one whose lips she could see was moving things round the table and talking as if they represented people and a van. She also thought he said the word "robbed".'

Trying to play devil's advocate, Jane wondered if the man could have been saying the name Rob instead of 'robbery', but the details were definitely beginning to mount up, particularly as the getaway car had been stolen in Tottenham.

'Did Rachel say anything else about these two men?'

Emma thought about it. 'She said they looked similar.'

Jane nodded. 'Anything else?'

'She thought one of them might be connected to the snooker or bingo hall in Bruce Grove.'

'Are they next door to each other?'

'No, they're in one building, which was originally a cinema. They converted the downstairs for bingo and the upstairs for snooker.'

'Why did she think one of the men was connected to the premises?'

'You can see the building from the cafe and Rachel said she'd seen him coming and going from there when she was in the cafe.'

'What hours does Rachel work in the sorting office?'

'Six a.m. to two p.m.'

Jane looked at her watch and saw it was 1.15 p.m.

'What Rachel lip-read on Monday could be connected to a robbery I'm investigating.'

Emma looked worried. 'Do you think the men Rachel saw in the cafe are the robbers?'

'It's possible, but I can't be certain until I speak to her in detail about what she was able to lip-read at the time. My car is parked up near the sorting office. If you are agreeable, we could meet Rachel outside and go to Tottenham Police Station, where I can speak to her in private and you could do the sign language for us. Would you be happy to do that?'

Emma nodded but she looked apprehensive. 'OK . . . if Mr Dobbs will let me go early.'

'I'm sure he will, and I'll stick to the verbal abuse and kids throwing food story for now. Do you think Rachel would be willing to make an official statement and attend an identity parade if necessary?'

'I don't know. She wasn't sure about me going to the police. She was worried they would find out who she was and where she works due to her Post Office uniform. That's why she wouldn't come into the station with me. I told her they could be planning a robbery and the right thing to do was tell the police. If she hadn't agreed I wouldn't have gone to the station, though I think she was actually relieved when no one contacted us.'

'I can assure you I won't pressure Rachel into making a statement or doing anything she doesn't want to. The same goes for you, Emma. But your sister's evidence could be really important.'

CHAPTER FIFTEEN

A light sprinkle of rain started to fall as Jane and Emma walked briskly along Tottenham High Road. Emma was wearing a warm black ankle-length mac and headscarf, and offered Jane her umbrella, but Jane moved closer and suggested they share it. As Emma transferred the umbrella to her left hand, Jane noticed that she had to place it into the palm, as her fingers were curled into a fist and she didn't seem to be able to move them.

'I know you don't want to report the abuse incidents you and Rachel have suffered to the police but you really should so there's an official record. You also need to explain you're worried any investigation would lead to further abuse. That way you'd also have the police on your side when you ask for a move.'

Emma stopped walking and looked at Jane.

'Could you maybe help us write a letter?'

'I'll do what I can to help, but the local police are your best bet for direct communication with the council. My current inspector worked at Tottenham CID before being moved to the Flying Squad – he might know an experienced detective there you could talk to. I'll have a word with him when I'm back at the office.'

'Thank you, Jane. I appreciate your help – and so will Rachel.'

'I don't want to appear nosy, but can I ask how you ended up in a flat on the Broadwater?'

'It was the only place Haringey Council offered us. We hadn't seen it and didn't know what the estate was like when we accepted it.' She pointed across the road. 'The sorting office is that way.'

Jane could see a railway bridge with a sign saying 'Bruce Grove', then as they walked under the bridge, the street sign for Moorfield

Road on her left and the Bluebird cafe on the corner of the junction with Bruce Grove.

'That's the cafe Rachel uses – the bingo and snooker hall are just up there on the other side of the road.'

Jane could tell from its shape and size that it had once been a large cinema.

As they turned into Moorfield Road, Jane noticed a menu stuck to the inside of the cafe window and pretended to look at it so she could see the layout of the interior. The premises were a reasonable size, with a lino floor and nine square wooden four-seater tables and chairs laid out in three rows of three. The tables were covered in red and white check plastic tablecloths, and on each one there was a red squeezy tomato-shaped sauce dispenser, pepper and salt shakers and a bowl of sugar lumps. The cooking and serving area were at the far end, and the cafe was about three quarters full of tradesmen having their lunch. Next to the menu was a notice saying: STAFF REQUIRED – MALE OR FEMALE – REASONABLE HOURLY RATES – APPLY WITHIN OR CALL NICK ON 808 9611.

As Jane got out her pocket notebook to jot down the name and phone number, two workmen got up from their table and left. The enticing smell of roast beef, potatoes and vegetables wafted out from the open door onto the street. One of the men did a thumbs-up to Emma and said, 'All right, luv?', but she ignored him. Jane recalled Emma had said that she'd never been in the cafe, but it seemed as if the man had recognised her.

Jane looked at her watch. 'It's nearly two o'clock, so we'd better make our way to the sorting office if we want to catch Rachel when she leaves work.'

'It's just around the corner. I'll nip in and tell her who you are first, if that's OK with you?' Emma said as they approached the building.

Jane started to make a drawing of the layout of the Bluebird cafe in her pocket notebook while she waited. A few minutes later she saw Emma come out of the sorting office with Rachel, and was instantly struck by the resemblance between them. The only difference was that Rachel's shoulder-length hair had some grey streaks in it and she was wearing a Post Office uniform under her open black mac.

'Rachel, this is Jane Tennison.'

'I'm pleased to meet you. It hadn't dawned on me you were twins,' Jane said.

'Born identical, but different now we're older,' Emma remarked.

Rachel, with her right hand closed in a thumbs-up position, brushed her thumb along her chin before holding her index fingers upright in front of her body. She moved her fingers towards each other, so they touched and then pointed them at Jane, who was unsure what she was signing, apart from 'hello'.

'Rachel said she's pleased to meet you,' Emma told her.

Jane smiled as she shook hands with Rachel, then spoke slowly, accentuating her lip movements.

'I'm very . . . pleased . . . to meet . . . you too—'

Emma interjected. 'It's OK, Jane, you can speak normally – it's actually easier for Rachel to understand what you're saying if you do.'

'I'm sorry, I hope you weren't offended.'

Rachel shrugged her shoulders and did some sign language to Emma.

'She said she can't hear you – so no offence taken.'

Jane smiled awkwardly at the joke. 'Are you happy to talk to me about the men you saw in the cafe on Monday you thought were talking about a robbery?'

She looked anxious and did some more sign language to Emma, who translated.

'I told her you were investigating a robbery. Rachel's very nervous and doesn't want to talk about it near the cafe or in the police station.'

Jane looked at Rachel. 'That's totally understandable. We can do it at your flat if you like?'

Rachel nodded.

'My car's just up the road. Where do you live?'

'She lives with me on the Broadwater Farm.' Emma turned away from her sister and looked at Jane. 'While I was in the sorting office she told me the same two men were in the cafe this morning.'

* * *

Driving Rachel and Emma to Broadwater Farm, Jane knew that Teflon and Cam would think she was mad going there on her own and was worried about parking her car on the estate. But she knew that every time the sisters left their flat, they risked verbal or physical abuse, and if they didn't let it stop them going about their business, neither would she.

As Jane approached the estate, Emma told her it might be best if she left her car in a side street and they walked to the flat.

'Your car's really conspicuous and it might get damaged or stolen if you leave it on the estate.' Emma pointed to a street on the right. 'Your car will be safe down there.'

'As it happens, my boss thinks my car looks like a custard tart,' Jane remarked.

Emma laughed, turned to Rachel and repeated what Jane had said, but she didn't smile.

Jane checked the rear-view mirror and could see Rachel was frowning and looking out of the window. She looked forward as she spoke to Emma.

'Can Rachel talk at all?'

'Being deaf she can't hear what she says, so her voice is very monotone and sounds like she's got a really bad throat. At first she tried speaking, but got fed up with people looking at her as if she was mentally ill.'

Jane wondered if Rachel wasn't born deaf but felt awkward asking Emma, as if she was talking about Rachel behind her back.

Jane felt nervous walking through the estate, but thankfully there were only a few people about, who didn't pay any attention to them. The lift door at Tangmere House was still stuck open, and although the pool of urine in it had dried out, the smell was still overpowering. Rachel pinched her nose and pulled a face, implying how bad it was.

'Sorry about the state of the lifts,' Emma said.

'It's not your fault. Is there no caretaker to clean or repair them?'

Emma sighed. 'They've been advertising for a new caretaker for months, but no one wants the job. The engineers do come now and again to repair the lift but as soon as they have, the kids break it again.'

Jane shook her head sadly. 'I can understand why you want to move away from here.'

'The flats have been poorly maintained by the council, there are water leakages, damp and electrical faults. We recently had an infestation of cockroaches and me and Rachel had to deal with it ourselves. The walkways that connect the blocks are dangerous. They provide easy escape routes, so people often get robbed on them.'

As they walked up the stairs Jane realised how lucky she was to have a place of her own in a nice part of London. She'd taken a liking to Emma and Rachel, and it seemed so unfair that they should have to live on a rundown and crime-ridden estate. She suspected that even if she did put a word in with the council on the sisters' behalf, they probably wouldn't give them preferential treatment.

As Emma unlocked the flat door Rachel held her open hands, palms up, towards Jane. She bent her fingers back and forth at the knuckles in short, repeated movements, then put the tips of her fingers together to form the shape of a roof.

'She's welcoming you to our flat,' Emma said.

Jane smiled and said, 'Thank you.'

The kitchen was to the right and opposite it a cupboard storage space, next to which was a bathroom, then a separate toilet and another room, which Jane suspected was a bedroom. Opposite was a room with the door open, in which Jane could see two single beds with handmade multicoloured patchwork throws on them. At the end of the hallway Emma opened a door, which led in to a reasonably sized living room. As Jane walked into the room, she recognised the musty smell of dampness and could see a small area of black mould on the wall under the large wooden-framed double window. Emma turned on the electric fire.

'Sorry about the damp smell – once the room heats up it goes away. Rainwater's been leaking in through the window frame, which is starting to rot. We keep cleaning the mould off with bleach and water, but it always comes back.'

Rachel looked at Jane and mimed drinking a cup of tea from a saucer.

'That would be lovely,' Jane replied, and Rachel went to the kitchen.

'Let me take your coat and I'll put it in the hallway cupboard for now.'

While Emma helped Rachel make the tea, Jane looked around the neat and tidy carpeted living room. In front of the two-seater settee was a small wooden coffee table. On it were some coloured sketches of different styles of skirts, dresses and women's blouses, which Jane assumed were sewing designs. On the wall above the fireplace were some small black chalk figure drawings; there was one of a young girl kneeling and cleaning a floor, a similar one with an older woman doing the same thing and another of an old man digging in a field with a spade. The drawings looked familiar, but Jane couldn't remember where she'd seen them before.

At the back of the room was a four-seater drop-leaf wooden dining table with two wooden chairs. Up against the far wall were three tall mahogany bookshelves, which, like the dining table, looked as good as new. The shelves were filled with an array of books: classics by the Brontë sisters, Charles Dickens, Jane Austen and Thomas Hardy, as well as Shakespeare's plays and *The Canterbury Tales*. There were also books by Agatha Christie and horror stories by Bram Stoker and Mary Shelley, next to which were the twenty-three children's tales written by Beatrix Potter and some Enid Blyton stories.

'Do you take milk and sugar?'

Emma put a tray with tea things on the coffee table. Rachel followed behind with some biscuits and vanilla slices. Jane took one of the slices and sat down on one end of the settee, while Emma sat next to her in an armchair. Rachel moved the other armchair into a position where she could see their lip movements and sat down.

'You have a lot of books,' Jane remarked.

'We've always liked to read since we were very young, and haven't bothered with a TV due to Rachel's deafness. We like to go to book fairs and buy second-hand ones.'

'Did you make the furniture covers yourself?' Jane asked Emma.

'Yes, do you like them?' She poured Jane a cup of tea.

'They're lovely – and so are the sketches of the dresses and blouses.'

'Rachel's the artist – I explain my ideas to her and she brings them to life on paper, then I make them.'

Jane looked at Rachel. 'You are very talented.'

Rachel smiled. She held her closed right hand to her chest, then extended her index and middle fingers in front of her face before moving them downwards in a snake-like motion and proudly pointing to the chalk drawings on the wall. Emma was about to translate, but Jane instinctively knew what Rachel had signed.

'You did all those sketches.'

Rachel did a thumbs-up, then a scissors motion with her fingers by her left ear and pulled a sad face.

'I thought they looked familiar – are the sketches copies of Van Gogh's paintings?'

Rachel nodded.

'I remember them from art studies at school when I was sixteen. Your drawings are as good as the real thing!'

Rachel signed 'Thank you'.

Jane thought it strange that were no individual or family photographs in the room.

'Do you have any family in London?' she asked, and Rachel shook her head.

'Not that we know of. Our parents died in a car crash when we were six, then we stayed with our uncle in Wood Green before we were put into a care home,' Emma said, showing no sign of emotion.

'I'm sorry – I can't begin to imagine what it would be like to lose your parents when you're so young. It must have been awful for you both.'

'It was worse for Rachel. She was in a coma after the crash and not expected to survive. It wasn't until she came around that the doctors realised the injuries to her head had made her permanently deaf.'

Jane was surprised. 'You were both in the crash?'

'Yes. Not being able to hear anything after the crash made Rachel withdrawn and she stopped communicating with anyone, even me at first.'

Rachel nodded, then made some signs to Emma, and ended by touching her left wrist and holding her hand in a bent fist shape like Emma's. Jane thought she'd grasped what she was saying.

'Did you injure your hand in the accident?' she asked Emma.

'Yes, I had an open fracture, which, as you can see, never healed properly. But although my wrist movement is restricted, I can still use it well enough to work and do my sewing.'

Rachel made some signs to Emma.

'She's asking if your parents are still alive.'

Jane nodded.

'Do you have any brothers or sisters?'

'I had a brother, but he died when I was four. My sister Pam is married and has a little boy.'

Rachel held her hand open in a vertical position in front of her nose and mouth, and moved it downwards while making a sad face.

'She's sorry about your brother; it must have been very upsetting for you,' Emma said.

Jane felt she could be open with them after what she'd learnt about the sisters' parents' death.

'I'd just turned four and he was three when he fell into a neighbour's pond and drowned. I didn't really understand what had happened at the time but my parents were devastated. Sadly, I have very little memory of Michael, but I do have some photographs of him. Do you have any of your parents?'

Emma shook her head. 'Memories are all we have, Jane. When our uncle was looking after us, he cleared all our parents' belongings out of the house and didn't give us any pictures of them. Looking back, I think he thought it would be best for us to try and erase them from our memories.'

'Have you ever tried to trace him?'

'No. He never made any form of communication after putting us in care, so as far as we were concerned, he didn't want to know us,' Emma said bitterly.

Jane was curious about the twins' childhood, their time in care, and what had happened after that, but time was pressing, and she needed to get a result, be it positive or negative, for DCI Murphy by the end of the day. She got out her pocket notebook and pen and looked at Rachel.

'I'm not from Tottenham CID – I actually work for the Flying Squad. We investigate robberies and your details were passed to us by the sergeant Emma spoke to on Tuesday. Are you still happy to talk to me about what you saw and lip-read in the cafe on Monday morning?'

Rachel nodded and did a hand movement as if she was holding a pen and writing on her hand, then jumped out of her chair and left the room.

'Did I say something to upset her?'

'No, she's just going to get the pad that she made notes in.'

Rachel returned to the room and offered the notepad to Jane. Jane signalled for her to keep it.

'It would be better if I read what you've written after I've interviewed you. You can use your notes to refresh your memory of what happened as we go along. I was wondering what's the best way to do this. Should I speak to you direct, or to Emma, who can then sign the questions to you?'

Emma interjected, 'It might be best to do both, just in case she has difficulty with anything you ask. I can translate her replies for you if they're more than a nod or shake of the head.'

Rachel did a thumbs-up.

'As you tell me what happened, take your time, and if you change your mind about anything then please tell me. Firstly, Rachel, I just need to confirm that you're referring to the Bluebird cafe in Bruce Grove, Tottenham.' Rachel nodded, and Jane continued. 'And the date you saw the two men who might have been talking about a robbery was Monday the twenty-first of April.'

Rachel did another thumbs-up.

'Had you seen them in the cafe before?'

Rachel nodded.

'Do you know their names by any chance?'

'I asked her that the other night and she said she doesn't, but at one point the man whose lips she read referred to the man sat opposite him as Tommy.'

Rachel signed to Emma that Nick, the owner of the cafe, might know their names as the one who might be called Tommy often comes into the cafe in the morning.

'Does the other man go there often?' Jane asked.

Rachel shrugged and signed.

Emma looked at Jane. 'She said maybe once or twice a week, usually on a Monday or a Friday and sometimes both.'

'How long have you been using the cafe?' Jane asked Rachel.

Emma waited for her to finish signing. 'She said since she started working at the sorting office, which was about two years ago. She goes there most weekdays for her meal break, which is between nine and 9.45. The two men only started coming in about six months ago.'

'I drew a plan of the inside of the cafe earlier. Can you mark with an "R" where you were sitting and put "M1" and "M2" where the men were? The man you think might be called Tommy can be M2.' Jane handed Rachel her pocket notebook.

She marked up the cafe plan and made some hand signs to her sister.

'She said there were two young men sat at the table by the wall when the two older men came in, but they must have said something as the two young men quickly moved to another table, taking their food and drinks with them.'

'What age would you say the two older men were?'

Emma told Jane that her sister thought the one whose lips she'd read was late forties to early fifties, and the other man was late thirties to forty.'

Jane looked at the plan. The men were seated in the far top right-hand corner, with a wall behind them and a window to the left that looked out onto Bruce Grove. Rachel had marked herself as sitting in the middle row, two tables down from them.

'From where you were sitting, did you have a clear and unobstructed view of them both, and in particular the man who you lip-read?'

Rachel nodded, then signed. Emma said, 'Apart from when Nick, the cafe owner, walked past or was serving them breakfast.'

'I think it might be easier for now if we continued to refer to the men as M1 and M2, then at the end I'll get a detailed description of them. Emma, could you translate what Rachel says in the first person?'

'You mean as if it were her speaking?'

'Yes please.' Jane looked at Rachel. 'Can you start with the time you saw the men come into the cafe, then tell me what M1 said?' Jane held her pen to her pocket notebook.

Rachel did a thumbs-up and started signing to Emma.

'I'm not sure as I was reading my book, but I think it was maybe between quarter past and half past nine. At one point I looked up and M1 was taking sugar lumps out of the bowl, then instead of putting them in his coffee cup he put two down next to each other in front of him on the table. I don't normally lip-read what other people are saying as I don't want to be nosy, but I was curious because I thought he was going to do a trick with them.'

Jane looked at Rachel and asked her to continue signing. She looked at her notes, then to Emma, who translated.

'The men were leaning forward close to each other, as if speaking softly, so as not to be heard. M1 picked up the salt pot and put it down next to the sugar lumps and said, "When the van pulls up, I'll take the rear." He picked up another sugar lump, put it down on the other side of the salt pot and said, "You cover the front with . . ."'

There was a pause as Rachel spelt the individual letters of the name.

'W . . . E . . . S . . . L . . . E . . . Y?' Emma asked.

Rachel shook her head, then picked up her notepad from the coffee table. Leaning over to Jane, she pointed to what she'd previously written.

'M1 said, "You cover the front with Webley." Is that right?' Jane asked.

Rachel nodded, then Jane asked them to continue.

'M2 nodded and M1 picked up the pepper pot and slid it across the table and said, "We rob the van, J . . . U . . . D . . . G . . . E – Judge pulls up here and we fuck off."'

'Are you sure he said, "rob the van"?' Jane asked and Rachel nodded. 'And how positive are you that the names M1 said were Webley and Judge?'

Rachel raised her hand, tilted it from side to side and signed to Emma. Emma told Jane that names can be difficult to lip-read but her sister was reasonably sure M1 had said Webley and Judge and a hundred per cent certain he'd said the name Tommy.

'What do you think the sugar lumps, salt and pepper pots represented?' Jane asked, and Rachel looked at her as if it was a silly question. 'I appreciate it's reasonably obvious from the way M1 moved them, and what he said, but I don't want to influence your thoughts by asking a leading question.'

Rachel nodded that she understood, then with her index finger and thumb of her right hand held slightly apart, she moved them downwards in front of her body, before mimicking someone moving a steering wheel up and down.

'She said vehicles for the sugar lumps and people for the salt and pepper.'

Rachel frowned as she shook her head and waved her hand at Emma, indicating she was wrong, then repeated what she'd just signed.

Emma sighed. 'Sometimes she goes too fast for me. She said it's the other way around – sugar lumps for people and condiments for vehicles.'

Jane asked if M1 had said anything else, and Rachel slowed down as she signed to her sister.

'She couldn't recall all the conversation when she made her notes, but she thinks the two men were disagreeing with each other as M1 was shaking his head and said something about a loose cannon and three of them was enough.'

Jane nodded. 'Did they say anything else about how many men were involved?'

Emma spoke as Rachel signed.

'At one point M1 sat back in his chair, raised his hands and said, "All right, he's in." And something about helping with the boxes and doing what he's told. That's all she was able to see and lip-read as Nick brought them their breakfast and she had to go back to the sorting office.'

'Emma mentioned to me earlier that you thought one of the men might be connected to the snooker hall opposite.'

Rachel nodded and signed to Emma.

'She's seen him come out of the entrance quite a few times in the morning and cross the road to the cafe while she was there.'

'And I take it the bingo hall above would be closed at that time?' Jane asked, and Rachel nodded.

'What you've told me could be very useful to us, Rachel, and you and Emma did the right thing reporting it to the police.'

'Do you think they were involved in a robbery you're investigating?' Emma asked.

'It's possible, but I'll obviously need to do a bit more investigation to find out their identities . . .'

Rachel looked concerned and signed to her sister.

'She's worried that if you speak to the cafe owner, he might tell them she lip-read what was said and they will know she spoke to the police.'

'I have no intention of asking any questions about them in the cafe. The only other people who will know about our conversation are the detectives I work with on the Flying Squad. May I have a look at the notes you made of what happened at the cafe?'

Rachel looked more relaxed as she gave the notebook to Jane, who then read it and handed it back.

'Thanks, everything you've written down ties in with my notes of our conversation. I believe you went to the cafe this morning and the same two men were there?'

Rachel nodded and signed to Emma that as usual the cafe was busy and they were sat in the same positions as Monday. She sat on the table one down from them but could only see the lips of M1. Jane pointed to a table on the plan she'd drawn and Rachel nodded.

'Did they talk about a robbery again?' Jane asked.

Rachel shrugged and signed that she wasn't sure.

Jane got ready with her pocket notebook and pen.

'Well, while everything is still fresh in your mind let's go over what happened this morning. Go slowly and tell me exactly what M1 said.'

Rachel sat upright, put her hands on her lap, closed her eyes and started to move her head up and down and from side to side.

'Is she all right?' Jane asked Emma.

'It's her way of recalling what was said. Although Rachel can't hear she's got a fantastic memory. She sort of goes back in time and relives the moment.'

After a couple of minutes' silence Rachel opened her eyes and started to sign to Emma, who translated.

'She says they came in about half past nine again and M1 looked angry, then pointed his finger at M2 and said, "I told you Riley was a hothead." M2 said something but she couldn't see his lips and M1 replied, "Yesterday was a total fuck-up." M2 said something about having to get a loan for Tina's wedding as a monkey from the job wasn't enough.'

Jane held her hand up for Rachel to pause.

'How sure are you he said the names Tina and Riley?'

Rachel was sure about Tina, but not so confident about Riley.

Jane knew a monkey was London slang for five hundred pounds, and asked Rachel if she realised it meant a sum of money. She shook her head and signed that another man walked up to the table, but because of where he stood, she then couldn't see M1's lips. M2 moved along a seat to let the man sit down.

'Had you seen him in the cafe before?' Jane asked, and Rachel shrugged. 'Can you describe him and what he was wearing?'

Emma translated her reply. 'She says she never got a look at his face as he had his back to her. He was quite tall, maybe three or four inches more than you, with dark slicked-back hair that was neatly cut. He wore a knee-length brown camel hair coat, which had a black suede collar, and was carrying a black leather briefcase.'

'Did M1 say anything to him when he sat down?'

'Not at first. The man sat down, put the briefcase on the table, then opened it and took out a large brown envelope, which he handed to M1, who put it on the table beside him without opening it. Then M1 said something about not letting him down and they shook hands.'

Jane held her hand up for them to pause while she wrote in her pocket notebook.

'Did M1 and the man have any more conversation?'

Rachel signed to Emma.

'M1 said something about having a nice X ... J ... S on the front and asked the man if he was interested, and the man nodded.'

'Did you notice if there was a Jaguar car outside the cafe?'

Rachel looked puzzled. Emma explained that they knew nothing about the makes or models of cars, but she did see him get into a vehicle parked on the opposite side of Bruce Grove and drive off towards the High Road.

'Can you describe his car?' Jane asked.

Rachel shrugged as she signed to Emma.

'She said it was a shiny maroon colour, quite long, with one door on the side and expensive-looking.'

'Did you see his face as he left?'

Rachel shook her head and signed that Nick, the cafe owner, came to the table to take away her dirty plate and was wiping the table down as the man left, so she couldn't see his face clearly.

'Did M1 and M2 have any further conversation after the man in the camel hair coat left?'

Rachel nodded and signed to Emma.

'M2 tried to take the envelope from M1, but he pulled it away and said something about "champagne and caviar for life". He folded the envelope in half and put it in the pocket of his coat, which was on the back of his chair.'

Jane knew that the conversation M1 had had with M2 and the man in the camel hair coat wasn't obviously about a robbery. In fact, it seemed more likely they were discussing a business deal that had gone wrong and the man in the camel hair coat was offering them another one that could be more successful.

'Did M1 say anything else?'

Rachel shook her head and said that he just said some stuff about how Tina's wedding was costing him a fortune. Then she left the cafe and went back to work.

'Are there any other people you've seen sitting with M1 and 2?'

Rachel signed that a younger, attractive, blond-haired man, who was maybe late twenties or early thirties, had been in a few times when M1 and M2 were there. But she had never paid attention to any of them until Monday, when she saw M1 moving the sugar cubes and condiments about.

'What I need now is a description of M1 and M2. If it's easier than signing you can write them down in my pocket notebook for me. You've given me their ages, so all I need now is their height, hair and eye colour, any notable facial features and what they were wearing.'

Rachel signed to Emma.

'She said she could draw their faces for you if you like.'

'That's a great idea, but I'm a bit pressed for time right now as I have to get back to the office and type up a report. I could pick the drawings up from you at work on Monday, if that's OK?'

Rachel nodded. Jane asked if she would mind sitting beside her on the sofa, so she could read the descriptions, and if necessary, ask questions as she wrote them down. Rachel moved over beside Jane, who handed her the police pocket notebook and pen.

'Do M1 first.'

Rachel wrote:

5 ft 11 inches, brown swept back thick hair with grey streaks at the sides above his ears and dark eyes, brown or green maybe. Slim, well-built and looks fit for his age. Dresses smartly, often in a pin-stripe blue or grey suit, shirt and tie and sometimes wears a shiny green coat.

'When you say a green coat, can you describe it in more detail for me, please, like the length, style and number of pockets?' Jane was thinking about the Barbour jacket Rita Brown from Edgar House had seen.

Rachel thought about it for a few seconds, then wrote:

Mid-thigh length, with a brown corduroy collar, big pockets at the front and two breast pockets, and a zip fastener up the middle and I think some metal studs as well.

Jane smiled, pleased with how much detail Rachel could recall. Rachel then began writing a description of M2:

An inch or two shorter than M1, dark blond hair which covers his ears, with a parting to the right, sideburns, blue eyes, dimple chin and similar build to M1. Often wears a shirt, dark jumper and black trousers or a black button-up leather jacket and black roll neck jumper, with a long gold chain around his neck and gold pendant hanging from it.

'Can you describe it?'

Rachel held her hands in a fist shape and jabbed them back and forth.

'A boxer?' Jane asked. Rachel pointed to her hand, then made out she was putting something on it. 'A boxing glove?'

Rachel shook her head and held two fingers up.

'A pair of boxing gloves?'

She nodded with a smile and held her thumb up.

'Thanks, they're very good descriptions. What about the younger man you said sometimes joins them – can you describe him in a bit more detail?'

Rachel wrote:

Same height as M2, blue eyes, wavy blond hair down to his shoulders, slim and very good looking. Usually wears a T-shirt and jeans or a polo shirt with a little emblem of a crocodile or man on a horse on the left breast.

'I must say, you're very observant.'

'She is when he goes to the cafe. She's told me about him before and I think she fancies him,' Emma said, and her sister glared at her.

'He sounds a bit like M2 – do they look like they may be related?'

Rachel shrugged and signed they might be, and that she'd seen
M1 give the younger man a large bundle of money on one occasion.

'How big was the bundle?'

She held her fingers about six inches apart and signed that she
thought they were twenty-pound notes as they were purple.

'That's quite a big sum of money by the sounds of it. Have you
noticed if any of these men smoke?'

Rachel signed that M2 smoked cigarettes and M1 smoked a big
cigar, and she didn't like the smell as it put her off her food.

'This may sound like a silly question, but can you tell people's
accents from the way their mouths move?'

Emma answered for Rachel. 'Accents are really hard for lip-
readers to detect, but sometimes they can get an idea from the
words and phrases people use.'

'How do you mean?'

'Someone from Liverpool might say *hozzy* instead of hospital,
but I think it's safe to say from what my sister told us that M1 had
a London accent.'

Rachel nodded in agreement.

'I know you're not very good on vehicles, Rachel, but have you
ever seen M1, M2 or the young man you mentioned in a car?'

Rachel signed that the only one she'd ever seen in a vehicle was
the good-looking young man, when he was parking outside the
cafe in a big white van. Jane put her pocket notebook and pen in
her bag and told Rachel she'd like to take the notes she made back
to the Flying Squad office as evidence, in case it was related to her
investigation.

'Can you tell us anything about the robbery you're investigating?'
Emma asked.

'Yes. It's been in the papers and happened yesterday in Leytonstone High Road. A Securicor van was robbed at gunpoint and a
police car crashed into a house chasing the suspects,' Jane said,
deliberately not mentioning that guns had been fired.

'And do you think the men in the cafe might be responsible?' Emma asked.

'I can't say at this stage, but I can tell you that some of the things Rachel said are of interest to the investigation. Like I said earlier, there's no need for either of you to be worried. Believe me, you did the right thing by telling us – police work would be much easier if there were more upstanding citizens like you two. If there are any developments, I'll let you know. I may need Rachel to look through some police mugshot albums of known criminals at Scotland Yard. Would you be willing to do that, Rachel?'

Jane picked up the way Rachel nervously signed to her sister and there was a moment before Emma replied.

'Of course. It's the right thing to do,' Emma said, looking at her sister.

CHAPTER SIXTEEN

Jane decided to go to Tottenham Police Station and speak to the collator, a uniformed PC who maintained records of local criminals and gleaned information from various sources, including uniformed beat officers, the CID and the public. She knew that station collators had usually worked at least twenty years on a division, and often provided invaluable information to serious crime investigations. It was late afternoon and the collator was putting a coat on as Jane entered his office.

'Hi, I'm WDS Tennison from the Flying Squad. I'm following up on some information I was given and wondered if you could help me.'

'I'm sorry, Sarge, but I'm just about to go off duty. I've got a half four appointment at my doctor's and I'm running late as it is. You're welcome to look through the index cards, or leave the details of anyone you're interested in and I'll get back to you on Monday with the results.'

Jane wondered if she could persuade him to stay a while.

'I'm investigating the armed robbery in Leytonstone yesterday morning . . .'

He stopped and turned around.

'The one where the officers got shot and crashed the area car?'

'Yes.'

'I heard about it and read the teleprinter message – bloody miracle no one was killed. I'm PC Kevin Bottomley. How can I help you?' He took his coat off.

'I'm following up on some information I was given about a couple of possible suspects, IC1 males who use the Bluebird cafe in Bruce Grove,' Jane said, referring to the police code for white people.

'I know the Bluebird – I used to pop in there regularly for a cuppa when I was the home beat officer.'

'I was told the owner is called Nick.'

'That's right. He's owned the cafe for donkey's years. Runs it with his wife, but I heard she's not been very well recently – emphysema.'

'Has he got a criminal record?'

Bottomley laughed. 'No, he's as honest as they come, though he does get a few criminals in his place now and again – but that's not unusual for a cafe in Tottenham. When I was the home beat, he put some names my way about a gang who were nicking shed-loads of fresh meat from an abattoir and trying to sell it on to him. They were nicked thanks to him. I know he's helped a few other officers out with information as well. What's your suspects' names?'

He picked up a pen and opened his A4 notebook.

'Apart from the name Tommy, I don't know if the others are Christian or surnames – but the descriptions I was given are quite good.' Jane got out her pocket notebook. 'I must tell you, though, my informant is obviously worried about repercussions.'

'I totally understand. I don't need to know anything about your informant, and what you tell me will remain between the two of us.'

She handed Bottomley the descriptions Rachel had written.

'M2 may be the one called Tommy.'

He read them and handed Jane back the piece of notepaper.

'There's no one who springs to mind instantly among the armed robbers who live on the division. To be honest, there are only about ten I know of, and at least half of them are currently in prison. What I can do for you is look through my card index trays and compile a list of criminals in the same age bracket with similar features. But it will take me a day or so and I'm off over the weekend.'

'That would be very helpful, thank you.'

'Is there anything else you know about them – what sort of work they do or cars they drive?'

'Nothing about cars, but there's a possibility M2 may be connected to the Star Bingo Hall or Grove Snooker Hall opposite the cafe.'

'Oh yes, the snooker hall opened about six months ago.'

Jane nodded. 'From what I was told, that ties in with the time the two men started using the cafe.'

'The bingo hall opens at about midday, and from the description of your M2 I'd say he's much more likely connected to the snooker hall. Did you notice if the building had an alarm on it?'

'I didn't look, to be honest.'

'Not to worry, let's have a look in the keyholders' cards to see if it's registered.'

He walked over to the index trays.

Jane knew that many businesses were fitted with alarms registered with the local police. The keyholder was usually the owner, or an employee, who could be called out during closing hours, in case of a break-in, and reset the alarm if it went off by accident.

He pulled a card from the tray.

'The bingo hall's main keyholder has been the manager for the last two years, the secondary is a woman. There's two people for the Grove snooker hall. The primary holder is shown as the assistant manager, Aidan O'Reilly, of 94A Seven Sisters Road N7, which is on Wood Green Division, and probably above a shop, as that's a main road. There's a phone number for him as well.'

Jane stopped writing in her pocket notebook.

'Sorry – did you say O'Reilly?' She recalled Rachel mentioning the name 'Riley'.

'Yes.'

He handed her the keyholder's card. She recorded the details in her pocket notebook.

'Have you got an Aidan O'Reilly in your criminal index cards?'

He looked through the 'O' section and pulled out some cards.

'There's five O'Reilly's, none with the first name Aidan, and two of them are from the same family.' He pointed to the computer on his desk. 'I could run a criminal record check on the PNC, but you'll probably get hundreds of hits from all around the country.'

Jane knew she'd need a date or year of birth to narrow the search down on the PNC, and said she'd wait until she had more details about O'Reilly. The secondary keyholder on the card was a Maria Fernandez, with an address in Stamford Hill and a phone number, which she also recorded in her pocket notebook.

'There's no mention of the owner or manager on here.'

Jane handed him the keyholder's card. He put it back in the tray.

'That's not unusual – often they don't want to be woken up in the early hours of the morning if the alarm goes off, so they get a member of staff registered as a keyholder. Fernandez isn't on my index cards.'

'I suppose she might be the barmaid or some sort of hostess at the snooker hall.'

'Possibly. What were the other names?'

'Judge and Webley, that's all I've got, but to be honest I can't be certain about those names either.'

Bottomley stroked his chin. 'They don't ring any bells for me . . .' He looked in the index trays. 'I've got two with the surname Judges and one Judge, but they're either black or juveniles – and there's no Webley on record. It could be that none of the names you've given me live on the Tottenham police manor so they're not on my cards.'

'Thanks for your assistance, and I'm sorry if I've made you late for your doctor's appointment.'

He put his coat on. 'My pleasure, Sarge, and don't worry about the doc's. It might be worth phoning Companies House. If the snooker club is a limited company, the owner should be registered with them. If not, the tax office might be able to help – if they pay any!'

'That's a good idea. Do you have their number?'

'It's in the address book on my desk, along with the reference code, which you need to give them, then they'll know you're police. They close at five, so feel free to use my phone. I could put some feelers out about the snooker club for you, on the pretext we think there's illegal gambling going on – which wouldn't be unusual for those types of places.'

'Thanks, but I'd rather do a bit more digging first and see if Companies House or the tax office can help.'

'Feel free to call me if there's anything else I can assist you with.'

'What's your poison?'

'Jameson's Irish Whiskey, but you don't need to bother—'

'I want to. Where shall I leave it?'

'The bottom drawer of that filing cabinet over there is fine,' he said with a grin as he walked out.

* * *

Jane remained in the collator's office and got straight on the phone to Companies House. The result was positive and encouraging. The Grove Snooker Hall was a limited company set up seven months earlier by Thomas Anthony Ripley, aged forty-six, of 12 Connington House, Hatch Lane, E4. Although the recorded age was slightly older than Rachel thought, Jane considered that M1, who was likely called Tommy, might look younger than he is. She checked the R's in the criminal index cards, but there were none for Ripley. She looked in the A-Z on the collator's desk and estimated that Hatch Lane, which was on Chingford Division, was about six miles from the snooker club and just over four from Barclays Bank in Leytonstone High Road.

Jane phoned Chingford Police Station and asked to be put through to the collator's office. When he answered, she said who she was and asked if he could check his index cards for a white male named Thomas Ripley aged forty-six, and gave his address. She nervously tapped her fingers on the desk, awaiting his reply while he checked the cards. A minute later he was back on the phone.

'I've got two Ripleys – one's twenty-six, the other is eighteen, and neither is called Thomas. The electoral register for that address shows a Thomas Ripley as the sole resident at flat twelve.'

'Have you heard the name before?'

'No.'

'He owns a snooker club in Bruce Grove, Tottenham.'

'Still doesn't ring a bell.'

'What sort of properties are in Connington House?'

'It's a block of privately owned, and rented, one- and two-bedroom modern flats off Hatch Lane, built a few years ago by a property developer in a middle-class residential area. Anything else I can help you with?'

'Have you got access to a PNC?'

She was unable to use the one on the desk in front of her as she'd never done a PNC authorisation course.

'Yes, there's one here in my office.'

'I don't have a date of birth for Anthony Ripley, but from his age, and the date he registered with Companies House, he was probably born in 1934 or '35.'

'I'll run the name with a four year spread on the birth year.' He held the receiver between his shoulder and chin as he typed. A few seconds passed before he spoke. 'There's a few possibles with that name and years of birth – you got a middle name for him?'

'Yes, it's Anthony.'

'Got one. Thomas Anthony Ripley, born tenth of August 1934, height five foot nine inches. Last recorded conviction was twenty-one years ago for GBH – he pleaded guilty and was sentenced to five years in the Scrubs.'

'Any details about the commission of the offence or co-defendants?'

'No, but that's the norm for really old cases on the PNC. I can request his criminal record file be sent to you at Rigg Approach.'

'Yes, please.'

'Any other names you'd like to run a check on?'

'I'm interested in an Aidan O'Reilly. I haven't a clue about his age or description, but I'd guess he's anywhere between thirty to fifty and may live on Seven Sisters Road.'

Jane could hear the collator typing the details on the keyboard.

'There's over sixty on here from all over the country. I can print them out and put them in a dispatch envelope to be delivered to you.'

'It's OK, I can get our clerk to do it when I return to the office later. You have anything on the card index for a Maria Fernandez?'

'Let's see . . . No, nothing on her.'

Jane thanked him for his assistance and decided to contact Wood Green Police Station. She was told by the control room officer that the collator had gone off duty. She asked the officer if he could check the name Aidan O'Reilly and 94A Seven Sisters Road against the collator's cards and electoral register.

'I would if I could, Sarge, but the other radio operator has gone for refreshments and it's really busy here just now.'

'Is Wood Green nick far from Tottenham?' Jane asked.

'About three miles.'

'What street is it on?'

She opened the *A-Z* at the back pages streets index.

'It's in the High Road opposite Earlham Grove.'

'Thanks, I'll call in on my way back to the office.'

She put the phone down, looked at her watch and was surprised to see it was nearly five o'clock.

'Shit!'

She'd forgotten to call the office and give an update of her whereabouts, which would definitely please Murphy, as it would give him something else to have a go at her about. She looked in the back of her pocket notebook for the office number, picked up the phone and hurriedly dialled it.

She recognised Katie's voice. 'Hi, it's Jane Tennison. Has Murphy been asking where I am?'

'Yes, a couple of times, but I've covered for you and said you'd rung in.'

'What did you tell him?'

'I said you'd been to the Broadwater Farm estate and were making further enquiries at the Tottenham Co-op to trace Emma Wilson.'

'That's right – did you speak to Teflon?'

'Yes, he rang in and told me what happened at Broadwater Farm – which meant I didn't have to make anything up about where you were going next,' she said smugly.

'You didn't need to lie for me, Katie.'

'We cover each other's backs on the Flying Squad, Jane.'

'Thanks . . . I owe you one. I'm at Tottenham nick and just need to pop over to Wood Green, then I should be back at Rigg just before six.'

'I think Murphy's got another meeting to go to at the Yard, but I'll let him know you called in and are en route to the office.'

'Thanks, I'll be quick as I can.'

'Did you speak to Emma Wilson?'

'Yes.'

'Was there anything connected to the investigation?'

'She didn't actually hear the men talking about a robbery, but—'

'A waste of your time and effort, just like I thought it would be,' Katie interjected, sounding pleased.

'Not entirely—'

'I knew Murphy should have got the local CID to follow it up before allocating the enquiry to you.'

'To be honest, meeting the Wilsons was a bit surreal, but worth it.'

'What do you mean?' Katie asked.

'I need to get a move on, but I'll explain everything when I get back . . . Catch you later.'

She put the phone down and was about to leave when she realised there was one more check she should make before going to Wood Green.

She opened the collator's 'W' tray and was pleased there were no criminal record cards for Emma or Rachel Wilson. She also checked the electoral register, which showed them as residing at 68 Tangmere House on the Broadwater Farm estate.

*   *   *

Katie went straight to Murphy's office after the call. He was sitting at his desk reading the newspaper articles about the robbery.

'Tennison just phoned in,' she told him.

'About bloody time! What did she have to say for herself?'

'Only that the Wilson woman didn't hear anything in the cafe, and it had been a bit surreal—'

'Tennison's the one who's bloody surreal! Give me anything else that comes in looking like another dead-end enquiry – then I'll allocate it to her. At least I can mark her card for not phoning in earlier.'

'Not really, sir. I told her . . . that I told you that she'd called in twice.'

'Why'd you do that? Now I can't bollock her!'

'Because you wanted me to get on side with her. Besides, if you're not here when she gets back, I can tell her you were mad she didn't return to the office by 5.30 to update you.'

'I told her I wanted a result by the end of the day, not a time.'

'I could have sworn you said by 5.30,' Katie said with a sly grin.

'You've got a right cunning streak in you, Powell – you'd have made a good detective.'

'I'll take that as a compliment, sir. Will you be wanting the team to work over the weekend?'

'Yes, if it's necessary, but only eight-hour shifts – with no overtime.'

'Will you be coming in?'

'It's Kingston's turn to be the squad's senior duty officer this weekend. I'll be at home, but only call me if there's positive and corroborated information about the Barclays Bank suspects, which will identify, locate and allow us to arrest them – with the money, preferably.'

'Will you be back later this evening?'

'I doubt it, but then again I might pop in to see what Tennison has to say for herself.'

* * *

The rush hour traffic was moving slowly, and it took Jane nearly half an hour to travel the three miles to Wood Green. On checking the collator's cards, there were no local records for an Anthony Ripley, Aidan O'Reilly or Maria Fernandez, and the electoral register for 94A Seven Sisters Road showed an Anthony Ripley as the sole occupant. With the snooker club connection, this couldn't be a coincidence. Jane wondered if, when Ripley moved to the flat in Connington House, he'd sublet it to O'Reilly.

Jane didn't get back to the office until 6.30 p.m. It was empty apart from Katie, who was sitting at her desk typing up some statements.

'Everyone still out on enquiries?' she asked as she hung her coat on the stand.

'Yes, apart from DI Kingston, who's in his office.'

'Murphy not about?'

'No, he had a meeting to go to.'

'I only came back because he wanted a result about the Emma Wilson enquiry today—'

'It's just as well, Jane, as he's fuming that you weren't back here by 5.30 like he told you to be.'

Jane looked quizzical. 'He never said I had to be back here at a specific time.'

Katie looked sympathetic. 'I tried to tell him he didn't say a specific time, but he wouldn't listen.'

'I appreciate you sticking up for me, Katie, but I don't want you getting on his wrong side because he's got it in for me.'

'Well, you shouldn't have to put up with Murphy's behaviour. It's not right – and he knows it.'

Jane changed the subject. 'Anything positive come in from the rest of the team?'

'Teflon and Cam are still out taking statements from the area car crew and some civilian witnesses. The Colonel and Bax called in. They spoke to the owner of the car used in the robbery and are checking out what he told them.'

'Do they think he was involved?'

'Not in the robbery itself, but they thought there was something about his car being stolen that didn't add up.'

'What was it?'

'They didn't tell me all the details. They were just calling in.'

'Sounds like I'm the only one who forgot to do that.'

'Yes, but like I said, Murphy and the others don't know that. I told him you'd interviewed Emma Wilson and it turned out to be a waste of time.'

'It was actually quite productive—'

'I thought you said she didn't hear anyone talking in the cafe?'

'She didn't – her deaf sister did.'

Katie laughed. 'A deaf person heard them talking? Are you pulling my leg, Jane?'

'No, she can lip-read. On Monday she saw two men in a Tottenham cafe moving condiments and sugar lumps around the table. From what she told me I think there's a strong possibility it might be connected to our investigation.'

'I see what you mean now when you said it was a bit surreal. Sounds like you did a good job though.'

Katie was trying to keep a straight face, knowing Murphy would be rolling on the floor with laughter when he heard about it.

'It would have been a lot easier if the duty sergeant at Tottenham had done his job properly when he spoke to Emma Wilson. She went to the station on Tuesday evening and specifically told him it was her sister who was in the cafe and she was deaf, but he didn't tell us until Thursday night and deliberately left out significant details. I reckon he knows he messed up and giving you the bare bones was an attempt to cover up his cock-up.'

'I know Geoff Harris from when I was the CID clerk at Tottenham – he's one of the older sergeants and was usually very competent. I should have asked for more details when he phoned over the information.'

'It's not your fault, Katie, you can only go by what he told you.'

'Did you have a word with him about his attitude?'

'I thought about it, but I was in a rush to get to Wood Green and back here, so I didn't have the time. It's probably best to just let it go now I've spoken to the Wilson sisters – two sergeants having a head to head won't achieve anything.'

'Well, if Harris phones again I'll be giving him a piece of my mind.'

'What's happening about the weekend? Is everyone in, or half the team Saturday and half Sunday?' Jane asked, wanting to change the subject.

'Murphy told me to tell you to take the weekend off.'

'Just me, or everyone?'

'I don't know.'

'I was hoping to make some follow-up enquiries on what I was told today and some of the names I've uncovered. Do you think it would be worth phoning him at home later, or in the morning, to update him and ask if I could work a voluntary shift on Saturday and Sunday?'

'I wouldn't – he gets really annoyed if his weekends are disturbed over something trivial. Sorry, I didn't mean to imply what you just said is trivial, but Murphy only likes to act on really solid information, so you might want to reassess what you've got before speaking to him.'

'Fair enough. Guess I'll just have to try and get as much done as possible tonight – after I've typed up my notes.'

Jane picked up the typewriter from the Colonel's desk with a sigh and moved it to her desk.

'Is there anything I can do to help you?' Katie asked.

'Are you authorised to use the office PNC?'

'Yes. You want some checks done?'

'Yes please.' Jane grabbed a pen and piece of paper and wrote the details down. 'I just need a printout for Thomas Anthony Ripley, IC1, born 10.8.34, and a search on an Aidan O'Reilly, but I don't have a date of birth or any other details for him, and he could be anywhere between thirty and fifty.'

'You'll probably get loads of hits for O'Reilly. It's a pretty common Irish name.'

She handed Katie the details. 'I know, but the only way I'm going to narrow it down is by a process of elimination. Did you say Kingston was in his office?'

Katie nodded. Jane grabbed her pocket notebook, and Rachel's, from her shoulder bag and went to knock on Kingston's door.

'I think I should tell him about my enquiries today. At least I'll get some genuine appreciation from him,' Jane said with a smile.

Katie felt herself reddening.

'You'd better bloody not, you bitch!' she muttered to herself.

CHAPTER SEVENTEEN

Jane sat opposite Kingston as he carefully read her notes of the conversation she'd had with Rachel Wilson.

'These notes are very detailed and interesting, especially what was said by M1 on the Monday and today – you've done really well, Jane.' He smiled.

'Thank you, sir. I also have the original notes Rachel made about what she lip-read on the Monday, and the descriptions of M1 and M2 that she wrote down for me today.' She handed them to Kingston.

'I don't mind you calling me Stewart when we're talking one to one like this or off duty.' He read Rachel's descriptions.

'It was all from the horse's mouth, so to speak.'

'How reliable do you think her lip-reading is?'

'Very reliable, she's been doing it for years, though she did say that making out names can be difficult. But she was certain M2 was called Tommy and reasonably sure M1 said the names Webley and Judge.'

Kingston looked at the notes. 'The way I'm reading it, M1 would cover the back of the van with another person who's probably the loose cannon, M2 would cover the front with Webley, and Judge was the getaway driver in the Cortina.'

'Yes, that's what I thought as well.'

'Which adds up to five people being involved. But all our witnesses said there were only four, and one man covered the front – not two.'

'It's possible the other man never went on the robbery.'

'Or M1 might not have been talking about the Leytonstone bank robbery. You need to be open-minded and consider alternative possibilities.'

'I know, but this morning at the cafe, M1 said, "Yesterday was a total fuck-up" and "Riley was a hothead". We know that an off-duty PC got shot and the man in the front passenger seat of the Cortina fired at the area car with a handgun – maybe that's what M1 meant by a fuck-up.'

'Again, it might not have been a robbery he was referring to, but there's something else M1 said that could arguably link to our investigation. He said he'd have to get a loan for Tina's wedding as a monkey wasn't enough. Two grand was in the Securicor cash box they got away with – which, divided by four, is a "monkey" each.'

'Rachel thinks M2 might be connected to a snooker hall opposite the cafe. I've got some names from Companies House, which are all connected to the hall, and one of them has a criminal record.'

Jane looked in her pocket notebook and told him about her enquiries at Tottenham Police Station and the conversation she had with the collator there, and at Chingford Police Station, then finally her flying visit to Wood Green.

'Bloody hell, you have been ferreting away today.'

'Rachel may have been wrong about the name Riley. I think M1 might have said O'Reilly, and it's reasonable to assume Tommy may be Thomas Ripley. Aidan O'Reilly lives at 94A Seven Sisters Road, which is where Ripley used to live. Ripley also has a conviction for GBH – admittedly it was just over twenty years ago, but it shows a propensity for violence. I've ordered his case file and it should be here by Monday.'

'Any CRO records for O'Reilly or Maria Fernandez?'

'There's a load of possibles for O'Reilly and nothing on Fernandez, but she's shown as a secondary keyholder for the snooker club. Obviously, I'll need to do more work on all the names I've got so far. Finding out who M1 is key as it may reveal further connections to Ripley and O'Reilly. The collator at Tottenham knows the cafe owner and said he's an honest man who's given him information before.'

'Is the collator still Kevin Bottomley?'

Jane nodded. 'Yes, and the cafe owner's called Nick.'

'Kevin was the collator when I was the DI at Tottenham – he's reliable and trustworthy. It might be worth asking him to speak to the cafe owner, without giving too much away – or you could get Kevin to introduce you to him and do it together.'

'He did offer to speak to Nick, but I said not at the moment. Bottomley is off over the weekend, but I'll speak to him on Monday morning.'

'Rachel mentioned M1 said something to Camel Hair Coat Man about having "a nice XJS on the front if he was interested" – sounds like the sort of thing a car dealer might say.'

'Rachel knows nothing about the makes or models of cars, but she's got an excellent memory, almost photographic I'd say. Her description of Camel Hair Coat Man's car is good, so I was thinking of making up an album of lots of different sports type cars and see if she can pick.'

Kingston opened his desk drawer and took out what Jane thought was a newspaper and handed it to her.

'This is the latest issue of *Exchange & Mart* – it's full of new and used motors of all makes and sizes.'

Jane shook her head. 'Why didn't I think of that?'

'Because you're a woman, and you let your boyfriends, husbands or fathers buy cars for you,' he said with a smirk.

She laughed. 'I'll have you know I bought my car all on my own, thank you.'

'Which explains the colour. Can I see your notes again, please?'

She handed them to him.

'What are your feelings about the man in the camel hair coat?' he asked.

'On the face of it, the conversation M1 had with him didn't suggest they were talking about a robbery. It could have been something to do with a business deal, and the envelope he gave to M1 could have contained a contract or something like that.'

He looked at Jane's notes. 'Agreed, but M1 wouldn't show M2 the contents of the envelope and said something to do with "champagne and caviar for life". If they were to commit a massive robbery it would set them up for life – and you have to wonder why M1 was so guarded about the envelope and wouldn't open it in the cafe if it was just a business contract.'

'Do you think it might have contained plans for a robbery?'

'If the men in the cafe were involved in yesterday's botched job, they could be planning another one to make up for it.'

'Does that mean I can make further enquiries about them?' Jane asked.

'Murphy will have to make that decision, but as far as I'm concerned the answer's yes.'

'I'm not exactly his flavour of the month.'

'I can't see how he can ignore your information – especially as it's the only lead we've got that's worth pursuing so far. You've got the weekend to do some more digging—'

'Katie told me that Murphy said I was to take the weekend off.'

'On the basis of what you've uncovered so far I'm authorising you to work it.'

'Can I have that in writing?'

'I'm sticking my neck out for you as it is. You need to firm up what you've got so far and keep digging for more if you want to convince Murphy to put a surveillance team on Ripley and O'Reilly.'

'I could go to the snooker hall and have a snoop around.'

He laughed. 'No offence, Jane, but you'd stand out like a sore thumb – snooker halls are men's dens.'

'What about using Dabs? He said he plays snooker for the Met team.'

'That's not a bad idea – he's a short-arse and doesn't look like Old Bill. For now, just keep what you've told me between the two of us. Get someone else on the team to help you with your enquiries.'

'Teflon helped me this morning when I first went to Broadwater Farm. Can I use him and maybe Cam as well if I need him?'

'I'm fine with Teflon, but Cam's a driver, not a detective. You can use him to make phone enquiries if you want.'

'Will you be telling Murphy they're assisting me?'

'Stop worrying about what Murphy thinks, just do your job and let's see what else you might uncover before we talk to Murphy on Monday. The more ammo you've got to fire at him, the more difficult it'll be for him to ignore you.'

'I doubt he'll agree with me on anything.'

'I'll back you up.'

'Do you think he might authorise making some arrests and searching their homes – and the snooker hall?

'I doubt he'd go as far as arrests at the moment. Sadly Barclays informed us the cash that was stolen is untraceable and there's no solid evidence that the men in the cafe were responsible for the Leytonstone job. If they're planning another robbery, Murphy will want to nick them on the pavement with the goods in their grubby little hands.'

'Is it worth me taking Rachel to the Criminal Records Office at the Yard to look through the mugshot albums?'

'I'd hold off on that for now. Thomas Ripley's mugshot is twenty years old and if she failed to pick him out it wouldn't help the investigation. She's seen M1 and 2 regularly in the cafe, so identifying them from surveillance photos won't be a problem.'

'The cafe owner had an advert in the window for a waitress. If he took me on, and Rachel's in the cafe, she could give me the nod when the men we're interested in come in. I could nip out the back, radio the surveillance unit, then we'd know exactly who to photograph and follow when they leave.'

'You ever done any undercover work?'

'I was a decoy for a serial rapist. He attacked me, but I still managed to arrest him. And I was a waitress in my school holidays, so I know how to act the part.'

He rubbed his chin. 'It's risky, and I can't make that decision, Jane. I'd need to run it by Murphy first.'

'Thanks for your support, Stewart.'

'Keep up the good work and Murphy will have to change his mind about you.' He looked at his watch. 'You fancy discussing this further over a quick drink in the pub?'

'I would, but I've still got to write up today's report.'

'Do it over the weekend, you've had a busy day and deserve a drink.'

'All right, but just a quick one.'

'We use the Prince of Wales – it's just down the road by the river. I'll drive if you want.'

'I'll take my car, then I can head off home from there as it's en route. What about Katie?'

'What's she done now?' He sighed.

'Nothing, I just wondered if she'd like to join us.'

'Have you told her what you told me?'

'Not everything. She only knows that Rachel Wilson is deaf and lip-read what was said – plus I gave her a couple of the names to do PNC checks on.'

Kingston ran his finger around the collar of his shirt.

'It's not that I don't trust Katie, but she can be a bit of a rumour-monger. I'm worried that if we discuss the case in front of her, she might say something to Murphy. It's probably best to tell her that you're going home . . . and I'll do the same.'

'I don't like to be underhand. We could discuss it now and then ask Katie if she'd like to join us.'

Kingston looked a little annoyed. 'What else is there you need to tell me?'

'Rachel said the man Tommy wore a pendant round his neck with gold boxing gloves on it. As you were a boxer, I wondered if that type of thing was an award of some sort?'

'I doubt it. Usually you get a cup or a championship winner's belt. I've seen boxing glove pendants, but it doesn't actually mean he's a boxer.'

'I was just thinking, maybe if I speak to Nick over the weekend, and he's agreeable to me working as a waitress, then I could start Monday morning—'

'There's no rush, Jane. If Murphy approves it on Monday, we could start the surveillance on Tuesday.'

'Rachel said she's only ever seen M1 and M2 in the cafe together on a Monday or Friday. Why waste three days on an observation when we could identify them in one? We could put a surveillance team on them, get some good photographs and maybe ID their associates.'

He thought about it. 'Speak to Nick when the place is closed. If you think he's as trustworthy as Kevin Bottomley says, ask him if a couple of officers can use his upstairs flat as an observation point until we can find a single OP that overlooks both the cafe and the snooker hall.'

'Is that a yes for me to start waitressing on Monday if Nick agrees?'

He shook his head. 'No, I'm on duty over the weekend and Murphy's off. You can keep me updated and I'll decide on the next course of action. Anything else you want to talk about?'

'No, that's all I can think of for now.'

'Then let's go and have that drink.'

She picked up her pocket notebook and Rachel's notes, then returned to the main office, where she saw the PNC printouts on her desk.

'Thanks for these, Katie,' she said, picking them up.

'My pleasure. How'd it go with Kingston? Was he pleased with your information?' Katie asked, avoiding eye contact.

'Some of it, but he wants me to make further enquiries over the weekend – see if I can "firm up" what I've got before approaching Murphy.'

'That's sound advice. What have you got so far?'

She forced a smile as Jane unlocked the drawer in her desk and put in her pocket notebook with Rachel's notes.

'Not as much as I thought, but hopefully I'll uncover more. Kingston said to ask if you wanted to join us for a drink at the Prince of Wales.'

She locked the drawer and pocketed the key.

'I'd love to but I'm out tonight and I've got a couple of things to finish off here before I head home.'

'Maybe another time then – just the two of us.'

Still smiling tightly, Katie said, 'I'd like that. Be good to get to know each other a bit better.'

Kingston walked out of his office and looked at Jane.

'Ready to go?'

She picked up her coat and bag. 'Katie's out tonight so she won't be joining us.'

'That's a shame. See you Monday then.'

He walked past Katie without looking at her.

Once Jane and Kingston had gone, Katie went to the window and watched Jane get in her car and follow Kingston down the road. She waited a few minutes, then grabbed her handbag and coat and left the office.

* * *

Kingston paid the barman for a pint of lager and a white wine, then took the drinks over to Jane, who was sitting at a small round table by the window.

'You want something to eat?' he asked, before taking a sip of his drink.

'Are you having anything?'

'Their scampi and chips in a basket isn't bad – we could share if you're not that hungry.'

'One between us would be great.' She reached into her bag. 'I'll pay for it.'

'No, you won't.'

He put his hand on her shoulder before going back to the bar to order the food.

Jane wondered why such a nice bloke had got himself involved with Katie. It struck her that maybe he wanted out, but was worried Katie would react by telling his wife.

'I ordered some bread and butter to go with it,' he said as he sat down. 'I forgot to ask you this earlier, but have you done background checks on the Wilson sisters?'

Jane nodded. 'No trace CRO and the electoral register confirms them living at the Broadwater Farm.'

'What else do you know about them?'

'Not a lot, other than their parents were killed in a car crash, and they were badly injured – that's how Rachel became deaf. Their uncle looked after them for a bit, but couldn't cope, so he put them in a children's home. Beyond that I didn't go into any detail about their past.'

'Well, you need to check them out a bit more—'

'They seemed genuine enough to me; I've no reason to think they've lied.'

Jane was slightly vexed by his implication that they might be dishonest.

'I'm not saying they lied to you, but Murphy will want to know if they are credible witnesses – and the courts, if we get that far. It's to your advantage if they're whiter than white.'

Jane nodded. 'I understand, but I think they're decent people, and I do feel for them. They've been suffering verbal and physical abuse from some of the younger residents on the estate and are trying to get rehoused. They've written numerous letters to the council but each one's been rejected.'

'I know how tough Broadwater Farm can be. I was the DI at Tottenham for two years, so I know loads of residents apply for a move. It could just be they are well down the list.'

'I was wondering if you knew anyone on the council who has a sympathetic ear?'

'Can't say I do. Have they reported the incidents to the local plods?'

'No, they're worried if police start asking questions on the estate, they'll be subjected to even more abuse and intimidation. Are there any detectives at Tottenham who might be able to help?'

'There's a couple I can think of, but it depends on how you want it dealt with.'

'What do you mean?'

'Well, there's the heavy-handed approach – i.e. scare the shit out of the little bastards so they don't do it again – or the more subtle approach to the council, telling them that if they can't get the sisters a move they may well go to the press about the council's lack of care for the deaf community.'

'What about getting them a move under the witness protection programme?'

'You don't know for sure yet that what Rachel told you is reliable. If the men were arrested and/or charged as a result of her information, then that's a different matter. My advice would be to hold off on helping them for the time being. Then, if your further investigation pans out, we can review the situation and maybe get the witness protection unit on board.'

'Should I at least tell them to report the incidents to the local officers?'

'That would be a good start. I'll contact DS Rickman at Tottenham – he's the best man there to deal with it. I understand your feelings about Rachel and Emma, but you mustn't let it cloud your judgement.'

'Thanks for the advice.'

Jane took a sip of her drink. It was good to know there was some-one in the office she could trust.

* * *

Katie parked her car, then got out and put on her coat and headscarf, before taking a deep breath and walking down the road towards the Prince of Wales. From the other side of the street she looked through the large front window of the pub, where she spotted Jane and Kingston sitting close together, engrossed in conversation and appearing to enjoy each other's company.

* * *

The waitress came over with their food.

'Who's for the scampi and chips with bread and butter?'

'We're sharing, so just stick it in the middle please,' Kingston said. 'Is salt and vinegar OK or do you want any sauce?'

'This is fine.'

Jane unwrapped her cutlery from the napkin and stuck her fork in a chip. He picked up a chip and popped it in his mouth, then had to spit it out onto his hand as it was so hot.

Jane laughed. 'Serves you right,' she said, handing him a fork.

He pushed it into a piece of scampi and held it up.

'What do you call a crayfish with a messy room?' he asked Jane.

'I don't know ... What do you call a crayfish with a messy room?'

'A slobster!' he replied, and she couldn't help laughing.

'That's a stupid joke.'

'Yeah, but it made you laugh.'

* * *

Katie was rooted to the spot, transfixed by the sight of them laughing and joking together. Then suddenly she ran back to her car, slammed the door and started thumping the steering wheel with her fists.

'You bastards!' she shouted, before breaking down in tears.

* * *

'Thank you for the scampi and chips, they were delicious.'

'My pleasure. Have you got a boyfriend?'

'Gosh, that's a very direct question,' she said, laughing.

'Well?'

'Not at present.'

'You surprise me – it's hard to imagine an attractive young woman like you not being in a relationship.'

'I find they generally end badly – so I'm quite happy being single.'

'I was thinking, maybe we could go out for a meal one evening?' he asked, leaning across the table.

'By "we", do you mean just the two of us?' she asked guardedly.

He put a hand on her arm. 'Is that a yes?'

'No, it is not!' she said firmly, shrugging his hand off.

'I'm sorry, Jane, I didn't mean to upset you. It's just that I thought there was a bit of chemistry between the two of us.'

She leant towards him so they wouldn't be overheard.

'I never mix business with pleasure – and I certainly don't go out with married men,' she said with a tight smile, then picked up her coat and bag to leave.

'What's going on here then?'

The Colonel's unmistakable voice boomed across the room. Jane looked up to see the Colonel, Stanley, Cam, Bax and Teflon walking towards them.

'What are you doing here?' Kingston scowled, realising he should have gone to another pub with Jane.

'We've had a hard day and thought we'd enjoy a cosy drink like you and Treacle here.' The Colonel smirked.

'Actually, I was just leaving.'

Jane pushed past him and walked out of the pub.

'Who's rattled her cage?' The Colonel laughed. 'Looks like you won't be pulling her drawers down any time soon. You might as well give me that twenty quid now.'

'The bet's off,' Kingston snapped.

The Colonel snapped his fingers twice and held his hand out. Kingston took a twenty-pound note from his wallet with a scowl and handed it over.

'I'll have a pint of lager and whisky chaser.'

He downed the rest of his pint in one.

*   *   *

The office was empty when Katie returned from the pub. She threw her coat and handbag down on a desk, opened one of the steel cabinets by the wall and took out a large holdall. Inside was a range of equipment the team used to force entry into premises and to fit trackers and listening devices to cars and houses. She removed a twelve-inch jemmy, weighed it in her hand, then replaced it in the bag. She rummaged around until she found the assorted screwdriver case, then selected the two smallest ones. She crouched down by Jane's desk so the side drawer lock was at eye level. She inserted one of the screwdrivers into the lock and jiggled it about a bit, then tried with the smaller one. After a few twists and turns the drawer popped open.

'You can't hide things from me, Little Miss Perfect,' she said, reaching in to remove Jane's pocket notebook and Rachel's notes.

CHAPTER EIGHTEEN

Jane got in her car and took a few deep breaths to calm herself down. She'd been enjoying Kingston's company and thought there was a mutual respect between the two of them, but now it seemed it was all an act to get her into bed.

How could I have been so stupid?

It had probably been thoughtless to snub his advances so forcefully. Would he now back her up when they spoke to Murphy about the Wilson sisters and the possible surveillance operations? Did it mean, yet again, she'd have to fight her own corner?

'Why does this shit always happen to me?' she muttered as she started the engine.

She knew if she went straight home she was still so upset she wouldn't be able to get to sleep for ages. She decided to go back to the office and get her pocket notebook and Rachel's notes, so she could type up her report at home after a calming hot bath and a glass of wine.

* * *

Katie was busy photocopying and didn't hear Jane come in.

'I thought you'd have gone home by now,' Jane said and Katie jumped.

'You startled me. What are you doing back here?'

'I'm just picking up my notes so I can type my report at home.'

'Murphy doesn't like people to take their work home. You know, in case they lose it and it gets into the wrong hands,' Katie said quickly.

'It's all right,' Jane explained. 'The notes are in my pocket notebook, which like every police officer I carry with me on the streets when I'm out making enquiries and often take home.'

She got her keys out of her coat pocket and opened her desk drawer.

'What the fuck? Someone's been in my desk and taken all my notes!'

'You're joking . . .' Katie said, putting her hand to her mouth in apparent surprise.

'Has anyone been back to the office while I was out?'

'Only Murphy. I nipped out to the loo while he was here—'

'Well, he must have a skeleton key because I locked it,' she said, turning towards his office.

'I think he has. Maybe he's taken them with him to read.'

'He's got no bloody right to do that!' Jane snapped.

She went into Murphy's office and started to search his desk. Katie gathered up her photocopying, then put it in the bottom of her desk tray and started typing.

'Were they in his office?' she asked as Jane reappeared.

'No. As much of an arsehole as Murphy is, I can't believe he would be so underhand. Did the Colonel come back here earlier?'

'No, I've not seen or heard from him since this afternoon.'

Jane checked the Colonel's desk and trays. Then, as she scanned the room, she noticed two small screwdrivers on the table next to the photocopier. She looked at Katie, who was still typing with her head down. Jane thought it strange that she hadn't lifted a finger to help her search for the notes. She checked the office duty sheet and saw that the Colonel had booked off about ten minutes before he came into the pub.

'The Colonel must have been in as he's booked off duty,' Jane said, looking at Katie.

'Really? Well, he might have come in just after Murphy while I was on the loo, then left before I got back to my desk.'

Jane checked the duty sheet again and saw that Stanley, Cam, Bax and Teflon had booked off at the same time as the Colonel, meaning he wouldn't have been able to take her notes without the rest of them seeing. She also realised there was no way Katie couldn't have seen or heard all four of them in the office, even if she was in the toilet, as it was just a few feet away in the corridor.

'How did Murphy know my notes were in my top drawer?'

'I don't know – but it's an obvious place to keep them,' Katie replied nervously.

'You can tell me if you saw Murphy take them. I won't rat on you.'

Katie's mouth had gone dry and she licked her lips.

'Like I said before, I was on the loo, so he or the Colonel could have taken them.'

Jane remembered seeing Katie by the photocopier and recalled something she herself had inadvertently done a few times when using it. She lifted the lid and her suspicions were confirmed.

'You're not half as clever as you think you are, Katie,' Jane said calmly. 'You're also a shit liar.'

'What on earth are you talking about?' she asked, trying to look surprised.

'Cut the act, Katie. You were the last person to use the photo-copier – and look what you left behind.' Jane removed the piece of notepaper from the copier. 'This is the description of the men in the cafe – in Rachel Wilson's handwriting. How do you explain that?'

'Murphy or the Colonel must have left it there,' she said straight-faced.

Jane picked up the screwdrivers and banged them down on Katie's desk.

'You used these to unlock my drawer, didn't you?'

'I wasn't using the copier, I was trying to fix the top – it had a loose screw and I left the screwdrivers on the table.'

Jane snorted. 'You're the one with the loose screw. Now where are my notes?' she demanded.

'I haven't got your fucking notes!' Katie shouted, knocking her chair over as she stood up. 'I've done nothing wrong and won't be spoken to like this. I'm going home.'

She picked up her handbag and Jane ripped it out of her hand.

'You're going nowhere,' she said, standing between Katie and the door.

Kate was going red in the face. 'You have no right to keep me here against my will!'

Jane opened Katie's handbag and tipped the contents on the floor, but neither her pocket notebook nor Rachel's notes were there.

'You see, I haven't got them.'

Jane noticed Katie make a quick glance towards her desk. She started rummaging through Katie's filing trays and quickly found her pocket notebook and the rest of Rachel's notes, along with photocopies of them. She held them up for Katie to see.

Katie shrugged. 'I'll deny it and say you're lying. Murphy will have you kicked off the squad before you know it.'

Jane thought for a moment. 'Did Murphy tell you to take the notes and copy them?'

Katie said nothing, her eyes full of contempt. Jane decided to try and rattle her.

'I'll take your silence as a yes, but tell me . . . who do you think Kingston will believe – me or you?'

'He'll believe me. He wants rid of you just as much as Murphy and everyone else does.'

'That's not the impression he gave me in the pub earlier; he was all over me. He definitely didn't want you there to cramp his style.'

Katie began to shake with anger.

'You're lying – it was you that was all over him and he rejected you.'

Jane was taken aback. 'Were you spying on us at the pub?'

'If you think you can take Stewart from me you're wrong. He loves me.'

Jane laughed. 'If you think being fucked on a weightlifting bench is love you need your brains tested.'

Her eyes opened wide. 'You were watching us in the gym!'

'And I can't wait to tell the rest of the team—'

Katie screamed, launching herself towards Jane with her fingers splayed like a cat's claws.

Jane took a step backwards.

'You're a fucking bitch, Tennison!' Katie shouted as she stepped forward.

Acting instinctively, Jane blocked Katie's right hand with her left and landed a straight right on Katie's chin, knocking her off her feet and onto the floor. She lay there for a long moment, eyes wide open staring into space. Jane thought she'd knocked her out, but then she took a deep, rasping breath and started to cry. She put her fingers to her split lip and they came away bloody.

'You cut me,' she sobbed.

'You'll live,' Jane said, grabbing a wad of tissues from the box on Katie's desk. She helped her sit up and pressed the tissues against her lip. 'No more games, Katie. I want to know what's going on.'

Katie took a couple of deep breaths. 'All right. I was told to keep an eye on you and find out what you were doing in the hope you'd mess up.'

'Who told you to spy on me?'

'Murphy.'

'That doesn't surprise me. Was Kingston involved?'

'No, he didn't want any part of it. He stuck up for you and I was jealous because I thought he fancied you, so I didn't mind doing what Murphy wanted. Oh my God, my lip is split open!'

Jane realised there was at least some truth in what Katie said about Kingston. He had given her valuable advice. She grabbed another wad of tissues and dabbed some more of the blood off Katie's lip.

'My advice would be to break it off with Kingston. I know from personal experience work relationships are doomed to fail, especially when a married man is involved.'

Jane looked up to see Murphy framed in the doorway with a surprised look on his face.

'What the fuck's going on?' he exclaimed.

Jane glared at him. 'Why don't you tell me?'

* * *

Jane sat opposite Murphy as he read her pocket notebook and Rachel Wilson's notes. She could feel the adrenaline still coursing through her veins. At first, he'd accused Katie of lying, but when Katie said she would report him to the Commander in charge of the Flying Squad, and back Jane up, he quickly capitulated, though he was adamant he'd never told Katie to break into Jane's desk drawer. He didn't apologise to Jane, but did agree to listen to her about the Wilson sisters and the possible suspects in the robbery, and read her notes with an open mind.

Murphy turned another page of Jane's notes, then opened the bottom drawer of his desk and removed the bottle of whisky and two glasses. He poured some whisky into one glass, picked it up and took a sip.

'This is good stuff.'

'My notes or the Scotch, sir?'

'Both. Do you ever take a "wee dram"?'

'Now and again.'

He poured her a glass and slid it across the table. She picked it up and took a sip.

'Cheers.'

'I wish the rest of the team made notes that are as detailed and thorough as this.'

She wondered if he was being sincere, or just embarrassed about his underhandedness being exposed and trying to get back into her good books.

'Do you feel what I've uncovered so far merits further investigation?'

'I might. Have you discussed these notes with anyone else on the team?' he asked, handing them back to her.

She hesitated for a second. 'No, not yet.'

She didn't want to land Kingston in it, despite his behaviour in the pub.

He nodded. 'Fine. I've got a few more questions – then I'll decide the appropriate course of action.'

He topped up both their glasses.

CHAPTER NINETEEN

'How many cops does it take to throw a prisoner down the stairs?' the Colonel asked, grinning at the others seated around the table.

'None, he fell,' Cam answered, and everyone laughed even though they'd heard the joke before.

Stanley put his hand in the whip glass and removed some pound notes.

'Same again, lads?'

There were nods and yeses around the table.

'Stewart, phone call for you!' the landlord shouted from behind the bar.

The Colonel tutted. 'That'll be your missus wondering what you're up to.'

Kingston shook his head drunkenly. 'She don't know the . . . number for the . . . for the pub . . .'

'Must be Katie then,' the Colonel teased.

'I frigging hope not . . . Shee who it is while you're ordering the drinks, Stanley, and tell 'em I'm not here.'

Stanley went to the bar.

'Who's calling Stewart?' he asked.

The landlord handed him the phone and said, 'Bill Murphy.'

After a brief conversation, Stanley quickly came back to the table.

'Where's the bloody drinks?' Kingston asked.

'It was Murphy . . . He wants us all back in the office right away.'

Bax frowned. 'Bloody hell, we've had three pints each. He'll go apeshit.'

Kingston laughed. 'Three, is that all . . . ? Then why do I feel pished?'

''Cause you've been knocking back the whiskys as well,' Stanley said.

'We all booked off duty before going on the piss, so we're not here in job time,' the Colonel chipped in.

'Then let's have one for the road,' Kingston said, downing the rest of his beer.

Stanley shook his head. 'Murphy sounded in a bad mood – I think we should go now.'

'You're right. Get a pint of water and two Underbergs for Stu, then help me put him in my car,' the Colonel said, pulling Kingston up from his chair.

* * *

Jane was at her desk typing up her report when the Colonel, Teflon, Stanley, Cam and Bax returned from the pub.

'What's happening, Jane?' Stanley asked.

'I don't know. Murphy asked me where you all were. He wants an office meeting.'

'Well, thanks for spoiling our evening by telling him,' the Colonel moaned.

'My pleasure.' She grinned.

'Has he called everyone in?'

'Just you lot and Dabs, as far as I know.'

'It must be something big if he's brought Dabs in as well,' Teflon remarked.

'Has Murphy had a reliable tip-off about the Leytonstone robbery?' Baxter asked her.

'Could be.' She shrugged. 'He's in his office making some calls. I guess we'll find out when he's finished. Where's Kingston?'

'In the ladies' loo spewing up.' The Colonel grinned, but Jane didn't rise to the bait.

Teflon flicked the kettle on. 'I think we'd better get some coffee down us in case we have to go out nicking people tonight.'

'Make Kingston's strong and black,' Stanley told him.

A pale-looking Kingston staggered in, then put a hand to his mouth, turned around sharply and headed back to the toilet.

Stanley sighed. 'He's never been able to hold his drink. I'll go and see how he is.'

'If he's made a mess in the ladies', make sure you clean it up,' Jane said.

'You want a hot drink, Jane?' Teflon asked.

'No thanks.'

She pulled her finished report out of the typewriter.

Baxter looked up as Stanley walked back in. 'How is he?'

'He's still drunk, but much better than he was in the pub – said he reckoned some scampi he ate was off.'

Baxter shook his head. 'Yeah, right.'

When Kingston came back he'd washed his face and combed his hair. He looked a bit better. Teflon handed him a coffee and then walked a little unsteadily to the photocopier, spilling some of his own coffee along the way.

'About earlier . . . I'm really sorry and I can assure you it won't happen again,' he said, making an effort not to slur his words.

'I hope not,' she replied without looking at him.

'Can we put it behind us and move on?'

'I already have.'

He looked surprised. 'Really?'

'I don't bear grudges.'

'Thanks, I appreciate it. What are you copying?'

'My report about the Wilson sisters and the men in the cafe.'

'You going to show it to Murphy?'

'Yes.'

'I really think you should wait until Monday, Jane, especially if he's called us in because he's got some good suspects in the frame.'

'He has.'

She picked up the copies of her report and took them to Murphy's office.

'What's she up to?' the Colonel asked Kingston.

'I don't know, but I think Murphy might be about to lay into her.'

'Good, I hope he does it in here so we can all enjoy the moment.' The Colonel smirked.

A few minutes later Murphy came out of his office with Jane at his heels.

'Right, gather round and listen up.'

The room went silent with anticipation

'Before I brief you on the plan of action, I want you all to read WDS Tennison's report.'

He nodded to Jane and she handed them out.

'Is Katie coming in?' Baxter asked.

Murphy shook his head. 'Unfortunately, she fell over when she got home and cut her lip on a sideboard so she's not feeling too good.'

'Sounds like a lame excuse for I can't be bothered,' Baxter muttered.

Kingston noticed that Katie's desk was uncharacteristically dishevelled, but it was the bloodstained tissues in the bin beside the desk that really made him wonder what had happened while they were all in the pub. As Jane handed out her report, the rest of the team exchanged bemused glances.

'Stop gawping and get reading!' Murphy barked. He looked at Kingston. 'A quick word in my office, please.'

As Kingston followed Murphy out, the Colonel dropped Jane's report on the table and flicked the kettle on. Jane went over and stood beside him.

'Are you not going to read my report?'

He didn't look at her. 'What for? Murphy's just toying with you – he won't act on anything you've told him.'

'I wouldn't be so sure of that. Do you really think he'd call everyone in at such short notice if he was playing games? It's up to you whether or not you read it, but you might look stupid if you don't know what he's talking about.'

*   *   *

Murphy closed his office door then sat behind his desk.

'You look like shit.'

Kingston sighed. 'I feel like it, but I'll survive . . .'

'Hair of the dog?' Murphy offered, opening his desk drawer.

'No thanks. What's Tennison's report about?'

Murphy closed the drawer. 'Don't play the fool with me, Stewart. It's obvious she's already briefed you on it – even though she said she hasn't.'

'I haven't read her report—'

'That's because she's only just typed it up – but she inadvertently let slip she'd spoken to you about it.'

'How?'

'Some of her deductions, and the further enquiries she wanted to make, were too shrewd for someone who's only been on the squad for two days – and only you and Katie were in the office when I left.'

'I never meant to go behind your back. I just wanted her to try and get more evidence over the weekend, then speak to you.'

'That's fair enough. She's done a good job as it is, and given us something positive to work on – which is more than the rest of the team so far.'

'What's made you change your mind about her?'

'I haven't. I still don't want any women on the squad, but right now I need her as the go-between with the Wilson women. If their information turns up trumps, and we identify the blaggers with enough evidence to charge them, it's a good result.'

Kingston suspected Murphy meant a good result for himself and not the team.

'Did Tennison find out you told Katie to keep an eye on her?'

Murphy nodded.

Kingston looked surprised. 'Katie grassed you up?'

'She didn't have a lot of choice after Tennison punched her in the mouth.'

'Bloody hell. Tennison beat her up to get the truth out of her?'

'Not exactly – Katie lost her rag with Tennison and went for her and she just defended herself.'

Kingston now realised where the bloodstained tissues had come from.

'What made Katie go for her?'

Murphy shrugged. 'I don't know, neither of them would tell me. But I've got a feeling it might have had something to do with your . . . inclinations towards Tennison.'

'I can assure you there's nothing going on with Tennison. She's made it quite clear she doesn't mix business and pleasure—'

Murphy sighed. 'You need to learn to keep your dick in your trousers, Stewart. Now might also be a good time to break it off with Katie, before you get your fingers burnt – or something else cut off. You'd be a fool to ruin your career and your marriage for the likes of her or Tennison.'

'Will you be getting rid of Katie?' Kingston asked hopefully.

'No, she's good at her job and I don't have the time to go looking for a replacement. Right, let's get on with the meeting,' he said, standing up.

Kingston reckoned that Jane must have confronted Murphy about Katie spying on her, and that's why he was now playing nice – to stop any formal complaint or internal investigation. But it was clear he was only using her. As soon as they'd nabbed the men responsible for the Securicor van robbery, he'd find a way to get rid of her.

* * *

Murphy looked around the office.

'Anyone not finished reading Sergeant Tennison's informative and detailed report?' he asked as he entered the room with Kingston.

'Do you think Murphy fell over and banged his head?' Cam whispered to the Colonel.

'Either that or he wants to shag her.'

'Might be worth having twenty quid on him as well.' Cam smiled.

'Something you two want to share with the rest of us?' Murphy asked with a dark look.

Cam shook his head, but the Colonel had something to say.

'It beggars belief the men we're looking for would openly discuss their plans in a cafe – and the stuff about the envelope, and what might or might not be in it, that's all conjecture. Rachel Wilson could be making the whole thing up.'

Jane suspected he'd only skimmed her report.

'She could, but I don't believe she is. Rachel's deaf, so can't hear what's being said or going on around her, but the cafe was busy on both the Monday and Friday, so it would have been noisy – the perfect cover for discussing the robbery.'

'But the fact is you can't be sure it was a robbery they were talking about – even more so as your star witness couldn't actually hear them,' the Colonel retorted.

Jane just shook her head.

'That's enough, Colonel, I don't want to hear any more negative talk. Let me make it clear: we will be taking further action based on what Tennison has uncovered so far. Firstly, do any of the suspects' names or descriptions mentioned in the report ring a bell with any of you?'

There was a brief silence in the room, until Stanley spoke up.

'We could run it by our informants now we have some names and descriptions.'

Murphy shook his head. 'I don't want to risk our suspects being tipped off.'

Kingston thought differently. 'The Colonel's informant knows a lot of old school blaggers and he's given us some good tip-offs in the past.'

'I was going to see him first thing Sunday morning, Guv,' the Colonel added.

Murphy thought about it. 'OK, don't be up front with any names. Just see what you can tease out of him. And take Tennison with you.'

The Colonel frowned. 'Do I have to, Guv?'

Here we go again, Jane thought to herself.

'Yes. She's never dealt with any informants on these types of investigations. She needs to watch, listen and learn from someone as experienced as you.'

The Colonel wasn't happy, but knew it was pointless arguing with Murphy.

'Anyone else got anything positive to add?' Murphy asked.

Baxter put his hand up.

'Jane's report mentions M1 might be a car dealer. Frank Braun, who me and the Colonel interviewed this morning, owns the Cortina that was used as the getaway car in the robbery, but he also has a 3 series BMW injection and a nice three-bedroom semi in Tottenham.'

Murphy and the others exchanged puzzled looks.

'Forgive me for not being on the same wavelength as you, Bax – but what's all that got to do with anything?' Stanley asked.

Baxter sighed. 'I thought it was obvious. Braun's a fireman and seems to be living well above his means. If M1 is a car dealer maybe he gave Braun the BMW, or sold it to him cheap for letting them use his Cortina and reporting it stolen.'

Stanley nodded. 'OK. Good point, Bax.'

The Colonel had more to add.

'The PNC check we ran on Braun turned up negative and the crime report at Tottenham tied up with what he told us, but I still think there's more to him than meets the eye. He said he knew Paul Lawrence, the lab liaison DS, and was working a fire scene with him when the car was stolen.'

'Check it out with Lawrence, then revisit Braun and ask him where he bought the BMW and the Cortina—'

'I know DS Lawrence. I can call him and ask about Braun,' Jane suggested.

He looked at the office clock. It was nearly ten o'clock.

'OK. It's late but give him a call and tell him it's urgent.'

As the meeting continued Jane rummaged in her bag for her address book, then used the phone on Katie's desk. Lawrence answered after a couple of rings.

Murphy looked at Dabs. 'How are we doing on the forensics?'

'Ballistics confirmed the rifling on the bullets and firing pin marks on the cartridge cases showed they were all fired from the same handgun, which they reckon was probably a nine-millimetre Luger. Also, the blood we recovered at the crash scene and on the burnt-out Cortina was B negative, which is only found in about one point five per cent of the population.'

'What was the origin of the bullets from the casing stamp?' the Colonel asked.

'Germany, World War Two issue – like you said.'

Jane finished her conversation with Lawrence and returned to the group.

'Sergeant Lawrence has known Frank Braun for about five years, and he's socialised with him on a number of occasions. In his opinion Braun is honest and trustworthy, and he knows he isn't living beyond his means. He won nearly thirty thousand on the pools a couple of years ago.'

'That doesn't mean he's straight – even people with plenty of money get greedy for more.' The Colonel shrugged.

'As I said, go back and ask about the cars. Anything else to add, Colonel?' Murphy asked.

'There's something in Tennison's report that might be wrong, or possibly misconstrued—'

Murphy frowned. 'I said I didn't want any negative input.'

'It's not negative, sir, it's just a thought.' He looked at the report. 'When M1 said, "You cover the front with Webley", it might not be another man he's referring to. Webley and Scott make handguns and shotguns – weapons that are commonly referred to as a Webley. It could be that M1 was telling M2, or Tommy as we think he's called, to cover the front with a shotgun. If Webley isn't a person, that means one man was at the front of the van with a shotgun – as all our witnesses reported.'

'That's a reasonable assumption,' Kingston replied, and Murphy nodded.

Jane was surprised the Colonel had read her report, but knew he liked to show off when it came to his knowledge of firearms.

'On that basis, she may have been wrong with other names,' Cam suggested.

'Rachel was adamant about Tommy but said she could be wrong about Judge,' Jane admitted.

Murphy nodded. 'You'll all be working the weekend to see what else we can find out about these people. To that end I've paired you up where necessary and allocated the further enquiries I want made, which Sergeant Tennison will now brief you on.'

Jane lifted back the front cover of the flip chart, revealing the pairings and bullet points outlining their tasks.

'Tomorrow morning Teflon and I will visit Nick, the Bluebird cafe owner, to see what he can tell us, and we'll also look for a suitable single observation point that overlooks the cafe and snooker hall. The Colonel and Bax, apart from revisiting Braun, will also identify the car dealerships on Tottenham's division and check the keyholders' cards and Companies House to see if they can identify the owners or persons connected to the premises.'

'If you reckon Braun is kosher, show him the artist's impression of the getaway driver and the description the landlady gave us,' Kingston added. 'Same with the cafe owner.'

'Have you arranged for the landlady to look through mugshots at the Yard?' Murphy asked him.

'They're making an album up of convicted robbers matching the impression and description. She can only do Monday morning, but I'm in court, so maybe Jane could go with her as they've already met.'

'Fine, but I want it done and not put off to another day,' Murphy added.

Jane flicked over to the next page.

'Stanley and Dabs will be visiting the Bruce Grove snooker club on the pretext of joining—'

'What have they done to get the cushy job?' Bax asked.

'Dabs doesn't look like Old Bill and Stanley has a lot of previous experience in undercover work,' Jane replied.

'Is that a polite way of saying Dabs is a short-arse and Stanley's nondescript?' the Colonel asked, raising a few laughs.

Murphy looked at Stanley. 'I suggest you get rid of that Jason King moustache before you go there.'

'Have a heart, Guv – it took me ages to grow it,' Stanley pleaded.

'And it will take you less than a minute to shave it off,' Murphy retorted.

'What am I doing?' Cam asked.

'As Katie's off sick, I need someone to man the office.'

Cam's expression couldn't hide his disappointment.

Jane continued, 'There are some important background enquiries that need to be done on the phone regarding the Wilson sisters, and PNC checks on names the others may call in with.'

She went around the room handing out the action sheets.

'Are we working the weekend voluntarily or without notice for double pay?' Cam asked.

'Seeing as we've got something positive to go on, I'll allow time and a half and no more than ten hours max. If you work beyond that then it's got to be taken as time in lieu,' Murphy told him.

Cam smiled. 'Answering the phone doesn't seem quite so bad, then.'

'I've got a report you can type up if you get bored,' Bax joked.

Dabs raised his hand. 'If we can get a cup or glass that any of the suspects used in the cafe, I can dust them for prints and see if we get a match through fingerprint bureau.'

'Good thinking, Dabs,' Jane said. 'I was hoping to go undercover as a waitress in the cafe for a couple of days, so I could do it then.'

'That's a bit risky, isn't it . . . ?' the Colonel said.

Jane was quick to answer back. 'I did waitressing before I joined the Met, but if you feel you could do a better job in a wig and apron then be my guest!'

'I'm not having a dig at you,' the Colonel insisted. 'What I'm saying is if the men in your report are involved in the robbery, the slightest whiff of a copper could ruin everything.'

Murphy held a hand up. 'Let's not get ahead of ourselves. I'll decide if and when any UC work is to be done in the cafe, Tennison. For now, just ask the owner to put anything they've touched to one side after he clears their table.'

Jane was upset but didn't show it.

'I was going to visit Abby Jones at her home address and get a statement from her. She's the seventeen-year-old who witnessed the area car being shot at.'

Murphy looked apprehensive. 'Right now, I'd rather not put an unreliable teenager through the trauma of being a witness to an armed robbery. Let's see how the next couple of days pan out and I'll reconsider you visiting her.'

'Yes, sir,' Jane said, understanding his concern.

'Anything else?' No one said anything. 'Then I suggest you all head off home and get some sleep.' He closed his pocket notebook.

'We got much left in the whip, Sarge?' Bax asked Stanley.

'Enough for another round at least.'

'Guv, you fancy a quick pint before last orders?'

Murphy shrugged. 'Go on then, but no talking shop – you never know who's listening . . . or lip-reading,' he added with a smile.

'Anyone else up for it?' Stanley asked, and only Kingston declined.

'I'll give it a miss, thanks, my stomach's still a bit dicky.'

'Hair of the dog might help,' Jane suggested, wondering if he was trying to avoid being in her company.

'Go on then.' He smiled.

* * *

Back in the pub, all the tensions and disagreements about the investigation quickly evaporated – even the mystery of Katie's disappearance seemed to have been forgotten – as they got on with the serious business of drinking and taking the piss out of each other. It was only Murphy laying down the law, insisting the next round was going to be the last, that put a stop to the fun, knowing he didn't want them hung-over or stinking of booze when they were out making enquiries and dealing with the public the next morning.

Stanley nudged Jane with his shoulder.

'I thought I told you to chill out and settle in gently,' he said with a grin.

'And I told you I didn't need your advice and could make my own decisions.' She gave him a nudge back.

'You're like a dog with a bone when you get your teeth into an investigation.'

'I'm not sure I like that comparison.'

'No offence – you used to be a soft poodle, but now you're like a Rottweiler.'

'Well, I'll take that as a compliment.'

He looked around, then whispered, 'Seriously, though, you've done some solid work today. We all thought Murphy was sending you out on a dead-end enquiry, but you turned up trumps and the rest of the team's dead impressed.'

She whispered back, 'I don't get the impression the Colonel's that impressed with my work – or even wants me on the team.'

'Ignore him. The Colonel likes to think he's God's gift to the Flying Squad. He's just jealous that you came back with some strong leads and got Murphy's attention. He'll never admit you did a good job, but he did read your report and I'll guarantee he'll do everything he can to try and identify M1.'

She shrugged. 'Hope it goes well in the club tomorrow.'

'I'm looking forward to it – what other job would pay you time and a half to play snooker? Mind you, I might have to take a milk crate for Dabs to stand on so he can reach the table.'

Jane laughed at the thought of Dabs standing on a milk crate. It wasn't exactly how she'd imagined the Flying Squad going after bank robbers.

'Right, I'm off home.'

'One for the road?' Stanley offered.

'No, I'm bushed. It's been a long day and it'll be an even longer one tomorrow if things go according to plan.'

She went over to speak to the Colonel before leaving.

'What time and where are you meeting your informant on Sunday?' she asked.

'Between 7.30 and eight in Brick Lane Market, so I'll meet you at Rigg around seven.'

Jane knew the location. 'It's easier for me to go straight there as it's on my route in.'

'Fine, I'll meet you at the junction with Bethnal Green Road at 7.30, then.'

He raised his pint glass.

'You did a good job today. Safe journey home.'

Walking to her car, Jane allowed herself a pat on the back – and not just because of the leads she'd uncovered; the fact that the team were beginning to accept her and admit she was a good detective was an even greater achievement. She heard footsteps as she unlocked the car, then saw Kingston walking towards her.

'If you've come to apologise about earlier again, there's no need.'

'No, I just wanted to thank you for not telling Murphy you spoke to me before him. Turned out he guessed anyway and wasn't that bothered.'

'Maybe I'm finally winning his confidence.'

'Don't be too sure about that, Jane,' he cautioned. 'He still doesn't want a woman on the squad.'

She raised her eyebrows. 'Well, he didn't give me that impression. Why call an office meeting and praise my report in front of the team if he doesn't want me there?'

Kingston sighed. 'Look, Jane, Murphy told me you'd found out he was using Katie to spy on you, and about the fight you had with her. He knows you could drop him in the shit by making an official complaint and just wants to make sure you don't.'

Jane wondered if it was true, or if Kingston was just trying to make out he was on her side so she'd soften towards him.

'If you're just trying it on again, you can forget it – I'm not interested.' She got in her car.

He put his hand on the door as she tried to close it.

'I meant it when I said it wouldn't happen again. I like you as a person – and I respect you as a detective – but believe me, if what you've uncovered gets positive results, Murphy will take the credit for all your hard work then drop you like a ton of bricks.'

'Leave me alone!' she said, slamming the door shut.

He pulled his hand away just in time.

'Have it your way, but don't say I didn't warn you.'

She started the engine, shoved it into first gear and sped off, leaving him on the pavement, shaking his head.

On the way home, she nearly went through a red light. What Kingston said had really touched a nerve. She no longer felt so sure about anything. Either he was lying about Murphy to try and get her into bed, or Murphy was just using her until he could kick her off the squad. She even began to wonder if Stanley was playing games with her when he said the rest of the team were impressed with her work. Her good mood had definitely vanished.

'Screw 'em all!' she said to herself.

From now on she was just going to focus on the investigation and keep a detailed record of everything she did, to cover her back. That way, she knew, if it was her hard work that solved the Leytonstone robbery, then no one could take it away from her.

CHAPTER TWENTY

Jane had a cheese sandwich and a glass of wine when she got home, then went to bed, but she found it hard to get to sleep, unable to get what Kingston had said out of her mind. Eventually she gave up, got out of bed and switched on the TV, then lay on the sofa under her duvet to watch the late film. It was *New Face in Hell*, starring George Peppard as a private eye who's set up for a murder by Raymond Burr. It was odd seeing Burr playing a bad guy, as she always thought of him as Ironside, the San Francisco detective in a wheelchair. The film was gripping enough to take her mind off the evening's events but, feeling exhausted, she switched it off before the end and went back to bed. She fell asleep almost at once.

The sound of the phone ringing jolted her awake. She fumbled for the switch on the table lamp and saw the time on her alarm clock was 1 a.m. She got up to answer the phone, assuming it must be someone from the squad, but instantly recognised her brother-in-law Tony's voice. He sounded agitated and distressed.

'Something bad has happened, Jane – I didn't know who else to turn to.'

He sounded as if he was trying to control his breathing. She could tell he was close to tears.

'Are Nathan and Pam OK?' she asked anxiously.

'They're fine – it's me that's in trouble, Jane. I really need your help.'

'Take a deep breath, speak slowly and tell me what's happened, Tony.'

'I've been arrested for something I didn't do. I'm worried the police will frame me for it,' he said, sounding even more distraught.

'I need to know why you've been arrested before I can help, Tony,' she said.

There was silence on the other end of the line.

'What's so bad you can't tell me?' she asked calmly.

Tony took a deep breath. 'This woman said I sexually assaulted her . . . but I swear I didn't.' He started to cry.

Jane was stunned. 'Jesus Christ, Tony – what happened?'

She heard a male voice in the background.

'Time's up, son. You got to go back to your cell now.'

'Please, please help me, Jane,' he begged, sounding like a broken man.

'What station are you at?' she asked quickly.

'The one in Mayfair—'

The phone went dead, and Jane realised the officer she could hear must have put the phone down. She sat on the edge of her bed in total disbelief, wondering what to do. She knew there were a few police stations in the West End, but the only one with a Mayfair address was West End Central in Savile Row.

She ran into the living room and got her Met Police pocket diary out of her shoulder bag, then, looking in the alphabetical list of police stations at the back of it, found the number for West End Central. She went back to her bedroom and was about to pick up the phone, but hesitated, wondering what she should say, as she knew the custody sergeant wouldn't be obliged to tell her anything. She didn't even know if Tony had requested to speak to a solicitor, but doubted it as he would only have been allowed one phone call.

'Christ, this is all I fucking need right now!'

She wondered if she should go to Pam's house or call her. It seemed pointless, since she didn't even know what the evidence against Tony was. The one thing she did know was that Tony had never been a violent man and had, in her eyes, always been a faithful and loving husband. He had his faults, but he was certainly no rapist. Her mind was made up; she decided to drive to West End Central Police Station and see if Tony was there, then find out for herself what the strength of the evidence against him was.

* * *

It didn't take long to get to the police station, being just over a mile away from her flat. After parking in a back street, she was about to go through the foyer door to the front counter when she heard someone say her name.

'Are you Jane?'

She turned and saw a familiar-looking man in his mid-twenties sitting on the foyer bench.

'Do I know you?'

'I'm Noel Harper. I was Tony's best man. We met at the wedding and I remember him telling me you were a detective. Do you work here?'

'No. I take it you know he's been arrested?'

'Yes, I was with him at the time. I've been trying to find out what's happening, but no one will tell me anything.'

She sat down beside him. 'When you say you were with him . . . did you actually see what happened?'

'Yes and no, I guess. We were with a group of mates on a stag night in Leicester Square. When the pubs closed some of us went to the Empire Ballroom and this girl was all over Tony, but he wasn't really interested in her.'

She sensed he was trying to hide something.

'What do you mean by "not really interested"?'

'Tony had a few dances with her, then he came back to the bar. She followed him over and asked if he'd buy her a drink.'

'How many drinks did he buy her?'

'Just the one, I think.'

'Was Tony pissed?'

'Not really.'

Jane didn't believe him.

'I'm going to be straight with you, Noel – and I need you to be the same with me, because I'm already feeling like you're trying to protect Tony and that's not going to help him. He phoned me after he was arrested and sounded in a hell of a state. I don't know what the evidence is against him, but I don't believe Tony would do what he's accused of. If I'm going to try and help him, I need to know the truth. So, I'll ask again: was he pissed and how many drinks did he buy her?' she asked firmly.

'He was drunk but coherent and bought her two drinks.'

'Was he trying to get her pissed?'

'No, she was half-cut when we got there and wouldn't leave Tony alone. I think he thought she might piss off if he bought her a drink, but she kept holding him by the arm and kissing his neck.'

'And did he reciprocate?'

Noel sighed. 'Not at first, but when the slow music came on she dragged him back onto the dance floor. They stayed on the floor for a few songs and she was rubbing her body against his and they kissed.'

'Did he touch her sexually or anything like that while they were dancing?'

Noel nodded. 'He had his hands on her backside, but that was all. When they finished dancing, she went to the toilet and he came back to the bar.'

'Did he say anything about her?'

'No, but one of the lads said she was a slapper and Tony said he was just having a bit of fun and wasn't interested in her. I noticed he had make-up on his shirt collar and said Pam would kill him if she saw it. He went to the toilet to clean it off and the girl came back. She asked where Tony was and I said he'd gone home. She looked upset and stormed off.'

'Do you know her name?'

'No.'

'What happened when Tony came back from the toilet?'

'It was late and I didn't want to miss the last Tube home, and Tony was staying with me so I said we needed to go. He finished his pint, then as we left the girl he'd danced with suddenly appeared. She grabbed his hand and dragged him off down the alleyway at the side of the ballroom.'

'And I take it he didn't resist?'

'No, but he must have thought it was funny as he was laughing. I didn't go down the alley as I thought he'd come straight out. About a minute later a policeman and policewoman were passing. They stopped and looked up the alley and must have seen them. They went into the alley and the next thing I heard was a woman's voice screaming, "Help me, help me!" I looked to see what was happening and the policeman had Tony pushed up against the wall and was putting handcuffs on him. He looked like he was in a state of shock when the policeman brought him out. I asked why he was being arrested and the officer said for indecent assault. I couldn't believe it. I tried to tell the policeman she was lying but he told me to shut up or he'd arrest me for obstruction.'

'Did you see the woman again?'

'When the policewoman helped her out of the alleyway, she was crying, but I couldn't see any tears. I looked her in the eye, and she turned away – it was obvious she was lying.'

'Tony's been a fool and got himself in serious trouble – but if what you've told me is the truth, there are some things that don't add up.'

'What do you think will happen to him?'

'I don't know yet. The night duty CID will take a statement from the woman, then they may interview Tony or leave it to the early turn CID to take the investigation over. Are you happy to stay here for now?'

'I'm not going anywhere until I find out what's happening. Does Pam know he's been arrested?'

'Not as far as I know, though Tony would have had to give his name and address to the custody sergeant. I'm going to ask the CID to speak to you. Would you be willing to make a written statement if necessary?'

'Of course, but I'm worried they'll think I'm lying to protect Tony.'

'I won't deny that's possible, but I'm a detective and I believe you.'

'Tony's lucky to have you as a sister-in-law.'

'It'll need more than luck to get him out of the mess he's made for himself. If the investigating officer tells me to sling my hook, that's the end of my involvement—'

'Even if he's charged?'

'Yes. I'm putting my neck on the line as it is by being here.'

Jane went through the foyer door to the front counter, where she showed her warrant card to the duty sergeant and asked if the night duty CID were available. The sergeant told her DS Simon Boon was in the CID office on the first floor, and let her into the police side of the station.

Entering the CID office, she saw a man in his mid-thirties, dressed in jeans and a polo shirt, sitting at a desk typing.

'Sorry to disturb you. I'm WDS Jane Tennison from the Flying Squad. Are you DS Simon Boon?' She showed him her warrant card.

He nodded. 'A bit unusual for the Sweeney to be out at this time of night. What can I do for you?'

'I'm here about the indecent assault suspect you're dealing with—'

'He doesn't strike me as a hardened armed blagger,' a suspicious-sounding Boon remarked.

Jane was direct. 'Tony Harrison is my brother-in-law. He used his right to a phone call after his arrest to contact me at home. I'm just trying to find out what happened and if he's likely to be charged.'

Boon looked surprised, stopped typing and sat back in his chair.

'He told the arresting officers his name was Tony Durham and said he lived at thirty-three Melcombe Street?'

She sighed. 'That's my address. I suspect he doesn't want my sister Pam to know he's been arrested.'

'Well, he's certainly not done himself any favours by lying.'

'Tony's never been in trouble with the police before, so he's unused to this kind of situation and probably not thinking straight. I've always known him to be a devoted husband and father, who's never been unfaithful or aggressive.'

'That's debatable, considering the allegation against him and the state of the victim.'

'I know your investigation is none of my business, but all I'd ask is that you speak to his friend Noel Harper, who is in the station foyer.'

'I wasn't made aware that Tony was with any friends, but I'll speak to Mr Harper.'

'Thanks for your time and I hope you don't think I'm trying to interfere,' she said, not wanting to push her luck.

'For what it's worth . . . I'd be standing where you are now if it was my brother-in-law who got nicked. I appreciate you being up front about your connection to Mr Harrison, and not trying to tell me the victim is mistaken or how to run my investigation. You do appreciate that whatever I may tell you is off the record?'

She realised he was prepared to listen to her.

'As far as I'm concerned, we never spoke, and if anyone questions why I was here, you refused to tell me anything.'

'Good, then we both know where we stand. What's Mr Harper's version of events?' Boon picked up his pen and a piece of paper. 'I just want to be sure that what Noel Harper told you matches with what he tells me.'

'That's understandable.'

She told him everything that Noel had said. Finishing up, Jane emphasised the fact that the woman had dragged Tony up the alleyway and only started screaming for help about a minute later, when the uniformed officers walked towards them.

Boon put down his pen, folded up the notes and put them in his trouser pocket.

'I spoke to the victim, Laura Brooks, when she was first brought to the station. She was clearly distressed and emotional, and said she felt embarrassed talking to me. I got the WPC who was at the scene to take a statement from her, but I'll come to that in a moment.' He picked up the uniformed officer's incident report book, which contained the details of Tony's arrest.

'The arresting officers were passing the alleyway when they noticed a couple kissing and touching each other's genitals.'

'Outside their clothing?'

'No, Tony had his penis out and his hand was up the woman's skirt. Her bra was up over her breasts and he was touching them with his other hand. As the officers approached, the PC shouted out that they were committing a public indecency offence. Brooks looked at them and started shouting out for help and pushing Tony away. She told the officers she was walking through the alleyway when she was grabbed from behind by Tony, who ripped her blouse and sexually assaulted her. She also said she was paralysed with fear until she saw the police officers and thought she would have been raped if they hadn't come along.'

'Was her blouse torn?' Jane asked.

'Yes, at the top, and one button was missing, which was recovered in the alleyway.'

'Did the police doctor find any scratches or bruising on her consistent with an indecent assault?'

'No, and he also did an inner thigh and vaginal examination.'

'So, he found no evidence to support she was sexually assaulted?'

'Correct. He also thought she'd had more to drink than she said she had, though that doesn't mean she wasn't assaulted. In her statement Brooks said she didn't struggle as she feared being raped and beaten. She admits masturbating Tony, but only because he got his penis out and forced her to.'

'Did she say anything about meeting him in the ballroom, then kissing and rubbing against him while they were dancing?'

'She says he came on to her and touched her backside and she slapped him, and he must have been angry and followed her up the alleyway to attack her.'

'Was she with anyone who can corroborate her version of events?'

'She said her friend felt ill and had gone home, so she was alone in the nightclub.'

'How convenient. Tony was with a group of lads on a stag night. If what Noel Harper told me is the truth, they can corroborate his version of events.'

'If they're willing to make a statement I'll ensure the early turn CID speak to them.'

'What did the WPC who took the statement make of Brooks?'

'She was present when the FME examined her, and after taking the statement she said that although she couldn't prove Brooks was lying, she wasn't convinced her story was entirely true.'

'Why lie like that and accuse an innocent man of something he didn't do?'

'The WPC has a theory on that.'

'Which was?'

'She was frightened she'd be arrested for indecency in a public place and her husband would find out.'

Jane was surprised. 'She's married as well . . . Tony's more stupid than I thought.'

'I know it's of little consolation where Tony's concerned, but she wasn't wearing her wedding ring. The WPC noticed a white mark on her ring finger. When asked if she was married, Brooks became nervous and said she'd taken her wedding ring off because her finger had swollen up and it hurt.'

'Did you contact her husband?'

'The WPC asked Brooks if she'd like us to, but she said he was away on business and she'd tell him when he got back. She also declined a lift home and when she got in a cab I rang her home address. A man answered and said angrily, "Is that you, Laura?". I said I'd got the wrong number and put the phone down.'

'Sounds like Brooks panicked, thinking she'd be arrested for public indecency.'

'Possibly – if her allegation is false.'

'Will you be interviewing Tony, or will you hand the case over to early turn?'

'I'll interview him after I've spoken to Noel Harper. If their stories match, I'll release him on bail pending further enquiries and deal with the case myself. I'm back on day shift Monday.'

'I know I'm pushing my luck but is there any chance I can see him?'

'I'm not sure that's a good idea.'

'I won't mention I've spoken to you or Harper – I just want to speak to him about my sister and tell him to be truthful.'

Boon stood up. 'I'll tell the custody sergeant you're family and I've approved a short cell visit – but I'll have to be present.'

'Of course.'

* * *

As Boon opened the cell door, Jane saw Tony sitting on the bed with his head in his hands. As soon as he saw Jane he started to well up.

'I'm sorry, Jane – I really messed up. I'm so ashamed of what I've done.'

'So you should be, Tony – even more so for giving a false name and using my address.'

'I was worried Pam would find out I'd been arrested.'

'If you hadn't fancied a sordid quickie up a dirty alleyway, you wouldn't be here now. This is DS Boon, and he'll be dealing with the investigation and interviewing you.'

'I swear, Jane, I didn't assault her – she's lying.'

'I'm not here to discuss your arrest or persuade DS Boon you're innocent. He will decide what happens to you, but you must tell him the truth and give him the details of the friends you were with so he can interview them.'

Tony was surprised by her bluntness. 'I don't want to drag them into this mess.'

Jane could see through his apprehension.

'Only because you're worried your arrest might get back to Pam. You may need them as defence witnesses – especially if you end up in court. If a jury finds you guilty, you could get ten years in prison.'

She knew this would frighten Tony, but that was her intention.

He looked at her with fear in his eyes.

'Ten years?'

She nodded. 'And I don't think Pam would stand by you either—'

'Are you going to tell her?'

'Give me one good reason why I shouldn't.'

'I don't want to lose Pam or Nathan. I love them both with all my heart.'

'You should have thought of that before you went over the side with another woman!'

'I didn't mean to—'

'Oh, so you accidentally went down the alley and, without realising, fondled each other's genitals?'

'It just sort of happened . . . I'd had a few drinks and, liked the fact another woman fancied me.'

'Drink is not an excuse. Have you been unfaithful before?'

'No, never. But I haven't had sex with Pam since she had the baby. When the woman touched me, I felt aroused—'

'So, you're saying you would have had sex with her if the police hadn't come along?'

He started to cry. 'I guess so, yes.'

'You need to listen to Jane's advice, Tony. I'll go and call the duty solicitor so he can represent you during the interview.'

Boon felt that the conversation was getting personal and he should give them some time alone.

'Thanks, Simon. I won't be much longer.'

She sat down next to Tony.

'I know you're not capable of attacking or sexually assaulting a woman, Tony, but you created this mess and I can't get involved.'

'Are you going to tell Pam?'

'There's part of me that says I should as she's my sister, but I also feel you should tell her. Are the two of you having problems at home?'

'She was fine when Nathan was born, then after a couple of months she became distant and didn't want to have any form of physical contact with me. I thought at first she might be seeing someone else, but I knew I was imagining it and realised she was just worn out from looking after Nathan day and night. I tried to help Pam more with him, but she wouldn't let me and kept saying I didn't know what I was doing. She doesn't even like me picking him up in case I drop him.'

'Sounds like a bad case of the baby blues. You need to talk to her, Tony – tell her how you feel and try and resolve the situation.'

'It's worse than you realise, Jane. She screams and throws things at me. She goes berserk about silly little things that don't really matter. I dread going home after work – I'm even sleeping in the spare room.'

Jane was shocked. She knew Pam could be bolshie and hot-headed at times, but she hadn't noticed any drastic changes in her behaviour. She wondered if Pam was depressed, suffering in silence and keeping her feelings from the rest of the family.

'I'm not going to tell Pam. Whether or not you do is your decision, but like I said, the pair of you need to talk. Try and get her to speak to her doctor about her depression. He may be able to prescribe some medication that will help or arrange some form of counselling.'

'I promise I'll do what I can to help her.'

'You can ring me at home any time if you want advice or just need someone to talk to.'

'Thanks, Jane. I appreciate everything you've done for me. Do you think I'll be charged later and then released?'

'DS Boon seems a fair man to me. I'm confident he will look at all the evidence and re-interview the complainant before making a final decision, which means you'll be released on police bail pending further enquiries. However, if she sticks to her story, it's your word against hers, and our solicitors' department may feel you should be charged. Then it's up to a jury to decide who's telling the truth. Hopefully it won't come to that.'

'Should I wait and see what happens before telling Pam?'

'That's up to you. But even friends may let the cat out of the bag unintentionally, so even if the allegation is withdrawn, Pam might still find out. My advice would be to go back to your friend Noel's house first and take some time to reflect on what's happened before you go home to Pam.'

'I promise I won't ever look at another woman again.'

Jane smiled. 'It's all right to look, Tony.'

She gave him a hug and closed the cell door as she left him to think about what he was going to tell Pam.

CHAPTER TWENTY-ONE

It was 4 a.m. Saturday by the time an exhausted Jane got home. She didn't even bother to undress, and after setting the alarm for 7 a.m., she collapsed on her bed then fell into a deep sleep.

When the alarm went off Jane reached out with her hand, turned it off and thought she'd have another minute or two dozing before getting up. It was a bad mistake as she woke up again at 8 a.m. and realised she'd have to get a move on to be in work for 9 a.m. She had a quick shower and washed her hair and dried it. She decided to dress down and put on a T-shirt, roll neck jumper, jeans, black Puffa jacket and trainers. She was hungry, but didn't have time for breakfast, and was about to leave when the phone rang. She was going to ignore it but then thought it might be Tony.

'What time and where do you want to meet?' Pam asked.

Jane mentally cursed herself. 'I'm really sorry, Pam, I totally forgot we were going to go shopping and . . .'

She also realised that Pam was still unaware of Tony's arrest.

'You've got to work.'

'Yes, it's been non-stop the last couple of days and our DCI said we all have to work the weekend.'

Jane heard a sigh on the end of the line. 'Thanks a lot, Jane, I'd arranged for Mum and Dad to look after Nathan and told them you'd be round for supper.'

'Can you apologise for me, please?'

'No, I can't – you ring them. I'm tired of being the bearer of bad news where you're concerned.'

Jane tried to stay positive. 'We're only doing eight-hour shifts so I'll be finished by five and come over then – I should be there about six-ish.'

'And if I tell them that and you don't turn up, I'll get it in the ear.'

'All right, I'll ring them when I get to work.'

'Make sure you do.'

'Are you going shopping?'

'Yes, assuming Mum's still willing to look after Nathan.'

'Could you do me a favour and visit a men's outfitters and—'

Pam's tone changed from annoyed to amused. 'Got a new beau, have you? Not another detective, is it?'

'No, to both questions. One of our suspects in the robbery was wearing a grey newsboy cap—'

'A paper boy robbed the Securicor van?'

'No, stupid, it's a type of cap, that we want to show our witnesses. I'd be really grateful if you could get one for me and I'll pick it up this evening at Mum's and pay you back.'

Jane gave her a detailed description of the hat. Pam chuckled.

'Will that mean I'm on the Flying Squad?'

'Believe me, you might not want to be . . . Look, I've got to go, I'm running late. I promise we'll go shopping another time.'

Pam snorted. 'And pigs might fly.'

As she put the phone down Jane felt as if she had betrayed Pam's trust by not saying anything about Tony's arrest. She knew she'd told Tony she wouldn't, but feared if Pam found out she'd been to the station and then said nothing . . . Pam would never forgive her.

* * *

Jane got to work at just before nine and Teflon was already there. The Colonel and Bax were about to leave to visit Frank Braun, and Cam was sitting at Katie's desk reading the *Sun* with a coffee.

'You look like you've had a rough night – knock a few glasses of wine back when you got home, did ya?' Cam asked.

'No, I had a dodgy tummy and didn't get much sleep.'

'Dabs just rang in and said he forgot to tell you something about a lock last night.' He rummaged around the desk. 'Him and Stanley are going to meet outside the snooker hall later—'

'What did Dabs forget to tell me?' Jane asked impatiently.

'Keep your hair on, Sarge, I wrote it down but can't find the bit of paper . . .'

She sighed. 'Try under the bloody newspaper.'

He lifted it up. 'Oh, right. Here it is!'

'That's why he's only the fucking driver,' the Colonel muttered as he left the room with Bax.

Cam read out what he'd written: 'Dabs forgot to tell you that forensics said the lock on the burnt-out garage door was engaged when the fire brigade ripped it off.'

'OK. Any luck with the children's home the Wilson twins were sent to?'

'I'm waiting for Tottenham to get back to me with details of the homes on their patch, then I'll start ringing them.'

Jane suspected he hadn't even bothered to call them yet but thought it best not to pull him up on it, unless he didn't have a result when she got back.

'Is DI Kingston in yet?'

She needed to get to the bottom of what he'd said last night.

'He called in and said he had to deal with something at home, but he'd be in later.'

She walked over to her desk.

Teflon nodded. 'Morning, Jane. I rang Tottenham control room. The Bluebird cafe closes early on a Saturday, so it looks like we've got a few hours to spare before we can speak to the owner in private . . . You look a bit rough – you ill?'

'I'm fine,' she said tetchily, feeling a headache coming on from lack of sleep.

She got her pocket notebook out and looked at the notes of the conversation she had with Helen Clarke, the woman living at 40 Edgar House, then rang and asked her if she'd spoken to her husband about locking the garage. Helen apologised and said she'd forgotten to let her know he'd left the garage unlocked and empty as he didn't want thieves forcing entry.

Jane finished the call and turned to Teflon.

'The couple who own the garage where the burnt-out Cortina was found bought their flat through an estate agent's in Wanstead. The previous owner died, and the flat was sold on by one of her relatives. I'd like to visit the estate agents and see if we can find out who that relative was.'

'OK, but can I ask why?'

'It's a long shot, but the lab said the garage was locked after the Cortina was left in it and the estate agent only handed over one key for the garage to the present owners. It's possible there were two keys, and whoever has the other one may have used it to lock it after torching the car.'

Teflon nodded, impressed with her thinking. 'Sometimes the long shots pay off – so let's get going.'

'I'll drive,' Jane said.

'We'll take one of the squad cars – might stand out a bit less.'

'You don't like custard tarts, then?'

'Love 'em . . . just don't like being inside 'em.'

* * *

The Petty, Son and Prestwich office – 'Est. 1908' – was just off Wanstead High Street. As Jane and Teflon entered, a middle-aged man, smartly dressed in a blue three-piece pinstripe suit, white shirt and red tie, got up from behind a desk.

'Good morning. I'm Peter Petty, the grandson of our founder and current owner of the oldest estate agency in East London. Are you looking to purchase a property or rent?'

'Neither, sir. I'm WDS Tennison and this is DC Johnson.' They showed him their warrant cards.

'Is this about that abysmal O'Donovan family who rent the ground floor flat in Chaucer Road? The number of complaints I've had about their fighting and screaming at all hours is getting ridiculous. I'm just the letting agent, not the landlord, officer. I've asked them to keep the noise down, but Mrs O'Donovan always tells me to eff off.'

'No, it's nothing to do with that,' Jane assured him. 'We are trying to find out who the previous owner of flat forty Edgar House was. The current resident, a Mrs Clarke, said that your company dealt with the sale, which was about six months ago.'

'I don't recall dealing with that property myself – mind you, we do so many it's hard to remember them all.'

'Could you look in the file?' Teflon asked.

'Yes, of course. Hang on and I'll nip and get it.'

As they waited Jane looked at the pictures of the two- and three-bedroom properties for sale on the office walls.

'Are you thinking of moving, or just browsing?' Teflon asked.

'Bit of both, actually, but I don't fancy Wanstead.'

'Snaresbrook and Wood Green are just up the road. A mate of mine lives in one of the police accommodation flats in Snaresbrook and says it's a nice area.'

'Found it, officers . . . Julie Lane dealt with the sale but she's on maternity leave just now.'

Petty held up the file, then invited them to take a seat at his desk.

'Do you mind taking notes?' Jane asked Teflon, who got his pocket notebook and pen out of his coat.

Petty opened the file and took out the paperwork, then flicked through it before removing a page.

'Here we go – the previous owner of flat forty was a Mrs Elizabeth Smith. It says here she died of cancer and her son, whom I assume inherited her estate, sold the premises to the Clarkes for just under fifteen thousand pounds.'

'Do you have the son's details?' Teflon asked.

'Mr Graham Smith, flat forty Edgar House.'

'Is there any other address shown for him?' Jane asked.

'No, looks like he lived with his mother. There's a contact phone number if that's of any use.'

'Yes please,' Teflon said.

'01-808-3503 . . . Wanstead's on the 989 exchange, so that's not a local number.'

'Do you have any previous history of the premises prior to Mrs Smith buying it?' Jane asked.

'Only that it was owned by the local housing association when Mrs Smith lived in it, and then she bought it from them. I know the manager of the association, so I can make a quick call and ask him to check his files.'

'Thank you, Mr Petty, that would be very helpful,' Jane said.

Jane spoke quietly to Teflon as Petty called the association manager.

'The neighbour on one side of flat forty said Mrs Smith lived alone and a man in his mid-to late forties sometimes visited her. I didn't think anything of it at the time, but with what we know now it would be worth revisiting her to get a description of him.'

Teflon agreed and suggested they go to nearby Edgar House when they'd finished speaking to Mr Petty.

Petty put the phone down and looked at the notes he'd made of the conversation.

'Mrs Smith had lived in the flat for a number of years and the association knew Mrs Thatcher was going to introduce the government's "right to buy" scheme. They decided to test the waters and offered some long-standing residents the opportunity to buy their flats at a reasonable price – Mrs Smith being one of them. Her son paid just over ten and a half thousand pounds for it.'

Teflon whistled. 'That was a nice quick profit.'

'How did he pay?' Jane asked, wondering if they could locate him through a bank account.

'Cash.'

'All of it?' Jane and Teflon asked in unison.

'Yes.'

'How did Mrs Clarke pay him?'

'I don't know, the final exchange was dealt with by solicitors and they won't divulge that sort of information.'

'One last thing, Mr Petty . . . Do you know how many keys were given to Mrs Clarke for the flat?'

'He looked at the paperwork. 'Two flat door keys and one garage key.'

'Thanks for your assistance, Mr Petty, you've been very helpful.' Jane smiled. 'Could I have Julie Lane's contact details, please? I may need to speak to her.'

'Certainly. Is Mr Smith involved in some sort of fraud?'

'We think so, and we'd be grateful if you could keep what we've spoken about to yourself,' Teflon said.

'Of course – my lips are sealed,' he said, handing over Julie Lane's details.

'One more thing: do you sell property in Snaresbrook and Wood Green?' Jane asked.

'Yes, and beyond. Is there a particular premise or name you're interested in?' he asked, thinking it was crime-related.

'It's a personal question. I live in a one-bedroom flat in Marylebone and was thinking of looking for a house in those kind of areas – two, maybe three bedrooms with a garden.'

Petty looked pleased he finally had a potential customer on his hands.

'Please sit down and I'll show you what we've got.'

'Unfortunately, I've got another appointment to go to. Could I take some brochures with me?'

Petty quickly went through some filing cabinets and removed a number of sales brochures, which he put in a folder and handed to Jane.

'If you'd like to view any let me know and I'll make sure it's arranged for a time that's convenient for you. We can help as well in selling your flat and I'll halve our normal fees, as we do for all police officers we deal with.'

Jane nodded her thanks and they left.

'That long shot sounds like it was worth it – you thinking Mrs Smith's son might have the other key?' Teflon asked as they walked to the car.

'Could be, but if he's got rid of it there's no way I can prove he used it to lock or unlock the garage before the fire.'

'It's still worth making some more discreet enquiries about him. Sounds like he's crooked if he can stump up ten and a half K cash for a flat.'

'I totally agree. Can I borrow your pocket notebook please? I want to ring Cam and ask him to make enquiries with the Post Office and trace the owner and address for that 808 number Mr Petty gave us.'

He handed Jane his pocket notebook and she used a public phone booth to call Cam.

'I'll get straight on it and let you know the result when you next call in or return to the office.'

'How's the Wilson twins enquiry progressing?'

'I've got the details of two children's homes in Tottenham and was just about to ring one of them.'

'Good – I'll expect the results to be typed up by the time I get back!'

* * *

'What now?' Frank Braun asked when he saw the Colonel and Baxter at his front door.

'We just need to ask a few questions about your car,' the Colonel said.

He folded his arms. 'I've told you everything there is to know about the Cortina.'

'Actually, it's the BMW we're interested in—'

'My wife's out in it with the kids doing the shopping. I can assure you it's not on false plates or stolen, and it's insured and MOT'd,' he said bluntly.

'We'd like to see the documents,' Bax said.

'For Christ's sake, please have the decency to tell me what's going on as right now I'm beginning to feel really pissed off!'

Bax looked at the Colonel, who nodded.

'We're interested in who you bought the BMW from and how much you paid for it,' Bax said.

'An authorised dealer in Essex. It was two years old then and I paid a fair price for it.'

'We spoke to Paul Lawrence and he told us about your thirty-grand win on the pools. Did you use the money to buy the car?' the Colonel asked.

'Sure, and to buy this house – I can show you all the relevant documents to prove everything is legit.'

'Yes please,' the Colonel replied.

'Fine. Give me a moment and I'll dig them out.' He left the room.

'He sounds genuine,' Bax said.

'Yeah, looks like Lawrence was right. I've a feeling whoever nicked his wife's car key from her handbag must have seen something with their address on it.'

'Whoever nicked it must be connected to the blaggers,' Bax remarked.

'This is turning out to be a dead end here. I'll check the paperwork then we'll be off.'

Braun returned with a blue folder.

'All the documents for both cars are in here, and this is my bank statement that shows the deposit of the pools money and purchase of the car.'

He handed it to the Colonel, who read out the details of the garage where the BMW was purchased while Bax wrote them in his pocket notebook. The Colonel looked at the MOT for the BMW and noticed the 'GR Motors Ltd' inspecting stamp. He looked through the documents and found the MOT for the Cortina, which was also stamped 'GR Motors'.

'Is this a local garage?' He showed Braun the MOT.

'Yes, it's in Lordship Lane.'

'Do they sell cars?'

'Yes, second-hand ones. They do repairs and servicing as well as MOTs in a garage at the back.'

'What sort of cars do they sell?'

'Jags, Mercs, BMWs, Range Rovers – but it wouldn't surprise me if the mileage was clocked.'

'Do you know what GR stands for?'

He shrugged. 'No, I only use the place for MOTs and servicing as it's a lot cheaper than going to an authorised dealer.'

'Both MOTs are signed by a G. Smith, who presumably examined the vehicles and passed them as roadworthy. Can you describe him?'

'I've never met them and only used the place twice. Each time I made an appointment over the phone. I dropped the car keys off with the receptionist, Tina, and went back later to get the car.'

'Do you mind if I keep the Cortina MOT?'

The Colonel handed Braun the documents folder.

Braun shrugged. 'Feel free.'

'Is Bruce Grove near the garage?' Bax asked.

'Yes, it's just down the road. You think someone from the garage might have nicked our car for the robbery?'

'I can't say. And I'd ask that you keep this conversation between the three of us.'

'No problem. And should you need me as a witness, I'm happy to make a full statement and attend court.'

Bax showed him the artist's impression made from Fiona Simpson's description of the man driving the Cortina.

'Do you recognise this man?'

Braun squinted at the drawing. 'No, can't say I do.'

'Fair enough. Can I use your phone to call our office?' the Colonel asked.

'Help yourself. I'll put these back in the drawer,' he said, leaving the room.

'Looks like this wasn't a dead end after all,' Bax said.

The Colonel kissed the MOT.

'You little beauty. This bit of paper is a bloody gold mine, Bax.'

CHAPTER TWENTY-TWO

Dabs and Stanley entered the Bruce Grove Snooker Hall just after 11.30 a.m. It was already busy, with seven of the twelve snooker tables being used, and two of the six pool tables. At the far end there was a bar, behind which an attractive olive-skinned woman in her early thirties, with hazel eyes and long dark hair, was filling up the small refrigerators with bottles of beer and mixers.

'How can I help you, gentlemen?' she asked in a noticeable Spanish accent as they approached.

'We're thinking of becoming members,' Stanley said.

'You don't have to be a member to use the tables, but it works out cheaper if you play a lot. The first hour is on the house, so you can have a game, see what you think of the tables, then decide if you want to join.'

'Which table can we use?' Dabs asked.

'Help yourself to one. Would you like a drink?'

Stanley ordered a pint of lager and Dabs asked for a bitter shandy. As the barmaid was serving them a tall muscular man in his early thirties, with short dark brown hair and rugged features, came over and spoke to her. He was dressed in a black suit and white shirt and Stanley assumed he was the club bouncer.

'Maria, Tommy wants a word wit ya in his office,' he said in a distinct Irish accent.

'Will you mind the bar for me while I go see him?'

'Sure.'

'These two gentlemen are interested in becoming members and are going to have a game before deciding.'

'That's great. I'm Aidan, the club manager. If ya want ta join let me know and I'll get ye the forms ta fill in.'

As they set up the snooker table with the balls, Dabs whispered to Stanley, 'Did you notice the cut on his forehead?'

Stanley nodded. 'It looks recent.'

'We found a blood trail in Woodville Road and on the passenger sill of the Cortina. Jane and I thought it was possible the man who shot at the police car injured himself on the dashboard or window when the Cortina hit a parked car, then braked sharply.'

'The paddy is obviously Aidan O'Reilly and the barmaid Maria Fernandez,' Stanley said, and Dabs nodded.

'You've got to admit, this investigation is finally getting somewhere and it's all thanks to Jane,' Dabs remarked.

'I know, but don't keep looking over at the bar, you twat.'

'Sorry, I'm not used to all this undercover stuff.' Dabs got a coin out of his pocket. 'Heads or tails for who breaks off.'

He flicked the coin in the air and Stanley called tails.

* * *

Jane and Teflon had a wasted journey to Edgar House. The woman at number 42, who had seen a man visiting Elizabeth Smith, wasn't in. With time to spare they stopped at an off-licence so she could get a bottle of Jameson's Irish Whiskey for Kevin Bottomley, the collator, as she'd promised. They then went to Tottenham Police Station and had a light lunch before walking to Bruce Grove to look for suitable observation points and speak to Nick at the Bluebird cafe.

'I don't think using the cafe as an OP will work, Jane,' Teflon said. 'If the suspects park in Moorfield Road we won't be able to get photos of them going in or out of the cafe. That newsagent's on the corner would be better as it overlooks both the cafe and snooker hall.'

'You're right. We could see what Nick can tell us about the owner. The closed sign's up, so let's go and talk to him.'

Inside, a short, balding man in his late forties was picking up used plates with one hand, while using a cloth in the other to clean the table. He puffed on a cigarette that dropped ash on his food-stained chef's coat. Jane and Teflon checked no one was coming, especially from the snooker hall, before knocking on the cafe door. The man turned and glared, stubbed the cigarette out in an ashtray, then put the plates down.

'He looks like Friar Tuck,' Teflon remarked.

He opened the door a few inches.

'*Madonna mia*, can you no read the sign? It a say we are CLOSED!'

He started to close the door.

'Is Nick in?'

'Why you wanna know?' he asked warily.

Jane showed him her warrant card.

'I'm WDS Tennison and this is DC Jackson. We'd like to speak to Nick.'

'You a lookin' at him. My name is Nicola Bianchi, but I pay my taxes and don't allow no stolen property to be sold on my premises. *Che vuoi da me?*'

She smiled. 'It's nothing like that. We'd like to talk to you about some men who use your cafe—'

'You gonna take long, because I have to clean the place up, then go to the shops for supplies? This business doesn't run itself, you know.'

'We'll try not to take up too much of your time,' Jane said.

Nick opened the door and ushered them inside the cafe.

'*Alla tavola . . .*'

Nick gestured to a table and pulled a chair out for Jane.

'Is there somewhere out the back we could talk more privately?' she asked.

Nick looked surprised. 'What's this about?'

'If we could go somewhere more private I can tell you.'

'OK. My wife's is away just now, so we can go upstairs to the flat.'

'That would be ideal, thank you. PC Bottomley mentioned your wife hadn't been well – he asked me to send his regards to you both.'

'That's kind of him. My a wife's is suffering from breathing problems – she's staying with her brother in Southend. I'm hoping the sea air will do her good.'

As they walked through the downstairs kitchen the smell of cooking oil and fried food was almost overpowering. The living room was small, with a two-seater sofa, two armchairs and a four-place dining table. It was neat and tidy but, like the kitchen below, smelt heavily of cooking oil and fried food.

'Please sit down. Who are these men you wanna know about?'

Nick sat down in an armchair. Jane sat on the sofa with Teflon, who got out his pocket notebook to take notes.

She smiled. 'We were hoping you could help us with that. From our enquiries we know they are white, in their mid-forties to early fifties, and usually use your cafe on Monday and Friday mornings.'

She didn't want to give away too much information until they'd gauged Nick's willingness to help.

'I'm full of customers at that time: there's a decorators, plumbers, electricians, engineers – you name it, I get them all in my place.'

'These men like to sit at the far end, at the table by the wall,' Teflon told him.

'I need a some more clues if I'm gonna be able to help you,' Nick said, lighting a cigarette.

'One of them wears a chain with a little pair of gold boxing gloves,' she added.

His eyes lit up. 'Ah, OK, that's a gotta be Tommy, *il pugilatore* – he tell me he used to be a champion boxer. He owns the new snooker club over the road.'

'And the other man?' Teflon asked.

Nick shrugged. 'There's a few people I've seen sittin' with Tommy . . . but I think is probably his brother George you talkin' about. He's a bit older and sometimes has breakfast with him.'

'Does George smoke?' Jane asked.

Nick frowned. 'Yes, the big fat Cuban cigars. The smell upsets some of my regular customers as his cigar make more smoke than my bloody frying pans—'

'Do you know their surname?' she asked.

'No, they've only been coming in here a few months. I have a little chat sometimes with them, I like a *due chiacchiere* with my customers – is good for business.'

'Is George involved with the snooker club?' Teflon asked.

Nick shrugged. 'He could be, but I never ask him what he do and he never tell me. Have they done something bad?'

'We don't know . . . Some information we received suggests they might have, but for now we're just trying to find out more about them,' Jane told him.

'You said there are a few people you've seen sitting at that table with Tommy. Do you know their names?' Teflon asked.

'When the inside of the snooker club was being built, he used the cafe like it was his office and discuss the building work – so he was talking to lots of different people.'

'I meant more recently . . .' He turned to Jane. 'Have you got that description of the white lad who wears the designer polo shirts?'

She got her pocket notebook out of her bag and looked for the relevant entry.

'He's late twenties to early thirties, five feet eight tall, slim, with blue eyes and wavy blond hair down to his shoulders.'

Nick looked more curious. 'I thought you said you just wanted to know about two men?'

'We're also interested in their associates – any information about them could also be helpful.'

'Are you the CID from Tottenham?'

Jane and Teflon looked at each other, wondering who should answer and how much they should divulge. PC Bottomley had given Nick a clean bill of health, so Jane decided they could risk being more open with him.

'We're from the Flying Squad at Rigg Approach.'

Nick's bushy eyebrows shot up. 'You're from the bloody Sweeney!'

'We didn't want to alarm you – that's why I didn't mention it initially.'

'I don't know anything about any robberies . . . *Madonna mia!*'

He took a long drag on his cigarette, shaking his head.

'At present we have no hard evidence that either Tommy or George are involved in a robbery. We are just following up on some information received.' Jane tried to make it sound as routine as possible.

Nick looked concerned. 'I understand you have a job to do, but my wife, she is very ill already. If she knew you'd been here asking about a robbery, she would get upset and it would make her breathing worse. *Ti prego*, enough,' he said, waving his finger.

Jane nodded. 'I understand, and we've no intention of speaking to her. What you've told us is just background information and nothing incriminating against Tommy or George.'

'What a robbery you investigating?'

'A Securicor van,' Teflon told him, 'outside Barclays Bank in Leytonstone on Thursday morning—'

Nick's eyes narrowed. 'Was that de one on the news, where the policemen were shot and they crash the car?'

'Yes—'

'*Vigliacchi bastardi!*' he said with a look of anger in his eyes.

Jane quickly pressed their advantage. 'We want to arrest whoever is responsible before it happens again, and if these men are involved, we need your help.'

Nick stubbed his cigarette out, then ran his hand over his bald patch and took a deep breath.

'The young a man with long blond hair . . . I've a heard Tommy and George call him Carl – and George some time say, "You all right, son?". But I donna know if he is really son, you know?'

'Do they look like father and son?' Jane asked.

Nick thought for a moment. 'Not really, no.'

'Do you know if Carl works for Tommy or George?'

'Maybe George . . . I've seen him give Carl a big wedge of cash, but I dunno what for – and I don't ask.'

Jane looked in her pocket notebook. 'We're also interested in a white man who's about five feet eleven tall, with dark slicked-back hair. He wears a brown camel hair coat with a black suede collar.'

Nick smiled. 'I see him a couple of time in here, he's very smart and speak with, how you say . . . a plum in his mouth.'

'You mean he speaks with a posh accent?' Teflon asked.

'*Si*. I dunno his name, but he has a face I don't forget, 'cause he look alike the actor who play Dracula . . .' Nick paused to think of the name.

'Vincent Price?' Teflon suggested.

Nick raised his eyes. 'No, no Vincent Price – he never play Dracula . . . I mean the man in the black and white film.'

'Bela Lugosi?' Jane offered.

'Yes!'

'How old is he?' Teflon asked.

Nick shrugged. 'I dunno, he's dead now.'

'I meant the man in the camel hair coat,' Teflon said, stifling a laugh.

'He about fifty, fifty-five maybe.'

'Have you ever heard George talk to him – or anyone else – about a wedding?'

'Not to Mr Lugosi . . . but a few weeks ago Tommy ask a me if I can do catering for a big wedding at a cheap price as the caterers for a George's daughter's wedding charging a fortune. I know Tommy taking the piss so I ask how a many plates of full English breakfasts he wants. George no a look amused and told us both to eff off.'

'Do you know when or where the wedding is?'

He shook his head.

'Have you ever heard them talk about a robbery?' Teflon asked.

Nick looked offended. 'If I had, I would tell you. Mind you, sometimes when they talking, and I go to the table, they stop suddenly – so maybe they don't want me to hear what they saying.' He made to get up. 'If that is all, I need to start cleaning up now.'

'There's just a couple of other things . . .' Jane started to say.

Nick sighed. 'I already tell you all I know.'

'Do you know what types of cars any of the men drive?' she asked.

'I far too busy to look out the window and see what they drive.'

'The newsagent's on the corner of Moorfield Road – do you know the owner?' Teflon asked.

'*Si*, Paki Pete, he a good guy.'

'Is he trustworthy?'

Nick nodded. 'One hundred per cent.'

'I notice you had an advert in the window for a waitress,' Jane said.

'*Si*, but nobody applies yet. Why you ask?'

'Would you be willing to let me work undercover in your cafe for a few days?'

He looked surprised. 'Is no an easy job, and might be obvious to these men you after them if you make a mistake, you understand?'

'I did quite a bit of waitressing before I joined the police, so I know how to take orders and serve tables.'

'OK, if it help you find the *bastardi* who shoot the policeman, the job is yours. When you want to start?'

'Monday morning?'

'OK, I see you here at six, you can have a little practice, familiar-ise yourself with the menu, then we open at seven.'

He got up to show them out.

* * *

As soon as they got back to Tottenham Police Station, Teflon checked the names George and Carl Ripley on the PNC, on the assumption that they might be father and son, while Jane rang Cam to update him.

'Me and Teflon have spoken to Nick and—'

Cam wasn't listening. 'Murphy wants everyone back here now for a meeting.'

'Why, what's happened?'

'I can't explain it all on the phone. Let's just say there have been a few interesting developments.'

'Did you get a result on that phone number or the Wilson twins?'

'Yes, and I've spoken to the two children's homes.'

'What did they say?'

'I'll tell you when you get back.'

'You haven't done it, have you?' she snapped.

'I have, Sarge, so stop getting your knickers in a twist and get back here.'

She was about to make an angry retort, but he'd put the phone down.

'Everything all right, Jane?'

'That bloody Cam's a rude, lazy sod.'

'I won't argue with that.'

'Still, looks like the others have got some good results. Murphy said he wants us all back at the office asap, so we better get going.'

'I've run the name George Ripley on the PNC with a forty-five to fifty-five age spread and got a few possible hits—'

'Leave it for now, we'll have to do it back at Rigg.'

Teflon shut down the computer.

'Looks like your gut feelings about what the Wilson sisters told you were right.'

Jane thought back to what Kingston had said about Murphy.

'I hope so . . . But something tells me the road to getting our suspects charged and convicted is going to be a long and bumpy one.'

CHAPTER TWENTY-THREE

When Jane and Teflon walked into the office, they instantly felt the buzz of excitement in the room. Everyone looked focused as they got on with their work, whether it was on the phone or even just typing up their reports of the morning's events. The first thing she wanted to do was have it out with Cam, but he was making notes while on the phone. She was surprised when the Colonel, who was writing some notes, looked up and gave her an approving nod.

'All right, Sarge?'

'Yes, thanks. How'd it go with Frank Braun?'

'Good. I was wrong about him being hooky; I think he's straight up.'

She wanted to ask him what he'd found out, but he looked busy and she knew she'd find out in the meeting anyway.

Dabs was standing next to Stanley, who was talking on the phone.

'How was the snooker?' she asked.

'We played three frames: first one Stanley bets me a pound and loses, so he says double or quits, and I win the next two frames as well. The only thing positive for Stanley was meeting Aidan O'Reilly.' Dabs grinned.

'Why was that?'

Stanley nudged Dabs. 'Nip over to the fax machine, they're just about to send over the results and want to know if they're coming through our end. Give us a shout when it starts printing off.'

'Sorry, Jane.'

Dabs brushed past her to get to the fax machine.

She sighed. It looked like everything would have to wait until the meeting. Cam finally put the phone down and she marched over. Before she could speak, he handed her an information sheet.

'That's the result from the Post Office on the phone number—'

'And the Wilson twins?'

'That was the children's home I was just talking to. There's a few things about them that don't add up and I—'

'What do you mean "don't add up"?'

'It's just that they might not be who they say they are.'

'Are you playing games with me?' She glared at him.

'For fuck's sake, I did what you asked and you're still moaning.' He picked up a notepad and tore off the top sheet. 'They lived in St Cuthbert's, a Catholic home. The address and phone number's on there – you can ring them yourself if you don't believe me.'

He walked off towards Murphy's office before she could reply. She was sure he was going to complain about her to Murphy. She watched anxiously as he knocked on Murphy's door and opened it, but didn't go in.

'Everyone's back in the office, Guv.'

'Thanks, Cam, we'll be out in a second.'

'Guv wants to start the meeting,' Cam said loudly.

Everyone stopped what they were doing and turned their chairs towards the centre of the room.

Jane felt bad for misjudging him.

'I'm sorry for snapping at you earlier. What did St Cuthbert's say about the Wilson sisters?'

Cam shook his head. 'I'll tell you after the meeting.'

Murphy strode into the room, followed by a subdued-looking Kingston.

'Right, I'm going to ask the Colonel and Bax to start.'

He nodded to the Colonel to start, but the fax machine began whirring and humming as it printed off an incoming fax.

'Somebody turn that bloody thing off!' Murphy barked.

'It's some urgent information I requested. It shouldn't take long,' Stanley said.

Murphy sighed. 'Carry on, Colonel.'

'We spoke to Frank Braun and it's safe to say he's no longer a suspect,' the colonel said. 'I examined the documents for both his vehicles, and everything was in order.' He held up the MOT. 'But this little beauty is the MOT for his Cortina and I seized it as evidence.'

'You just said his vehicle documents were in order,' Cam said, looking puzzled.

'They are, but the garage stamp on the MOT was "GR Motors Ltd", located in Lordship Lane and close to Bruce Grove.'

Bax took over. 'We did a casual drive past and the premises has a "front", with about twenty high-end second-hand cars on it, like Jags, Mercs and BMWs. At the back there's a servicing, MOT and repair garage, as well as a separate office area, where, according to Braun, a young receptionist called Tina works.'

Murphy looked in his pocket notebook.

'The name Tina was lip-read by Rachel Wilson, wasn't it?' he asked Jane.

She nodded and looked in her pocket notebook.

'M1 said to M2 in the cafe, "If yesterday hadn't been a total fuck-up I could have paid our Tina's wedding off in cash."'

Murphy looked pleased. 'Interesting. Do we know who owns the garage?'

The Colonel shook his head. 'We're still working on it, Guv. Companies House isn't open until Monday, but I reckon there's a good chance GR could be the initials of the owner, so it could be Ripley.'

'What about the keyholder's card for GR Motors?' Murphy asked.

'There's no alarm on the premises or keyholder's card at Tottenham. The authorising vehicle inspector's signature on the MOT is "G. Smith".'

'You reckon he might have had a key cut in order to steal the car?' Dabs asked.

Bax nodded. 'The traffic officer's conclusion also supports that theory.'

Teflon looked at Jane, who nodded.

'Jane and I got some stuff that ties in with what the Colonel just said re GR. Nick, the cafe owner, said M1 is George and M2's called Tommy and they're brothers. He also said Tommy was the new owner of the snooker club, who we know, thanks to Jane, is Thomas Anthony Ripley.'

'That's good information, but we need some documentary evidence to prove GR Motors is owned by or connected to George Ripley. Have you run a PNC check on him?' Murphy asked.

'Yes, sir, and I got a few hits. I was going to print them off and go through them after the meeting. We also got some information about a Graham Smith from an estate agent's in Wanstead,' Teflon said.

'I don't recall authorising any enquiries at an estate agent's . . .' Murphy frowned.

Jane interjected. 'It was my idea to go there and make enquiries about the previous owner of forty Edgar House. I thought I'd mentioned it at the last meeting, but obviously I didn't,' she said, knowing that she'd informed Kingston and he'd told her to visit the estate agent's.

Murphy sighed. 'OK, tell us about Graham Smith.'

'He bought flat forty for his mother Elizabeth about a year ago and paid just over ten thousand pounds cash—'

'That's a lot of dosh,' Stanley remarked.

Jane continued, 'Then he inherited it when she died, and sold it through the Wanstead estate agent's for a tidy profit. Garage twenty-nine was owned by Mrs Smith, who, as far as I'm aware, didn't have a car, though she may have rented the garage out – or her son Graham could have used it and kept a key when he sold the flat.'

'That's all very interesting, Tennison, but Smith is not exactly an uncommon name, and you don't have any firm connections between the Colonel's G. Smith and yours.'

'I think she does, sir . . .'

Everyone looked over at Cam.

'Sergeant Tennison asked me to check out a phone number with the PO – it turned out to be registered to GR Motors Ltd in Lordship Lane.'

'Bloody hell, this gets better and better!' Baxter exclaimed.

'The estate agent had it as a contact number for Graham Smith when he was selling the Edgar House property,' Teflon added.

'Another thing you forgot to mention to me, Tennison,' Murphy growled.

'She didn't know – I forgot to give her the result when she got back to the office,' Cam explained.

She gave him a subtle nod of thanks and made sure the bit of paper with the phone number details was still in her pocket.

'Any description of your Mr Smith, Tennison?' Murphy asked.

'Not yet, sir.'

'Make it a priority to get as much as you can on him.'

'Yes, Guv. Would you like me to go over what the cafe owner told us?'

'After we've heard what Alex Higgins and Ray Reardon have to tell us,' he said drily, raising a few chuckles of laughter.

Stanley put on a stern face. 'The most important thing I have to tell you, sir – and everyone else in this room – is don't play snooker for money with this short-arsed bandit!'

'Didn't you know Dabs played for the Met?' the Colonel laughed.

'No, I did not!' He scowled at Dabs, who grinned back.

'Apart from you getting fleeced, what happened at the snooker hall?' Murphy asked.

Stanley gave detailed descriptions of Aidan, the manager, and the Spanish barmaid, Maria. Based on the registered keyholders for the snooker hall, he concluded that they were Aidan O'Reilly and Maria Fernadez.

Dabs emphasised the recent cut to O'Reilly's forehead and the blood trail at the Woodville Road scene and on the door sill of the Cortina, suggesting that the passenger in the getaway car had sustained a head injury.

'Any sighting of someone that might be Tommy Riley?' Jane asked.

Stanley shook his head. 'No, but Aidan told Maria that Tommy wanted to speak to her in his office, so he must have been on the premises.'

Murphy looked pleased. 'Good work, you two. Keep digging and see what else you can find out about them.'

'If O'Reilly is involved in the robbery, and the one who started shooting at the police car, it's hard to believe he hasn't any previous convictions,' the Colonel remarked.

'He could be using a false identity,' Bax suggested.

'It's possible, but when we were in the snooker hall it struck me that the Aidan O'Reilly we ran a PNC check on might not come up if he's only got a criminal record in Northern Ireland or the Republic – their PNC systems aren't linked to ours. I tried the Garda in Dublin first, but it was like pulling teeth – their systems are from the Stone Age. I then tried the RUC criminal records office in Belfast based on the detailed description and age range I gave them – they had four hits on the surname O'Reilly. I asked them to send the results through with copies of their fingerprints – that's why the fax machine's been whirring away.'

'Have you got something to compare the prints to?' Murphy asked.

'O'Reilly served me a drink, so I nicked the glass. I've already dusted it in my office and managed to lift a couple of good prints onto acetate, which I can compare to the ones the RUC fax over.'

'Nice work, Dabs. You and Stanley get the stuff off the fax and have a look through it while we continue the meeting.'

Dabs nipped out to get the fingerprints he'd lifted, while Stanley grabbed the sheets of paper from the fax machine and started to go through them.

Murphy looked at Jane. 'Let's hear what else the cafe owner had to say.'

She went over the details about the younger man, Carl, and the man in the brown camel hair coat.

'Is Carl related to any of them?' Murphy asked.

'He could be, but Nick didn't know for sure,' Teflon replied.

'Maybe Carl's the man who's marrying George's daughter Tina,' Dabs suggested as he examined the fingerprints.

'Did you find out any more about the wedding?' the Colonel asked.

'Nick knew about it, but not when or where it's going to be,' Teflon said.

'What about using his cafe for surveillance?' Murphy asked.

'It wasn't suitable due to the viewing angles, but the newsagent's on the corner of the road overlooks the cafe and snooker hall. We spoke to the owner, who's happy for us to use the upstairs and didn't ask any questions.'

'I asked Nick about doing some UC work as a waitress,' Jane added. 'He said I could start Monday—'

'That's an option worth considering, but let's not get ahead of ourselves—'

'We got a fucking hit!' Stanley shouted, waving one of the fax sheets in the air. 'Connor Aidan O'Reilly, aged thirty-six, born Belfast 1944, six feet four inches tall, with dark brown hair.'

He handed the sheet to Murphy, who squinted at the photo of O'Reilly.

'This mugshot looks old and the fax is blurry,' Murphy complained.

Stanley wasn't fazed. 'I know, but I can tell you it's him – and Dabs reckons the prints match, too.'

Dabs held up the sheets. 'I can't make a full sixteen-point identification – the prints aren't clear enough on the faxes.'

Stanley frowned. 'Are you now saying they're not a match?'

'From what I've got in front of me I can only identify twelve points that are the same, so—'

'That doesn't answer my question, Dabs.'

'Calm down and let me finish, will you? What I can say is that the source of the fingerprints on the glass is a highly probable match to the prints held on file by the RUC . . .'

'Christ! So they are a match!' Stanley snapped.

'In my opinion, yes,' Dabs explained patiently. 'But I need a second fingerprint expert to confirm it for any arrest or court purposes. A decent copy of the prints from the RUC would help.'

Murphy held his hand up. 'All right, stop bickering . . . For now I'm happy with your "expert opinion" that the prints are a probable match. Get the RUC to send a decent copy to fingerprint bureau at the Yard, then another expert can examine them. What sort of criminal record has O'Reilly got?'

Stanley looked at the rap sheet. 'Not a lot, and mostly when he was a teenager – just theft and a couple of burglaries. There's one for reckless GBH when he was eighteen, though. He did three years for that.'

'Doesn't exactly sound like the headcase we're looking for, though,' Cam remarked.

Stanley picked up another faxed page marked 'confidential'.

'It's what he *hasn't* been convicted of that's more interesting. According to his intel file he's a bare-knuckle fighter with a reputation as a hard man and "fundraiser" for the UDA.'

'Who the fuck are they?' Bax asked.

The Colonel shook his head in disbelief.

'Christ, you're an ignorant fucker, Bax. The Ulster Defence Association – they're a paramilitary loyalist group who protect Protestant districts from IRA attacks. The reality is both sides are just a bunch of murdering thugs.'

Stanley continued, 'O'Reilly was suspected of running a protection racket in Belfast, where he blackmailed and extorted money for the UDA from construction firms, building sites, pubs and shops.'

'Now that does sound more like the guy we're interested in,' Cam remarked.

'It gets better,' Stanley said. 'In 1978 three businessmen decided to testify against him on the condition their identities remained hidden. Someone leaked it to O'Reilly and one of them was shot dead by a masked gunman in front of his wife and children. The others then withdrew their allegations and the case against him collapsed.'

He handed Murphy the intel fax.

'Was O'Reilly arrested for the murder?' Teflon asked.

'Yes, but he was given an alibi by two of his henchmen, which the RUC couldn't disprove, so they had to release him.'

'Why did he come to London?' Teflon asked.

Stanley shrugged. 'Don't know. The intel report doesn't mention it, so the RUC may not even know he's here.'

'Could be he needed to lie low for a while,' Bax suggested.

'Or he was worried the RUC would fit him up.' The Colonel grinned.

Murphy handed the fax back to Stanley.

'O'Reilly could have come to London for any number of reasons; it's what he's up to right now that we need to focus on. He's clearly a dangerous criminal who will undoubtedly be surveillance conscious.' He paused for thought, then looked at Teflon. 'Print off the PNC hits on George Ripley for me, and the recorded convictions.'

'Yes, Guv,' Teflon replied, thinking he meant later.

'Now, please. I want to see if he has any joint convictions and who with.'

Teflon went over to the PNC terminal, sat down and started to type in George Ripley's details while Murphy continued with the meeting.

'You've all worked hard today and proved that good teamwork produces positive results. I think we can all agree there's evidence, albeit circumstantial, that the Ripley brothers, Aidan O'Reilly and most probably Graham Smith are involved in the Leytonstone robbery. We need to find out who Carl is as he may be part of the gang; likewise the man in the camel hair coat, and what was in the envelope he handed to George Ripley.'

'Are we gonna nick 'em, Guv?' Bax asked.

'Although Rachel Wilson appears to be a credible witness and her evidence is enough to arrest and interview them on suspicion of robbery, I believe—'

Cam interrupted. 'I'm not so sure about the Wilson sisters being credible, Guv.'

'Why?' Murphy asked.

Cam went to Katie's desk to get the notes of the conversation he'd had about the twins.

'I spoke to a nun at St Cuthbert's children's home, who remembered young twins coming there in 1958 after a car crash, but their names were Emira and Rasheda, the children of Mehmet and Emine Osman, Turkish Cypriots who came to the UK in the early fifties and lived in Wood Green.'

'Are you saying the Wilson twins are those two girls?' Jane asked.

'Yes. The nun told me Rasheda became deaf as a result of the crash and Emira had a deformed left hand.'

Murphy turned to Jane. 'Does Emma Wilson have a deformed left hand?'

'Yes, she does, she injured it in the car crash when her parents died,' she replied.

'OK, carry on, Cam.'

'Emine Osman didn't die in a car crash – but I'll get to that in a minute. I managed to speak to a home beat PC at Wood Green who's been there nearly thirty years. He told me Mehmet Osman used the name Micky Osbourne, and had a fearsome reputation in the Turkish community as a loan shark and slum landlord. He exploited and harassed his tenants with physical violence and threats to get what he wanted. Sometimes he'd kill their domestic pets and hang them from a lamp post with their entrails dangling out. No one was prepared to stand up to him, but then he went overboard with his fists and put Emine in a coma. He told the hospital she fell down the stairs, but the doctor told the police her injuries were not consistent with a fall and she wasn't expected to live, so Osman was circulated as wanted. Two days later a patrol car stopped him on the A20 heading towards Dover. The radio operator approached on foot and was standing by the driver's door when Osman stuck a gun in his stomach and shot him dead. A pursuit followed and Osman crashed head-on into an HGV, went through the windscreen and died instantly. No one knew his daughters were in the back of the car until afterwards.'

'Bloody hell, our star witness is the daughter of a cop killer,' Bax said.

'Looks like you might have been lied to, Tennison,' Murphy said with a hint of a smile.

'But surely you can understand why they might want to hide their past . . .' she argued.

'Did those girls ask for any favours in return for making a statement?' Murphy asked.

She was in two minds about whether to lie, but she'd already spoken to Kingston about helping the twins get a move off the Broadwater, and he might have told Murphy.

'Emma's manager at the Co-op told me that she and Rachel were being harassed by local youths. He'd helped her write some letters to the council to get a move, but nothing happened—'

'You're not answering my question, Tennison,' Murphy interrupted. 'Did either of them ask *you* to help them?'

Jane knew she was in a corner.

'Emma asked if I could write a letter to the council. I advised her it was best to report the abuse incidents to Tottenham CID, as the local police would be in a better position to assist them.'

Murphy frowned. 'They never reported any of these alleged abusive incidents?'

'Only because they feared further harassment if they did.'

'This raises serious questions about Rachel Wilson's credibility as a witness. And offering to help her could be regarded as an inducement for her to lie.'

'Rachel never told me about the abuse incidents or asked me to write a letter to the council—'

'She could have been encouraged by her sister to make the whole thing up after they read about the robbery in the paper,' Murphy said.

Jane tried hard to keep her emotions under control. She knew Murphy didn't really believe what he was saying; it was just a way to belittle her in front of the team. But she was determined not to let him.

'What she lip-read in the cafe was on the Monday before the robbery. If she's making it all up, she seems to have got a lot right.'

Teflon stepped forward and handed Murphy a PNC printout.

'I don't think she could make this up. I just got a hit on a George Ripley aged fifty. Previous conviction for robbing a jeweller's when he was twenty-six and his co-defendant was Graham Smith, then aged twenty-four. Both men used hammers to threaten the staff and smash open the glass jewellery showcases – they both got ten years in Pentonville. They've also got form for handling stolen goods, theft and burglary. George Ripley's been off the radar since the robbery, but Smith got nicked two years ago for assault on a customer while working at GR Motors. He claimed self-defence and was found not guilty. He fits the age, hair colour and height range from Fiona Simpson for the man driving the getaway car. The mugshot taken when he was charged with the assault is remarkably like her artist's impression.'

Jane watched Murphy's eyes widen when he looked at the mugshot. He then handed it to Kingston who, for the first time during the meeting, had something to say.

'Simpson also said he's got long sideburns, which he clearly has in this photo. If it wasn't for Tennison interviewing the Wilson sisters, we'd still be chasing our tails.'

There were nods and mutters of agreement around the room, but Murphy remained stone-faced. Jane now realised Kingston's warning about Murphy had been genuine and gave him a grateful smile. Kingston gave her a quick nod in return, then turned to Murphy.

'It might be best if Jane spoke to the Wilsons and asked about their parents before we make any judgement.'

'Fine, but with another officer present.'

'You could always consider re-interviewing Rachel Wilson with a court-approved sign language interpreter present,' Kingston suggested.

Murphy frowned. 'I'll think about it, if and when we need her as a court witness. For now just find out more about her family background.'

'Jane, did you say Rachel Wilson reckoned George Ripley said the name "Judge"?' Stanley asked.

She looked in her pocket notebook.

'Yes, he picked up the pepper pot, then slid it across the table as if it represented a vehicle and said, "Once I've robbed the van, Judge pulls up here, we fuck off and change motors up the road."'

Stanley grinned. 'A common nickname for someone called Smith is "Smudge" or "Smudger". Maybe she lip-read Smudge as Judge.'

Kingston had more to add.

'Another positive is the Graham Smith mugshot. We can put it into an album for Fiona Simpson to view at the Yard. If she picks him out it's a massive leap forward, as we'll have one of the gang positively identified.'

'I want Fiona Simpson taken up the Yard tomorrow morning,' Murphy said. 'It's Sunday, so she won't be opening up until midday – plenty of time to get her up there and back.'

'I'll give her a ring after the meeting and arrange to pick her up in the morning, early,' Kingston agreed.

Murphy shook his head. 'I want you here in the office with me tomorrow, planning the surveillance operation starting Monday morning.'

'We'll need to call in support from the other Flying Squad units if we're going to carry out static and mobile surveillance on all the suspects,' Kingston suggested.

'I know. We can also ask the central surveillance unit at the Yard to help out. I want the rest of today and tomorrow spent finding out where Graham Smith and George Ripley live, and double-check the addresses we have for O'Reilly and Tommy Ripley.'

'Are we going to arrest Smith if Simpson picks him out?' Stanley asked.

'It's an option, but not one I'm keen on pursuing. Right now I want to know more about them, and in particular their finances. That snooker hall will have cost Tommy Ripley a good few quid. I want to know if he paid cash or got a loan. Same with George Ripley, as their businesses could be a front to launder the proceeds of their crimes. The Leytonstone robbery was a disaster for them, and they made peanuts out of it, so my guess is they're planning something big.'

Jane looked in her pocket notebook.

'According to Rachel Wilson, George Ripley did say on Friday in the cafe, "If yesterday hadn't been a total fuck-up I could have paid our Tina's wedding off in cash and had enough left over for her bloody honeymoon." But then again, she might have made it up,' she added with a straight face.

'If we nick them on the plot, we won't need her as a witness,' Murphy retorted. 'Cam, draw me up a list of all the phone numbers we've got so far that are connected to our suspects and I'll ask for authority to wiretap them. Colonel and Bax, concentrate on George Ripley, Stanley and Cam on Tommy and O'Reilly, Teflon and Tennison, take Simpson up the Yard and revisit the Wilson twins. All of you see if you can find out more about Carl and the man in the camel hair coat.'

'Does that mean I'm manning the phones tomorrow?' Dabs asked.

'Yes, but I want you to do a full forensic report on everything we have so I can use it as supporting evidence when I apply for the wiretaps. Anyone else got a question? Good, now get to work. We need to nail these bastards before they have a chance to organise another job. Next time somebody might get killed.'

CHAPTER TWENTY-FOUR

Jane looked at her watch as Teflon drove to the Broadwater Farm estate; it was half past four, and she figured she could still get to her parents' for supper by six. She wondered if Tony would be there and what state of mind he'd be in. She hoped he wasn't, in case he inadvertently let slip he'd recently seen her.

'Thanks for agreeing to see the Wilson twins with me today.' she said.

'No problem. It will give us more time to concentrate on our other enquiries tomorrow.'

'I've got to go with the Colonel to meet his informant, but that's at 7.30 in Brick Lane, so I should be back at the office before nine. Then we can collect Fiona Simpson and take her to see the albums.'

'The man she saw in the driver's seat of the Cortina has to be Graham Smith.'

'I just hope she picks him out.'

'Even if she does, Murphy won't arrest him yet. He wants them all bang to rights, cash and guns in hand on the plot, so he can put them away for a long time.' He paused, then gave her a side-on glance. 'You've done well, Jane.'

'Thanks.'

She smiled over at him and for a moment their eyes met. She quickly turned away, feeling herself flushing. He was a handsome man, and she couldn't help being attracted to him, but another relationship with a police officer – let alone one of the Flying Squad – was definitely not in her plans.

Why don't I ever meet anyone nice outside the job? she wondered.

'For now, I'm not going to tell Rachel, or Emma, anything about the suspects we've identified or what we know about them,' she said, bringing her focus back to the job in hand.

'I agree with you. Looking ahead, it might be better not to put Rachel through the experience of giving evidence in court against men like them. I'll park here in Willan Road; it's only a short walk to Tangmere House.'

'Kingston was very quiet at the meeting,' Jane remarked as they got out of the car.

'According to the Colonel he had a massive bust-up with his wife last night.'

'I hope it wasn't too serious,' she said, hoping he'd say more.

'Keep it to yourself, but apparently when she got home last night, Katie decided to tell her boyfriend she was having an affair with Kingston. He then phoned Kingston's wife while we were all in the pub, so no surprise all hell broke loose when he got home.'

'Bloody hell,' Jane said, wondering what else Katie had said.

'Kingston's a good detective and a decent bloke – but he's only got himself to blame when it comes to his home life. His wife is a lovely, attractive woman. For the life of me I can't understand why he goes out looking for a burger when he's got steak at home.'

Jane didn't much like what the analogy implied about her, so she quickly changed the subject.

'I know Murphy wanted you there when I speak to the twins about their family, but I was thinking it might be best if I spoke to Emma alone.'

'That's fine by me. I could go through the cars section in *Exchange & Mart* with Rachel while you do that,' he said. 'What a surprise – looks like the lift's working.'

A young couple stepped out of it as they entered the foyer. Jane winced at the thought.

'I'd rather walk up the stairs.'

Teflon smiled, turning away from the lifts. 'You might be right.'

When they got to the right floor, Jane knocked on the door of flat 68 and it was quickly opened by Emma.

'Hello, Jane, please come in.'

'Thanks. This is my colleague Lloyd Johnson.'

Emma shook hands with him.

'How's your investigation going? Were the men in the cafe involved in the robbery?'

'The investigation is progressing well, and thanks to Rachel's information we have some interesting leads.'

Emma looked pleased. 'That's good news. She's in the living room doing some drawings and will be eager to know what's happened. I've been sewing and stitching a little present for you.'

'You didn't need to do that.'

'It's not much, just a way of thanking you for offering to help us with the council.'

'Get out of that one,' Teflon whispered.

Rachel was sitting in an armchair with her back to the living room door and wasn't aware anyone had entered the room. She was drawing in an A4 sketchbook. Emma walked in front of Rachel and signed that Jane and her colleague had come to see them. Rachel jumped up with a smile as she signed 'hello', then gestured to them to sit down on the sofa. As they sat down, she showed them her drawing of a man's face. Jane was astonished by how lifelike it was, and her eyes were instantly drawn to the pair of boxing gloves on a chain around the man's neck.

'Is that M2?'

Rachel nodded and turned back a page, revealing another drawing, then wrote M2 next to it with a pencil.

'They're brilliant, Rachel, and they'll be very useful to us,' Jane said.

'Definitely better than most police artists' impressions,' Teflon remarked.

'She has a photographic memory,' Jane said.

Rachel flicked back another page, which had a drawing of a young man with hair down to his shoulders.

'I take it that's the good-looking man who wears the polo shirts with a crocodile on them?' Jane asked.

Rachel had a twinkle in her eyes as she smiled, and nodded her head repeatedly with a childlike innocence.

Emma looked at Teflon. 'She likes him . . . a lot.'

Rachel frowned at her sister and handed Jane the sketchbook.

Jane opened her shoulder bag and took out the *Exchange & Mart* paper Kingston had given her. As Jane spoke Emma signed to her sister.

'I'd like you to go through the cars for sale section with my colleague Lloyd and see if you can identify the car the man in the camel hair coat was driving.'

Rachel nodded and signed to Emma.

'She said she can try and draw it if you want.'

'Look through the magazine first, then if you don't see the car do the drawing. Meanwhile I'll help Emma make a nice cup of tea for us all.'

'Can I have a coffee with milk and sugar please?' Teflon asked.

Jane followed Emma to the kitchen.

'Is something wrong, Jane?' a worried-looking Emma asked.

'What makes you think that?'

'You didn't say anything about your investigation to Rachel and seemed eager to be alone with me.'

Jane realised Emma was more perceptive than she thought.

'Actually, there is something I need to speak to you in private about.'

'Do those men know it was Rachel who told you about them?' she asked, with a genuine look of concern.

Jane shook her head emphatically. 'We haven't spoken to them and only my team know about you and Rachel.'

'Was it them that committed the robbery and shot the police officers?'

'We don't know for certain, and even with what Rachel told us we haven't enough to arrest them – so there's nothing for you to worry about.'

'That's a relief. Can I tell Rachel?'

'Of course. What I want to speak to you about concerns yours and Rachel's childhood.'

'There's not much to tell, really. As you know, our parents died in a car crash and we were raised in a children's home.'

'Was it St Cuthbert's in Tottenham?'

'Yes, why do you ask?'

'A colleague of mine spoke to a nun at St Cuthbert's. She told him about twin girls called Emira and Rasheda Osman, who were sent there in 1958 after a car crash.'

'I've never heard those names before.' Emma looked away nervously.

'The nun said one girl was deaf and the other had a deformed left hand as a result of the crash. To me, there can be no doubt she was talking about you and Rachel.'

Emma sighed and looked at Jane. 'After the crash we were both in hospital for some time, then our uncle looked after us for a week while he finalised the arrangements for us to go to St Cuthbert's. The Mother Superior decided to change our names to Emma and Rachel Wilson. Rachel was withdrawn and isolated in a world of deafness, she needed me to support her, but after a year and a half I was sent to live with a family and Rachel remained at the home.'

Jane was stunned. 'They split you up? Why on earth did they do that?'

'They liked to foster children out whenever they could, though some siblings were kept together.'

'After what you and Rachel had been through, I would have thought it crucial you were kept together.'

'I still remember one of the nuns at the home telling me no one wanted a deaf and dumb girl to look after. Even though I was eight by then, I knew she was expressing her own feelings as well. I missed Rachel terribly and asked my foster parents if they would take me to the care home, but they told me it wasn't a good idea as it would make me miss her more, and the same for her.'

'You obviously kept looking for her, though.'

'Of course . . . I eventually found out she'd been moved from St Cuthbert's, but no one would tell me where. I was beginning to feel there was nothing else I could do. When I was twenty-one I worked as a seamstress at a dressmaker's in Hackney and rented a single room in a bedsit. One day, out of the blue, a girl came up to me while I was in Woolworths shopping and started waving her hands at me. I hadn't a clue what she was doing, until an older woman with her said she was using sign language.

Jane smiled. 'Oh my God! Was it Rachel?'

'No, the girl was with her mother and thought I looked exactly like a deaf friend of hers. It dawned on me she might have thought I was Rachel so I spoke to the mother, who told me her daughter had been a day pupil at the Asylum for the Deaf and Dumb in Lower Clapton. It turned out Rachel was sent there from St Cuthbert's, and it was a proper school where she'd been a resident pupil for years. The mother told me Rachel was still there and teaching sign language. I couldn't believe we were living a mile apart in the same area and never knew it. I went straight to the school to see her.'

'It must have been a wonderful feeling when you saw each other again after all those years apart.'

There was a broad smile on Emma's face. 'It was beyond belief, Jane. It's hard to explain the mixed emotions when you find someone you thought you'd never see again. We both cried floods of tears as we hugged each other and vowed we'd never be parted again.'

'If you were both living in Hackney, how did you end up on the Broadwater?'

'When Rachel started working at the Tottenham sorting office it made sense to apply to Haringey Council for accommodation. We'd been orphans at St Cuthbert's and I'd spent my teenage life living with different foster parents in Haringey. I applied to the council and they immediately offered us a flat on the Broadwater Farm – we didn't know what the estate was like.'

'The nun at St Cuthbert's also told us your father, Mehmet, was being chased by police when he crashed the car with you and your sister.'

Emma's eyes narrowed at the mention of her father, but there was also a sadness in her face.

'Did the nun tell you he killed our mother and a police officer?'

Jane nodded. 'I can understand why you and Rachel didn't want to tell me the truth about everything that happened . . . It's OK.'

'Rachel lost her memory as a result of the car crash. The nuns said it was best I never told her how Mama died, and they led her to believe she was killed in the car crash. My father beat her to death in front of us. I'm glad Rachel doesn't know the truth, and as long as I live I'll never tell her.'

Jane was shocked. 'You witnessed the assault on your mother?'

Emma nodded. 'We cowered in a corner, holding each other tight, as Mama screamed in pain and begged him to stop. The last thing I remember was the way she tried to reach out to us as she lay on the living room floor in a pool of blood. I put my hand out towards her, but he stepped between us and shouted at us to go to our room.'

'Did you see him shoot the policeman as well?'

Emma looked close to tears as she recalled the painful events of her past.

'The bastard didn't care about anyone but himself – our lives were ruined because of him. He'd take a belt to us if we misbehaved, Mama would cry and he'd blame it on us, then when he hit Mama with a belt, we just accepted his behaviour as normal . . .'

She paused and took a deep breath before continuing. Jane could see the hatred for her father in her eyes.

'But when I saw what he did to Mama that day with his fists, I realised he was evil – just like those men in the cafe.'

'I'm so sorry, Emma . . . I can't begin to imagine what effect that must have had on your lives.'

'My father was punished by God for his sins,' Emma continued. 'But the reality is he got away with nearly killing me and Rachel, and murdering Mama and the policeman. I'm glad he died, but part of me will always feel he should have been tried and sent to prison.'

'I understand now why you wanted Rachel to tell me about the men in the Bluebird cafe.'

Emma looked imploringly at Jane. 'Promise me you'll never tell her the truth about our father and what he did to Mama . . . It would break her heart.'

'You have my word on it. We'd better finish making these drinks and take them through, or Rachel will wonder what's going on.'

As they walked into the living room Rachel signed to Emma, asking if everything was all right.

'We were just chatting about your drawings, then I showed Jane some of my dress patterns.'

Emma handed her sister a cup of tea. Jane could tell from the look on Rachel's face she suspected her sister wasn't being truthful. She handed Teflon his coffee.

'Any luck with the car?'

'Looks like your Camel Hair Coat Man was probably driving a Jensen Interceptor.'

'That's a sports car, isn't it?'

He grinned and shook his head. 'Saying that would be sacrilege to a Jensen owner. The cars are classed as GTs, which means Grand Tourer, from the Italian *gran turismo* – luxury high performance cars that are designed for long-distance driving, like Aston Martins,

Ferraris and Maseratis. Jensen stopped producing cars in 1976, but a new one back then would have cost you around eight grand.'

Jane smiled. 'I didn't take you for a car buff.'

'I'm not, but my dad is. He gets *Classic Cars* magazine every month and lets me have them when he's finished. I like to dream about cruising an alpine road in an Aston Martin.'

Rachel signed and Emma translated.

'She said, "You never know, one day you might win the pools or Premium Bonds and be able to buy one."'

'I'd get stopped by the police every five minutes if I was driving a Jensen – or any expensive car for that matter,' he said wryly.

Emma signed while Jane explained to Rachel that her information about the men in the cafe had proved useful and was still being followed up, but there was no direct evidence to suggest they had committed, or were about to commit, a robbery. Rachel smiled and signed that in some ways that was a relief. She was worried about using the cafe after telling Jane what she had lip-read.

'I want you to know, if you use the cafe on Monday morning, I might be in there working undercover as a waitress. If I am there it's important that you don't do anything that might give away you know me.'

Rachel looked anxious and signed quickly.

'She's worried you told Nick about her.'

Jane shook her head. 'Don't be. He doesn't know that you've spoken to me and, like I promised you, he never will.'

Rachel sighed with relief and signed, asking if Jane would like her to stop using the cafe for a bit.

'It's entirely up to you, Rachel, but I'd be grateful if you'd continue going in and lip-reading what the men talk about.'

She looked at Emma for advice.

'I think you should if it will help their investigation, but like Jane said, it's up to you.'

Rachel licked her lips as she thought about it, then agreed that she would go to the cafe on Monday morning.

* * *

As Jane and Teflon walked towards the stairwell to leave, Emma called out to them.

'I wasn't entirely truthful with you about why I needed to get away from the estate. We did suffer abuse from some local teenagers, and occasionally a few adults. We even had "weirdos" and "psycho twins" painted on our front door. I genuinely feared reporting it to the police would make matters worse, so we chose to ignore it and tried to avoid the people responsible when we were coming and going from the flat. Then one day everything suddenly changed. Someone had repainted our front door and the abuse stopped. If the kids saw us coming, they'd walk off or look the other way.'

'Sounds like "someone" had a word in their ear and told them to stop. Do you know who it might have been?' Jane asked.

'At first, I didn't, but after a few weeks I discovered it was Uncle Asil, our father's brother.'

Jane looked perplexed. 'The same man who abandoned you twenty-two years ago?'

Emma nodded. 'He worked for my father and returned to Cyprus after his death. He came back to England a few years ago and found out where we lived. I wrote the letters to the council about a move to get away from him . . . Asil is a criminal, just like my father was.'

'It sounds like you've spoken to him.'

'He waited for me outside my work one day. I didn't know who he was at first, but he called me Emira and I could see the resemblance to my father. I told him I wanted nothing to do with him and walked away, but he begged me to hear him out and said he only wanted to help me and Rachel. I said we were fine and didn't need his help, but he followed me and said he was already helping us.'

Jane guessed what Asil had done.

'He'd threatened the people on the estate who were abusing you.'

'Not him directly. He hired some people to find us, they witnessed it and he told them to sort it out.'

'So you did talk with him.'

'Yes, I couldn't get away from him. He told me he never worked for my father and sent us to St Cuthbert's because he was unable to raise us on his own. Now he'd returned to the UK he wanted to make amends, but I told him Rachel and I would never forgive him and not to come near us again or I would call the police. He handed me a large envelope and said it contained twenty-five thousand pounds, which we could use to buy a place of our own. I told him I didn't want his ill-gotten gains and threw it back at him. Then he handed me a business card and tried to convince me he owned a company in Cyprus that exported fruit for big supermarkets. I knew he was lying, tore the card up and walked away.'

'When did you speak to him?'

'About two months ago.'

'And you haven't heard from him since?'

'No, but I'm sure he's watching us. You have to understand I can't risk Rachel finding out the truth. If we can get moved off the estate then he won't be able to find us.'

'He has already, and he will again if he wants to. The good thing is that so far he hasn't turned up here. I'm grateful you've told me the truth, Emma, but knowing what I do now puts me in a difficult position. I can't lie to the council to help you get a move—'

'And I can't tell them the truth for Rachel's sake.'

'Leave it with me for now. My detective inspector was arranging for a local detective to speak to you next week. I'll have to tell him about our conversation today and seek his advice about the best way forward, then I'll let you know what he suggests.'

On the way back to the car Jane told Teflon about her conversation with Emma in the kitchen.

'That puts everything in a different light,' he remarked.

'I wouldn't want Rachel standing up in court where the defence could use her family past against her and she wouldn't have a clue what they were talking about.'

'In that case, do you think you did the right thing by asking her to keep helping us?'

'We can use what she tells us as intelligence and not evidence. That way we won't need to call her as a witness and can protect her identity.'

'That's good thinking, but I'd run it by Murphy first and let him make the decision.'

He opened the driver's door. She got in the passenger seat and looked at her pocket notebook.

'Do you want to get off home now or are you happy to carry on working?'

'I'm easy. Where do you want to go?'

He started the car and prepared to drive off.

'I was thinking of visiting Abby Jones. She's the young girl who saw the man shooting at the police car—'

'Didn't Murphy say to hold off on her for now?'

'Yes, but I've a gut feeling she may have seen O'Reilly's face. What she said to me at the scene doesn't add up.'

He frowned at Jane. 'That will piss Murphy off big time – and that's not something you want to do right now.'

She checked something in her pocket notebook.

'I asked Abby to describe the tall man who got out of the passenger seat of the Cortina. She told me he was wearing a balaclava, even though every other witness said he was wearing a brown stocking mask.'

Teflon shrugged. 'The poor kid obviously made a mistake – which is understandable when there are bullets flying round your head and police cars crashing in front of you.'

'From where the getaway car stopped in Woodville Road there were two trails of blood. One ran to the middle of the road, where several drops were confined to a small area, which indicates someone was standing there. The fired cartridge cases were near there as well, and the direction of the other blood trail was returning to where the car had been—'

He was starting to get frustrated with her stubbornness.

'I think maybe it's best we call it a day.'

But Jane wasn't going to be deterred.

'If the man who fired the handgun at the police car had a cut to his forehead, you'd expect the stocking mask to soak up the blood and maybe leave a few drops here and there.'

'What's your point, Jane?'

'If the blood was being soaked up by the stocking it would spread like ink on blotting paper, making it difficult to see. We think O'Reilly was the man who fired the handgun, and we know he has a cut to his head. I believe he took the stocking mask off before he got out of the getaway car because he couldn't see with it on. Abby wasn't mistaken; she lied because she was frightened. But if she can identify O'Reilly in a line-up, we've got him. Likewise, if Fiona Simpson can identify Graham, plus we can link them to the Ripley brothers—'

'Even if Abby Jones agrees to do an ID parade, she might bottle it on the day, then you're left with nothing. You nick them on the plot, and they're all fucked in one hit.'

'That could happen, but we won't know unless we speak to her. If she agrees to look at an ID parade, we can tell Murphy, then he can decide on the next move.'

'He'll still be pissed off.'

'God forbid the next robbery our suspects commit should go wrong again. Like Murphy said, one of us – or worse, an innocent bystander – could get killed ... all because we want to make a pavement arrest.'

He sighed and shook his head. 'Christ, you can be infuriating at times . . . What's Abby's address?'

'Number six Leybourne Road, Leytonstone.' She grinned. 'And don't worry, I'll take the blame if Murphy gets his knickers in a twist.'

CHAPTER TWENTY-FIVE

Jane rang the doorbell of a terraced, two-bedroom Victorian property and Abby opened the door. She looked worried when she saw
who it was.

'Hi, Abby.' Jane smiled. 'You remember me? This is my colleague
DC Johnson. Are your mum and dad in?'

'No, they're both out,' she said with a frown.

'I wonder if we could come in and have a quick word with you
about what you saw on Thursday morning in Woodville Road?'

'I've already told you everything.'

'Have you told your parents about it?'

'Yes, and my dad was angry with me, he said I shouldn't have
spoken to you without his permission.'

'If you'd still been sixteen that would be true – but now you're
seventeen we don't need his permission.'

Teflon threw Jane a warning glance, but she ignored him.

'There's just a couple more questions I'd like to ask you, then
we'll be on our way.'

Abby sighed and opened the door.

They followed her into the living room, where her son Daniel
was asleep in a carrycot on the sofa. Abby sat down next to him
with a surly look on her face and her arms folded.

'What do you want to ask me?'

Jane decided to get straight to the point.

'I have reason to believe that the tall man you saw firing the gun
at the police car wasn't wearing a mask and I—'

'He was so, it was a black balaclava with eye and mouth holes,'
she insisted.

Jane spoke softly. 'Every witness to the bank robbery said the tall
man with the gun was wearing a brown stocking mask.'

'So? He might have changed into a balaclava after the robbery.'

'Our forensic officer found drops of blood in Woodville Road leading to and from where the Cortina was parked. He believes the man with the gun took his stocking mask off before he got out of the car.'

Abby started biting her thumbnail. 'I'm not a liar, you know.'

'I can understand why you're scared, Abby – but I can assure you those men will never know who you are. By telling us the truth you'll be helping us to make sure they never do anything like that again and go to prison . . . for a very long time.'

Jane looked to Teflon for support. He rolled his eyes, then crouched down so Abby had to look at him.

'If you did see his face and would be able to recognise him again, it would really help us.'

Abby started to cry. 'OK, his head was bleeding, right, then just before he started firing the gun, he wiped the blood with a stocking . . .' Her voice trembled as she remembered the moment.

Jane sat down next to Abby, handed her a tissue and put her arm around her.

'That's great. you're doing really well.'

Abby looked at Jane with floods of tears running down her face.

'After he'd fired at the police car, he saw me looking at him and pointed the gun at me . . . I thought he was going to shoot me—'

'What the fuck is going on here?' Mr Jones's voice boomed as he marched into the room, quickly followed by his wife.

'It's OK, Mr Jones. We're CID,' Teflon said quickly.

'Get away from my daughter!' Mrs Jones shrieked, pushing Jane away.

'Is this the detective woman you spoke to the other day, Abby?' Mr Jones asked, and she nodded. He glared at Jane. 'How dare you come to my house harassing my daughter without my permission.'

'I wasn't harassing Abby, Mr Jones, I was just asking her—'

'I don't care what you were asking her,' Mrs Jones snapped.

Jane took a deep breath. 'Abby just told us she saw the face of the man who fired at the police car and he pointed the gun at her. Understandably she's frightened, but I think she might recognise him if she saw him again.'

She looked at Teflon, who raised his eyebrows and shook his head. It was obvious he thought she was not helping the situation.

Mr Jones turned to his daughter.

'Did you see the man's face?'

She nodded, wiping the tears from her eyes.

'But you wouldn't be able to recognise him again, would you?'

'No, Daddy.'

Mr Jones pointed to the door.

'Get out of my house, the pair of you!'

'I'm just doing my job, Mr Jones. Your daughter, or other innocent members of the public, could have been seriously hurt. All I'm asking is—'

Teflon decided he'd had enough. He grabbed Jane by the arm and led her towards the front door.

'I apologise for any distress we have caused you and your family, Mr Jones – we won't bother you or your daughter again,' he said as they walked out.

'You'd better not!' Jones shouted as he slammed the door shut.

'You can take your hand off me now,' Jane told him icily. She brushed her arm down. 'I know Abby saw his face . . .' She held her finger and thumb a couple of inches apart. 'We were that close to getting her on our side—'

'Shut up and get in the bloody car,' Teflon told her through gritted teeth.

He said nothing as he drove off, then took the first left turn and came to an abrupt halt, making Jane lurch forward.

'For Christ's sake!' she exclaimed.

He shook his head in disbelief. 'Can you not see Jones was only trying to protect his daughter? You should have walked away as soon as Abby told you he was mad that you'd spoken to her without his permission.'

'Maybe, but—'

'Then you go and tell him the suspect pointed the gun at her and she could have been killed. After hearing that I wouldn't let my daughter go anywhere near a bloody witness stand.'

'I said hurt, not killed, and I was just being honest with him.'

'Sometimes honesty isn't the best policy. Put yourself in his shoes . . . He already knew our suspects are hardened criminals who don't give a toss about anyone or anything and are not afraid to commit murder to get away with their crimes.'

'You don't need to lecture me,' she retorted. 'I've dealt with witnesses to murder and many other serious crimes, so believe me I know what it's like for them.'

'Dealing with witnesses to armed robberies is different from a murder investigation. We've had loads of people in witness protection, but lost in court because of physical assaults and intimidation of their families and members of the jury. Even if Abby identified O'Reilly in a line-up, a good defence barrister would have destroyed the poor girl in court – and alleged that you coerced her.'

Jane threw her hands up. 'Fine. You're right – we shouldn't have gone to see Abby.'

'I should never have let you talk me into going there. Part of me wonders how much you just wanted to rub Murphy's nose in it by getting Abby to admit she saw O'Reilly's face.'

'I said I'm sorry – and I can't change what's just happened.'

'Next time think before you dive in head first, Jane. Why throw all your hard work away on a seventeen-year-old kid, who you already suspected had lied before you got there? If Murphy had told you to go and interview her then the blame for that fiasco would have been on his shoulders – not yours!'

He started the car and moved off.

Neither of them spoke on the journey back to Rigg Approach. Jane had time to think about what Teflon had said and she realised he was mostly right. Her biggest dilemma now was whether or not to tell Murphy what had happened.

* * *

As she drove home, Jane felt more and more annoyed with herself, knowing the fiasco at the Joneses' house had damaged all her good work over the last three days and dented the respect Teflon had for her. She parked her car in a back street and trudged up the stairs to her flat. She'd never felt so tired and looked forward to a hot bath and going straight to bed. She managed to open the door a few inches before it got stuck and, after pushing harder, she opened it enough to squeeze around the door into her flat. She saw a plastic House of Fraser bag wedged between the door and carpet, and realised it must have been pushed through the letterbox. After closing the door, she picked the bag up and saw a bit of paper with Pam's handwriting on it.

> Bought this for you earlier and thought I'd drop it off before going to Mum and Dad's for supper as I wasn't sure if I'd see you later. If you've seen this before I've told you about it then you probably got stuck at work . . . or forgot about supper . . . AGAIN! See you when I see you . . . Your long-lost sister Pam. PS You owe me £3 and the receipt's in the bag.

Jane opened the carrier bag and took out the grey newsboy cap. 'Bollocks,' she said to herself, annoyed she'd forgotten about going to her parents' for supper. She picked the phone up and started to dial their number, but put the receiver down and banged her hand against the wall in frustration. She knew her mother and Pam would accuse her of putting her job before the family, which would be somewhat ironic after what she'd done for Tony. She couldn't face any of her family after everything that had happened in the last twenty-four hours and just wanted to be alone.

She went into the kitchen, poured a large glass of wine and drank half of it down in one. As she topped up the glass, she thought of Emma and Rachel cowering in a corner, watching their mother being beaten to death. Alone in the silence of her flat it was as if she was there herself, unable, like them, to do anything to stop it. She remembered Emma saying how her mother had tried to reach out to them as she lay on the floor in a pool of blood. Jane felt herself welling up with guilt. She snatched a tissue from a box in the kitchen and hurried to the phone. She dialled her parents' number and her mother answered.

'I'm so sorry, I let you all down tonight, I should have been there . . .'

'That's all right, dear. I didn't make anything special, it was only roast chicken with mushroom sauce.'

Jane sniffed, trying not to cry. She realised that deep down, she had been worrying that one of her parents was ill, before a different explanation for Pam's behaviour had become apparent.

'Are you all right?' She could hear the concern in her mother's voice.

'I've had a distressing day, Mum, it's all been a bit much and I'm really tired. I just feel so bad about not turning up again.' She blew her nose loudly.

'Don't get so upset, sweetheart, your father and I understand how important your work is to you and we're very proud of all you've achieved.'

'Thank you, Mum, that means a lot to me.' She wiped her eyes with a tissue.

'We're always here for you, Jane. You know we both love you very much.'

'I love you too, Mum.'

'Well, I've always been a good listener, and I want you to tell me what's upsetting you.'

She knew she couldn't say anything about Tony, but could still be truthful.

'Oh, Mum, it's just that I've been dealing with twin girls whose mother was murdered by their abusive father and they were put into a convent. One of them is deaf and mute, and I just thought how fortunate I am, and always have been, to have you both and I just feel so bad about not having your chicken and mushroom sauce.'

'Well, I can cook that any time for you. Pam wanted to know if the cap she dropped off was the right one?'

Jane took a deep breath. 'Yes, Mum, the cap was exactly what I wanted. Is Pam there so I can thank her?'

'No, Tony picked her and Nathan up a little while ago. I'd hoped they'd stay for a bit longer. Your father and me love being with Nathan.'

'I haven't seen Tony for a while – how is he?' she asked, hating how deceitful she sounded.

'Funny you should ask, but he looked tired and was very withdrawn, which is unusual for him. I hope he's not coming down with the flu. I wouldn't want him to pass it on to Nathan.'

'He's probably had a hard few days at work and is feeling exhausted . . . like me.'

'I know Tony works hard to provide for Pam and Nathan. Mind you, sometimes I feel she's a bit harsh with him.'

'Goodnight, Mum, thanks for your support.'

Jane put the receiver down and wondered if Tony was currently confessing to Pam. The thought that he might reveal her involvement worried her deeply.

CHAPTER TWENTY-SIX

It was 11 p.m. and Jane hadn't been asleep long when she heard the doorbell ring. She turned on the bedside light and got up to see who it was repeatedly pressing the bell.

'Hang on, I'm coming!' she shouted as she walked up the hallway.

She opened the door, which was on a safety chain, and, peering around the gap, saw a distraught-looking Pam holding Nathan on one shoulder and a small holdall over the other. Jane could see Pam had been crying and realised it would seem strange if she didn't ask why. She undid the chain and opened the door.

'What on earth are you doing here?'

Pam started to cry. 'Tony's admitted having sex with another woman and I've left him. I didn't want to go to Mum and Dad's – can I stay with you please?'

'Oh my God. Of course you can.' She took the holdall from Pam's shoulder. 'Put Nathan in my bed for now.'

Jane wondered what Tony had said, but knew if he'd mentioned her involvement at the police station Pam would have flown off the handle and confronted her right away.

'Do you want a cup of tea?'

'Have you anything stronger?'

'I've got some brandy.'

'That and a coffee would be nice.'

While Pam settled Nathan down in bed, Jane poured two large brandies and prepared two cups of coffee while the kettle boiled. She wondered if she should be up front and tell Pam about speaking to Tony after his arrest, or wait and see what Pam said, and if Tony had lied about his arrest, then tell her the truth.

Pam came into the kitchen, tore off a piece of kitchen roll, wiped her eyes and blew her nose. Jane handed her a glass of brandy and she took a sip, then licked her lips.

'I'm sorry to turn up on your doorstep like this, Jane, but I didn't know who else to turn to.' She sounded miserable.

'I'm always here for you, Pam . . . you know that.'

'I told Tony I wanted him out of the house, but he refused to go and kept saying we needed to talk. I told him I didn't want to be anywhere near him and he begged me to stay, but I packed a bag, took Nathan and left in a cab.'

'Does he know you're here?'

'No, is that a problem?'

'I'm just concerned he'll be worried about you and Nathan.'

'Let's take our drinks through to the living room.'

Jane sat opposite Pam, who took another large sip of brandy.

'How did you find out Tony was seeing another woman?' she asked.

'I knew something was wrong in the car on the way back from Mum and Dad's. When I asked him how the stag night was, he seemed nervous and couldn't look me in the eye. I knew he was hiding something and confronted him after I'd put Nathan to bed. At first, he said he'd had a lot to drink and felt embarrassed because he was sick on the dance floor and got thrown out of the club. I've never known Tony be sick through drink and told him to stop lying to me. I picked up the phone and said I was calling his friend Noel to ask what happened.'

'What did Noel say?'

'Tony broke down and confessed before he answered the phone.'

Jane needed to know if Tony had told the truth.

'Confessed to what?'

'That he'd met some slut called Laura on the stag do last night while they were at the Empire disco in Leicester Square. He screwed her down a dirty alleyway and even tried to blame her for leading him on.'

Jane wondered if her sister may have misinterpreted some of what Tony told her, due to the heartbreak and rage she must have felt at the time of his confession.

'He actually admitted having sex in an alleyway?'

'He said they just kissed and touched each other, but I don't believe him. If it wasn't more than that, then why go down the alley in the first place?'

'I'm not condoning what he's done, Pam, but he must have felt some remorse to confess—'

Pam looked upset. 'Whose side are you on, Jane? Tony lied and cheated on me. He only confessed because I forced him into a corner.'

'I know, but he might have been frightened to say anything at first, for fear of losing you and Nathan. If it was just a kiss and cuddle it's not the end of the world—'

'I can't believe I'm hearing this. Especially from a woman who's never been married and had a string of disastrous relationships – one of them with a married police officer with children, as I recall.'

'That's not fair and you know it. I was a naive young probationer at the time, and if I'd had any idea he was married I would never have had a relationship with him.'

'As I recall, it only ended because he got killed in an explosion during a bank raid.'

Jane was appalled by Pam's contemptuous remark, but kept calm.

'That's a horrible thing to say. He was a respected police officer who died doing a job he loved.'

'How do you think his wife would have felt if she knew about your affair?'

'Why are you being so vicious, Pam?'

'I've been hurt, and you don't seem to care.' She sniffed.

'I do care, and the last thing I want to see is you and Tony break up. Being a single parent is not easy and it would be tough on Nathan, too.'

'You know nothing about raising a child, Jane – so don't pretend you do.'

'Maybe not, but I've dealt with parents and children who have been affected by broken marriages.'

'That doesn't make you a fucking expert! You hardly ever see Nathan because you're always too busy with your work. In case you'd forgotten, you're supposed to be his godmother.'

'Does it make you feel better, having a go at me?'

'Yes, especially when you speak to me like I'm the one who's in the wrong.'

Jane was beginning to realise that Tony's concerns about Pam's erratic behaviour were valid.

'I've never said you did anything wrong, Pam . . . I'm just worried about you, that's all.'

'I don't need your or anyone else's sympathy.'

'Have you been suffering from any sort of anxiety or depression—?'

'Of course I'm fucking depressed! Wouldn't you be?' Pam shouted.

'If you'd let me finish, I was going to say before Tony was unfaithful.'

The phone started to ring, and Jane wondered if it might be Tony trying to find out where Pam was.

'I better answer that in case it's work.'

'Who else would it bloody well be? Where's the brandy?' she asked, holding up her empty glass.

'In the kitchen, but do you really need another drink?'

Pam ignored her and went to the kitchen while Jane picked up the phone and took it into her bedroom on a long extension lead to take the call.

'Who's calling?' she asked quietly so as not to disturb Nathan, who was sleeping with a pillow either side of him.

'It's Dad. Tony's just phoned asking if Pam was with us. Your mother said no and asked him what's happened. He said he'd had a row with Pam and she'd walked out with Nathan and he doesn't know where she's gone. Your mother's worried sick.'

'It's OK, Dad, Pam and Nathan are here with me and they're both fine.'

'Thank God for that . . . Why are you whispering?'

'Because Nathan's asleep next to me and I don't want to wake him. Tell Mum not to worry and Pam will call her in the morning.'

'Why can't she speak to her now?'

'She's sleeping and I don't want to wake her.'

'What the hell's going on, Jane?'

'They've had a big row and she just wanted someone to talk to, that's all.'

'Has he been having an affair?'

'I don't know what they argued about.'

'I spoke to him on the phone and asked him straight if he was. He said he'd been stupid and kissed another woman, but I could tell it was more than that. I'm not an idiot, Jane. Pam wouldn't take Nathan if it was just a silly kiss, and I know she always confides in you.'

'If they want to tell you what it's all about, that's up to them – not me.'

Nathan was waking up and starting to grimace. Jane used her shoulder to hold the phone against her ear and turned Nathan slightly on his side. She supported him with one hand and gently rubbed his back with the other, which relaxed him and made him gurgle.

'I asked Tony if he'd called you and he said he didn't want to bother you late at night, which seems a bit strange. I would have thought you'd be the first person he would call if he was so worried about Pam and Nathan.'

'He's probably not thinking straight. I'll call him in a minute and tell him Pam and Nathan are with me.'

'Why didn't you call him when she first got there?'

'Because I thought she'd told him she was going to see me.' Suddenly the penny dropped. 'Are you seriously thinking I might be the "other woman"?'

He was slow to answer. 'No, but I feel you're hiding something.'

She knew he was suspicious because of the relationship she'd had with a married officer.

Jane sighed. 'For Christ's sake, this is all getting out of hand. I haven't got the time or inclination to explain everything to you tonight, Dad – but let me assure you I'm not having an affair with Tony.'

'What are you doing with my baby?' Pam snapped as she entered the bedroom.

'I thought you said Pam was asleep,' her father said on hearing her voice.

'Give him to me.'

Pam snatched Nathan from the bed, making him wail.

'Be careful, Pam.'

'Don't you tell me how to look after my baby!' she shouted, walking off into the living room.

'What's going on, Jane?' her father asked, hearing Pam's distress.

'Everything's fine—'

'No, it's not. Your mother and I are on our way over.'

'You'll make matters worse, so stay at home and let me deal with this. Call Tony and tell him Pam and Nathan are fine and with me,' she said bluntly, then put the phone down and went to the living room.

Pam was crying and kneeling on the floor, holding a distressed Nathan, who was still wailing. As she rocked back and forth to comfort him, Jane knelt beside Pam and put her arm around her.

'Everything will be all right, Pam. Come and sit on the sofa with me.' She helped her sister up. 'Have you got any milk for Nathan?'

Pam nodded. 'His plastic cup's in the holdall, along with a carton of milk.'

Jane filled the cup with milk and Pam gave it to Nathan, who instantly fell silent as he sucked on the spout.

'There you go, he was just hungry.'

'I'm sorry, Jane, I didn't mean to shout at you. I just feel so tired and irritated all the time, and this mess with Tony just sent me over the top.'

'I think you might be suffering from the baby blues, Pam.'

'I know I am . . . but I don't know what to do about it.'

'Once Nathan's settled, we can talk about the best way forward.'

When Nathan was asleep Pam put him to bed and Jane made her another coffee. In the kitchen she saw the large brandy Pam had poured for herself and tipped it down the sink.

'How long have you been feeling like this?' Jane asked.

'A few months now, but it comes and goes. Some days are good, some are bad and others are just a blur.'

'Depression and a feeling of hopelessness are symptoms of post-natal depression, Pam.'

'But I was fine for the first few months after Nathan's birth, then suddenly everything went downhill.'

'Did you say anything to Tony about it?'

'No, but I took my emotions out on him. It's probably what drove him into the arms of another woman.'

Jane sighed. 'It wasn't just your mood swings, Pam, and he knows what he did was wrong, but I truly believe it was a one-off and he wasn't the instigator.'

Pam looked surprised. 'Was that him on the phone just now?'

'No, it was Dad. Tony was worried and phoned the house to see if you and Nathan were there. I told Dad you were both fine and staying the night with me.'

'Do they know what we argued about?'

'Tony said he'd kissed another woman and you were upset, that's all.'

'So he lied again.'

'Dad forced it out of Tony, but understandably he didn't want to tell him everything that happened last night—'

'What do you mean, "everything that happened"? When did you speak to Tony?' Pam scowled.

Jane took a deep breath. 'Last night at the police station after he was arrested.'

Pam sat up. 'Arrested? Why didn't you tell me?'

'Tony asked me not to tell you because he wanted to.'

'Well, he clearly didn't!' Pam said, becoming agitated.

'I think he was going to, but you walked out with Nathan before he could.'

'Oh, so it's my fault again. I thought I could confide in you, Jane, but all the time you're sneaking behind my back and lying to me.'

'You need to calm down and listen to me or you'll wake Nathan,' Jane said sternly.

Pam folded her arms. 'Go on, then.'

'Tony was arrested after what I believe to be a false allegation of indecent assault. He called me at home and I went to the station to find out what was happening.'

'He was arrested for indecent assault and you didn't tell me?'

'I'm sorry, but it wasn't up to me and—'

'You were just worried about Tony's arrest affecting your bloody job, weren't you?'

Jane had had enough of being the scapegoat.

'I put my job on the line for Tony and I'd do the same for you if ever you were arrested. I was just trying to help. You can let me explain everything or go to bed – the choice is yours.'

'I'm all ears,' she replied flippantly.

Jane went over everything, from start to finish, about her involvement in Tony's arrest and why she went to the station. She was blunt and to the point, and even told Pam about the conversation they'd had in the cell about Tony's emotional state due to Pam's erratic behaviour.

'Tony's been a fool to himself, and he knows it. But put yourself in his shoes for one minute and think how you'd feel if someone made a false allegation like that against you.'

Pam started to well up. 'I understand why he called you and not me . . . and he's right about the way I've been treating him.'

'I hated myself for not telling you, Pam, but you and Tony need to sit down and talk, and seek some medical advice about your condition.'

'Do you think Tony will end up in court over the assault allegation?'

'I'm pretty certain the DS dealing with the case believes Tony and Noel's version of events. He's going to see the woman again and re-interview her. Hopefully when confronted with the truth she'll withdraw her allegation. If not, he could be charged and face trial.'

CHAPTER TWENTY-SEVEN

Jane let Pam sleep in her bed with Nathan, while she slept on the couch. She got to bed at 2 a.m. and hardly slept before the alarm went off at 6 a.m. On waking she was on autopilot as she showered, then dressed for work. Her vision was slightly blurred, and when she looked at her eyes in the bathroom mirror, they were baggy and slightly bloodshot. She used some moisturiser and did some facial stretches, but it didn't make much difference, so she put on a bit more make-up than usual.

Before leaving she popped in to see Pam.

'You OK?'

'Yes, I'm fine.'

'I'm off to work now, so make yourself at home. There's bacon and eggs in the fridge and cereal in the cupboard.' She leant forward and kissed Nathan, and then Pam's cheek. 'You can invite Tony over here if you want to have a heart-to-heart.'

'Thanks, but I'll go home. It would be better under our own roof . . . for Nathan as well.'

'Forgiveness is never easy, but I know you'll work things out. Tony's a good man and he loves you both dearly.'

'I know, and I love him.'

'Let me know how it goes.'

Jane started to leave the room.

'I love you as well, Jane. I know I can be a silly cow at times, but I really appreciate what you've done for Tony and the advice you've given us.'

'That's what sisters do, Pam – they help each other through thick and thin.'

* * *

It was a fresh, sunny spring morning as Jane parked her car in a back street near Brick Lane, famous for its array of Jewish, Bangladeshi and Indian restaurants and its Sunday flea market. As she crossed Bethnal Green Road she saw the Colonel walking towards her, and couldn't help letting out a big yawn.

'You look like you've been up all night,' he remarked.

'I have,' she replied, yawning again.

'Then a nice hot coffee and a salt beef bagel is what you need to wake you up.'

'I've got to be back at Rigg for nine to meet Teflon and take Fiona Simpson up to the Yard.'

'It's only half seven – we've got plenty of time.'

'All right then . . . I haven't had a salt beef bagel in ages, and a black coffee wouldn't go amiss.'

As they walked down Brick Lane, some vendors were still setting up their stalls with second-hand goods and putting price tags on them. As they approached the busy Jewish cafe, the smell of salt beef filled the air. They found a free table in the corner.

'My treat,' he said, and went to the counter.

Jane saw him get a brown envelope out of his pocket and tear it open. He removed two ten-pound notes, handed one to the waitress, and put the other in his wallet. As he did so, she remembered Murphy saying he'd authorised twenty pounds out of the informants' fund for the Colonel's "snout".

'There you go.' He put her food and drink down on the table.

'Can you tell me anything about the informant we're going to meet?'

'His name's Gentleman Jim, he's done time for armed robbery and now he's out he sells antiques in the flea market,' he said brusquely.

'Why's he called Gentleman Jim?'

The Colonel laughed. "Cause he was always polite when he robbed a bank . . .' He put on a posh voice. '"Please don't press the alarm, and I'd be very grateful if you'd be so kind as to put the money in the bag." Then, having scared the shit out of the bank staff with a gun, he'd say "Toodle pip" before leaving.'

'What were the rest of the gang like?'

'Jim was always a lone blagger; figured he wasn't going to be grassed on if he did things by himself.'

'Is he meeting us here?'

'No, he runs a stall further down the lane.'

'So how does it work on the squad with informants?'

'You give them a nickname and you have to register them with Murphy and fill in a report for secure filing every time you have a meet.'

'And what about paying them?'

'Fill in a payment request form and give it to Kingston, who then gets Murphy to check it. If he approves it, Kingston can give you the money out of the office safe. If you get good info that results in a conviction, the snout gets a big wedge out of any reward fund.'

Jane wondered to herself if the money the Colonel had in the envelope was meant for Gentleman Jim.

'You can't beat a good salt beef bagel.'

He took a large bite of his second one.

'Do you think Jim might know something about the Leytonstone job?'

'Well, we ain't here to buy an antique clock from him. You don't half ask a lot of questions, Jane.'

'Well, you're supposed to be the teacher.'

'Then just watch and learn when I speak to Jim.'

Brick Lane was fuller now, with people who had come out early to try and grab a bargain. As they walked down the lane the Colonel stopped at some stalls and enquired about the merchandise or picked things up to have a look at them, trying to appear like a normal punter. He stopped at a stall and picked up a doll dressed in an old-fashioned sailor's outfit, with a ring in one ear and realistic features. The stallholder was an overweight, elderly balding gentle-man with a thick moustache, who smelt strongly of stale sweat. He wore a white shirt, grey pinstripe trousers and a black waistcoat with a pocket watch.

'Is sir interested in the doll?'

'I might be. What sort of doll is it?'

'It's German, known as a bisque head, made circa 1875 from bisque porcelain,' he said in a posh voice. 'The matt finish gives it a rather lifelike look, don't you think?'

'How much?'

'Fifty pounds – but if it's for your good lady I'd be prepared to drop the price to forty-five.' He smiled at Jane.

'Fuck off, Jim – I bet you've got a box full of replicas in the back of your van.'

He shrugged. 'I gotta make a fucking living, Colonel.'

'This is Jane. I'm teaching her the ropes.'

'I'd listen to every word he says, my dear – if only to see what rubbish he talks.' He sneered.

The Colonel took a five-pound note out of his pocket and held it towards Jim.

'You know anything about the Leytonstone job on Thursday just gone?'

'Not for a fiver I don't. A score is my going rate.'

'The Guv'nor cut the funds down. I'll give you another five out of my own pocket if it's worth it.' He took another note out of his wallet.

Jim sighed. 'It'll have to do for now, I suppose.'

He went to take the money and the Colonel pulled it back from his grasp.

'Info first, my friend.'

Jim sighed, then spoke softly. 'Rumour 'as it a big Irish UDA guy who recently came over 'ere is involved. 'E's got a reputation for being a fuckin' nutter.'

Jane noticed that Jim's accent had suddenly become proper cockney.

'Age?' the Colonel asked.

'Late twenties, early thirties.'

'Was his name—?' Jane began.

The Colonel cut her off abruptly. 'I'll ask the questions! What's your source?' he asked Jim.

'Pub talk. The paddy was pissed and gobbing off to a mate about turning over a Securicor van.'

'What pub was it?'

'I can't tell you that, Colonel – if your mob start snoopin' aroun' in there, I'm brown bread.'

'This paddy say anything else?'

'Only that 'e was managin' a snooker 'all in North London.'

The Colonel didn't react to any of the information. He paused, waiting for Jim to say more, then handed him the two five-pound notes.

'Keep digging, Jim. You find out any more, you know where to reach me.'

'Make it a twenty next time an' I'll see what I can do.'

'It's up to the Guv'nor – and keep your nose clean on this one.'

Jim raised his eyebrows and spoke in a posh voice.

'Good Lord, Colonel ... Why would an upstanding gentleman like me want to partake in criminal activities?'

'Because you're greedy and got sticky fingers.'

Jim shrugged. 'To each his own, my friend.'

As they walked back up the market the Colonel said nothing.

'Looks like Jim's talking about Aidan O'Reilly and the Bruce Grove Snooker Hall.'

The Colonel stopped and looked at Jane.

'Don't ever give a snout information like names or they may lead you on. Let them do the talking and never tell them if they're right or wrong. You run them – it can never be the other way around or they end up tapping you for information.'

'Sorry, you're right. I noticed his accent changed during the conversation.'

'The posh thing is all an act. He used it when he was robbing banks, to fool the victims and police. He started again when he got into the antiques business, where it's good for selling dodgy gear to naive punters.'

'He seemed to know his stuff.'

'Self-taught from books while he did a five stretch in the Scrubs. I'll see you back at the nick,' he said as they reached Bethnal Green Road.

Jane thought about the money the Colonel had given Gentleman Jim for his information. If the twenty pounds in the envelope was from the informants' fund, it seemed he had pocketed a tenner of it for himself and the 'extra' fiver from his own wallet wasn't in fact his. She sighed. It wasn't significant in the greater scheme of things, but it was still theft of the Commissioner's money.

* * *

Jane had parked her car and was walking towards the squad building when she saw Teflon rush out of the front entrance with car keys in his hand.

'Kingston said Fiona Simpson is willing to attend albums, so we may as well go straight to the pub to collect her.'

'What's the rush?'

'Cam said Murphy's on his way in and he's got the hump.'

'What about this time?' she asked, hoping it wasn't anything to do with the Jones family.

'Who knows?' Teflon shrugged as they both got in the unmarked police car. 'How'd it go with the Colonel's informant?' he asked, doing up his seatbelt.

Jane smiled. 'He's quite a character. I think he might be on to something with O'Reilly.'

'Take my advice – let the Colonel deal with his informants on his own.'

'Why do you say that?'

'Because his snouts often tread a fine line between giving an officer information about a crime and participating in it.'

Jane thought back to the Colonel telling Gentleman Jim to 'keep your nose clean on this one', and decided it might be best to change the subject.

'How was Kingston this morning?'

'I dunno, he's asleep in his office. He called me from a payphone last night – it sounded like he was in a pub and had had a few. Probably drowning his sorrows with the Colonel as usual.'

'I was with the Colonel earlier and he didn't appear to have a hangover.'

'The Colonel can drink more than the lot of us put together and still be sober.'

'Kingston's not doing himself any favours by going on the piss and getting home late.'

'That's his problem, not ours. Sorry I snapped at you yesterday; you were only doing what you felt was right.'

'I was wrong, and I don't blame you for telling me – in fact, it gave me a wake-up call. I'm going to speak to Murphy after we've been to the Yard and tell him what happened.'

'I'll do it with you if you want.'

'It was my screw-up, not yours.'

'I could have refused to drive you there.'

'I'd have gone on my own anyway.'

'Well, I'm not going to blab to anyone in the office about it.'

'Thanks, I appreciate it.'

* * *

Jane repeatedly rang the doorbell at the lounge bar entrance to the Crown pub in Leytonstone High Road, but there was no answer. She checked her watch – it was just after 8.30 a.m. – then she went to the saloon bar entrance and knocked on the door, but still there was no answer. She stepped back into the street to look up at Fiona Simpson's flat above the pub; the curtains were open but there was no sign of movement. There was a high brick wall, with a thick wooden door leading to the beer garden and rear of the pub. It was locked. She looked through the window and could see the lights were on inside, before returning to the unmarked police car. She tapped on the driver's window.

'What's up?'

'I've rung the doorbell and banged on the door but there are no answer.'

'Maybe she had a late night and she's still sleeping it off.'

'It doesn't look like the place has been cleaned up – there are dirty glasses and unemptied ashtrays on the bar.'

Teflon called the office on the radio and asked Cam to phone the pub.

'Tell Fiona Simpson we're waiting outside for her.'

Jane went back over to the lounge bar door and listened to the phone ringing for nearly a minute before it stopped.

'Cam said there was no answer – maybe she's locked up and gone out already.'

'Kingston gave me the impression she wasn't afraid to be a witness. Do you reckon you can get over that wall into the beer garden and check the back door?'

'Piece of cake.'

With a run and a jump he was up and over the wall.

'Bugger off or I'm callin' the police on you two!' a shrill female voice shouted.

Jane turned and saw a frail elderly woman with a hunched back, clutching a copy of the *News of the World*.

She got her warrant card out.

'It's all right, Betty, we are the police.'

Betty tilted her head and her eyes narrowed.

'Then why's that darkie jumpin' over the wall?'

'He's my colleague; we've come to see Fiona. She wasn't answering our calls and we think her front doorbell may be broken, so now we're trying the back door.'

'Right, fair enough, but you can't be too careful these days, you know.'

'You're quite right, Betty.'

'Is it about the robbery? I saw it as well, you know.'

'Yes, I heard you tell Fiona about the gun going off and the young man lying on the pavement.'

Jane nodded, watching for Teflon to come back over the wall.

'One of 'em bastards nearly knocked me for six before they robbed the van. When's one of your lot gonna come and see me about it?'

'Sorry, Betty, what did you say?'

'I said, when's one of your lot gonna come . . . Never mind, luv, you obviously ain't interested in what I gotta say.'

She started to walk off.

Jane grasped the gist of what she'd said.

'Did you say one of them knocked you over?'

'I said *nearly*. As a police officer you should pay more attention, you know. I was walkin' up the road when this bloke opens a car door and nearly 'its me bad 'ip. After the robbery Fi told me she saw it 'appen and 'e was the one who drove the car.'

'Has no one from the investigation been to see you?'

Betty frowned and shook her head. 'Not a soul.'

Jane glanced across the road and saw Teflon inside the lounge bar, opening the door. She got her pocket notebook and pen out.

'What's your address, Betty? I'll come and see you later, probably this afternoon sometime.'

'Fifteen Dacre Road – it's down there on the right. Don't come between five and six as the *Antiques Roadshow* is on and I don't like to miss that.'

She limped off.

Jane recalled wanting to speak to Betty on the Thursday afternoon, when she first met her, but not bothering as Fiona said DI Kingston was dealing with her. From what Betty had just said it seemed he hadn't spoken to her, which didn't make sense as Kingston had told her Betty was 'a bit senile and not very reliable', and in his opinion it wasn't worth getting a statement from her. She had no reason to doubt Kingston. As she watched Betty limp down the road, she wondered if she had dementia and had forgotten about the whole thing. Or maybe she just liked the attention and wanted to talk to another policeman.

'We need to get the local CID down here.'

Teflon sprinted towards the car.

'What's happened?' Jane asked, hard on his heels.

'The back door was open, and the keys were in it. There's a woman at the bottom of the cellar and blood on the floor – looks like she fell backwards and hit her head on the concrete.'

'Have you called an ambulance?'

'No, she's dead.'

'Are you sure?'

'I checked for a pulse. I'm assuming it's Fiona Simpson.'

He opened the car door and picked up the radio.

'Call a divisional surgeon to pronounce life extinct and a lab liaison sergeant as well – ask for Paul Lawrence to attend, if he's on call,' Jane told him.

'I was going to get the local lads to deal with it.'

Jane shook her head. 'Locals can hold the scene until a lab sarge gets here – they know more about suspicious death scenes than a divisional SOCO or CID ever do.'

'You reckon it's suspicious?'

'Paul taught me to treat every unexplained death scene as a possible murder – we don't know yet whether she fell or was pushed. I'm just going to take a quick look and see if there's anything that needs urgent preservation for forensics.'

She pulled a pair of latex gloves out of her shoulder bag.

'You always carry those around with you?'

'Yep, a couple of pairs at least. If you go around touching things at a scene without them, you could destroy or contaminate potential evidence. If the locals turn up before I'm back, you tell them to stay out of the pub.'

Jane stood at the top of the short flight of steep stone steps leading to the cellar and crouched down. The light was on and she could see the dead woman's face, her eyes wide open as if frozen with fear. A two-foot pool of blood surrounded her head and the outer few inches of the pool had congealed, indicating to Jane that Fiona had lain there motionless for some time. She looked closely at the steps and the carpet in the hallway leading to the cellar, but there was no sign of any blood trail or droplets. She made notes in her pocket notebook of her observations, and the fact that the cellar light switch was in the hallway by the cellar door. Then she checked the saloon bar door, which was bolted shut, top and bottom, as was the public door to the beer garden. There were dirty beer glasses on the tables and bars, and no sign of any disturbance to indicate a struggle might have taken place.

Jane went into the beer garden through the private rear door, to look at the gate in the wall. It had a Yale lock, which could only be opened from the inside by turning the oblong knob. She made some notes before removing the set of keys from the private back-door Chubb lock, which she put in an empty plastic coin bag she found next to the till.

She went to speak to Teflon, who was talking with a PC. Jane asked the officer to man the lounge bar door and not let anyone in without her permission, and to record the names and times any authorised persons entered and left the premises.

'Is it Fiona Simpson?' Teflon asked.

'Yes. Did you have to unbolt the lounge bar door to get out?'

'Yes. Is there a problem?'

'It seems she'd locked up the lounge and saloon bar doors before she died, but she left the back door open, which makes me wonder if someone other than Fiona opened the back door to leave via the beer garden.' She held up the coin bag with the keys in it. 'With a bit of luck, we might get a fingerprint off the Chubb key or Yale lock on the garden door. Was the cellar light on or off when you found her?'

'On. You reckon she was murdered?'

'It's too early to say for sure, but it's something we have to consider.'

'Well, if she was, and it's connected to the robbery, then maybe the driver of the getaway car saw her looking out of the upstairs window at him.'

'Could be. Anyway, it's all speculation until forensics examines the scene.'

Teflon nodded. 'Local CID and div surgeon are on their way, along with DS Paul Lawrence. I told Cam what I found, and he said he'd inform Murphy. I'll let him know it's Fiona Simpson.'

'I'm just going to pop down the road and speak to that old lady again. She said she's a regular at the pub, so she might know who was working behind the bar with Fiona Simpson last night. I don't want anyone else entering that scene before Paul – not even the divisional surgeon.'

Jane knocked on the door of Betty's 1930s, brick-built, one-bedroom terraced house.

'I wasn't expectin' you until later, dear. Come on in, make yourself at 'ome. You wanna cup of Rosie Lee?'

'No thanks, Betty.'

She followed Betty into the small living room, which was stifling, with a three-bar electric fire on and the window closed.

'Sorry about the cold, luv, but I ain't got central 'eating – I can turn the fire up if ya like.'

'I'm fine, thanks.'

Jane looked around the room. It had two armchairs and an old side cabinet with various black and white, and colour, family photos arranged on it. In the corner of the room there was a small dining table, on top of which there was a half-completed jigsaw depicting a shallow river, with a man driving his horses and cart through it.

It looked familiar.

'What's the jigsaw you're doing, Betty?'

'Don't know, I just liked the picture on the box, so I bought it. Me 'ip's 'urtin', luv, so I needs to sit down.'

She lowered herself gingerly into an armchair.

'Are jigsaws your hobby?' Jane asked, picking up the box lid. Of course, she thought: *The Hay Wain*, by Constable.

'Pretty much since me Albert died. We used to like goin' out to the countryside on the train when 'e was alive; now 'e's gone the jigsaws remind me. I don't get out much as me 'ips are so bad . . . Doing jigsaws 'elps keep me mind tickin' over and brings back 'appy memories. I got loads of 'em in me cabinet there.'

'You said no one had been round to take a statement off you about the robbery . . . ?'

'Not a dicky bird, luv. The only person who spoke to me about it was Fi, cause she seen the driver as well, like.'

'Did she tell you she'd made a statement?'

'I don't know about a statement, but she did say she'd spoken to a detective and 'e might want to speak to me.'

'Did she say who the detective was?'

Betty paused. 'It was King, I think.'

'Could it have been Kingston?'

She pointed a finger. 'That's the name. Fi said 'e was a nice chap and told 'er not to tell anyone that she saw the driver's face. She said I should keep schtum about it as well.'

'And have you?'

'On me life, sweetheart, I ain't told a soul,' Betty replied firmly.

'What happened when the driver opened the car door?'

'I was on me way to get some bits an' bobs from the shops an' the bastard nearly knocked me off me effin' feet when 'e was getting out of 'is car. Brown, it was. The car . . . I told him to mind what 'e was doin' an' use 'is bloody eyes, but 'e just pulled 'is cap down an' walked off. I called 'im a rude word, but 'e still ignored me.' She looked angry.

Jane asked her to describe the man, and she confirmed the details they already had: the newsboy cap, sideburns and ruddy cheeks.

'Would you recognise him if you saw him again?'

'Me 'ips is bad but me eyes ain't – an' I got a good memory for faces.'

'Did you see anything else?'

'When I came out of the shops the robbery was takin' place. I nearly had an 'eart attack when the gun went off an' that poor lad fell to the ground. Then quick as you like the brown motor pulls up an' the three robbers jump in an' piss off. The driver was wea-rin' a balaclava this time, but I know it had to be the same bloke in the cap, because of what Fi told me.'

'When did you last see Fiona?' Jane asked.

'Yesterday evening at six, when I popped in for my usual two bottles of Mackeson.

'Did she have anyone helping her behind the bar, Betty?'

'No, she was on her own . . . has something happened to Fiona?'

Jane took a deep breath, crouched down beside Betty and took her hand.

'I'm sorry to have to tell you Fiona is dead.'

Betty started to rock back and forth, her eyes open wide with disbelief.

'No, no, not my Fi, she can't be dead . . . It's gotta be a mistake.'

'I'm so sorry, Betty, but we're sure.'

She squeezed Jane's hand and started to cry.

'Oh my poor, poor Fi . . . She was like a daughter to me . . . What 'appened?'

'It looks like she fell down the cellar stairs and hit her head on the floor.'

Jane did her best to comfort her, then once she'd stopped crying she made her a cup of tea.

'Is there a neighbour you'd like to come and sit with you for a bit?'

'No thanks, luv, I'd rather be on me own right now,' Betty said with a sniff.

She shuffled over to the dining table, where she sat down and started doing *The Hay Wain* jigsaw without another word.

Jane walked back to the pub with a heavy heart, but also feeling puzzled. It was abundantly clear Betty was far from being senile, and she couldn't for the life of her understand why Kingston had dismissed her as a credible witness. When she got to the car, Teflon was talking to a young man. Teflon turned to Jane.

'This is DC Reid, early turn CID from Leytonstone. The divisional surgeon's pronounced life extinct to Paul Lawrence, who's in the pub, and Murphy is on his way. Did Betty say who was working behind the bar?'

'She was on her own when Betty saw her at six. Poor thing's absolutely heartbroken about Fiona's death. I'll go and have a word with Paul.'

'I filled him in about our investigation and Simpson being a witness. He said he's looking forward to seeing his young protégée.'

Jane stood at the top of the cellar stairs and could see Lawrence, with his back to her, crouched down over Fiona's body and bending her arm at the elbow joint, testing for rigor mortis.

'How's it going, Paul?'

'Hello, Jane.' He gently released Fiona's arm.

'Can I come down?'

He grinned up at her. 'Of course you can.' He opened his arms as she came towards him and they shared a tight hug. 'How's life as the first female on the Flying Squad?'

'Well, I've only been on it since Thursday, but I think it's going to take some time before they accept me as one of "the Dirty Dozen".'

'"The Dirty Dozen" – what's that all about?'

'I won't bore you, but some of them have the mentality of a child at times.'

'You'll win them round, you always do.'

'I'm not so sure this time. What was the state of rigor?'

'She's cold and stiff. Considering she'd probably have closed the pub between eleven and twelve last night, the rigor fits with her being dead eight to ten hours.'

'Any signs she was pushed down the stairs?'

Jane went over her earlier observations with Paul about the cellar light being off, the locked doors and the beer garden gate. She then showed him the set of keys.

'I didn't have an exhibits bag so I had to put them in this coin bag; whoever last used the Chubb key on the back door might have left their prints on it.'

'Good thinking.'

He pulled out an exhibits bag from his pocket and dropped them in.

'I'm worried her death might be connected to our robbery?'

'Why?'

'Just a gut feeling at the moment. If I'm right, there are only two ways our suspects could know she was a witness – one, the getaway driver saw her looking at him, or two, someone told them.'

Paul tilted his head and raised his eyebrows.

'Are you implying you've got a leak on the squad?'

Jane sighed. 'I don't know, Paul, but there are one or two things that don't add up. Then again, I could be jumping to conclusions and seeing things that aren't there.'

'That sounds familiar,' he remarked with a grin. 'You've already observed that there's no sign of any struggle or assault in the bar or hallway area leading to the cellar. It's the same down here, and there are no broken bottles, which means she wasn't carrying anything up or down the stairs at the time. There are quite a few footprints, but they could be from any number of people who've been down here recently. From the blood pooling and position of her body, I'd say she fell backwards and smashed her skull on the ground.'

'Do you think she could have been pushed?'

'I can't say. There's no bruising on her face or lower arms to suggest she was punched or grabbed, but the post mortem might reveal bruising on her chest or shoulders, which could be consistent with being pushed.'

Paul went over to the beer barrels and gently lifted each one an inch or two off the ground. He said nothing as he walked upstairs.

'What are you doing?' Jane asked, following him.

In the lounge bar he picked up a clean beer glass and handed it to her.

'Pour me a pint of Heineken, please.'

'Are you serious?'

'You should know by now there's always a method in my madness.'

She held the glass under the spout and pulled the tap forward. At first there was the sound of air, then a few small foamy splutters of beer coughed their way out of the spout, followed by a large sputter, which hit the beer already in the glass. It splashed back up and almost over Jane.

Paul smiled. 'As I thought . . . The Heineken barrel in the cellar is a fresh one and hasn't been run through the pipes to ensure an uninterrupted flow of lager from the keg to the glass.'

'What the hell do you two think you're doing?' Murphy shouted.

An embarrassed Jane quickly put the glass on the counter, wishing the ground would open and swallow her up. But Paul knew Murphy of old.

'Good morning, sir. I'm demonstrating to Sergeant Tennison that Fiona Simpson most likely changed a beer barrel just before her death.'

'What are you talking about, Lawrence?'

'It's not a great revelation, but it could be relevant to her time of death.'

'Get to the point and don't give me all the Sherlock Holmes shit!'

'Someone changed the Heineken barrel and it hasn't been used, until now. It would explain why Fiona Simpson went down the cellar, but not if she fell or was pushed on her way back up.'

'Show me the body,' Murphy said.

'My pleasure, sir.'

Lawrence showed Murphy the body and repeated his and Jane's observations.

'The bottom line is you don't know how she died?' Murphy asked, leading the way back up to the bar.

'Correct. However, my advice would be to secure the scene, remove the body to the mortuary and have a post mortem this afternoon. If the pathologist finds any sign of a struggle, or contentious injuries, then the coroner will decide if a suspicious death or murder investigation is required.'

'OK, arrange for the PM and finish what you need to do here.'

'Will you be attending?' Lawrence asked.

'No . . .'

'May I?' Jane asked.

Murphy glared at her. 'Not unless you'd like an instant transfer back to division?'

'What do you mean, sir?'

'The Flying Squad don't deal with suspicious deaths or murder. Division can deal with it and inform me of the PM result.'

'But one of our suspects might have pushed her.'

'Right now, you're pushing me to the limit, Tennison. I had the duty inspector on the phone to me at home last night, about a Mr Jones who made an official complaint about you and Teflon interviewing his daughter without his permission.'

'She's seventeen, and legally an adult.'

'I don't give a toss what age she is – I specifically told you not to speak to her and you disobeyed me. I want you and Teflon to go back to the office right now.'

He marched off, and Lawrence could tell Jane felt she'd been deliberately humiliated in front of him.

'Ignore him, Jane, he's always been an overbearing twat.'

Jane sighed heavily. 'He's been on my case since day one and is determined to get rid of me. He told me I was only transferred to the squad as an experiment.'

'What do you mean?'

'I'll tell you later. Is it OK to ring you at home this evening?'

'You know you can call me any time, day or night. But the best way to shove two fingers up at Murphy is to do what you do best – and that's being a damn good detective.'

'I'm trying, Paul. Believe me, I'm trying.'

CHAPTER TWENTY-EIGHT

Jane was still preoccupied by Murphy's dressing-down as Teflon drove back to Rigg Approach.

'That's what he must have had the hump about when he spoke to Cam this morning.'

'Murphy bent my ear before he spoke to you in the pub.'

'I hope you told him it was my fault.'

'I told him you were right about Abby Jones lying, then repeated what she told us at her house – that the gunman wasn't wearing a mask and had a cut to his head.'

'How did he take that?'

'I think I hit a nerve. He asked me if I thought Abby would be able to identify him. I said I was almost certain she could, but her father pressured her to lie and say she couldn't.'

'What did he say to that?'

'Just that he'd speak to the pair of us later. I think he's just testing your mettle to see if you're up to the job. Murphy told me Jones attended the station *wanting* to make an official complaint, which suggests the duty officer persuaded him not to and we'll be given words of advice.'

'He might still make a formal complaint.'

'So what? It's not a sacking offence; worst we can get is a slap on the wrist and a pocket notebook caution for disobeying him, which means it's the end of the matter.'

'I'm not so sure he'll do that with me—'

'Nah, I backed you up. He can't treat us any differently.'

'Thanks for your support, it means a lot to me—'

He shrugged. 'That's what we do on the squad – we watch each other's backs.'

Now that Jane could feel a mutual respect growing between her and Teflon, she wondered if she should tell him about her conversation with Betty, and how Kingston had dismissed her as an unreliable witness. Stranger still was the fact he'd never mentioned Betty's evidence in any of the office meetings. She looked out of the passenger window, sighed to herself and decided not to say anything to him, worrying that all it might accomplish would be to damage the bond that was forming between them if she were to question Kingston's integrity. Which meant she either had to keep her suspicions to herself or confront Kingston about it face to face.

* * *

Murphy sat at his desk writing a misdemeanour caution in their pocket notebooks, while Jane and Teflon stood to attention. Jane felt like she was back at school, standing in front of the headmistress and being told off for her bad behaviour in class. Teflon gave her a side-on glance and a 'told you so' smile. She tried not to smile back in case Murphy looked up.

'Next time I won't be so lenient.' He handed back their pocket notebooks. 'You're lucky the Leytonstone duty officer persuaded Mr Jones not to make a full-blown complaint. I suggest you find out what he drinks and buy him a bottle . . . *each*!'

'Yes, sir,' they replied in unison.

'Type up a detailed report of your conversation with Abby Jones and her father, then file it as NFA.'

'Excuse me, sir,' Jane said, 'but I wondered if this would be a convenient time to tell you about our visit to the Wilson sisters yesterday?'

'Was the result as bad as the Joneses?' he asked in a sarcastic tone.

'To be honest . . . yes and no,' Jane admitted.

'Let's hear it then . . .'

Jane gave him a summary of what she'd learnt about the twins.

'Bloody hell, those girls have had a tragic life,' Murphy remarked.

'I think the reason they've managed to come through it is because they have each other,' Jane said. 'Would you like me to make some enquiries about the uncle?' she added.

'No, pass on all the details to Tottenham CID and they can see what he's up to. Our priority now is the Ripley brothers and the other Securicor van robbery suspects.'

'Yes, sir. Rachel did these drawings of the Ripley brothers and the suspect named Carl.'

She got them out of her bag and handed them to Murphy.

'Bloody hell, these are detailed. Make a load of copies for the surveillance operation.'

He handed them back to her.

'Are you happy for Rachel to continue using the Bluebird cafe?' she asked.

'Yes, I want her to continue lip-reading what our suspects say, then report back to you.'

'Will you be using her as a prosecution witness if we get to trial?' Teflon asked, knowing it was a concern for Jane.

'Not if I can help it. She's a reliable source of information, but I don't want her facing some obnoxious defence barrister who's going to attack her honesty. I've called the squad back in for a meeting about the surveillance operation, so let me know when everyone's in.'

Jane and Teflon turned to leave.

'One other thing, Tennison.'

She turned, steeling herself for another rebuke.

'I want you working undercover in the Bluebird from tomorrow, OK?'

'Thank you, sir. I'll get my old waitress uniform out of the wardrobe.' She smiled.

'Don't go overboard. Now go get that Jones report done.'

* * *

As she walked back into the office, Cam called out to her.

'A DS Boon from West End Central called this morning while you were out.'

'Did he leave a message?'

'Yeah, he just said that the complainant in a case you were interested in withdrew their allegation and there'll be no further action against the suspect.'

'Thanks, Cam,' Jane said, suppressing her delight.

She got straight on the phone and Pam answered.

'Have you heard the good news?'

'Yes, DS Boon called Tony. The woman changed her mind and said she didn't want to press charges or give evidence.'

'Tony's learnt a lesson, Pam – albeit the hard way. How's it going between you?'

'We're getting there, and we won't be breaking up.'

'I'm pleased for you both. I've got to go as I'm in the office.'

She ended the call and phoned Nick at the Bluebird cafe. She was relieved to find he was still happy for her to work as a waitress. She asked if she should wear a waitress's outfit and he laughed, telling her it wasn't the Ritz. She should just wear jeans and a T-shirt, and he would give her an apron.

She then went to speak to Cam, who was sitting at Katie's desk doing some of her paperwork.

'I was just wondering if that PC you spoke to at Wood Green about Mehmet Osman mentioned anything about his brother Asil?'

'No. Why do you ask?'

'Emma Wilson said he was involved in her father's criminal activities before going back to Cyprus, but he's come back to London claiming to be a successful fruit exporter.'

'Drugs, more like. I'll ring the PC and see what I can dig up.'

'If you don't mind, that'd be great.'

'Looks like I'm going to be stuck driving Katie's desk for a while, as she's gone sick.'

'What's wrong with her?'

'Apparently she had a big bust-up with her boyfriend over Kingston. I reckon she's too embarrassed to come in.'

'Sorry to hear that . . . Is Kingston in his office?'

'He's been in it all day – looks like he's spent the night there.'

'Does he know about Fiona Simpson's death?'

Cam nodded. 'I told him after Teflon called it in.'

'How'd he take it?'

'He seemed quite shocked. He was at the pub yesterday evening talking to her about going to the Yard.'

'He told you he was at the pub?'

'Yes, why?'

'We were trying to find out who else was working behind the bar . . . so he might know.'

Jane went to her desk and sat down. She started typing her report, then stopped.

'It's now or never,' she said to herself, getting up.

She knocked on Kingston's office door and put her head around.

'I just wanted to talk to you about Fiona Simpson.'

'Sure, come in. I heard you and Teflon found her body.'

'Yes. Paul Lawrence is examining the scene and arranging a post mortem for this afternoon.'

'Does he think it's suspicious?'

'Too early to say. There were no signs of a struggle at the pub, so she either fell or was pushed down the cellar stairs, probably after changing a barrel. Cam said you were there last night, about her visiting albums.'

'Yeah, she was keen to do it.'

'Do you know who was working behind the bar with her?'

'There was just one other girl while I was there. I think her name was Sarah, but Fiona let her go about half ten as the pub was so quiet.'

She thought about asking Kingston what time he left, but didn't want to appear over-inquisitive.

'Lawrence thinks she died around midnight.'

'Then she must have closed up and been on her own.'

'Or one of our suspects hid in the pub waiting for everyone to leave.'

'I left just before closing time and there was only about five people still there. As I recall two of them were young guys playing darts in the saloon bar, and the other three were a group of old boys in their fifties – none of whom looked like our suspects.'

'I'm probably letting my imagination run away with me,' she said nervously, still unsure about mentioning Betty.

He tilted his head as he looked at her. 'What is it you're not telling me, Jane?'

'What do you mean?'

'Something's bothering you, isn't it?'

'Nothing's bothering me.'

'Do you know about Katie's boyfriend calling my wife?'

Jane sighed. 'Yes.'

'Well, if that's what you're worried about, I've spoken to Katie and she didn't tell him about the fight with you.'

'Her boyfriend should have spoken to you; what he did was a cheap form of revenge.'

'Maybe, but I doubt Katie did much to try and stop him.'

'Does Murphy know what happened?'

'Yes, I told him first thing this morning. He wasn't exactly pleased, but he was even more pissed off with you about speaking to Abby Jones.'

'He gave me and Teflon a pocket notebook caution.'

'You were lucky – if you'd gone there on your own, he would have served you with a 163 disciplinary action. Basically, Teflon saved your bacon.'

Jane couldn't hold back any longer.

'I spoke to an elderly woman this morning who was walking past the getaway car before the robbery. She said the driver opened the door and nearly knocked her for six. She saw his face and from her description I believe it's our suspect Graham Smith.'

Kingston leant back in his chair and laughed.

'For fuck's sake, is that what's bothering you?'

She frowned. 'I don't see what's so funny. Betty said you never interviewed her, but you told me you did, and that she was an unreliable witness. As far as I can see she's as bright as a button and the only identification witness we've got, now Simpson's dead and Abby Jones won't help us.'

'Fiona Simpson saw what happened from the pub window, so she told me about Betty.'

'Then why didn't you mention it in any of the meetings?'

'Simpson asked me not to use Betty as a witness because she's elderly and recently lost her husband. I agreed not to unless it was absolutely necessary, so I kept her name out of my report.'

She looked at him uncertainly. 'Betty was adamant that neither she or Fiona Simpson told anyone they saw the driver's face—'

He pointed his finger at her. 'Whoa! Stop right there before you dig a big hole for yourself. I'll give you ten out of ten for tenacity, but you're way off base if you think I or anyone else on this squad is a leak or has anything to do with Simpson's death.'

'I never said that.'

'No, but you're insinuating it. For your information I told Murphy about Betty straight after I first spoke to Simpson. He agreed with me about keeping her out of it – if you don't believe me go and ask him.'

Jane was taken aback. 'I'm sorry—'

'Look, I was shocked to discover Fiona Simpson was dead – and of course it's crossed my mind that it might be connected to our investigation – but I'm on the fence until we get the post mortem result and Lawrence finishes examining the scene.'

'I shouldn't have doubted you.'

'You're not the first and you won't be the last – but at least you were up front with me.'

Jane felt a sense of relief, mixed with shame, that she'd jumped to the wrong conclusion.

'I heard the money I gave the Colonel was well spent,' he said.

'Sorry, what are you talking about?'

'The money from the informants' fund for his snout.'

'Yeah, looks like Gentleman Jim was talking about Aidan O'Reilly.'

She was now certain the Colonel had stolen a ten-pound note.

There was a knock on the door and Cam looked in.

'Guv's ready to start the meeting.'

* * *

Jane was not the only one eager to hear what Murphy had to say.

'As you all know, our witness Fiona Simpson is dead. Her post mortem is scheduled for three p.m., but whatever the outcome, Division will deal with the investigation and keep us informed. If her death is deemed to be suspicious, only me or DI Kingston will speak to Division, as there is obviously sensitive information that I don't want disclosed at this time. Before I speak about the surveillance operation, has anyone anything further to add about our suspects?'

The Colonel raised his hand.

'DI Kingston told me about your snout's information – it looks promising, but we need more.'

'He's working on it. I also got an address from Companies House for George Ripley—'

'How'd you get that on a Sunday?' Murphy interrupted.

'You don't want to know, Guv.'

'I do, Colonel.' He frowned.

'I told the security guard I was Commander Drury from Scotland Yard and needed to check some files urgently.'

'Drury's in prison,' Stanley said.

'Then he won't know I used his name, will he?' The Colonel grinned.

'George Ripley's got a big house in Gravel Lane, Chigwell, called Farthings,' he continued. 'Which is ironic as a farthing was worth a quarter of a penny. We did a drive-by recce and the house has big iron gates and a high wall at the front with a long gravel driveway. There's woodland at the back and a field opposite, so the only way you can do surveillance on the place is in an OBO van, but it's a country lane and you'd stand out like a sore thumb.'

Murphy wrote down the details in his pocket notebook.

'What about setting up road or gas works?' Kingston asked.

'Again, a bit obvious. You can only go left or right out of the property, so a surveillance vehicle at either junction could pick up the target.'

'Problem is, without a fixed OP on the house we won't know when Ripley leaves,' Murphy reflected.

'You could stick a CROPS officer in the field opposite the gates or woodland in the grounds,' Stanley suggested, referring to highly trained Covert Rural Observation Post Surveillance officers.

'Good thinking, Stanley,' Murphy said. 'You ever do CROPS work when you were on the surveillance squad?'

'Thankfully I wasn't trained to that level – I never fancied living in a hole for days with my own piss and shit to keep me company.'

'That's not true – I remember your room in the section house before you got married,' the Colonel quipped, to a roar of laughter.

'All right, enough of the jokes!' Murphy barked. 'Anything else on George Ripley?'

Bax had some information. 'All Saints Church is at one end of Gravel Lane, so on the off chance we popped in and had a quick word with the vicar about any forthcoming marriages. We struck lucky – Tina Ripley is getting married there this Saturday at three o'clock, but the vicar didn't know where the reception is being held.

I also got George and Tommy Ripley's home phone numbers from the PO.'

Murphy looked pleased. 'Excellent work. You two have been busy.'

'Did the vicar ask why you wanted to know about that particular wedding?' Kingston asked.

'Yes, but we didn't say who we were interested in and assured him we wouldn't disrupt the service or reception. He gave us his word he wouldn't tell anyone we spoke to him.'

'Is Tina Ripley marrying our suspect Carl?' Jane asked.

'No, it's a bloke called Duncan Sharpin, who's no trace CRO.'

'Hope he knows what sort of family he's marrying into,' Teflon joked.

Murphy asked Stanley how he'd got on regarding observation points for the other suspects. He said he had secured a suitable observation point in a two-storey house, owned by an elderly couple, in the next road down from GR Motors. He'd been in the house and from the back bedroom there was an unobstructed view of the car sales front, offices and repair garage.

Murphy made some more notes, then asked Stanley to continue.

'Cam made some enquiries yesterday on Maria Fernandez's address in Stamford Hill. She doesn't live there any more, but the mail forwarding address she gave the Post Offices is twelve Connington House, Chingford, which is where Tommy Ripley lives. I couldn't find a suitable OP there, but an OBO van with two other surveillance vehicles should be enough to follow him to and from the premises. I also secured an OP in a flat above an off-licence that overlooks O'Reilly's place in Seven Sisters Road. There are side streets for the surveillance vehicles to park up and wait for the "off" shout from the OP. It's a busy area, so if he travels on foot or by bus it will be easy to follow the target. I checked out the view from the newsagent's opposite the Bluebird – it's a good one that takes in the snooker hall as well. That covers all the addresses we have so far.'

'Good work. We can tail Graham Smith when he leaves GR Motors, and hopefully we'll get a visual sighting of the suspect Carl and can then tail him. Any more on the man in the camel hair coat, Tennison?'

'Rachel Wilson identified a vehicle in *Exchange & Mart*. I'll let Teflon tell you about it as he's the car guru.'

'She picked out a silver Jensen Interceptor Mark 3, but said the one she saw was maroon in colour. She was confident it was the car and possibly a convertible, but she wasn't sure. The company folded in '76, but they only sold a few hundred a year, so we might be able to backtrack on maroon ones sold to London residents.'

'That'll take a long time,' Cam remarked, knowing he'd have to do it.

Murphy agreed with him.

'Let's try and pick up the Jensen on surveillance first. The surveillance operation will commence at six a.m. tomorrow and the targets will be followed until it's safe to assume they've gone to bed. I've got other CO11 units to assist us with the surveillance and permission for wiretaps on the Ripleys and Aidan O'Reilly's home and work phones. DI Kingston and I just need ten minutes to finalise the details of who will be in the static OPs, or armed in vehicles on the ground, then I want you all to go home and get some rest before tomorrow. You'll be working long hours for at least the next four weeks, then the squad commander will review the surveillance operation. The bottom line is we don't know if, when or where our suspects will carry out another robbery, but if they do, we have the element of surprise on our side. Some Level 1 officers from D11 Firearms Command will be working with us, but as you all know, our suspects are trigger-happy and will be armed with handguns and sawn-offs – so don't hesitate to shoot the bastards if you feel your life is threatened. Just make sure you hit the bloody target!'

* * *

When Jane left the office at 4 p.m., the result of Fiona Simpson's post mortem hadn't come in, but she knew the examination of the body could take two to three hours and she could ring Paul Lawrence later in the evening. She was still feeling on a high after the office meeting. The last few days had had their ups and downs, but everything was coming together, and although Murphy was giving her a hard time, the others seemed to have accepted her as part of the team. Thinking about the suspects being ambushed and arrested 'on the pavement' was exhilarating, and she hoped it would happen sooner rather than later. Not being authorised to carry a gun, Jane knew she wouldn't be part of the arrest team, but she hoped at some point Murphy would let her go on a firearms course. She smiled to herself, thinking of her mother's shock if she found out her daughter carried a gun and was involved in the arrest of armed men in the middle of a robbery. Thinking of her mother, she wondered if she ought to go and see her parents after the stressful situation with Tony and Pam. She decided against it, as she didn't fancy repeating everything she'd told Pam and needed an early night.

When she got home Jane got a pair of jeans, a white T-shirt and red roll neck jumper out of her wardrobe to wear in the cafe. She then had a hot bath, put on some tracksuit bottoms and a T-shirt, and poured herself a glass of wine. Feeling hungry, she cooked herself a large portion of spaghetti bolognese and some garlic bread, then turned on the TV. She flicked through the channels, but there was nothing on she wanted to watch, so she decided to read some more of *Medea* instead. The story about a woman's revenge on her husband couldn't help but make her think about the goings-on in the office. She hoped Kingston's wife didn't start poisoning people like Medea had.

The phone rang and she quickly answered it.

'Hi, it's Paul – we've just finished the PM.'

'What was the result?' she asked eagerly.

'Inconclusive, I'm afraid. She died from an acute subdural hae-matoma.'

'In layman's terms, please.'

'When her head hit the concrete, it cracked her skull open and probably knocked her out. But it also ruptured a vein, which then filled the brain with blood and ultimately led to her death. If she'd got immediate treatment, she might have survived.'

'Was she pushed?'

'There's no bruising on her body to support that conclusion—'

'But she could have been?'

'Yes. I found some footprints in the men's toilets—'

'How on earth is that going to help? Dozens of people must have been in there.'

'Christ, you can be impatient at times, Jane. The prints were on the cubicle toilet seat, which I don't believe you need to stand on to have a crap.'

Jane could suddenly see it.

'Oh my God, someone must have been hiding in there when she locked up.'

'It's possible. They look like trainer marks, but I can't say when they got there, plus someone might have stood on the seat to fix the cistern. I've removed the seat and I'll take it back to the lab for a closer examination.'

'What about the Chubb key? Do you think you'll get a print off it?'

'I'm going to try a new technique using superglue.'

'Superglue? How does that work?'

'I'll put the keys in a glass tank next to a tray with some super-glue in it. Heating the glue makes it vaporise and releases fumes into the container. The vapours adhere to any fingerprints, mak-ing them visible, then I can enhance them by using dyes or pow-ders. However, it's a bit of a slow process and can take a day or two.'

'Fingers crossed you get something, and it's not Fiona Simpson's print.'

Jane thanked Paul and ended the call. As she got ready for bed, the image of a man hiding in the toilets, calmly waiting until his victim was alone, wouldn't leave her mind, and she wasn't sure if she would sleep.

CHAPTER TWENTY-NINE

All the observation points were operational by 6 a.m.: OP1 was the newsagent's in Bruce Grove, manned by Bax; OP2 was George Ripley's house, the entrance to which was being watched by a CROPS officer from a hide in the field opposite; OP3 was Tommy Ripley's flat, being watched by Stanley in an OBO van; OP4 was GR Motors, being manned by Teflon; and OP5 was Aidan O'Reilly's flat, being manned by CO11. Each OP also had three CO11 surveillance officers ready to do foot follows, and two unmarked vehicles nearby with officers ready to tail the suspects' cars. Motorcycle surveillance officers were also parked up near the Ripleys' addresses.

Kingston and the Colonel were carrying revolvers and parked up at Tottenham Police Station, with firearms officers from D11 in two unmarked cars, ready to pounce on the suspects if they committed a robbery. Murphy was with Cam at Rigg Approach controlling the operation. Their call sign was 'Gold'. George Ripley was Target 1, Tommy Ripley Target 2, Aidan O'Reilly Target 3 and Graham Smith Target 4. If the suspect believed to be Carl was seen he would be Target 5, and the man in the camel hair coat Target 6.

* * *

Jane parked her car in a back street away from the cafe.

Nick opened the door when she arrived. '*Buongiorno*, officer Tennison.'

'*Buongiorno*, Nick. I think it would be best if you called me Jane.'

'OK, Jane. You wanna cappuccino?'

'Yes please.'

'*Bene*, you gonna make it on the machine, and I watch you.'

'Straight in at the deep end, eh? I've never used an espresso machine, but I'll give it a go.'

'You better learn quick, cause we open in an hour.' He handed her a short-waist black apron with pockets in it for a pen and order pad. 'I tell you how to make the cappuccino.'

Under Nick's guidance she poured some cold milk into a metal steaming pitcher, then held it under the tip of the steaming wand on the espresso machine and turned the dial, releasing the steam.

'Not too much or you burn the milk.'

She turned the steamer off, and with a little help from Nick made a single shot of espresso, which she poured into a large cup. She picked up the steamed milk and went to pour it into the cup.

'*Aspettare, aspettare*, you have to give it a tap first. You tap the bottom of the pitcher on the counter to bring the foam to the top.'

She finished making the cappuccino and Nick took a swallow.

'*Molto buona . . .* Is good.'

'Would you like me to do any cooking?'

'No, *il cucinare* is my job – you just take and serve the orders.'

Nick spent the next half hour going over the menu, then showed Jane how the till worked and where everything was kept.

'Any problem you just ask me, but from what I see so far you are very good.'

* * *

Everyone on the surveillance team was maintaining radio silence as they waited for the suspects to appear. It was 8.30 a.m. when the CROPS officer's voice was heard over the radio.

'All units from OP2, Target 1 has left premises in gold Mercedes 450SL convertible, index X-ray, Papa, Echo 264 Sierra. Vehicle has turned left towards junction with Abridge Road.'

'OP1 from Central five two, we have eyeball on Target 1 vehicle and ready to follow,' the detective said.

There was another period of radio silence, until one of the CO11 officers watching Aidan O'Reilly's flat piped up.

'All units from OP5, Target 3 has left premises and waiting at bus stop on north side of the road. Officers on foot have eyeball and are following.'

It wasn't long before Stanley, in an OBO van at Chingford, came on the air.

'Target 2 in red Mini, X-ray, Lima, Oscar 67 Romeo, being driven by IC1 female. Now in Hatch Lane heading towards roundabout.'

'Central solo six four has eyeball,' the plain clothes motorcycle officer said as he started to follow the Mini.

'LJ to Gold, receiving, over?' Teflon said.

'Go ahead, LJ,' Cam replied.

'IC1 male matching Target 4's description opening garage at premises opposite OP4. His vehicle is a dark blue Mark 3 Capri Ghia, index Victor, Hotel, Kilo 499 Tango.'

He started to take some photographs with a zoom lens camera. Cam did a vehicle check on the PNC as he listened.

'Vehicle's shown as registered to Target 4,' he told Teflon.

Murphy was standing next to Cam.

'Good, all our main targets are on the move. Looks like Maria Fernandez is driving Tommy Ripley to work.'

'The Mini is registered to her at Tommy's Hatch Lane address. Jane said a witness at Edgar House saw a man matching George Ripley's description driving a gold Mercedes,' Cam reminded him.

Murphy picked up the radio. 'All units from Gold . . . Female driving mini will be Target 7.' He turned to Cam. 'Let's hope the Ripley brothers are going to the Bluebird.'

* * *

Nearly half an hour passed before Bax spoke on the radio and Dabs started taking photographs.

'All units from OP1, the Mini has parked around the back of the snooker hall and Targets 2, 3 and 7 have just gone in . . . Stand by . . .' He paused as the gold Mercedes drove around the back of the hall. 'Target 1 has just turned up and driven into the car park.' He waited, then watched as George Ripley appeared. 'All units, Target 1 has entered hall.'

As soon as Bax had finished, Teflon had an update from OP4 regarding the suspect Carl.

'An IC1 male matching Target 5's description has just turned up at the garage driving a white Ford Transit van, Oscar Mike Echo 547 November.'

Cam did a PNC check and spoke to Teflon.

'The vehicle is registered to the garage – Gold said to assume the driver is Target 5 for now.'

'Received,' Teflon replied.

* * *

Jane had just finished clearing and wiping down a table when Rachel came in and sat down.

Nick gave her a wave and whispered to Jane, 'She a *sordomuto* – you have to give her the pad and she write down what she want.'

Jane thought it was funny that he was whispering, then went over to Rachel and handed her the pen and notepad. Rachel wrote down what she wanted and handed the pad back to Jane, who, without thinking, started to read out her order of a bacon and egg sandwich for Rachel to lip-read it was correct. Rachel looked at her, wide-eyed, and started to tap her ears and mouth, indicating she couldn't hear or speak. Jane tore the order off the pad and handed it to Nick, who shook his head.

'I just tell you she deaf and you talk to her when she no can understand what you a say.'

Jane felt herself reddening. 'Sorry, I won't do it again.'

As Jane gave Rachel her cup of tea, the cafe door opened and the Ripley brothers walked in. Glancing around, she was instantly struck by the likeness to the drawings Rachel had done of them. George was wearing a green waxed Barbour jacket just like the one Rita Brown had described, and a blue open-neck shirt with grey Farah slacks. Tommy was dressed in a black roll neck jumper, black trousers and wearing the gold boxing gloves pendant Rachel had spoken about. Jane was surprised how normal they looked. It was hard to imagine them carrying shotguns and threatening people, though George did walk with a confident swagger. Tommy, by contrast, shuffled along meekly behind him.

A young man sitting at their usual table by the wall moved when he saw them. Jane felt nervous but, knowing she had to appear calm and natural, took a deep breath and went to take their order.

'Good morning, gentleman, what can I get you?'

'Bloody hell, makes a change to see a pretty face serving up in here, darlin',' Tommy said.

She smiled. 'Thanks . . . darlin'.'

Tommy winked. 'My pleasure.'

George laughed. 'A bit of sass as well. You having the full English?' His brother nodded. 'Same for me, and two coffees.'

'Cappuccinos, latte or—'

'None of that shit – just normal with milk.'

As Jane took their order over to Nick, she thought George was ill-mannered as he never once said 'please' or 'thank you'. She noted that, like the Securicor guard had mentioned, George had a gravelly voice and brown eyes.

While making their coffees she glanced over and could see them leaning towards each other, as if discussing something in private.

She looked over at Rachel, who had a hardback novel open on the tabletop and was writing in a notebook as if making notes for an essay, while looking out of the corner of her eye to try and lip-read what George was saying.

When the Ripleys' full Englishes were ready she took the food over to them.

'I like your boxing gloves pendant,' she said as she put the plate down in front of Tommy.

'It's eighteen carat gold and worth a few bob,' he boasted.

'Did you win it in a fight?'

He laughed. 'No, me girlfriend Maria bought it for me. We just won tin cups or a belt when I was boxing.'

'My dad did a bit of boxing.'

'Where was his club?' Tommy asked.

'Above the Thomas A Becket pub in the Old Kent Road,' she said, remembering it from when she worked in the CID at Peckham.

He looked impressed. 'That's a well-known club – it's produced some famous boxers. Henry Cooper trained there six days a week for fourteen years, and Muhammad Ali and Joe Frazier sparred there.'

'My dad wasn't that good. He told me he spent more time on the canvas than on his feet.'

Tommy laughed. 'I know the feeling. My old club produced a few amateur champions, but I wasn't one of them.'

'Where was your club?' she asked.

'Chingford, at the TA drill hall.'

She felt her stomach churn as she remembered the photograph of Kingston in his office, with CHINGFORD AMATEUR BOXING CLUB 1958 on it, and him telling her the club was at the Territorial Army drill hall.

'Get us some more brown sauce, darlin', this 'un's empty,' George said, handing her the bottle.

* * *

Teflon watched as Carl got in the Transit van and a plume of black smoke spluttered out of the exhaust as he started the engine.

'All units from OP4, Target 5 is on the move in white Transit van.'

'Received by Central five six, we will follow with a solo.'

A few minutes later Bax was on the radio.

'Target 5 parking Transit outside hall and out on foot towards cafe.'

*   *   *

George looked out of the window and spoke with a mouthful of sausage.

'We better change the subject. Carl's on his way.'

'Have you never thought about getting him on a job?' Tommy asked.

'Nah, he's a fucking mummy's boy.'

George took a mouthful of coffee to wash his food down.

'Why you always so hard on him?'

''Cause he's a retard and ain't from my loins.'

'It's not his fault he's backward,' Tommy said, looking serious.

George's eyes narrowed. 'What you mean by that?'

'Nothing, forget it—'

'Come on, spit it out – don't be a wimp like Carl,' he said aggressively.

'The boy's the way he is because you knocked him about.'

George shrugged. 'Weren't my fault he tripped and cracked his skull . . .' He looked over at Jane, who was behind the counter plating up some food. He snapped his fingers. 'Bring us another coffee, luv.'

Jane tried hard to keep a pleasant smile on her face as she put a spoonful of coffee in a clean cup, then saw Carl walk into the cafe wearing a blue boiler suit. He looked exactly as Rachel had described him: in his late twenties, extremely handsome, with sea-blue eyes and long wavy blond hair.

'You found a bird for the wedding yet after that tart gave you the boot?' George asked as Carl joined them.

'Not yet—'

'Well, you better do 'cause I've got to fork out the dosh for two hundred meals and I ain't having an empty seat in the marquee because of you.'

Jane put George's coffee on the table.

'What can I get you?' she asked Carl.

'A decent woman would be good,' George said with a deep guttural laugh. 'Come to think of it, gorgeous, what you doing this Saturday?'

Carl looked embarrassed.

Jane felt like telling him it was none of his business, but instead said, 'I don't know yet. Why?'

'You fancy going to a wedding with him?' George pointed his knife at Carl.

'But we haven't even met,' Jane replied.

'Another rejection, son. You'd probably get a yes from a poofter, though, with hair like yours.'

He smiled nastily, then lit a cigar with a gold Dunhill gas lighter with the initials GR on it.

Jane felt sorry for Carl, who looked hurt by George's gibes. He sounded totally dejected as he ordered a coffee and sausage sandwich.

'He's got errands to run, so he ain't got time for food,' George said, taking a large wedge of cash out of his pocket and a piece of notepaper. 'I want ya to go down the builder's merchants and get some stuff for Smudge.'

He handed Carl the note and some cash. Carl pocketed them and then got up to go to the toilet.

Jane picked up the dirty plates from the table and took them to the sink behind the counter. Rachel came up to the counter to pay for her food and Jane handed her the bill. She had a folded five-pound note in her hand, which she passed to Jane, along with a few bits of notepaper, which Jane slipped into her pocket under the counter.

She was wiping down a table when Carl came out of the toilet and approached her.

'I'm sorry about my stepfather – he likes to think he's funny, but he isn't.'

'It's all right, you've no need to apologise.'

'I was wondering if you would do me a favour.'

'And what would that be?'

'Would you come to my stepsister's wedding with me?' he asked awkwardly.

For a moment she was lost for words.

'Sorry, I'm being stupid. Of course you're not going to say yes – you don't know me from Adam.'

He started to walk off. Her first instinct was to let him go. After all, it was a pretty odd thing to do – to invite someone you'd only just met to a wedding. She wondered if he was a bit simple, or just determined to prove George wrong, but then she quickly thought what a great opportunity this could be to help the team identify other associates of the Ripley brothers.

'Go on, then. I love a good wedding. Where is it?'

His face lit up.

'All Saint's Church in Chigwell at three o'clock on Saturday, then the reception's in a marquee at my stepdad's house just up the road.' He smiled sheepishly. 'I don't know your name.'

'It's Jane.'

'I'm Carl. Would you like to go for a drink before Saturday? Then we could actually get to know each other a bit. Give you a chance to duck out of the wedding if you decide you don't fancy coming with me,' he added with a grin that Jane could see hid a touch of sadness.

'That sounds like a good idea. OK.'

'Do you have a number I can call you on?'

'Er . . . I don't have a phone – but I could meet you outside the Empire Ballroom in Leicester Square, say tonight at 7.30.'

'That'd be great – I'll see you then,' he said, beaming.

As he left the cafe Jane wondered what Murphy would say when she told him.

'Hey, Jane, what you doing?' Nick called out, interrupting her thoughts. 'These dirty plates won't clean themselves.'

'Can I just nip to the toilet?'

'*Mamma mia!* Go on then.'

She closed the toilet door, then got Rachel's notes out of her pocket.

M1 asked M2 if he had sorted the driver out for Saturday and M2 nodded. He also asked M2 if his man had spoken with the woman. I don't know what M2 said, but M1 looked angry and said, 'He was only supposed to put the frighteners on her.' Then he spoke about someone called Carl and said he was a retarded wimp.

Jane suspected George was referring to a wedding car driver for Saturday, but the reference to the man putting the frighteners on a woman sent a shiver down her spine. She was sure it was something to do with Fiona Simpson. She remembered Rachel telling her that George Ripley had said to Tommy that 'Riley' was a loose cannon. Since Aidan O'Reilly worked for Tommy Ripley, she wondered if he was the man George was referring to. If he was, then it followed that O'Reilly was in the Crown on Saturday night.

She suddenly felt nauseous thinking about Kingston, wondering if it was more than mere coincidence that he was in the same boxing club as Tommy Ripley. He'd also been in the Crown shortly before Fiona Simpson died, and said the pub was quiet. It struck her that if Aidan O'Reilly had been there, Kingston would have known, or at least suspected, it was him. Like everyone on the team, he'd seen the photo the RUC had faxed over of the six feet four O'Reilly, who now also had a cut on his forehead. Her mind was spinning and her stomach churning at the thought that Kingston may have deliberately distracted Fiona Simpson while O'Reilly slipped into the pub and hid in the toilet. The thought that he could be complicit in her death and leaking information to the Ripleys was beyond comprehension, and she didn't know what to do about it.

There was a knock on the toilet door.

'You all right, Jane?' Nick asked.

'Yes, just a bit of a queasy stomach.'

'OK, make a sure you spray the air freshener.'

When she came out of the toilet the Ripley brothers had gone. She took their coffee cups and tucked them away under the counter to take back to the office with her, so Dabs could fingerprint them.

*   *   *

Cam put the phone down and turned to Murphy.

'Fingerprint Bureau say the prints sent over by the RUC are a match for Aidan O'Reilly. George Ripley is in his office at the showroom, and CO11 tailed the suspect Carl to a builder's merchant where he purchased some boiler suits.'

'Do we know how many?'

'Three.'

'Looks like they're getting their outfits together for a robbery and Carl is their errand boy. After we nick 'em all on the pavement he might be the weak link and cough up about any other robberies they've done.'

'I also spoke to Tommy Ripley's bank manager. He took out a forty grand loan to buy the ground floor of the old cinema and turn it into a snooker hall. He's already late on the payments.'

'So, he's desperate for money. What about George Ripley?'

'According to the tax man he doesn't make a fortune, and certainly not enough for his kind of lifestyle.'

'He's probably got a hooky accountant and doesn't run every sale through the books. I'm just going to see how the wiretaps are going.'

He went into Kingston's office. Two officers from CO11 intelligence unit had five reel-to-reel recorders set up to tape any conversations on the Ripleys' work and home phones.

'Anything interesting so far?'

'No. A few calls to GR Motors about MOTs, servicing, et cetera, and O'Reilly ordering booze and crisps for the snooker club. Ripley's wife, Maureen, has been on and off the phone all morning to caterers and friends about the wedding. You'll like this – she's talking to a friend of hers about the flowers.'

The officer rewound the tape and turned it on. She spoke in a screechy cockney accent.

'The flowers are costin' a bloody fortune. I could 'ave a dirty weekend in Southend for the price of the bridal bouquet . . . I mean, it's a total load of bollocks, all this flingin' it over your shoulder to the single gals,' Maureen said.

'Oh, don't be mean, whoever catches it will have a future filled with love and happiness,' her friend replied.

'Well, I caught me sister's and she ended up shaggin' me first 'usband. All it did was fill me with a desire to cut 'is knackers off with a pair of scissors!'

Murphy laughed. 'Ouch, I wouldn't like to upset her. Let us know if you hear anything of interest.'

* * *

It was just after 3 p.m. The cafe was empty, and Nick put the closed sign on the door. Jane popped upstairs with the coffee cups and put them in a plastic bag in her shoulder bag. She then radioed in that the cafe was closing. Cam said Murphy wanted her to return to the station.

'You done good work today, Jane,' Nick said as she put her coat on.

She felt exhausted. 'It's been a long time since I was on my feet for so long. I wish I'd worn my trainers instead of my thin flat soles.'

'You gonna come in tomorrow?' he asked, opening the door.

'I expect so, but it's up to my boss. *Arrivederci*, Nick.'

Walking to her car, Jane thought about Kingston and wondered if he was corrupt and involved with the Ripley brothers. If he had lied, then Betty could be in danger. She knew if she told Murphy, or anyone on the team, she risked being ostracised for daring to question an experienced and respected officer's integrity. She took a deep breath and blew it out in an effort to unclutter her mind. Seeing a public phone box, she dialled the lab and asked to speak to Paul Lawrence.

'The Chubb key is still in the superglue chamber, but it looks like a finger mark is starting to develop.'

'What size was the footprint on the toilet seat?'

He looked in his notes. 'It's a nine to ten Nike training shoe. Why?'

'I thought one of our suspects called Aidan O'Reilly might have gone to the Crown last night to kill Fiona Simpson. He's six foot four, so that shoe size seems unlikely for a man that tall.'

'Height isn't an exact predictor for shoe size. We're all different – some tall people have tiny feet, some short people have huge feet. From my experience, a man that tall could wear a shoe size anywhere between a nine and a fourteen. Dabs told me about O'Reilly, so as soon as I get the fingerprint developed I'll check it against O'Reilly first and let you know the result.'

'Thanks. Catch you later.'

'Come on, spit it out, what's bothering you?'

'Nothing. I've literally been on my feet and hardly slept in the last two days, so I'm really tired and irritable.'

She desperately wanted to tell Paul her suspicions about Kingston, but knew he would say not to jump to conclusions and wait for the fingerprint result on the Chubb key.

'Then go home and get some rest.'

She gave a mirthless laugh. 'I wish life was that simple.'

She put the phone down.

As she walked towards her car, Jane saw two men sitting in a vehicle parked behind hers. The passenger was leaning to one side and looking at Jane's reflection in the wing mirror. She felt a sense of unease as the passenger opened his door and began to get out of the car. Her anxiety increased when he looked at her; she wondered if her cover had been blown and the Ripleys had sent someone to get her. The man was dressed smartly in a suit and tie but he had a menacing look about him. He started walking towards her and she knew she only had two choices – to run or to stand her ground. Her head was spinning, and she wondered if her physical and mental exhaustion was making her imagine things. The man put his hand inside his jacket and for a moment Jane was paralysed with fear. She closed her eyes, thinking this was the end.

'WDS Tennison? I'm Detective Chief Superintendent Leonard Bartlett.' He spoke in a West Country accent.

She opened her eyes to see he was holding up a warrant card, but she didn't recognise the police crest badge.

'That's not a Met warrant card,' she said nervously.

'I know, I'm from Dorset Police – same as DI Wickens, who's me driver.' He nodded towards the car. 'I appreciate you're very busy, but we'd just like to have a quick word with you.'

'What about?'

'I'd rather we spoke in the car.'

She remembered Dabs referring to Dorset Police as the 'Sweedy' when they first met.

'Are you from Operation Countryman?'

'Yes. I'm in charge of it, as it happens.'

'Why do you want to speak to me? I haven't done anything wrong.'

'I know that, Jane. You've sailed a little close to the wind at times, but from what I've heard you're as honest as the day is long – and the first woman ever to be on the illustrious Flying Squad.'

She didn't like his patronising manner.

'Have you been following me?'

'Only today – and not me personally.'

She realised he must have put a surveillance team on her.

'You could have blown my cover and put me in danger.'

'We're not that reckless. It's some of your colleagues you should be more worried about.'

'Like who?' she asked, immediately thinking of Kingston.

He opened the rear nearside door and Jane got in. Bartlett turned his body to face her.

'An underworld "supergrass" has claimed that members of the Flying Squad are receiving large sums of money for warning criminals of imminent arrests and police raids, and for dropping robbery charges. We also know that evidence is being fabricated by participating informants and their controlling officers so the reward money can be shared.'

Jane suddenly found herself thinking of the Colonel and the meeting with Gentleman Jim. She also knew that he and Kingston were close.

'I still don't see what this has got to do with me.'

'Do you suspect anyone on your team of corruption?' the DI asked.

Although Jane had her suspicions about Kingston and the Colonel, she wasn't about to risk her career by making unsubstantiated allegations without knowing who Bartlett suspected.

'I've only been on the squad since last Thursday, and to be honest, as a woman I haven't been made very welcome. The rest of the team aren't very open with me. It would help if you could give me some names.'

'Our source said he'd heard it was one or two members of your team but wasn't able to give us any names, but we're confident he will,' Bartlett said.

Jane wondered if they thought she was naive, and were just fishing for any sort of information that they could use to their advantage.

'If I had evidence that an officer on the squad was corrupt, I can assure you I'd do something about it.'

'That's why we wanted to speak to you. Do you have any suspects in your current robbery investigation?'

'You know I'm not obliged to tell you anything about our investigations.'

'I'll take that as a yes,' the DI said with a wry smile.

Jane didn't like his attitude.

'You can take it however you like . . . sir. Unless there's anything else you'd like to ask me, I've got work to do.'

Bartlett sighed. 'We don't like what we do, Jane, but it's vital to stamp out corruption in the Met. Here's my card. It would be to your advantage to contact me if you suspect anyone on your team of corruption.'

'What do you mean, to my advantage?'

'I'd hate to see an honest officer get dragged under by association with a dishonest one.'

She got out of the car and slammed the door.

'Fucking arseholes,' she said to herself.

She was disgusted with their veiled threats and underhand methods. Even if she did discover evidence to prove that Kingston, the Colonel or any member of the squad was corrupt, Bartlett and his cronies would be the last people she'd tell.

CHAPTER THIRTY

Returning to Rigg Approach, Jane's feet were so sore from wait-ressing that she trudged up the stairs using the safety pole to pull herself forward.

'Christ, you look knackered,' Cam said as soon as he saw her.

'I'll tell you what, it's a lot easier pounding the beat than being a waitress.'

She took off her shoes, sat down and started to massage her feet.

'How'd it go at the cafe?'

'Not much to tell, really.'

'I spoke to that PC at Wood Green this morning about Asil Osman. He made some enquiries and phoned back earlier. Asil wasn't part of Osman's gang, and helped the CID to locate his brother after he assaulted his wife. I won't bore you with all the details, but the fruit export company he owns appears legit. Here's the company name and address, and the PC's details if you want to speak to him about it.'

He handed her a bit of paper with the details.

Jane was surprised.

'So, his money isn't hooky?'

'He's opened a distribution warehouse over here and from the enquiries I've made with Customs and Excise it doesn't appear he's importing drugs.'

'Is Murphy in?'

Cam nodded, and she went straight to his office.

'Lost your shoes?' Murphy asked.

'Do you mind if I sit down? My feet are killing me.'

'Be my guest. What happened at the cafe?'

'I didn't hear what the Ripleys were talking about, though we did have some casual conversation while I was serving them. George is the more dominant, likes the sound of his own voice and thinks he's funny. Truth is he's an ignorant pig of a man with no manners, but Tommy seemed OK.'

'When he's not robbing banks with a sawn-off in his hand,' Murphy reminded her.

'Point taken.'

'Did Rachel Wilson turn up?'

'Yes.' She handed him the note. 'She slipped me this.'

He read it and handed it back.

'Doesn't tell us much . . . Banks are closed on a Saturday, so "sorting out the driver" probably refers to one of the bridal cars. The other bit about putting the frighteners on a woman is the sort of thing they do, but it could be anyone.'

She couldn't keep the surprise out of her voice.

'You don't think it's Fiona Simpson?'

'Jesus Christ, you've really got a bee in your bonnet about her—'

'Lawrence found some shoe prints on the toilet seat, which suggests someone might have been hiding in the toilets waiting for her to close the pub. I've got a gut feeling that it might have been one of our suspects.'

'I've spoken to Lawrence and I agree with you.'

'You do?' she asked, surprised.

'I've informed the divisional DI who's investigating her death that as soon as we've completed our operation, he is free to interview the Ripleys and the other suspects about Simpson's death.'

'Why can't we, if we arrest them?'

'Because we deal with robberies,' he said firmly, indicating the matter was closed.

Cam knocked on the door and popped his head in.

'The surveillance team are wondering if you want to put anyone on Graham Smith and Carl when they leave work.'

'Tail them and find out where they live. If they can find an OP or use an OBO van on Smith then watch him until he beds down, but don't worry about Carl. We haven't got enough officers for a static observation on him.'

'OK, Guv.' Cam left.

'Carl is George Ripley's stepson and Tina is his daughter,' Jane said. 'He speaks to Carl like he's a piece of dirt and treats him like an errand boy.'

'Well, your errand boy went to a builder's merchant's earlier and bought some boiler suits. You know, the kind of thing a robber likes to wear.'

'I was serving them when George Ripley gave Carl some money and said to get some "stuff for Smudge".'

'Well, he obviously knew what he meant when George said "stuff".'

'I'm not so sure. George gave him a piece of paper with what to buy written on it.'

'The fact is he bought four, and somehow I doubt they were all for Graham Smith. Anything else of value?'

'The wedding reception is being held at Farthings in a marquee.' He gave her a quizzical look. 'How'd you find that out?'

'Carl invited me to the wedding and—'

'Jesus Christ, I hope you said *no*,' he snapped.

'I was caught in an awkward situation. George Ripley had been ribbing him about not having anyone to take to the wedding and Carl asked me out of the blue. It was a bit odd, but I saw it as an opportunity to gather more information about the Ripleys. There's no OP at the church or overlooking the grounds of the house, so I thought I could blend in at the wedding and take photographs of the guests with a pocket camera.'

'Well, you bloody well thought wrong. I'm not risking you giving the game away and screwing this operation up in a honey trap! The answer is no and that's final.'

'Do you still want me to work in the cafe?'

She already suspected what his answer would be.

'No, I want you in the office where you can't screw things up. Tell Cam you're replacing him and he can drive Kingston and the Colonel, then book off duty and go home.'

'I need to write up my report.'

'Do it tomorrow. Now get out of my sight before I really lose my temper.'

Jane bit back an angry retort and walked out of Murphy's office, silently fuming. She picked up her jacket and shoes, then slung her bag over her shoulder.

'Murphy said you're back driving the car and I'm in here, as from tomorrow morning.'

'Why, what you do?' Cam asked.

'My fucking job!'

She stormed out of the office.

*   *   *

Jane's anger hadn't abated by the time she got home. In fact, if anything she was even more furious. She went straight to the fridge and poured herself a glass of wine. She took a large mouthful, then banged the glass down on the kitchen counter and went to her bedroom. She opened the wardrobe and looked through her dresses, then took one out and held it up against her body as she looked in the mirror.

'Fine, I won't go to the bloody wedding. But nobody said anything about going out for a drink, did they?'

She turned one way and then the other.

'Nope, too dowdy.' She threw the dress on the bed and grabbed another one. 'Too short.' She threw it on the bed, said, 'Out of fashion' with the next, until finally, after taking out six dresses, she decided on the one to wear.

*   *   *

George Ripley closed up GR Motors at 6 p.m. and drove home. His daughter Tina had not been seen at work by Teflon, who'd been keeping observation on the garage. However, the CROPS officer in the field had seen Maureen Ripley and a young woman, who was assumed to be Tina, leaving and then returning to Farthings in a green Range Rover. Murphy guessed that Tina had the week off work before her wedding and was shopping with her mother. Graham Smith was tailed to a three-bedroom semi in Enfield. The CO11 officers following him remarked that he drove his Capri 'like a madman' but knew how to handle the car. Carl was followed to a one-bedroom flat in Stoke Newington. And a subsequent check in the electoral register revealed his surname was Winter and he had no criminal record. Murphy stood the firearms officers down at 5 p.m. as the banks were all closed. Tommy Ripley left the snooker hall at 6 p.m. with Maria Fernandez and returned home to his flat in Chingford, while Aidan O'Reilly remained at the snooker club, which closed at 10 p.m. on weekdays.

'Can you fucking believe it? Going to the wedding with Carl Winter? Either she's mad or she thinks I am.'

Murphy slugged down a mouthful of whisky and offered the bottle to Kingston. Kingston filled his glass.

'She's got plenty of spunk, that's for sure.'

'It's not funny, Stewart. I'll admit she's better than I ever imagined she'd be and as tenacious as hell, but she acts on impulse without thinking about the consequences.'

'Tell me about it . . . But letting her go to the wedding might not actually be a bad idea.'

'Whose side are you on?' Murphy scowled.

'Yours, of course, Guv. But don't go cutting off your nose to spite your face. Pulling her out of the cafe is going to look suspicious if the Ripleys turn up again and find she's not there.'

Murphy had to admit he was right.

'For fuck's sake, get Cam to ring her and tell her to get her pinny out again.'

* * *

Jane decided on a pastel and floral midi-dress, which had a pleated skirt and loosely nipped-in waist. She chose a chunky brown belt to go with it, and a blue jacket as there was a slight nip in the air. She knew if she'd managed to tell Murphy about the drink with Carl he'd have said no to that too, but Murphy hadn't given her the chance. She was on thin ice, but her anger had made her reckless.

* * *

Leicester Square was busy, with a crowd of people outside the Empire Ballroom watching some street entertainers doing a juggling act. She looked at her watch: it was nearly 7.45 p.m. and she wondered if Carl wasn't going to show up, then about fifty metres away she saw him jogging towards her. He was smartly dressed in a blue blazer, white open-neck shirt, black trousers and black ankle boots.

'I'm really sorry, I had to get a bus, and then it got stuck in traffic.'

He was out of breath and Jane could see a few drops of perspiration on his forehead.

'It's all right, I've only just got here myself.'

'You look lovely,' he said with a nervous smile.

'Thank you, and you look very smart too.'

'Would you like to go for a drink or something to eat?'

'I'm quite hungry as it happens.'

'Anything you especially like?'

'I love Chinese.'

'Well, we're spoilt for choice with Chinatown around the corner.'

'Let's go then,' she said, slipping her arm into his.

'Did you have a busy day at work?' she asked as they walked up Wardour Street.

'Same as usual, really: running errands for my stepfather George, picking up car parts and working in the garage.'

'Are you a mechanic, then?'

'Yeah.'

'How long have you been doing that?'

'Since I left school at sixteen. George owns a car sales showroom and his mate Smudge runs the repairs, servicing and MOT side of it. If you've got a problem with your car, whatever it is, I can fix it for you.'

'I'll remember that.'

'Shall we try this one?'

He pointed to the Lotus Garden.

Inside, the waitress led them to a table for two and Carl pulled out a chair for Jane to sit on before gently easing it forward. Carl ordered a pint of lager and Jane said she'd have a half. They looked through the menu in silence as the waitress served their drinks.

'Cheers,' he said, raising his glass.

'Cheers.' She clinked her glass against his.

'Do you want to choose your own or have a set meal for two?'

'Meal B looks good to me.'

'Some crispy duck pancakes to start?'

'My favourite!'

He called over the waitress and she took the order.

'So, you've just started at Nick's cafe?'

'I'm only there for a week or so, just helping out until he gets a new waitress.'

'Oh, that's a shame. What do you do otherwise?'

'I work for my father as his secretary. He's an accountant, but I used to do waitressing during my school holidays.'

Carl made a sour face. 'I hope he's nicer than my stepfather.'

'I have to say, I didn't like him. He was really rude, and I thought the way he spoke to you in front of me was appalling.'

'He does it all the time; he's an ignorant bully.'

'Why don't you work somewhere else?'

'I can't afford to just now. He bought a shitty one-bedroom flat to get me out of the house and charges me a nominal rent to live there. I've been saving every penny I can as I'd like to start a garage of my own, or maybe buy a van and do mobile servicing and repairs.'

'That's a brilliant idea.'

The waitress served the crispy duck.

'Tuck in.'

He offered Jane a pancake.

The food was delicious, and Carl behaved like a perfect gentleman. There was a part of her that felt bad about what she was doing, but it was her job. Now Jane knew Carl disliked George, she wondered if he would say more that might be useful.

'Your uncle Tommy seemed a bit nicer.'

'He's OK, but him and George are as thick as thieves, like my father and Smudge, which is another reason I want to get away from the garage.'

'You make it sound like they're up to no good.'

He hesitated for a moment. 'George and Smudge were in prison together.'

'What for?' she asked, feigning surprise.

'I didn't know at the time, but I later found out it was for robbing a jeweller's. I was seven when George went in and fourteen when he got out. Prison changed him. He was a bitter man and I was on the wrong end of his anger on a regular basis.'

'He beat you up?' Jane asked, genuinely shocked.

He nodded, clearly disturbed by the memory. 'Usually with a leather belt and sometimes his hands ... It stopped when I was about eighteen, but the verbal abuse didn't.'

'Did your mother know what he was doing to you?'

'Yes, but he also knocked her about, just not as often. She told him to stop or she would leave – but in the end she likes the good life too much: nice car, big house and plenty of money.'

'Does he hit your sister?'

'God, no, he treats her like a princess. What Tina wants, Tina gets.'

'If he was in prison how did he end up doing so well for himself?'

'I don't know, and I definitely don't ask. George likes to make out he's the bad boy done good, but once a criminal, always a criminal, I reckon. He sells high-end second-hand cars like Jags, Mercs and BMWs. I'm pretty sure Smudge clocks the mileage. I've seen people hand over cash when they buy them.'

Jane wondered if other criminals were laundering the proceeds of their crimes by paying cash for George's cars.

The waitress served them their set meal of chilli beef, chicken with cashew nuts, stir-fried vegetables and egg fried rice. The food was so good they didn't talk much as they ate. Jane was already convinced that Carl was nothing to do with the robbery or part of the 'gang'. He clearly suspected the Ripley brothers and Smudge were still committing crime, but for his own self-preservation turned a blind eye to it and didn't ask questions. She wanted to probe Carl more and ask about Tommy's snooker hall to see if he knew anything about Aidan O'Reilly, but worried she might be pushing her luck and making him suspicious.

Jane changed the subject to daily life, and as they spoke about films and sports they liked she realised they had a lot in common. They had another drink and spent nearly two hours in the restaurant. He seemed much more relaxed when he wasn't speaking about his family, and had a sharp sense of humour. When the waitress gave Carl the bill, he insisted on paying and wouldn't take no for an answer.

'Would you like to go for a drink somewhere?'

'I'd love to, but I've got to be up early and be at the cafe by seven.'

'How are you getting home?'

'On the Tube from Charing Cross.'

'I'll walk you to the station.'

He got up and removed her jacket from the back of her seat and helped her put it on.

As they cut through Leicester Square a busker playing a guitar was singing 'Lyin' Eyes' by the Eagles. Carl took some change out of his pocket and dropped it in the busker's guitar case.

'That song reminds me of my last girlfriend.'

The song, about a woman who cheats on her husband, also hit a nerve with Jane. She wasn't cheating on Carl, but she was certainly lying, and her smile was a thin disguise to get information out of him. As they walked to the station, Jane wondered if she should make an excuse and tell him she couldn't go to the wedding. Standing him up on the day would be really hurtful. She had to remind herself that, nice bloke though he seemed to be, she was doing this to help catch the robbers.

'Would you like to go out again before the wedding?' he asked.

'Sorry, I've got to do some typing and filing for my dad in the evenings. He was a bit miffed that I went out tonight, actually.'

'Sure, I understand.' He took a bit of paper out of his pocket and handed it to Jane. 'I did a little map of where the wedding and George's house are. The service starts at three. I could come over and pick you up—'

'It's fine, I'll make my own way to the church and meet you there,' she said, forcing a smile.

He leant forward, gave her a quick kiss on the cheek and nervously stepped back.

'Thanks for a lovely evening, Jane.'

He turned around and walked away.

Jane put her hand on her cheek where he'd kissed her. She didn't feel offended; it was a nice gesture. Part of her wanted to call out to him to stop, so she could tell him the truth, but she knew it was too late for that.

Sitting on the Tube to Baker Street, Jane felt miserable. What she'd thought would be nothing more than a fact-finding evening had turned into something she'd never expected. Once she'd stopped trying to get information out of him and relaxed, she'd found herself genuinely enjoying Carl's company.

You really know how to mess things up when it comes to men, don't you? she thought to herself wryly.

CHAPTER THIRTY-ONE

It was Tuesday morning and the surveillance operation was up and running again from 6 a.m., with all officers in their allocated positions. All the suspects left their premises and went straight to work, arriving at about the same time as they had the previous day.

Jane got a call from Cam at 6 a.m., telling her that Kingston had persuaded Murphy to put her back in the cafe. Cam also said he'd tried to contact her the previous evening but she must have been out.

Driving to the cafe, she couldn't stop thinking about her date with Carl and what a fool she'd been to go over Murphy's head. She'd discovered nothing that might implicate the Ripleys in the Leytonstone or any future robbery, and clocking the mileage on motor cars was hardly a serious offence. There was no way she was going to tell Murphy what she'd done, and she hoped to God he never found out as he would undoubtedly throw her off the Flying Squad.

She got to the cafe just after 7 a.m., and by 8 a.m. it was very busy. Rachel came in just after 9 a.m. and Jane slipped her a thank you note for her information while serving her. Neither of the Ripley brothers came to the cafe, but Carl unexpectedly walked in at mid-day.

'Hi, I was just passing by and thought I'd drop this off for you. It's an official invite to the wedding. I didn't know your surname, so I just put Jane.'

'Thank you. It's a beautifully designed card.'

'Like I said – only the best will do for Tina.'

'Would you like something to eat and a drink?'

'No, I can't stop. I've got to pick up some engine parts and get them back to the garage. Thanks again for last night, I really enjoyed your company.'

He leant forward to kiss Jane's cheek and she pulled her head away.

'Sorry,' he said.

'It's OK. It's just that people are watching us and I'm quite shy about things like that.'

'I understand, I won't do it in public again,' he said, then walked out.

Jane sighed. Reaching across a table to pick up a dirty plate, she knocked a half-full coffee cup, spilling some onto a customer's lap.

'Watch what you're doing, you silly cow!'

The young man grabbed a napkin and started wiping himself down.

'I'm really sorry. It was an accident. I'll get a clean cloth for you.'

'These are my best jeans and you've fucking ruined them!'

Nick strode over, a look of anger in his eyes, and picked up the young man's plate of half-eaten food. Jane thought he was going to tell her off.

'Getta out of my cafe!'

'What for?' he asked.

'No one a speak to my staff like that! Now *vaffanculo*.'

Jane assumed that was 'fuck off' in Italian. As the man walked to the door, Nick told him never to come back.

'Thanks,' Jane said.

'Is OK, accidents they happen, and I no like ignorant *bastardi* in my place.'

* * *

The day passed without any movement by the suspects from their work, until they returned home at the same time as the previous evening. The phone taps were also uneventful, with most calls being made by a stressed Maureen Ripley trying to organise the wedding. The man in the camel hair coat had not as yet been seen or identified.

Murphy wasn't troubled. He knew that surveillance was often a long drawn-out waiting game, but he also knew Tommy Ripley needed money to pay his debts and George was greedy. He was certain they were planning something big after re-reading Jane's report of what George said to Tommy, after the man in the camel hair coat handed over an envelope.

'. . . *champagne and caviar for life.*'

Murphy was already aware that over the next few weeks several security vans in London would be transporting large amounts of money, some with over a million pounds in them. He strongly suspected one of them would be the Ripleys' target, and they might already have done a recce of the place they would hit. He knew that surveillance was a waiting game, which required the utmost patience, but when the day came his team would be ready to pounce, without fear, and take the Ripleys and their gang down.

* * *

It was Wednesday 30 April, and all the suspects went about their business as usual, arriving at work at the normal time, not making any suspicious detours or discreet phone calls. Although the members of Murphy's team and officers from CO11 were feeling tired, they were buzzing with adrenaline, knowing that today could be the day.

Murphy and the surveillance teams, working on a lone radio channel, were blissfully unaware when, at 11.30 a.m., six heavily armed members of the Arabs of KSA group stormed the Iranian embassy in South Kensington. The gunmen quickly overpowered the armed police officer guarding the embassy and took twenty-six hostages. They demanded the release of Arab prisoners in Khuzestan and their own safe passage out of the United Kingdom.

* * *

Cam ran into Murphy's office.

'Guv, the shit's hit the fan. The CO11 commander wants his officers back at the Yard right away.'

'Why, what's happened?'

Cam explained about the embassy siege.

Murphy picked up the phone.

'We'll see about that – I'm not having a bunch of towel heads ruin my operation.'

It wasn't long before a solemn-looking Murphy walked into the main office and spoke to Cam.

'Stand the CO11 officers down and tell them to go back to the Yard.'

'All of them?'

'Yes, apart from the CROPS officers. The Anti-Terrorist Squad want as much support as they can get to locate where the KSA cell were staying and anyone connected to them.'

'What about the guys listening to the phones?'

'Them as well. They're going to put listening probes in the embassy walls, so they'll be needed for that. Tell the rest of the team I want them to come back here for a meeting when the Ripleys get home.'

'How are we going to man our OPs and carry out surveillance without CO11 support?'

'Where there's a will, there's a way.'

He went to his office to think.

* * *

When she'd finished at the cafe, Jane went to the Co-op in the High Street to speak to Emma Wilson.

'Are you sure?' a doubting Emma asked.

'Yes. I spoke to the PC myself after my colleague told me. Your Uncle Asil was never part of your father's criminal activities. Some people thought he was and were out for vengeance for what your father had done to them. According to Customs and Excise, his current importation business is genuine and they don't suspect him of being involved in any criminal activity.'

'But he still abandoned us to save his own skin.'

'Maybe he was worried about what might happen to him, or he feared for your and Rachel's safety if he looked after you. It could be that he put you in the care of St Cuthbert's because he felt, at the time, it was the best thing to do.'

'If he wants forgiveness, I can't give it to him – not after all these years.'

'After your mother was seriously assaulted, Asil helped the police to try and find your father. Perhaps his remorse is genuine.' She handed Emma a bit of paper. 'This is a contact number for Asil if you want to speak to him.'

She looked at the details, then held the note tightly in her hand.

'What do you think I should do?'

'It's not for me to decide, Emma. We all make mistakes in life and do things we deeply regret. Forgiving your uncle won't change the past, but it could change your and Rachel's future, without her ever knowing the truth about your mother's death.'

'I'll speak to him – but it doesn't mean I've forgiven him,' she replied with a tear in her eye.

Jane put her hand on Emma's shoulder and gave her a gentle squeeze of reassurance, then left.

* * *

She got back to the office at 4 p.m. and was shocked when Cam told her about the embassy siege.

'Was anyone killed?'

'No, but the terrorists are saying they will shoot hostages if their demands aren't met. We've lost all the CO11 officers.'

'I bet Murphy's pissed off.'

'He was at first, but he knows the Anti-Terrorist Squad's work always takes precedence. Paul Lawrence called and left a message. He wants you to ring him at the lab,' Cam told her.

Jane went to her desk, picked up the phone and called him.

'Did you get anything off the key?'

'We got a thumb and fingerprint mark, which don't match any of your suspects.'

Jane felt a sense of relief. 'Whose was it?'

'No ident yet, but Fingerprint Bureau are still checking. Division are treating her death as murder, but they don't think it's connected to your investigation.'

'Are they thinking it's a burglary gone wrong?'

'Yes, and I'd say that's a reasonable conclusion under the circumstances.'

She had a thought.

'Could you get the RUC bureau to check the prints against their files? Just in case there's a connection to Aidan O'Reilly.'

'You don't let things go, do you?'

She smiled. 'You shouldn't have taught me so well.'

* * *

All the team were in the office by 7 p.m. With the surveillance and intelligence officers having to return to the Yard, the mood was bleak.

Murphy strode out of his office looking positive.

'For Christ's sake – you lot look like you let the Ripleys get away with another robbery.'

'The way things are going it could happen, Guv,' Bax remarked.

'Not on my watch they won't. If all else fails, revert to plan B.' He held up a piece of paper. 'We can do this without CO11. It will be harder, but it's doable.

'We've lost the firearms officers as well, and the CROPS officers won't be working the bank holiday weekend. Colonel, you will be driving the gunship with DI Kingston on board and tailing George Ripley. The second gunship will tail Tommy, and be driven by Cam with Stanley on board. Bax and Dabs continue at the Bruce Grove OP and Teflon on GR Motors. We can pick up eyeball on Graham Smith and Carl Winter when they arrive at the garage, but don't worry about a tail on Winter for now. Tennison, I'm going to have to pull you from the cafe to work in here.'

She wasn't pleased about it, but knew he had no choice as their numbers had been severely depleted. He did, however, say he would use Kingston's office and listen in on the phone conversations as they were being recorded, as there were four phones to monitor.

'Did the intel guys listening to the phones pick up anything interesting today before they went back to the Yard?' Kingston asked Cam.

'I had a quick look through their logs. There's nothing of significance, mostly Maureen Ripley moaning and groaning. She phoned George and gave him a right ear-bashing about playing golf on the Saturday morning before the wedding.'

'He's playing golf before his daughter's wedding? That sounds a bit dodgy,' Teflon remarked.

Cam picked up the relevant log from his desk and flicked through it.

'George phoned the golf club straight after Maureen had a go at him to confirm a seven a.m. tee-off time, Saturday morning, for four people.'

'I play golf – I can do a tail on Ripley,' Bax suggested.

'Shut up,' Murphy told him, shaking his head.

'Sounds legit. Does the log say which course it is?' Kingston asked.

Cam looked at the log. 'The person who answered the call said, "'Royal Epping Forest".'

'That's a private, members-only club – not cheap either,' Bax said.

'Sounds like the sort of place Ripley would join to impress people,' Stanley said.

'Maybe Camel Hair Coat Man is a member there as well,' Dabs suggested.

Murphy nodded. 'Anyone know if there's anywhere near there we could park an OBO van, or surveillance car, to get a few pictures of George Ripley's playing partners?'

There was silence and shaking heads.

'I'll scout it out first thing in the morning,' the Colonel said.

'I don't need you all on duty Saturday or Sunday, and Monday is the May Day bank holiday, which reduces the pressure on us as no Securicor vans will be making cash deliveries to the banks during the long weekend.'

'What about covering the wedding?' the Colonel asked.

'Is there anywhere on the grounds of the church we can use as a static OP?' Kingston asked, knowing the Colonel had been to the church.

'No, and it's right by a country lane, so an OBO van would stick out like a sore thumb.'

Murphy looked at Kingston, who shrugged his shoulders, as if to say, 'It's up to you.'

'Tennison will be going undercover at the wedding.'

Jane looked up, wide-eyed.

'That could be a bit dangerous, Guv,' Stanley remarked.

'It's a risk I'm prepared to take. We still haven't identified the man in the camel hair coat and there may be other people attending who could be of interest. She'll be able to take photographs of the guests and their cars without it looking suspicious.'

'There'll be a load of criminals there. If she's nicked one of them before and he recognises her, it could blow the whole operation,' the Colonel argued.

Jane wasn't worried. 'I last worked north of the river over four years ago, and never arrested anyone who I'd consider to be involved with the likes of the Ripley brothers. It doesn't appear they've sussed who I am, and they're expecting me to be there. Carl Winter invited me while I was working in the cafe.'

'Well, that makes it all hunky-dory then,' the Colonel said, clearly unconvinced.

Murphy looked at Jane. 'Wear a wedding hat and keep the brim down, consider sunglasses if it's a bright day. If at any time you feel your cover might be blown, pull out.'

'If she leaves it will look suspicious,' the Colonel said.

'There are two hundred people going to the reception and more coming in the evening, so I doubt they'll miss one person leaving. If I need to, I'll tell Carl Winter that I'm not feeling well and leave.'

'Anything else anyone wants to add?' Murphy asked.

'The banks usually take in extra cash before a bank holiday weekend. It seems strange that none of our suspects have been out plotting up their place for a hit.'

'They could have done a recce before we started our surveillance or have been given the details by Camel Hair Coat Man,' Murphy said. 'Apart from that, George Ripley may actually have a heart and not want to risk another robbery going pear-shaped and getting nicked before his daughter's wedding.'

'Hmm, we'll see about that,' the Colonel said darkly.

'Right, we resume at six a.m. tomorrow,' Murphy said, dismissing them.

* * *

Thursday was another uneventful day, and some on the team began to wonder if the Ripleys knew they were being followed. Murphy's experience told him otherwise, and his thoughts were confirmed on the Friday at midday when Teflon spoke on the radio from his OP overlooking GR motors.

'All units . . . all units . . . Targets 1 and 4 leaving garages in gold Mercedes.'

'Central 888 has eyeball and will follow,' Kingston replied, and continued with a running commentary. 'Vehicle turning right into Bruce Grove and maintaining thirty miles per hour.'

'Received by Gold,' Jane said from the office with Murphy standing beside her.

There were a few minutes of silence before Kingston spoke again.

'Target 1 has turned left and is entering rear of hall.'

Bax came on the air.

'OP1 has eyeball and holding.' Several seconds later he spoke again. 'Targets 1 and 4 entering hall.'

'Looks like they're having a meeting.'

Bax came back on the radio, sounding excited.

'All units from OP1 . . . Male in camel hair coat wearing brown snap brim trilby has just got out of a cab and entered hall. Unable to give description as eyeball on his back.'

'Christ, I wish we had a listening device in there,' Murphy said.

'You could send Dabs in again,' Jane suggested.

Murphy took the radio from her.

'OP1 from Gold . . . receiving, over . . . ?'

'Yes, go ahead.'

'Have you access to a phone?'

'Yes, there's one right next to us.'

'Call me in the office.'

A few seconds later the phone rang, Murphy answered it and asked Bax if there were many 'punters' in the club. He told him there were about six unidentified men who had entered the club since it opened, and some were carrying snooker cues. Murphy asked to speak to Dabs.

'Yes, Guv, what's up?'

'I want you to go in the snooker hall, make out you want to join or practise on a table and see what's happening – then phone me back later.'

'On my way, Guv,' Dabs replied enthusiastically.

'That was a good shout about Dabs, Jane.'

Murphy handed the radio back to her.

He'd called her by her Christian name for the first time.

I'm finally doing something right, she thought.

* * *

As Dabs entered the snooker hall he saw the Ripley brothers, Smith, O'Reilly and the man in the camel hair coat by a table at the far end of the room. Maria Fernandez was behind the bar. Dabs approached her with a smile and his chequebook in his hand.

'I came in the other day and decided I'd like to join.'

She picked up a membership form and handed it to him.

'Fill this in and make the cheque for twenty pounds payable to Bruce Grove Snooker Club.'

'Is it all right if I do it here?'

'Sure.' She handed him a pen. 'Do you want a drink?'

He asked for a half of lager and leant on the counter to fill in the form. The suspects were too far away for him to hear what was being said, but he deliberately took his time so he could glance up occasionally and see what they were doing. After a few minutes he'd seen enough and returned to the OP, where he called the office. Jane answered and handed the phone to Murphy. She wanted to listen in, so pointed to the headset and Murphy nodded. He was concerned that Dabs hadn't been in the snooker hall very long.

'I thought it was best to leave as O'Reilly looked over, but I think it was because he'd met me the other day when I was in there with Stanley. Anyway, I said I wanted to join the club and Maria gave me a form and—'

'For God's sake, Dabs, I don't care about that. Did you hear what they were talking about?'

'No, but from what I saw they were clearly planning something. While I was filling in the form, I—'

'Just tell me what they were bloody well doing!' Murphy barked.

'They were all stood around a snooker table. George Ripley was moving some of the balls and talking to the others.'

Murphy sighed. 'So, they were just playing snooker?'

'No, none of them had a cue in their hands. George was picking up different coloured balls and placing them in a pattern on the table, just like he did with the condiments and sugar cubes in the cafe last week. I think he was demonstrating how the robbery would be carried out.'

'You little beauty, Dabs, well done.' Murphy beamed.

'Thank you, sir. The man in the camel hair coat does look like Bela Lugosi, by the way – he's even got the greased-back hair.'

'Make sure you get some good photos of him when he comes out.'

Murphy put the phone down.

'You think they're going to do the robbery this afternoon?' Jane asked.

'I doubt it, but what Dabs just said makes me feel even more confident that it will happen, and they obviously haven't a clue we're watching them,' he said with a sly grin.

Bax spoke on the radio.

'All units, all units, Camel Hair Coat Man leaving hall with Targets 1 and 4.' He turned to Dabs. 'Quick, get some pics of them.'

Dabs pointed the Nikon zoom lens camera at the targets and pulled the winder back to advance the film and take a picture, but there was no resistance.

'Shit, I forgot to put a new film in before I went to the snooker hall,' he said, hurriedly opening the back and removing the film.

'Hurry up, he's hailing a taxi.'

'I'm going as fast as I can.' He fumbled the new film as he tried to fit it to the winder teeth. 'Right, I've got it.'

'Too late, he's gone.'

'OP1 to Central 888, are you tailing Camel Hair Coat Man?'

'No, we're on Targets 1 and 4,' Kingston replied.

'Murphy's going to kill us,' Dabs said forlornly.

*   *   *

Murphy called everyone back to the office after the Ripleys returned home. The atmosphere was highly charged as he spoke about the suspects meeting at the snooker hall and George Ripley strategically placing the snooker balls on the table.

'How long will it take to get the photos developed at the lab?' Murphy asked Dabs.

'There was a slight problem, sir. The shutter jammed when I tried to take a picture of Camel Hair Coat Man. By the time I got it working he'd got in a taxi and left.'

He waited for a rollicking from Murphy.

'Shit happens. At least you and Bax have seen his face. Pity he didn't turn up in the Jensen as we might have got an address for him. If you see the car tomorrow, Jane, make sure you clock the registration. And take plenty of film with you,' he added with a shake of his head.

Murphy looked in his pocket notebook.

'Colonel and Stanley, I want you to take the OBO van out in the morning and see if you can get some pics of who Ripley's playing golf with. If it's too risky then don't bother. Teflon, you pick up Jane from her flat at 1.30 in the undercover black cab, then take her to the wedding. The rest of you can have the day off.'

'What about Sunday and Monday?' Bax asked.

'Sunday, they'll all be hung-over from the night before,' Stanley remarked.

'And the banks will be closed until Tuesday,' Cam added, hoping they could have at least one day off.

Murphy laughed. 'All right, all right, you all deserve a bit of R and R. Sort it out among yourselves, but I want at least three of you in the office both days – the rest of you, be near your home phone in case I need to call you in. Otherwise it's six a.m. Tuesday and noses to the grindstone.'

CHAPTER THIRTY-TWO

The Royal Epping Forest Golf Club was in Forest Approach, Chingford. It was 6.30 a.m., and the Colonel and Stanley sat in the back of the OBO van, which had JB Plumbers written on the side, spy holes and a one-way rear-view window. They were parked at the rear of Chingford Masonic Hall, opposite the club entrance, and had a good view, with binoculars, of the first tee and the eighteenth green by the club house.

'I'll bet the Ripleys are Freemasons,' the Colonel remarked.

Stanley agreed. 'And so are a few senior detectives, but thankfully none of them are on our squad. The rubber heelers and Countryman think any officer who's a Freemason must be corrupt.'

'Anybody that says I'm corrupt can kiss my Porsche!' the Colonel joked.

Stanley had to put his hand over his mouth to stifle his laughter from being heard outside the van. He nudged the Colonel.

'Look up, here comes George in the Merc . . . He's got someone with him.' Stanley took a photograph.

'It looked like Tommy,' the Colonel said, looking out of the rear window.

Five minutes later Stanley saw a dark blue Mark 3 Capri Ghia approaching the golf club.

'I don't bloody believe this – the Ripleys are playing golf with Smith and O'Reilly.'

The Colonel looked out of the window. 'Jesus, I thought you were taking the piss. I'll call it in.'

'They might just be having a meeting in the car park. Let's wait until we see who George actually tees off with.'

Just before 7 a.m. the four men approached the first tee, two men carrying a set of golf clubs each, the others pulling theirs along on a trolley.

'Do you reckon they're just socialising or discussing a robbery again?' the Colonel asked.

'How the hell should I know? I'm not Rachel Wilson, I can't bloody lip-read.'

They watched as George teed off and hit a decent drive down the middle of the fairway, as did his brother Tommy. Aidan O'Reilly was next to tee off.

'Gold from KG, receiving . . . over?'

'Yes, go ahead, over,' Bax replied.

The Colonel told him who was playing golf and asked how long a round took, as he'd never played the game.

'Depends if it's nine or eighteen holes they're playing, how good they are and if there are any hold-ups by the golfers in front of them.'

'There's no one in front of them.'

The Colonel watched O'Reilly hit the ball hard but slice it into the rough on the left.

'You're looking at about four hours then.'

Graham Smith made two air shots, missing the ball completely, and on his third attempt the ball scooted about fifty metres along the ground.

Stanley sighed. 'This could take all fucking day the way Smith plays.'

'I'll nip out when the coast is clear and get some coffee and sandwiches.'

'Get some newspapers and magazines as well.'

'*Hustler* or *Penthouse*?' the Colonel quipped as he got out of the van.

*   *   *

Jane woke early after a restless night thinking about her undercover role at the wedding. She felt nervous, not just about what she was doing, but also at the thought of seeing Carl again. Although part of her looked forward to it, she felt she was prolonging the agony for herself – and Carl – before she walked out of his life. She wondered if, after the Ripleys were arrested, she should tell him the truth, and that although she had lied to him she genuinely thought he was a nice man. It was all too much. As she sat in the kitchen eating her breakfast, she began to wonder if she should have told Murphy that she didn't want to go to the wedding.

After a lot of indecision going through her wardrobe, she finally decided what to wear. She chose a knee-length pleated floral print dress in shades of pink, blue and yellow, with ruched shoulder straps that could be worn on or off the shoulder. To go with the dress, she chose some pink flat-soled shoes with a matching ribbon on them, and a beige wide-brimmed hat with an organza flower bow.

Before ironing her dress, she had a bath and washed her hair, then blow-dried it and put in some sponge curlers. Looking at the clock, she realised she still had five hours before Teflon would be picking her up. She put on her dressing gown, lay on the sofa and went back to reading *Medea*.

* * *

The day shift guard got out of his car with the engine running and pressed the intercom of the gated entrance to the Security Express depot in Curtain Road, Shoreditch.

'It's me, Harry. Open the gates, will ya?' Archie said. 'And stick the kettle on.' Harry checked the TV screen linked to the front gate camera and, satisfied it was his work colleague, pressed the button to open the large electric gates. Archie drove in, then parked his car in the corner of the yard and heard an Irish voice call out.

'Excuse me, my son, I was wondering if ya can help me.'

Archie saw an elderly, grey-haired, bearded man with stooped shoulders shuffling towards him as the gates closed. He was dressed in a black suit and shirt, and wore thick-rimmed brown glasses and black leather gloves.

'You can't come in here, mate,' Archie said, warily holding his hand up.

'Oh, I'm sorry, my son, it's just that I'm a bit lost and can't find the church. I'm the stand-in priest and supposed to be taking the service in fifteen minutes.'

Archie noticed he was wearing a dog collar, and carrying a Bible and rosary beads in one hand and a map in the other.

'What's the church you're looking for, Father?'

'St Leonard's in Shoreditch High Street.' He showed him the map.

'Are you in a car?'

'No, I'm walking.'

'You need to go up Curtain Road, then turn right into Bateman's Row and keep going until you come to the T-junction and the church is up on the left. It's about a five-minute walk.'

Harry could see Archie was talking to a priest and giving him directions. He got up and put the kettle on.

'Bless you, my son, you're a guiding angel to be sure.'

'My pleasure, Father. I'll let you out.'

The priest held up the Bible and started to open it. Archie thought the old man was going to read a passage and bless him. It was only when he felt the gun pressed against his stomach that he realised the Bible had concealed a gun.

'One fuckin' wrong move and you're a dead man, ya understand me?'

Archie nodded. The priest made him walk to the entry door to the building and stood close to him with the gun in his back. Archie entered the key code, opened the door and the priest put a small wooden wedge in it so it didn't close. They walked up the stairs, then, as Archie opened the control room door, the priest smashed him over the back of the head with the gun and let him fall to the ground. On seeing the gun, Harry instantly stuck his hands in the air and backed off. As Archie sat up groggily the priest got a thick roll of duct tape from his inside jacket pocket and threw it down on his lap.

'Tape his hands, legs and eyes, then gag him.'

With the gun pointed at Harry, the priest told him to lie face down on the floor and put his hands behind his back. When Archie had finished, the priest kept the gun pointed at him while he checked that the tape was secure.

'Open the gate,' he told Archie.

He did as he was told and a green Ford Transit van, with Security Express logos on the side, drove into the yard and reversed into the loading bay. Four men dressed in blue boiler suits and balaclavas got out of the vehicle while the driver, also wearing a balaclava, lay across the front seats. One was carrying a sawn-off shotgun and the other three had handguns. Two of them ran up to the control room and one remained in the downstairs corridor by the entry door. When they arrived, the priest dragged Harry to the toilet, then took off his glasses and put on a balaclava and stayed with him.

The man with the sawn-off pointed it at Archie.

'When the supervisor arrives to do his check, you let him in, or I'll blow your fuckin' brains out,' he said in an Irish accent.

A terrified Archie nodded repeatedly as he was pushed down into the control desk chair, while the other man held the gun to his head.

'The keys to the cash vault are locked in the safe and we don't know the numbers for it,' Archie said.

The man with the gun slapped the back of his head hard.

'If yer hand so much as twitches towards that panic button, I will pull the trigger.' He also had an Irish accent.

Archie folded his arms, squeezed them tight to his chest and began to shake with fear.

At 8.30 a.m. on the dot the supervisor pulled up at the gate, got out of his car and pressed the intercom. The man with the shotgun ran down the stairs and joined his colleague.

'Morning, Archie.'

'Morning, boss.'

'Has Harry not gone home yet?' the supervisor asked, noticing his car was still in the yard.

Archie felt the gun being pressed hard against his head.

'Answer him.'

'He's just having a cuppa and a chat with me.'

'OK, make me one, will ya?'

Archie pressed the button to open the gate and before he knew it, he was dragged out of the chair, slammed to the ground face down and a pillowcase was put over his head. He was then tied up with duct tape and dragged to the toilet by the man with the handgun. The priest let the two blindfolded guards know he was with them, so not to bother trying to escape.

As the supervisor opened the ground floor door and stepped into the corridor, he saw the masked man pointing the sawn-off shotgun at him. He wasn't aware of the other man behind the door, who kicked it shut and stuck a gun in his back.

'Top of the mornin' to ya, mister supervisor,' he said in a deep, calm voice.

The supervisor was forced upstairs to the control room and tied to a chair. The man with the deep voice spoke to him, while his colleague held the shotgun to his head. The third man with them watched the monitor in case anyone came to the gates.

'What's the code for the safe dat holds the vault keys?'

'I don't know,' he said nervously.

'Don't fuck me about, son, or I'll be toasting yer fuckin' head.'

'I swear to God, I don't know the code – only the depot manager does and he's not in today.'

'Well, I'm the god of hellfire,' he said menacingly.

He got a can of lighter fluid out of his boiler suit pocket and squeezed the flammable liquid over the supervisor's head. The terrified hostage could smell the fluid as it trickled down his face. He began to shake uncontrollably as the man got a gold lighter out of his pocket and flicked the top open.

'Believe me, son, this is gonna hurt. And you'll be disfigured for life.'

He flicked the friction wheel with his thumb, releasing a spark, which lit up the tiny stream of butane gas. He moved the flame towards the supervisor's head.

'All right, all right, please don't burn me! It's 200258.'

He flicked the lighter lid back down and lightly patted the supervisor's cheek.

'Good boy ... Now ye can go be with your friends in the shithouse.'

The man with the shotgun then duct-taped the supervisor's mouth, put a pillowcase over his head and dragged him to the toilet. The priest stayed with the guards, while one man watched the TV monitor and the other two got the keys from the safe, then opened the vault.

'Jesus Christ, there has got to be millions here!' the man with the sawn-off said with delight.

'I told you there would be – most of it'll be from the Ideal Home Exhibition,' the man with the deep voice said. 'Open the loading bay door and get the holdalls from the van.'

His colleague did as he was told and quickly returned with six large holdalls. They hurriedly filled them with cash and the man with the deep voice looked at his watch.

'One more each and we gotta go,' he said.

'There's still loads here.'

'It's too risky, we need to do everything to plan and stick to my timing. We've got enough to make us rich for life.'

'The Costa Brava, champagne and caviar, what more could a criminal want?' The man with the sawn-off chuckled.

Once they had loaded the bags in the van, one of the men went to get his two colleagues and the priest warned the guards they were still being watched before quietly leaving the toilet. Before leaving they ripped the false Security Express signs off the side of the Transit van and threw them in the back.

* * *

'Christ, I'm bored. What time is it now?' the Colonel asked, looking through binoculars at the eighteenth green.

Stanley was reading the paper. '10.35.'

'How can anyone play a game that takes so long?'

'Stop moaning. A cricket match can take five days.'

'I wouldn't mind if we were doing something positive, but this is like watching paint dry. Tell you what – I'll bet you a quid the guy on the green misses this putt.'

'Go on then.'

As the ball fell into the cup, the Colonel sighed, fished a pound note out of his pocket and handed it to Stanley.

'That bloody siege is still going on,' Stanley said. 'They've threatened to shoot a hostage if they don't get what they want. I wouldn't want to be that poor PC they grabbed. He'll probably be the first.'

Stanley folded the paper, put it down and took over watching with the binoculars. At ten to eleven he saw the four men walking up to the eighteenth green.

'They're on the green,' he said.

Teflon picked up the camera and started taking photographs.

'The way that Smudge bloke plays, I thought they'd be a lot longer,' he remarked.

They watched as the four targets finished their game and shook hands with each other. Ten minutes later they all left the course in the same vehicles they had come in.

CHAPTER THIRTY-THREE

It was nearly 1.30 p.m. Jane stood in front of her bedroom mirror, put her wide-brimmed hat on and did a left and right half-twirl.

'You look good,' she said to herself with a smile. She went to the living room, looked out of the window to the street below and saw Teflon pull up in the black cab. She picked up her coat, then checked her Kodak Instamatic camera was in her clutch bag, along with a spare film, before leaving the flat.

Teflon waved when he saw her walking towards the cab.

'You look absolutely stunning,' he said, his eyes wide.

'No need to look so surprised,' she laughed, getting in the back. 'I last wore this outfit when I was godmother at my nephew's christening.'

'Where to, lady?' Teflon asked in a cockney accent, as if he was a real cabbie.

'All Saints Church, Chigwell, please.' She smiled.

'Right you are,' he said and moved off.

* * *

Teflon drove slowly so he didn't arrive at the church too early.

'You be careful, Jane. No matter what Murphy said, the wedding surveillance isn't worth putting your neck on the line for. All we really need is the camel hair coat guy's car registration so we can identify him. If he doesn't turn up, then you may as well call it a day.'

'I was only intending to stay until the evening reception starts, then I'll make an excuse to pull out.'

He nodded. 'I'll wait in the canteen at Chigwell nick. Call me when you want picking up.'

He handed her the station phone number.

* * *

The sun was shining and there wasn't a cloud in the sky as they pulled up on the road outside the church. Jane saw Carl outside, anxiously pacing up and down the gravel path. He had a top hat in his hand and was wearing a black and grey morning suit. As soon as he saw her he smiled broadly and waved.

'You look gorgeous, Jane,' he said as he helped her out of the cab.

'Thanks. You look very elegant in your suit.'

She winced as if feeling a sudden sharp pain.

'You all right?' he asked, looking concerned.

'It's just a bad stomach cramp.'

'Is it something you ate?'

'No, it's just that time of the month.'

He looked embarrassed. 'Oh, right, I see . . .'

'Don't worry, I'm sure they'll go away.'

'We'd best go into the church. Tina will be here soon.'

She followed him inside, feeling bad that she was lying to him about period pains, but she needed to lay down an excuse she could use later. Carl escorted her down the aisle to the front row on the left. It hadn't crossed her mind that he would want her to sit next to him and his family. He introduced Jane to his mother, Maureen. She shook Jane's hand limply.

'Pleased to meet you, darlin'. My Carl can't stop talkin' about you. He was right, as well – you're a real looker.'

Jane sat at the end of the pew and a minute later she felt a tap on her shoulder, making her jump. She turned around and saw a smiling Tommy behind her with the much younger Maria Fernandez, who was wearing a red dress with a low cleavage that showed off her full figure.

Tommy whispered to Jane, 'Thanks for coming, luv, you've made Carl's day. I've not seen him as happy in a long while. This is Maria, me girlfriend. Maria, this is . . .' He paused, awaiting a reply.

'Jane. Pleased to meet you, Maria.'

As they shook hands, Jane recognised Graham Smith and Aidan O'Reilly from the surveillance photographs. They were sitting in the row behind Tommy. O'Reilly still had visible signs of the cut to his forehead, but he also had a rash all over his face, which he was rubbing with his hand.

The room was suddenly filled with the sound of the organ playing Mendelssohn's 'Wedding March' and everyone stood up. Jane thought Tina looked beautiful in her wedding dress, though she felt nothing but contempt for George Ripley when she saw him. She wondered if Tina knew what her father was really like, and how the proceeds of crime had probably paid for her extravagant wedding.

*   *   *

The service was over in half an hour. Carl linked arms with Jane as they walked out of the church, then shook the vicar's hand and said it was a lovely service. The bride and groom, bridesmaids, best man and ushers had a few pictures taken outside the church, and George announced that the family's and friends' photos would be taken in the grounds of Farthings.

Jane scanned the church car park to see if the Jensen Interceptor was there, but couldn't see it. She looked around the guests for a man resembling Bela Lugosi, but again with no joy.

When the photos were done, Jane travelled with Carl to the house in a wedding limousine. The six-bedroom mock Tudor house was approached via electric gates and a sweeping gravel driveway, and surrounded by over an acre of land, with a small fishing lake and woods at the bottom of the vast gardens. The impressive marquee was close to the house and several waitresses and waiters were serving champagne and canapes. Carl picked up two glasses from a tray and handed one to Jane.

'Thanks again for coming, it really means a lot to me. George reckoned you'd give me the boot after our first date.'

'Well, he reckoned wrong . . . Cheers.'

She raised her glass and he did the same.

George's booming deep voice filled the air.

'Right, listen up, you bunch of reprobates. If anyone wants a piss, the ladies' is in the entrance hallway to the left of the staircase, and the gents' is in the utility room off the kitchen. Have an enjoyable day and make sure you drink all the booze.'

The photographer called out that he'd like the Ripley family to gather around for a photograph.

'Come on, Jane,' Carl said, taking her gently by the hand.

'I'm not part of your family, Carl, I wouldn't feel right being—'

'Maria will be in it and she's not family. Please, I'd like a proper photo of us together.'

She didn't have the heart to say no, and also realised she could use the moment to her advantage. She handed her pocket camera to a guest and asked if they'd take some pictures for her. Carl asked the guest to take a quick one of him and Jane before they joined the family.

Although Jane forced a smile, inside she was mortified – standing in the Ripley family photograph next to Tommy, with George only a few feet away. After the photograph was taken she started to move off, but the photographer told everyone to stay where they were, then asked for close friends of the bride's family to join them for a group shot. It went from bad to worse as she watched Graham Smith and Aidan O'Reilly join the group and stand right behind her.

'You should put some of Maria's make-up on that rash for the photo,' George told Aidan and laughed, as did Tommy.

'Now we know why he prefers the soft touch of nylon,' Tommy added in a simpering voice.

'Fuck off, the pair of ya,' Aidan grumbled.

'Right, everyone smile at the camera,' the photographer said.

Jane thought how surreal it felt to find herself dressed up to the nines and standing in the middle of a group of hardened criminals who hated the police and would have shot her without a second thought.

As the photographer took the pictures, Jane saw a maroon Jensen Interceptor, with a man and a woman in it, coming down the driveway towards the house. She felt her heart rate increase as the Jensen pulled up by the house. The man and woman got out and walked across the lawn towards the assembled guests. The man was carrying a large gift-wrapped box, and wearing the exact same coat as Rachel described – a knee-length brown camel hair coat with a black suede collar. He did look like Bela Lugosi, too. He was nearly six feet tall, in his early fifties, with dark slicked-back hair that she suspected was dyed. He wore a blue three-piece pinstripe suit and walked with an air of confidence. The woman with him wore a wedding ring and was about the same age, elegantly dressed in a figure-hugging red dress and hat.

When George saw him, he went straight over and shook hands. Tommy Ripley, Smith and O'Reilly also greeted him warmly with big smiles. The man handed George the present, and he asked one of the waiters to put it in his study next to the lounge.

Jane looked at the registration of the Jensen, HLT 354N, and memorised it by repeating it over in her mind using the mnemonic HiLT-35-4 Nick. If and when she got the opportunity, she'd try and take a photograph. She managed to take a few photographs of the guests as they gathered for the large group photo and, holding her camera down by her side, took a few risky potshots of the man in the camel hair coat.

The professional Master of Ceremonies, dressed in a red jacket and black trousers, called everyone into the marquee and announced that the meal was about to start. The receiving line consisted of the bride and groom and both sets of parents. Jane felt her stomach churn as she shook hands with George.

'Lovely service, Mr Ripley,' she told him.

'You the girl from the cafe?' He smiled.

'Yes, Carl invited me.'

He looked her up and down. 'You're far too good-looking for him, darlin'.'

Jane forced a smile and moved on.

She was about to look at the seating plan when Carl came over and said she was on the end of the top table with him. In some ways she felt relieved. At least it was better than sitting with Smith and O'Reilly.

Jane looked at the menu card. A prawn cocktail starter, a main course of chicken breast with vegetables and boiled potatoes, followed by Black Forest gateau, then coffee, cheese and biscuits. As she put the card down on the table, she felt an eerie sense of unease, as if someone was watching her. She scanned the marquee and saw the man in the camel hair coat sitting at a table in the middle of the room. He was looking at her with his head tilted to one side and tapping his lips with his left index finger.

'Who's the chap that owns the Jensen?' she asked Carl casually.

'Tony. He's a nice guy. He's in the same Masons' lodge as George. Lovely car, isn't it? Me and Smudge do the servicing and MOT. He let me have a drive of it once; it's fast but drinks petrol. I could ask him if he'd let me take you for a drive some time.'

'That'd be nice.'

Jane was apprehensive about questioning Carl further about Tony. Knowing he was sitting at table 8, she thought she'd sneak a look at the seating plan by the marquee entrance to find out his surname.

'I'm just going to the toilet.'

'It's in the hallway by the stairs,' Carl told her.

She walked slowly, then stopped briefly by the seating plan, which had Mr A. Nichols where Tony was sitting. She went to the toilet, then returning to the marquee she suddenly felt her left wrist being grabbed from behind. She spun around, thinking it was Carl, and found herself face to face with Tony, who tightened his grip on her wrist.

'Do I know you?' he asked with a nasty expression.

'Let go, you're hurting me,' she said, trying not to show she was scared.

He let go of her hand and smiled. 'Sorry, I thought we might have met before.'

'I don't think so, you must have got me mixed up with someone else.'

'Maybe, but I never forget a pretty face,' he said, walking off to the marquee.

Jane was shaking, desperately trying to think where or when they might have met. She went back into the house to phone Teflon and, seeing the study room door open, made sure no one was about and nipped in. She picked up the phone and noticed a long metal case tucked under the large oak writing desk and gift-wrapping paper in the bin. She called Chigwell Police Station, then asked to be put through to the canteen and Teflon answered.

'I need you to pick me up outside the house in about half an hour.'

'Will do. You all right?'

'The man in the camel hair coat thinks he knows me.'

'Come out right now, Jane,' Teflon insisted.

'I can't. It would look suspicious.'

She put the phone down.

She was about to go back to the marquee when curiosity got the better of her. Realising the metal case was the same size as the present Tony Nichols had handed George, she pulled it out from under the desk, put it on the top and opened it. Inside the silk-lined case were the barrel and stock of a Purdey shotgun. Jane got her camera out of her clutch bag and took a picture.

She returned to the marquee and saw Tony standing beside George at the top table, leaning down and whispering in his ear. As she walked to her seat, she tried not to look at them, but out of the corner of her eye she could see George glaring at her.

'I thought you'd done a runner for a minute,' Carl said. 'George is about to start his father of the bride speech.'

'I'm really sorry, Carl, but I've got to go. My stomach cramps are killing me and my period's really heavy.'

'You can have a lie-down in the house if you want.'

'No thanks, I'm worried about staining my dress.'

'I understand. I'll call a cab for you.'

'I did it while I was in the house. You stay for George's speech and I'll see myself out.'

'When can I see you again, Jane?' he asked, a little forlornly.

'I'll be in the cafe next week. I'll see you then.'

She kissed him on the cheek, feeling ashamed.

* * *

It was still light as Jane walked along Gravel Lane. One second she was thinking about the Ripleys and Tony Nichols, and the next about Carl. Part of her was excited that she'd identified the infamous 'Camel Hair Coat Man', but she wondered if in doing so she'd jeopardised the whole operation and the Ripley gang now suspected they were being watched. But worse than that was the thought of the danger she'd put Carl in if George suspected she was a police officer.

She saw Teflon approaching in the cab and waved him down. He stopped and she got in.

'You look awful.'

'I feel awful.'

'What happened?'

'I'll tell you on the way home.'

* * *

The speeches finished and the DJ was setting up his equipment for the disco.

George smiled as he approached Carl.

'All right, son? Where's your girlfriend?'

'She wasn't feeling well and went home.'

'That's a shame. She seemed a lovely girl.'

'She is. I really like her.'

'I'd like to have a word with you in my office.'

'What about?'

'Your future. I know I've been a bit hard on you over the years, but you're a good worker, Carl. I'd like to give you a little something to show my appreciation.'

His eyes lit up. 'Really? What is it?'

'Just a few quid to help you—'

'Set up my own business?'

'You can do what you like with the money – maybe get a flat of your own. I'll see you in the study in a minute, after I've had a word with your uncle Tommy.'

George patted Carl on the shoulder.

* * *

After a few minutes, George walked into the study, smiled at Carl, then closed the door behind him and quietly locked it. He got a key out of his pocket and opened the desk drawer, which was filled with bundles of cash. He took a few out and placed them on the table.

He picked up the nine-inch letter opener by the point, and flipped it up and over so the wooden handle was in the palm of his hand.

'There's two grand for you, son.'

'I don't know what to say, George,' Carl said as he went to pick up the money.

Before he knew it, George had grabbed him around the back of the neck and slammed his head down hard onto the desk. He turned Carl's head sideways and pressed the tip of the letter opener against the skin by the side of his eye.

'Your fucking tart's a rozzer.'

'She's not, she's a secretary,' Carl said, his voice trembling with fear.

George slowly applied more pressure on the letter opener.

'Well, whatever she is, you'll never be able to see her again if I take your eyes out.'

'She never asked me anything about you or Tommy,' Carl said, realising he made it sound as if she had.

'You dumb shit! Don't fucking lie to me!'

George lifted Carl off the table and punched him hard in the stomach. He fell to his knees, gasping for breath. George stood over him.

'What did you tell her?'

'Nothing . . . I didn't tell her nothing,' he pleaded.

George slapped him hard across the face.

'Your precious Jane doesn't give a toss about you – she even asked me if you were a retard.'

Carl looked at up at him. 'I don't believe you.'

George slapped him again. 'She used you to watch me and Tommy because she thinks we're criminals.'

'You're not going to hurt Jane, are you?' Carl wept.

'Not as much as I'm going to hurt you.'

He removed his thick leather belt, then held it so the metal buckle end was dangling over Carl.

'Please, no, don't,' he begged.

'Don't you dare scream.'

George raised the belt and brought it down hard on Carl's back. He let out a muffled scream, then fell to the floor and curled up in a ball. George whipped him again and again across his back and legs, leaving him shaking and sobbing. When he'd finished, he looked down at Carl and sneered.

'Take the money and get out of my flat. If I ever see your face again, I'll kill you.'

He put his belt on and kicked Carl in the stomach, then ran his hands through his hair, brushed himself down and left the room.

* * *

George was at the bar speaking to Tommy and Smudge when Maureen came over.

'I just seen Carl leavin' in 'is car,' she said, looking concerned.

'That tart he brought to the wedding gave him the boot and he's gone running after her.'

'Fuckin' bitch. Wait till I get me 'ands on 'er!' Maureen snapped, her eyes filled with rage.

* * *

Teflon parked up outside Jane's block of flats and got in the back of the cab with her.

'Come on, stop beating yourself up about Carl.'

'I can't help it.'

'Are you sure you've never seen Tony Nichols before?'

'Nowhere I can think of.'

'Like you said, he might be mistaken, but it does sound like he sussed you were Old Bill. You're going to have to tell Murphy.'

'I know.'

'Granted he'll be pissed off, but at the end of the day he chose to send you in there. What you did took a lot of guts.'

'I feel like shit about what I've done to Carl. George Ripley's used him as a punchbag for years. If he so much as thinks I'm a police officer, I dread to imagine what he might do to Carl.'

'Look, I know it's tough, but sometimes when you're doing UC work, people on both sides get hurt. At the end of the day you were doing your job.'

'That's easy to say.'

'You have to forget about Carl; think about why we're doing this. We're trying to put away some violent criminals. There's going to be a few tears along the way.'

CHAPTER THIRTY-FOUR

Jane tossed and turned in her sleep, dreaming that she was walking through London Fields late at night, when suddenly a man in a stocking mask jumped down from a tree with a knife in his hand, and held it to her throat.

'Don't scream or I'll cut your throat,' he said, unzipping his trousers.

Terrified she was about to be raped, Jane kicked as hard as she could towards his groin, and the sudden jerking of her foot woke her up. Her heart was beating fast as she switched the light on, then went to the living room, picked up the phone and called Paul Lawrence.

'I'm sorry to bother you, Paul . . .'

'For Christ's sake, it's four o'clock.'

'I know, but this is really important.'

He let out a deep sigh. 'Go on then.'

'You remember years ago when I was a decoy and arrested that rapist Peter Allard?'

'Yeah, he got off the rape but pleaded guilty to assaulting you.'

'That's right, then we nicked him for the murder of Susie Luna.'

'I'm not really in the mood for war stories—'

'Was his barrister a guy called Tony Nichols?'

'Let me think . . . Yeah, he was Queen's Counsel, but got disbarred about three years ago for false legal aid claims.'

'Do you know what he's doing now?'

'I haven't a clue.'

'Thanks. Sorry to bother you.'

'Wait a minute . . . What frying pan have you got yourself into now?'

'It's a long story, but Nichols is tied up with the Ripleys and our other suspects.'

'Did you get the message I left for you yesterday afternoon?'

'No, I was at a wedding.'

'The RUC got a match on the Chubb key to a Patrick O'Dwyer. He's got a criminal record for violence and was in the same UDA unit as Aidan O'Reilly. Looks like you were right about Fiona Simpson's death being linked to your investigation.'

'I'll let Murphy know. Thanks again, Paul.'

She put the phone down.

Jane thought about why she had failed to recognise Tony Nichols. She had only seen him once before the wedding, when he had cross-examined her for half an hour at the Old Bailey. Although it was six years ago, she now remembered he was chubby-faced, had greying dark hair with a side parting, and wore thick-rimmed gold glasses. Since then he had undoubtedly lost weight, dyed his hair black and, she assumed, replaced his glasses with contact lenses. It didn't seem to her to be a deliberate effort to disguise himself, more the act of a vain man who wanted to look younger.

* * *

Jane arrived at the office just after 9 a.m. Bax was the only one there, working at a desk catching up on his reports.

'How was the wedding?'

'A right den of thieves. I saw the Jensen – a disbarred barrister called Anthony Nichols owns it.'

'Makes sense.'

'I've got the registration for the Jensen. Can you do an owner check, please?' She gave him the details. 'Is Murphy in yet?'

'He was, but he got called out. There was an armed robbery at the Security Express depot in Shoreditch yesterday morning. The security guards were tied up and no one found them until this morning.'

'I didn't hear anything on the radio about it.'

'That's because the press haven't been informed yet.'

'What? Does Murphy think it's the Ripleys?' Jane asked with alarm.

Bax laughed. 'If it is, the whole squad will be back pounding the beat. Luckily Stanley and the Colonel were watching our four suspects play golf when it went down.'

'That's a relief. What happened at the depot?'

'All I know so far is four tooled-up blokes with dodgy Irish accents forced their way in there, tied up the guards and stole the money from the vault.'

'How much?'

'Four or five million, they reckon – in non-traceable notes.'

Jane let out a whistle of surprise. 'That's twice as much they got away with in the Great Train Robbery. Is anyone with Murphy?'

'Just Teflon,' Bax said.

'Do you think they'll need some help?'

'I wouldn't bother. It happened on our patch, but Murphy said he's going to hand the job over to the Tower Bridge team since we're tucked up with the Ripleys.'

'I may as well catch up with my paperwork, then.'

Jane went to her desk while Bax did the vehicle check.

'The Jensen's registered to Nichols. The address is fourteen Westbury Lane, Buckhurst Hill, which isn't far from George Ripley's house.'

*　*　*

Murphy and Teflon returned to the office just after midday.

'Well done on identifying our Camel Hair Coat Man.'

She looked at Teflon, realising he must have said something to Murphy.

'Could I have a word with you in your office, please, sir?'

'Yes, if you make me a black coffee first.'

She was putting the coffee powder in a cup when Teflon came over for a quiet word.

'He asked me what happened at the wedding on the way to the Shoreditch robbery. I told him you'd ID'd Nichols, but I didn't mention he might have sussed who you are.'

'I'm now positive he did.'

She poured the hot water in the cup.

'Shit. Why are you so sure?'

'Six years ago he was the defence barrister in a murder trial when I gave evidence. He's changed so much I didn't recognise him.'

'Then the Ripleys definitely know we're on to them.'

Jane nodded, picked up the coffee, and took it into Murphy's office. He was on the phone, but waved her in and pointed to a seat as he continued the conversation.

'One of them was dressed as a bloody priest and all the guards said they had Irish accents, which might have been faked. It was clearly well planned and executed, and they had insider information as they clearly knew the guards' routine. Anyway, I've got some statements I'll fax over to you now, then you can get one of your team to pick up the originals.'

Murphy put the phone down.

'That was the DCI at Tower Bridge. Tell me all about the wedding, then, and how you got the name of our Camel Hair Coat Man.'

Jane got straight to the point and told him about Anthony Nichols being a disbarred QC who knew she was a police officer.

'I had to come out when I saw Nichols speaking to George Ripley. Ripley was looking daggers at me.'

'I appreciate you being up front and honest, Jane. If I was in your shoes and a lone officer among the Ripley gang, I'd have been out of there in the blink of an eye.'

'I'm sorry if I've ruined the whole operation, sir.'

'Look, Jane, you did your job and got the information I asked for. Against the advice of some members of the team, it was my decision to send you in there alone, so the reality is I'm responsible for what happened – not you.'

What he said was reasonable, but she still didn't understand why he wasn't more pissed off about the way things had gone. They were never going to nick the gang on the pavement now.

'I've got an address for Nichols in Buckhurst Hill.' She handed him the details.

'As I see it, we're left with two options,' Murphy said. 'Nick them all now, or carry on with the surveillance for a few days and see what happens.'

'Paul Lawrence said the fingerprints on the Chubb keys matched a UDA man called O'Dwyer.'

'I know, I spoke to the DI investigating. His team are trying to locate O'Dwyer, but even if they do, I can't see him implicating O'Reilly in anything.'

'There's always Betty, the old woman who saw the getaway driver close up.'

Murphy nodded. 'DI Kingston spoke to me about her.'

'She's sharp as a tack and would make a good witness despite her age. I'm convinced she'd pick out Smith on an ID parade. Then there's Abby Jones . . .'

'That's a non-starter after the fiasco with her father.'

'But if we arrest the suspects and you spoke to him, he might be more willing to let Abby be a witness.'

'I'm aware of all the ifs and buts, thank you. I need to speak to the Commander. In the meantime, get Bax to call everyone in and ask Teflon to fax the statements over to Tower Bridge.'

*　*　*

Bax was gloomy as he picked up the phone.

'Sounds like he's going to arrest them today if he's calling everyone in. If we don't find some solid evidence connecting them to the Leytonstone robbery, I can't see how Murphy can charge them.'

'How'd he take the news about Tony Nichols?' Teflon asked her.

'I thought he was going to scream blue murder, but he basically said it was his fault.'

'Bloody hell, that's a first. I take it you didn't tell him about the date with Carl?' he whispered.

'No, and I'm not going to,' she whispered back. 'Carl Winter's not involved and doesn't have a clue about what George or the others have been up to. Can I have a read of the statements for the Shoreditch job after you've faxed them?'

He nodded. 'Wait till you see what they did to the supervising guard – it'll give you nightmares.'

* * *

Jane was sitting at her desk reading the statements in chronological order when Bax answered the phone.

'Jane, it's Paul Lawrence for you.'

He transferred the call to her.

'Hi. You still mad at me?'

'I wasn't mad . . . just bloody knackered. I made some enquiries about Anthony Nichols with a QC who's prosecuted a few murders I've given evidence in. He didn't know him personally, but made some phone calls. Apparently Nichols is working for a dodgy firm of solicitors—'

'I thought he was disbarred?'

'He was, but that doesn't stop him from overseeing cases or attending a police station as a suspect's advisor. He just can't appear in court as a legal representative.'

'The law's an ass. Did your friend know which firm?'

'Russell and Cartwright – they're in Curtain Road, Shoreditch.'

'Did you say Curtain Road?'

'Yes.'

'OK. Thanks, Paul.'

Jane grabbed the office Yellow Pages. She flicked through the directory to the Solicitors section and found the address for Russell and Cartwright, then phoned City Road Police Station and spoke to the duty sergeant. Her hunch was right: the offices of the solicitors' firm Tony Nichols worked for overlooked the Security Express depot.

She read through the statements slowly, making notes as she went. She thought the statement lacked fine detail and realised a local detective must have taken it, as the officer's name wasn't familiar to her. She wrote down the heights of the robbers as given by each guard. They all fitted within the range of the Ripley brothers, Graham Smith and, most notably, Aidan O'Reilly, who was six feet four. The supervisor said the man who threatened him had a deep voice, like George Ripley.

'Teflon, I need your help.'

He walked over to her desk. 'What with?'

'These statements. There's details here that make me think the Ripley gang may have done the Shoreditch job.'

Teflon laughed. 'You're becoming obsessed with them, Jane. They were all playing golf.'

'The heights of the men all fit, one had a deep voice and repeatedly used the word "son" in a colloquial manner – just like George Ripley does.'

'So do lots of people, Jane.'

She wasn't going to be put off.

'The supervising guard said in his statement that the tall man who was watching the TV monitor kept scratching his face through the balaclava. At the wedding I was in a group photo. Tommy was standing next to me and Smith and O'Reilly were directly behind me. O'Reilly had a red rash all over his face and Smith made a joke about it, then Tommy said, "Now we know why he prefers the soft touch of nylon."'

Teflon looked bemused. 'What's your point?'

'We know Aidan O'Reilly wore a stocking mask in the Leyton-stone robbery – stockings are made of nylon and balaclavas of wool,' Jane explained. 'If O'Reilly's allergic to wool, he would get a rash on his face.'

'So why would he wear a balaclava this time?' Teflon asked dismissively.

But Jane knew she had the answer to that.

'He had a cut to his head that would be visible through a stocking mask. A balaclava doesn't give away any features apart from eye colour, and both the supervisor and the guard, Archie, said the man with the sawn-off had blue eyes . . . just like—'

'Tommy Ripley,' Teflon said.

'Bax, how long did it take our suspects to play their round of golf?'

Bax looked in the observation log.

'They teed off at seven a.m. and were on the eighteenth at 10.50. Stanley said Smith was a shit golfer, so I would have thought they'd take a bit longer than that.'

'That's if they were actually playing golf,' Teflon said, catching on to Jane's idea. 'Does the Royal Epping golf club have woodland on it?'

'It's called the Royal Epping *Forest* – the clue's in the name,' Bax replied sarcastically.

'Can you look in the *A-Z* and see if there are any roads by the course that you could get to through the woods?' Jane asked Teflon.

'I'm on it.'

'What are you two doing?' Bax asked.

'Jane's on to something big,' Teflon said as he opened the *A-Z*.

'What?'

'I think the Ripley gang did the Shoreditch job,' she said.

Bax started to laugh but Teflon was on her side.

'She's serious, Bax, and there's evidence in the guards' statements that backs her theory up.' He looked at Jane. 'There's three roads with sections of woodland that lead to the course where they could have left and returned.'

'I reckon it would take about thirty to thirty-five minutes to get from the course to the Security Express depot in Shoreditch on a Saturday morning at seven o'clock,' Jane said.

'How could they leave the course and return nearly three hours later without other golfers seeing them?' Teflon asked.

Bax grinned. 'Easy. You just need to make sure there's nobody playing behind you when you go back on. When I was younger, we used to sneak on and off the local course and never got caught once.'

'Then they must have had someone in a vehicle parked up nearby waiting for them,' Teflon said.

'That makes five robbers, and the guards all said there were four,' Bax remarked.

'The driver would have stayed in the van while the others did the robbery,' Jane suggested. 'If they did, my guess is it's a guy called Patrick O'Dwyer. He's connected to O'Reilly and his prints were on Fiona Simpson's keys.'

Jane did some calculations on a piece of paper.

'The robbery started at eight o'clock, when the guard arrived at the depot. If they cut through the woods and got in a van on the second hole it would be about 7.15, which means they'd get to Shoreditch before eight and had at least two hours to do the robbery. If they left the depot at ten, they'd be back at the course by, say, 10.30 at the earliest to 10.45 latest.'

'Which would mean they'd have to sneak back on the course at the seventeenth or eighteenth to finish at 10.50,' Bax said.

Jane looked on the back of the supervisor's statement to check the provider's address and phone details. She picked up the phone and called him.

'Hello, is that Mr Bridge?'

'Yes, speaking.'

Jane turned on the speakerphone for Bax and Teflon to listen in.

'It's WDS Tennison from the Flying Squad. Some of my colleagues were with you this morning.'

'What can I do for you, officer?'

'I'm sorry to bother you after such a traumatic experience. I just need to ask you a couple more questions about the robbery.'

'Certainly – I'll do whatever I can to help catch those bastards.'

'You said in your statement that the man with the deep voice, the one who threatened you, had a gold-coloured lighter in his hand.'

'Yes, that's right.'

'Was it butane gas, or a fluid lighter like a Zippo?'

'Definitely gas – I watched the bastard light it in front of me, ' he said, a tremor in his voice.

'How did he light it?'

'The way you do any lighter – by flicking the spark wheel with your thumb.' He sounded bemused by the question.

'And was the spark wheel on the top or side of the lighter?'

'The side.'

'Could you see if it had any writing on it?'

'No, his hand was covering it.'

'Can you describe the lighter to me in detail?'

'It was about two or three inches long, an inch wide and chunky-looking.'

'Thanks for your time, Mr Bridge.' She put the phone down.

'What was that about?' Bax asked.

'I've seen George Ripley use a gold lighter with his initials engraved on it in the cafe.'

'That doesn't mean the man who threatened the supervisor was him,' Bax replied.

'George's lighter also had a spark wheel on the side.'

'It's just a bloody lighter – it doesn't prove anything.'

'I know it was George Ripley,' Jane said tersely.

Bax sighed. 'No, you don't. They all wore masks, so none of the guards can identify them. Everything you've said is valid, Jane, but it's guesswork – not bloody evidence.'

'Bax is right, Jane. If no one saw them leave or return to the golf course, then Stanley and the Colonel have unwittingly given them the perfect alibi.'

CHAPTER THIRTY-FIVE

By midday the Rigg Approach office was filled with another fifteen detectives from the Tower Bridge Flying Squad, who had been
called in to assist the arrest operation. Most of them were carrying
revolvers in side holsters and everyone in the room was tense, waiting for Murphy to address them.

Jane had already spoken to Murphy about the Ripleys, and
explained why she thought they were responsible for the Security
Express robbery. He agreed there were parts of her analysis that
pointed to them being responsible, but he felt her theory was based
on conjecture and worried that she was making the suspects fit
the crime. He told her that, although he had decided to arrest the
Ripleys, Smith and O'Reilly, the only way they could prove the
Ripleys themselves were responsible for both robberies was to find
some actual physical evidence, at their homes or work premises,
connecting them to the robberies.

Jane realised she was the only female in the room and overheard
one of the Tower Bridge officers say he hoped he wasn't with the
'plonk' when they made the arrests. It made her hope she would be
the one to arrest George Ripley or Tony Nichols.

Murphy came out of his office with the Tower Bridge DCI and
DI Kingston. The room went quiet.

'Firstly, I'd like to thank the Tower Bridge officers for coming out
to assist us with the arrests.'

'Don't worry, Guv, we'll happily show your lads how it's done,' a
Tower Bridge officer called out and his colleagues laughed.

'Yeah – and pigs might fly,' the Colonel retorted.

Murphy waited for the laughter to subside.

'I know, as dedicated Flying Squad officers, you would have
wanted this to be an operation where we carried out an armed

ambush on the suspects while they were committing the crime. However, circumstances beyond our control have dictated that we arrest them today in a co-ordinated hit that will take place at two p.m. precisely. I have split you into teams and armed officers from my squad will lead each team and make the arrests, supported by officers from Tower Bridge. Me and DI Kingston will arrest George Ripley at his home address, DS Stanley, Graham Smith at his home address and DC Baxter, Tony Nichols at his home address.'

'Yes, Guv,' they replied almost in unison.

'Our SOCO is presently working undercover in the Bruce Grove Snooker Hall and called me just before the briefing. Tommy Ripley, Aidan O'Reilly and Maria Fernadez are all there, apparently looking like they've got almighty hangovers from the wedding. The Colonel and Cam, with extra backup, will arrest them.'

'What if any of them leave before we get there?' the Colonel asked.

'Dabs is going to come out of the hall at five minutes to two and meet you outside the sorting office in Moorfield Road with an update. I want two teams from Tower Bridge to hit their home addresses at the same time. I've arranged for uniform officers to go to the garage at two p.m. and secure it, then we can search it later.'

Jane and Teflon looked at each other, wondering what they would be doing.

'WDS Tennison and DC Johnson will arrest Carl Winter. He, like Maria Fernandez, may or may not be involved in the planning or commission of the robberies, but they could be a useful source of information – especially Winter.'

Teflon could see that Jane was about to say something.

He gave her a discreet dig with his elbow and whispered, 'Don't say a word or he'll crucify you in front of everyone.'

'I want all the suspects taken to Leytonstone Police Station for interrogation, and continual updates given to me over the radio throughout the operation. Any questions?'

There were none.

Murphy went to his office with the Tower Bridge DCI and Kingston to have a quick glass of whisky before the armed operation.

Teflon took Jane to Dabs's office to speak to her.

'Not letting us be involved in any of the main suspects' arrests is Murphy's way of punishing us for what happened with Abby Jones.'

'Carl is not in any way, shape or form a criminal,' Jane said angrily. 'I should be the last person to have to arrest him and Murphy knows that.'

'Stop feeling sorry for yourself. Murphy's arresting Carl for the right reasons, not to spite you. Even if it was someone else on the team making the arrest, it's inevitable during questioning Carl will find out you're a police officer. If you feel so bad, then this is your opportunity to make him realise you meant him no harm and were just doing your job.'

* * *

Dabs met the Colonel outside the sorting office just before 2 p.m. and told him that O'Reilly was in Tommy's office and Fernandez was still behind the bar. The Colonel radioed Murphy.

'Gold from KG, receiving . . . over?'

'Go ahead . . . over,' Murphy replied.

'All three targets still in hall.'

'All units from Gold, are you in position?'

He waited until the last unit responded.

'Attack, attack, attack!' Murphy shouted.

* * *

A traffic police Land Rover pulled up outside the gates of George Ripley's house. The passenger jumped out and quickly connected a cable to the gates.

'Go, go, go!' he shouted.

The Land Rover drove off at speed, ripping the gates from the brick pillars.

George was in his study and heard the noise. Looking out of the window he saw Murphy and his team coming down the driveway, sirens blaring. George grabbed the phone to call Tommy.

The unmarked police cars slid through the gravel as they came to a halt. An officer jumped out with a battering ram and smashed it against the Yale lock on the door, which splintered and flew open.

Murphy, Kingston and two other armed officers raced in, shouting, 'Armed police! Stay where you are!'

Tommy didn't answer. George put the phone down, calmly picked up the *News of the World* and started reading it as Murphy and Kingston rushed in, pointing their guns at him.

'Don't fucking move, George,' Murphy said.

He smiled and slowly put the paper down.

'If you'd rung the doorbell, I'd have let you in. Who should I send the repair bill to?'

Kingston holstered his gun and got his handcuffs out. George put his arms out and held his wrists together ready to be cuffed.

'Is the lovely Jane not with you?'

Murphy and Kingston ignored him.

'Is she a good fuck?' George smirked.

Kingston punched him hard in the stomach, knocking the wind out of him.

'George Ripley, I am arresting you on suspicion of armed robbery. You are not obliged to say anything unless you wish to do so, but what you say may be put into writing and given in evidence.'

'You ain't got fuck all on me,' he gasped, then spat on the ground at Kingston's feet and got another hard punch to the stomach for his disrespect.

As they led him towards the front door, the normally truculent Maureen stood quietly in the hallway. She'd known the day would

come when George would be arrested again. This time she hoped
they had enough evidence to lock him up and throw away the key.

'Maureen, phone Tony Nichols and tell him I've been nicked,'
George told her.

She nodded.

'Save yourself the bother, luv – Tony Nichols will be in the cell
next to him,' Murphy said with a satisfied smile.

* * *

Tony Nichols was returning to his house with his wife after a pub
lunch. She was driving her BMW and he was in the passenger seat.
As they approached their house, he suddenly pulled the lever to
drop the seat back so he couldn't be seen.

'Keep going, don't park at the house,' he snapped, having spotted
the unmarked police cars nearby.

'Why? What's wrong?'

'Just do as I say – keep going.'

When they were well away from the house, he told her to stop.

'Go back on foot. If the CID come calling, tell them you've been
out for a walk and you don't know where I am.'

She looked scared. 'What have you done now, Tony?'

'Just give me the bloody keys and do as I say. I'll call you later.'

* * *

The Colonel and his team walked casually into the busy snooker
hall, their guns held by their sides. Dabs pointed to Tommy's office
at the end of the room while Cam arrested Maria Fernandez. Two
armed officers followed the Colonel. When they were just a few
feet from Tommy's office door it was opened by Aidan O'Reilly. He
quickly tried to shut the door, but the Colonel put his shoulder to
it and they barged in.

'Armed police! Stay where you are!'

The Colonel pointed his revolver at Tommy Ripley, who was sitting at his desk with his hands in the air. The Colonel looked around for Aidan. A door behind Ripley was open, leading to a fire escape stairwell. He ran across the room and could see him halfway down the escape. He shouted for him to stop and sprinted after him, but by the time the Colonel was halfway down O'Reilly was nearly at the bottom.

'Bollocks!' the Colonel said to himself, climbing over the railing. 'Why didn't we know there was a bloody fire escape?'

Holding his gun in one hand, and with the other gripping the railing, he launched himself off just as O'Reilly stepped onto the tarmac and managed to knock him to the ground. As the Colonel tried to stand up, his ankle gave way and he collapsed in a heap. O'Reilly was back on his feet and reaching into his jacket pocket.

'Don't do it!' the Colonel shouted.

'Fuck you!'

O'Reilly pulled out a Luger handgun.

The Colonel lifted himself up into a half sit-up position, then fired three rounds into O'Reilly's chest before the Irishman could get off a shot of his own. O'Reilly was dead before he hit the ground.

* * *

Jane trudged up the threadbare stairs behind Teflon and knocked on the door of Carl Winter's flat, but there was no answer. Teflon called Murphy, who told them to wait in the car for Winter to return.

Half an hour passed before they saw a forlorn-looking Carl shuffling up the road towards his flat, carrying a suitcase. As he got closer Jane could see his nose was swollen and he had a cut beside his left eye. Teflon said what Jane was thinking.

'Looks like George took his anger out on Carl.'

'And it's my fault,' she added.

'Give him a minute to go up to his flat.'

*   *   *

Jane knocked on the door and Carl opened it. She held up her warrant card.

'We need to speak to you, Carl.'

He looked at her in amazement. He seemed close to tears.

'I'm sorry, Carl, I never meant to hurt you. Did George hit you because he found out I was a police officer?'

Carl didn't say anything. He just kept looking at Jane.

'We've arrested him,' Teflon said.

'Good. I hope he goes to prison for ever.'

Teflon went to search the bedroom and let Jane be alone with Carl.

'I had a job to do, Carl. But it turned out I enjoyed your company. You're a nice guy.'

In the bedroom Teflon saw an empty suitcase on the bed and next to it Carl's clothes, neatly folded and laid out ready to be packed. He noticed a brown A4 envelope by the pillow and looked inside.

'Jane, have you got a second?' he called out.

He held up two large wads of cash and whispered, 'There's two grand here, and he was about to pack his case.'

Jane felt her head spin, wondering if Carl was not the straightforward man he appeared to be.

'I think he's had you fooled. We need to arrest him,' Teflon said.

'No, there has to be an explanation. Let me talk to him first.'

She took the money from him.

'Have it your way, but when I've finished searching this room, I'm nicking him.'

As Jane left the room, Teflon opened the door in the corner of the bedroom and saw that it led to a small bathroom, with a shower, basin and toilet. He closed the door and unzipped his pants.

'Where did you get this money, Carl?' she asked, showing it to him.

'George gave it to me. He told me to get out of his flat and never come back.'

'Is that the truth?'

She put the money on the table.

'Look what he did to me,' he said, taking off his shirt.

She gasped when she saw the red and blue welts all over his torso. He had been lashed so hard the belt and buckle had cut into his skin, leaving imprints of their shape.

Jane was so transfixed she wasn't aware Tony Nichols had crept into the flat and was listening to the conversation from the kitchen. She put her hand to her mouth.

'Oh my God, Carl. What have I done?'

'It wasn't your fault.'

'Of course it was. Tony Nichols told him who I am and he took it out on you.'

Carl sniffed. 'I know where George and Smudge hide things.'

'What things?'

'Stuff they steal.'

Nichols quietly picked up a large carving knife from the kitchen counter, then crept up behind Carl and plunged it hard into his back before Jane even knew what was happening. Carl fell to the floor, groaning and gasping for air as blood pooled around him. Jane instinctively moved forward to help him but Nichols pointed the knife at her, making her back off. She stopped herself from glancing towards the bedroom, hoping Nichols didn't know Teflon was with her. Nichols picked the money up and put it in his coat pocket.

'I couldn't let him tell you where the money is – and I'm afraid I can't let you tell anyone what I've done,' he said menacingly, as he moved slowly towards her.

'Don't hurt her,' Carl moaned, making a feeble attempt to get up, but he'd already lost too much blood.

Jane wondered why Teflon hadn't come to her aid and then she heard the toilet flush. Nichols realised she wasn't alone and raised the knife. She screamed for help as she kicked the small coffee table towards him, making him stumble. She lunged forward and grabbed his right hand with both of hers. She tried to pull him forward and down to the ground, but he was stronger than her and managed to regain his balance.

Teflon was just washing his hands when he heard Jane scream. He grabbed a large bottle of Brut aftershave off the bathroom shelf and ran into the lounge. Nichols had broken free of Jane's grasp, and was about to stab her with the knife when Teflon smashed the bottle over his head, knocking him to the ground. He punched Nichols repeatedly in the face until he was totally subdued. Jane rushed to Carl's aid as Teflon turned Nichols over and cuffed his hands behind his back.

'Get an ambulance!' she shouted.

Teflon ran to the car to use the radio. Jane knelt over Carl, who was still lying on his back, his face pale.

'I'm going to try and stop the bleeding, so I'll need to turn you over.'

There was a look of fear in his eyes.

'Jane,' he whispered, and she leant closer to him. 'It's in the pit.'

His breathing was shallow and erratic, and he started to cough up blood.

'All that doesn't matter now. You need to stop talking and concentrate on your breathing.'

She rolled him over, grabbed a towel from the kitchen and applied pressure to the stab wound on his back. Teflon came back into the room.

'An ambulance and uniform officers are on their way. How is he?'

'Not good,' Jane said. 'His breathing's getting shallower and he's cold to the touch. Take over doing this, please.'

Jane moved around so she could see Carl's face and try and keep him awake by talking to him. She got on her knees and leant forward.

'You're going to be OK, Carl. You can use the money to buy a van and start your own business now.'

But there was no movement to suggest he could hear her. Teflon felt for a pulse, but it was weak. Jane could hardly hear him breathing and his eyes were fluttering. She held his hand.

'We could go for another meal, Carl . . . maybe Italian this time. Do you like Italian?'

His eyes closed and his body went limp. Teflon felt for a pulse.

'I'm sorry, Jane . . . he's dead.'

Jane started to rock back and forth on her knees as the tears ran down her face.

'No, no, no . . . What have I done?'

Teflon helped her up and held her as she wept on his shoulder.

CHAPTER THIRTY-SIX

Teflon used the radio to request CID from Stoke Newington, and a lab liaison sergeant, attend Carl's flat as it was now a murder scene. He then called Murphy and told him what had happened. When he heard Jane was suffering from shock he told Teflon to take her home – or even better, to her parents' or sister's so they could look after her.

'O'Reilly's dead as well,' he added.

A uniformed van took Nichols to Leytonstone Police Station, and when the local DI arrived Teflon filled him in.

'Is she all right?' the DI asked, looking at Jane.

She was sitting in the car with Carl's blood on her hands and clothes, looking numb and staring into space.

'Nichols was going to kill her. It scared the shit out of her, but she's a tough cookie. She'll come through it.'

Teflon didn't want anyone to know the real reason behind her troubled state of mind.

'Lucky you were there, then,' the DI remarked.

'Yeah, I guess so.'

Teflon got in the car and said her name, but she didn't respond. He gently shook her arm.

'Jane?'

She slowly turned her head and looked at him.

'He said it was in the pit.'

'You have to stop thinking about Carl, Jane. You're in shock and need someone to look after you. Murphy wants me to take you to your family. Where do your parents live?'

'I don't want to go there,' she said, sounding more coherent.

'Murphy said—'

'I don't care what Murphy said. Carl's last words were: "It's in the pit." If he knew where George and Smudge hid it, then it makes sense it was at their house or the garage.'

'It could be anywhere, Jane. Murphy is having every suspect's house and work premises ripped apart by search teams. If the money's there they'll find it.'

'What do you think he meant by "the pit"?'

Teflon shrugged. 'If he's a mechanic then it could be the vehicle examination pit in the garage.'

Jane nodded as it suddenly all fell into place.

'Nichols came here for the garage keys because he knew Carl had a set. He was going to take the money for himself . . . We need to go to George's garage right away.'

'Murphy's in charge of the searches and has the garage under control.'

'Carl wanted me to find the money.'

'I'll go and get the keys from Carl's flat.'

He shook his head in disbelief at what he was doing.

*   *   *

When the Colonel saw the Luger next to O'Reilly's body, he realised why he'd run. He didn't want to be caught with a gun that ballistics would match to the bullets recovered at Woodville Road after he'd shot one of the police officers in the area car.

*   *   *

Tommy Ripley said nothing and didn't resist arrest. When he was being booked in at the station he demanded to see his solicitor. His jaw nearly hit the ground when he saw a bloodied and beaten Tony Nichols brought into the custody suite in handcuffs. The PC who'd brought Nichols in told the custody sergeant he'd been arrested for the murder of Carl Winter. Tommy exploded with rage and before anyone could stop him, he lunged at Nichols, punching him so hard it broke his nose and knocked him unconscious.

* * *

The other man in Tommy's office at the time of his arrest had an Irish accent. He told the Colonel his name was Danny Grogan and he was just having a friendly chat with Tommy and Aidan. There was something about Danny the Colonel didn't like, so he arrested him. As soon as they arrived at the station, Dabs took a set of fingerprints from Danny and checked them against Patrick O'Dwyer's – they were a match.

* * *

Graham Smith was out for a drive in the countryside with his wife when Stanley and his team forced entry to his house. Smith returned home just after 3 p.m., casually parked his car in the driveway, got out, and with a look of disdain said, 'How can I help you, officers?' When they arrested him, just like Tommy, he said nothing.

* * *

Teflon unlocked the servicing garage, opened the large metal sliding door and switched the lights on. There was a green Ford Transit van over the inspection pit with keys in it. As Teflon got in and reversed it out, Jane saw some mechanic's disposable gloves in a box on a worktop and pulled four out. She handed Teflon a pair.

'We'd better put these on, so we don't leave our prints on anything.'

They stood side by side and looked down into the long, eight-foot deep inspection pit. It had a concrete base and small drainage hole, with sheet metal sides. Teflon grabbed a crowbar, a hammer and some screwdrivers from the toolbox.

'If it's hidden down there it'll be behind the metal. Ladies first,' he said with a grin.

Jane climbed down the steps and started knocking on the metal on one side of the pit while Teflon did the same on the other side. At the far end Jane noticed a change. It suddenly sounded hollow.

'I think it's hidden behind this section.'

The piece of sheet metal was three feet square and held in position by Phillips screws. Teflon handed Jane one of the screwdrivers and they undid the screws together. When they removed the sheet there was a square hole. Teflon picked up the inspection pit lamp, turned it on and handed it to Jane.

'Carl wanted you to find the money.'

She held the light by the entrance and could see a large open area to the right that stretched back a good six or seven feet. She felt nervous; it was as if she was about to enter a tomb looking for hidden treasure. She crouched down, moved forward a few inches, then stopped and looked back at Teflon.

'Do you think it might be booby-trapped?'

He shrugged and Jane moved forward, then held the lamp up and her eyes opened wide at what she saw. She was overjoyed, yet filled with sadness, knowing how Carl had led her here. She unzipped one of the holdalls, which was filled with banknotes. After a quick look in a smaller holdall she shuffled backwards out of the hole.

'It's an Aladdin's cave in there. There's holdalls filled with cash, balaclavas, guns, a priest's outfit, a fake beard and boiler suits.'

She handed the lamp to Teflon to have a look.

His voice echoed from inside.

'There's a sawn-off shotgun in a plastic bag and some screwed-up Security Express van logos as well – they must have put them on the van they used at the Shoreditch job.'

Jane was grinning from ear to ear.

'We got them, Teflon. George, Tommy and the rest of the gang will be going to prison for a long time.'

* * *

Jane and Teflon went to see Murphy at Leytonstone. He was over the moon when he heard what they'd found at the garage.

'Well done, you two. We've got those bastards bang to rights now.'

'Would you like us to help with the interviews?' Jane asked.

'It's all right, me and DI Kingston will do them. You two can go back to Rigg Approach and write up your statements, then have the bank holiday Monday off.'

Jane realised that Kingston, having arrested George Ripley, couldn't have been involved with him or Tommy, as any connection to them would have been exposed by the brothers. It was also clear he was not involved in the death of Fiona Simpson. She was glad she'd been wrong about him, and realised that subjective suspicion is worthless without objective evidence to back it up. She didn't think the Colonel was corrupt, but he was a tad dishonest when it came to paying an informant a small amount of money and she decided to tell him not to do it again.

* * *

As Jane and Teflon walked out of the front of the station, they saw Maureen Ripley getting out of her car. As soon as she saw Jane, she exploded with rage.

'You fuckin' bitch! My son is dead because of you! I 'ope you rot in 'ell!'

She ran forward and spat in Jane's face. Jane wiped the spit off with her jacket sleeve and walked on.

'Don't walk away from me, you cow!' Maureen screeched, grabbing Jane by the wrist.

Jane pulled free of her grip, spun around and pushed Maureen up against the wall with the palm of her hand.

'I'm not proud of what I've done, but your son is dead because of George, not me. Tony Nichols stabbed Carl to stop him telling us where the money from the robberies was hidden. I watched a decent, kind man die because your husband is a filthy criminal. Carl told me you did nothing to stop the beatings he suffered from George – all because you liked the high life. Well, now you've got nothing but misery and shame ahead of you.'

As Jane walked away, Maureen stood frozen with shock. Then she started to cry, knowing what she'd been told was the harsh truth.

* * *

It was midday on the Monday and Jane was getting ready to go to her parents' for lunch when the phone rang.

'Sorry to spoil your day,' a gloomy Teflon said, 'but Murphy wants to see us right away in the office.'

'Why, what's happened?'

'The Ripley job's gone pear-shaped – Tony Nichols is alleging our search of the garage was illegal under Judges' Rules.'

'That's rubbish.'

'Murphy's fuming. Because we knew there was no one there on a Sunday and weren't making an arrest, we should have got a warrant.'

'But we were searching as a direct result of their arrests and didn't need one!'

'That's what I thought ... If the cash, guns and other stuff we found is ruled inadmissible as evidence, the whole lot of them will walk out of court free men – apart from Nichols.'

Jane was mortified.

'I'll be there in half an hour.'

She phoned her mother. 'I have to go into work, but hopefully I can come over later.'

'That's all right, dear. I'll keep a plate of food for you and warm it up when you get here. I read in this morning's paper about those men you arrested for the Security Express robbery. You must feel so proud.'

'I did, but it looks like I've messed up and they could get off.'

Jane heard an intake of breath on the other end of the line.

'Oh dear, that doesn't sound good.'

*　*　*

Jane trudged up the stairs to the office, knowing that Murphy was going to give her hell and probably then kick her off the squad. She opened the door and walked in.

'Welcome to the party, Treacle!' the Colonel shouted, raising his beer can.

Jane looked around the room. The whole squad was there, smiling and raising their cans.

'You bastard, Teflon – you had me worried sick!'

'I knew it would get you here quickly.' He grinned.

'We always have a piss-up after a good result and thought you needed cheering up,' Stanley said.

Murphy tapped his beer can on the table to get everyone's attention.

'I want to thank you all for your hard work over the last few days – especially you, Jane. We wouldn't have been able to charge the Ripley gang if it hadn't been for your tenacity and attention to detail. Welcome to the Flying Squad.'

He raised his glass, then everyone clapped and cheered loudly and toasted her. Teflon opened a can of lager and handed it to Jane.

'Murphy's recommending the Colonel and me for the Queen's Police Medal for bravery,' he said.

'You deserve it – I wouldn't be here if it wasn't for you. Cheers!'

She tapped her can of beer against his.

'I was wondering if you'd fancy going out for a drink or to the pictures some time?'

'Yeah, I'd like that, but just on a friendly basis.'

'I'm fine with that,' Teflon agreed.

'We got you a little present, Treacle.'

The Colonel handed her a large rolled-up poster with a red ribbon tied around it.

Jane unrolled it and everyone laughed. It was a blow-up of the Ripley family and friends photograph taken at the wedding, with her smiling and surrounded by the gang of criminals. Above it was the heading: A ROSE AMONG THIEVES. The Colonel took it from her and pinned it to the wall next to the Dirty Dozen poster.

Dabs approached her. 'I had the pictures you took developed and thought you might like to have this one.'

It was the picture of a happy-looking Carl with his arm around Jane, taken by a guest at the wedding with Jane's camera. She felt herself welling up.

'Thank you, Dabs.'

Jane gently touched the photograph of Carl and put it in her bag. For the moment, she was enjoying the thrill of finally being accepted as one of the Flying Squad. But she knew that once the elation had worn off, she'd have to ask herself whether it really was the right job for her. She'd seen some things that she'd never be able to forget, however hard she tried.

'You've certainly changed your tune about Tennison,' Kingston said.

Murphy shrugged, taking out a bottle of Scotch and pouring two large glasses.

'She's a good detective, but a woman on the Flying Squad will always be a liability. She'd never have been able to take down O'Reilly or Nichols like the Colonel and Teflon did, or be any good in a street fight with people like the Ripleys. I'll be telling the Commissioner's office their little experiment isn't working and I'm asking for a male replacement.'

*   *   *

The office celebrations were in full swing and Jane was feeling a little drunk when she went over to the Colonel to have a quiet word in his ear about the ten pounds he'd pocketed.

'Why did you only give Gentleman Jim a tenner when it was supposed to be twenty?'

He smiled. 'You're a sharp cookie, Jane, but I didn't nick it. If I'd had to have paid Jim a score I would have, but I decided to front him out and gave the tenner back to Kingston. He didn't want it, though.'

'So, what did you do with it?'

'You're drinking it, Treacle.'

She smiled and wagged her finger at him. 'You're as slay as a fox, Cooonel,' she said, slurring her words.

Stanley turned the radio up and the sound of the Bee Gees' hit 'Stayin' Alive' filled the room. He jumped up on the table, then started doing point-and-shake moves and gyrating his hips like John Travolta. There was a loud cheer in the room, and everyone clapped and whistled to the music.

'Can you jive, Jane?' Teflon asked, holding out his hand.

'Can a duck swim?' She took hold of his hand.

There was a loud roar of encouragement from her colleagues as she did a walk-through move and a twirl with Teflon.

It suddenly hit her that despite their rough edges, they were not only a great bunch of guys, but bloody good at what they did. And one thing was guaranteed: there was never a dull moment in the Flying Squad.

Yes, she thought, *the Flying Squad is where I want to be.*

Lynda La Plante

Readers' Club

If you enjoyed *The Dirty Dozen*, why not join the
LYNDA LA PLANTE READERS' CLUB by visiting
www.lyndalaplante.com?

Dear Reader,

Thank you very much for picking up *The Dirty Dozen*, the fifth novel in the Jane Tennison thriller series. I've been so pleased by the response I've had from the many readers who have been curious about the beginnings of Jane's police career. It's been great fun for me to explore how she became the woman we know in middle and later life from the *Prime Suspect* series, and I hope you have enjoyed reading this book as much as I enjoyed writing it.

In *The Dirty Dozen*, Jane has started a new job in the Sweeney – a boys' club who dub themselves 'the Dirty Dozen'. Throughout her policing career, Jane, like many other women in the 1980s, has faced barriers to climbing the career ladder, and these difficulties are what have helped her to become the tough woman she is at the beginning of the book. The Sweeney is a whole different ballgame, though, and Jane really struggles to prove herself, before eventually being instrumental in taking down the criminals. As I've consistently said, I very much enjoy writing strong female protagonists, and it's been wonderful to have the opportunity to keep delving into Jane's story and to see her going from strength to strength in her policing career.

If you enjoyed *The Dirty Dozen*, then please do read the first four novels in the Jane Tennison series, *Tennison*, *Hidden Killers*, *Murder Mile* and *Good Friday*, which are now available in paperback, ebook and audio. The next book in the series, *Blunt Force*, will be published in August. There is also a lot more going on. I reworked my first ever novel, *Widows*, which was published in 2018, and was also turned into a major feature film written by Steve McQueen. I followed this up with *Widows' Revenge* and then *She's Out*. I'm now working on a whole new series, a spin off from *Widows*, with a central character who has really taken hold of my imagination. The first book in the new series, *Buried*, will be coming in April 2020 and I'm looking forward to sharing it with you all.

If you would like more information about what I'm working on, or about the Jane Tennison thriller series, you can visit www.bit.ly/LyndaLaPlanteClub where you can join My Readers' Club. It only takes a few moments to sign up, there are no catches or costs and new members will automatically receive an exclusive message from me. Zaffre will keep your data private and confidential, and it will never be passed on to a third party. We won't spam you with loads of emails, just get in touch now and again with news about my books, and you can unsubscribe any time you want. And if you would like to get involved in a wider conversation about my books, please do review *The Dirty Dozen* on Amazon, on GoodReads, on any other e-store, on your own blog and social media accounts, or talk about it with friends, family or reader groups! Sharing your thoughts helps other readers, and I always enjoy hearing what people experience from my writing.

With many thanks again for reading *The Dirty Dozen*. I hope you'll return for *Blunt Force* and my new series in 2020.

With my very best wishes,

Lynda

Read on for an extract from Lynda La Plante's
brand new book

BURIED

Coming April 2020

CHAPTER ONE

Rose Cottage had lain empty for eight months. It was a neat, two storey, white stone building with thick, black wooden lintels above the central front door and each of the five small windows – three up, two down. On the more sheltered, west side of the front wall, the ivy had completely taken over and was lifting the slate from the roof, but on the exposed east side, the stonework was bare and had been flattened by centuries of strong winter winds swirling down from the hills. From some angles the cottage looked as though it was leaning to the left.

As the cottage was rural, with stables and a hay barn, the land surrounding it had been fairly unkept even before it was left empty, but a small area directly outside the front door had been landscaped into narrow, winding footpaths circling rose beds. The wild roses, left to their own devices, were still fighting against the changing seasons, but today they looked particularly beautiful. In fact, they were the only real reminder of how lovely the cottage had once been.

Suddenly, the small downstairs windows to the left and right of the front door exploded under the immense pressure from the heat inside, sending glass and wood showering into the multi-coloured rose heads. Flames quickly took hold of the black wooden lintels and, within seconds, the smoke from the fire had blackened the white stone wall.

Inside, the furniture had been moved into the centre of the room, just in front of the hearth. A heavy wooden chest of drawers and two bookshelves surrounded a two-seater, horse-hair sofa, which had four occasional tables piled high on top of it. Some of the books from the bookshelves had been forced into the gaps of this makeshift bonfire, and the rest had been thrown into the hearth on top of a huge stack of paper.

The fire had taken hold extremely quickly, and the small lounge was soon consumed by flames, which rose to the ceiling beams, travelled to the wooden staircase and up the stairs. They eventually pushed their way out between the slate roof tiles from the engulfed wooden ceiling beams beneath, and it wasn't long before a spark leapt across to the hay barn, which was full of bales of hay, despite the horses being long gone. The barn went up like a roman candle and, from that point onwards, there was no stopping the fire.

* * *

A quarter of a mile away, in a small housing estate, the first of the 999 calls was finally made. Neighbours watched as the dark brown smoke billowed into the clear blue sky. When the house had been occupied, the smoke from the chimney had always been the expected light grey, but this was different. It looked heavy and rancid, and just kept coming.

Speculation was rife as to how the fire had started. Was it 'that bloody tramp' trying to keep warm again? Was it kids taking their games too far?

Fourteen 999 calls were made in total, sending two fire engines racing towards Rose Cottage from Aylesbury Fire Station. By the time the engines arrived, the contents of the cottage had almost gone and the hay barn was a pile of rubble and ashes. However, the stables, which were furthest away from the cottage, were still fully ablaze, with the flames heading for the surrounding trees.

When the fire brigade arrived, they split into two teams – one to tackle the fire inside, and a second on the stables to prevent the flames from jumping to the woodland beyond. The stables were easier to gain control of because, once the wooden frames had gone, there was nothing left to fuel the fire. The interior of the cottage, however, kept re-igniting as the fire found new fuel on the upper floors and from the wooden roof beams. It didn't take much to give the flames a new lease of life.

By nightfall, the grounds resembled a muddy swamp and the rose beds had been completely destroyed by four hours of torture from eight pairs of heavy fire boots walking backwards and forwards. Much of the furniture had been thrown into the front garden, to avoid further re-ignition inside the property, so the once beautiful rose garden looked like a fly-tipping site.

'Stop!' the Sub Officer shouted as he emerged through the hole that used to be the front door. 'Nobody goes back inside!'

Sub reached for his phone and dialled Sally Bown. It was late and the phone rang for quite some time before it was finally answered. 'Sal, this one's for you. We've got a body. Bring your CSI.'

* * *

Fire Investigation Officer, Sally Bown, arrived at the scene at 11 p.m. From the neck down, she was kitted out in her well-worn Fire Officers' Uniform, but from the neck up, she was immaculate. Her long brown hair was in a loose, low braided bun, held in place by an antique hairpin of white beads and silver leaves, and her light make up enhanced her natural beauty. The whole crew fancied her on an average day, so this post-bridesmaid look was definitely making their arduous night better. She didn't mind. They respected her position, so them watching her arse every now and then didn't bother her in the slightest.

'It's way better than men *not* watching my arse,' was her response to any woman who objected to the glib sexism that came from the male fire fighters. And Sally looked at them, too, so she thought it only fair.

At Sally's side was a child of a CSI with puffy eyes and bed hair. He carried a case almost as big as himself, and he stuck to Sally's side like glue. He wasn't quite used to shift work yet, but if he'd been called by Sally Bown, then he was good at his job. He'd learn the rest.

In the lounge of Rose Cottage, the pile of heavy wooden furniture was now destroyed. The brass hinges and handles from the chest of drawers lay on the floor, just in front of the hearth and, on the obliterated sofa, part-melted into the springs, lay a dead body, charred and blackened beyond recognition.

'Jesus,' muttered Sally, as she got out her camera and filmed the scene, starting at the front door and moving methodically towards the centre of the lounge and the dead body. Her young CSI waited outside until instructed to do otherwise.

'Sally, stop!' Sub shouted. Sally stopped dead. Sub was a man of very few words and everyone who worked with him knew that he only really spoke when he had something important to say. 'Retrace your steps, Sal. Now. Please.'

Sally didn't question his instruction. She started walking backwards, toe to heel, following exactly the same path as she'd taken to come in.

There was a deafening crack from directly above Sally's head. A hand grabbed her belt and she flew backwards with the force of a recoiling bungie rope, to be caught by Sub's waiting arms. Once he had a firm hold on her, he fell backwards onto the floor, taking Sally with him, and in the next split second an iron bedframe dropped through the air and landed right where Sally had been standing. A cloud of ash and debris flew into the air and took an age to come back down. When visibility returned, Sub was still seated on the floor, Sally between his legs and his arms gripped tightly round her waist. The two legs of the bed that were closest to them had smashed deep holes through the lounge floorboards, and the other two were straddling the remains of the sofa and the charred body, which was still, luckily, in one piece.

Sub momentarily tightened his grip around Sally's waist, before letting go completely. That tiny squeeze reassured her that she was safe and protected. As Sally gripped Sub's raised knees to use them as leverage to stand, and he eased her forwards with his hands politely in the small of her back, she couldn't help but think to herself what a massive shame it was that he looked so like her dad.

* * *

When he arrived on the scene, Detective Inspector Martin Prescott was frustrated to be held back from entering Rose Cottage until the risk assessment had been done. He couldn't imagine three more infuriating words in the English language than 'risk-fucking-assessment'!

Prescott had been Senior Officer to Sally Bown's older sister for more than twenty years, and so the families were naturally close. This was not unusual for rural Aylesbury, or for the local emergency services. Sally knew he'd be impatient, so, whilst the fragile ceiling and crumbling walls were shored up and made safe, she kept him occupied by showing him the video footage of the interior.

'We initially thought he could be a vagrant,' Sally told Prescott.

'He?' Prescott smiled as he corrected Sally's assumption. It was very clear from the video that there was no way of knowing the gender of the charred remains at this point.

Prescott always made Sally smile without even trying. She thought his thick Yorkshire accent made him sound happy, even when they were disagreeing with each other.

'Sorry,' Sally corrected herself. 'We initially thought that the body could be that of a vagrant unlucky enough to have set fire to himself after lighting candles to keep warm. There's no electricity in the cottage, and we found several tea lights scattered around the lounge – on the mantle and in the hearth – but when I looked more closely at the debris on the floor directly next to the sofa, it was clear that the furniture had been piled up around him. I mean, around the body.'

'So, the body was there first?'

'That's for you to decide, Martin.'

'Accelerant?'

'Undetermined as yet.'

Prescott was disappointed when the video footage ended. 'That all ya got?'

Sally started to play a second video, which began by showing the iron bedframe sitting squarely astride the sofa. Prescott closed his eyes and sighed heavily at the sight of his crime scene being buried under a double bed. The quiet breath he exhaled formed the words, 'fuck me!'.

Prescott took a moment to gather his thoughts. When he was thinking, his eyes flicked from side to side as though he were seeing the various scenarios flashing past inside his head. He appeared to be a very laid back man, but had an intensity bubbling away underneath the surface.

Sally knew that Prescott took this action because he was mildly dyslexic and, soon after joining the force, had made the decision to never write anything down in public. Instead, he had to remember everything, and in a brain that full, it could sometimes take a little longer to process what he was seeing. But Prescott was a clever man, and it was always worth waiting for him. He hid his intellect under Northern glibness, but Sally's older sister had shared all of his secrets with Sally over the years.

'Right, well, ya know the rules, Sal. It's a suspicious death, so I 'ave to assume murder til the evidence tells me otherwise.' Prescott walked away from Sally before she could counter and headed for Rose Cottage to see if he could at least peek in through where the widow had once been. 'And if it's murder, then I'm wastin' valuable time standin' out here doing naff all!'

Sally raced ahead and stood in his way, forcing him to stop. 'This may be your crime scene, DI Prescott, but you are *not* going into Rose Cottage until I say it's safe for you to do so.'

Prescott looked down at Sally. She was at least four inches shorter than him, but she was a feisty woman, just like her sister, and her calling him DI Prescott instead of Martin told him that she wasn't going to back down.

'And anyway . . .' Sally added, '. . . I hadn't finished.' Sally fast forwarded the second video, stopping it at seven minutes and thirty-two seconds. On the wall above the hearth the word PERVERT could be seen scrawled in red paint. It was mostly covered in a thick layer of black soot, but the letters could still just be made out. 'It looks like you could have a dead sex offender. And I doubt he got here on his own.'

Prescott got his vape out of his left-hand jacket pocket and said, 'See, I know that should make me feel better about havin' to wait to gain access to me crime scene. I mean, a dead perv 'int supposed to be as bad as a dead anybody else, but it just annoys me more. I don't know if that word relates to this dead body or not, do I? So now I'm more frustrated than before you showed me.' He dragged on the vape, but couldn't for the life of him get it to work. He put it back into his pocket and, from the other jacket pocket, he got a packet of cigarettes and a lighter. 'You follow ya rules and get that place scaffolded up asap and I'll be over 'ere shortenin' me life.'

* * *

Six hours had passed and Martin Prescott had been donned in a blue paper suit and shoes for the last fifty minutes. His white paper face mask sat round his neck as he watched Sally pointing at the partially collapsed roof and muttering to Sub. Sub nodded and Prescott immediately put on his mask. The man of few words had spoken.

Inside Rose Cottage, scaffolding held up the charred ceiling beams and the loose stones from the walls had been removed, leaving behind a relatively solid and safe structure. Visually, the scene was as Prescott expected, based on the preview he'd got from Sally's videos, but nothing ever prepared him for the smell of a body. The stench of burnt flesh and bones overpowers every other sense and, even through his face mask, he could smell and taste the distinctive miasma of 'long-pig'.

'Long-pig is what cannibals call human beings,' Sally had explained on their first ever meeting, more than fourteen years ago. 'By all accounts we taste like barbequed pork and, as we cook, we definitely smell like it.'

'Fuck me,' Prescott had mumbled through his face mask. 'No wonder you're single.' And from that day forwards, Prescott and Sally had got on like the proverbial house on fire.

Prescott and Sally paused just inside the jagged hole in the wall that used to be the front doorway of Rose Cottage and watched the dog handler lead her spaniel through the rubble. The dog wore tiny red canvas boots, velcroed in place around the ankles and with thick rubber soles that protected her paws from smouldering embers and sharp debris, allowing her to work safely and comfortably. The single repeated command of, 'show me, Amber,' was all that could be heard inside Rose Cottage.

Amber's handler kept her off the sofa, as the charred body was still there. The dog worked hard, sniffing and moving around the remnants of furniture. Her tail wagged, her tongue lolled, she jumped and rummaged, but she didn't make one single indication that an accelerant was present.

'Maybe the fire burnt intensely enough to destroy any accelerant?' Sally speculated. 'Or maybe a less common one was used. The dog only knows the most common ones, such as petrol or household flammables. Your Forensics people might still find accelerant on the items you collect.'

'I'll make sure I've got a tennis ball in me pocket if they do.' Prescott signalled for his blue suited CSIs to descend on the scene. He pointed at the sofa. 'There's a body in there, fellas, but it's goin' nowhere, so don't rush and don't compromise evidence just to get it out.'

A sea of nodding blue paper heads dispersed around the room and set about collecting anything and everything that might be useful – wood, brass hinges, plaster, bed springs. All items were individually double-wrapped into nylon bags to preserve any traces of accelerant.

Now that Prescott was inside his crime scene, he had the patience of a saint. He could see the wheels of the machinery turning, see his officers working and progress being made. He followed his CSIs deeper into the mess, allowing them to clear and preserve the way in front of him, and Sally followed after. This was *his* scene now, and she totally respected the shift in authority.

Eventually, and in relative silence, Prescott and Sally made it as far as the sofa. The iron bedframe, which was now gone, had missed the body when it fell. Even so, the body was massively damaged. The face was not only burnt down to the skeleton, but the cheekbones and lower jawbone were smashed and many of the teeth were missing.

'Could that damage to the skull be from falling debris?' Prescott asked.

Sally leaned in to get a better look. 'The ceiling was largely gone by the time we arrived, so God knows what might have fallen through and landed on the sofa. The cleaner looking skull fractures around the temple area could be heat stress. The skull can sometimes just pop, depending on the intensity of heat the fire achieves.'

'Damn shame this fella's teeth are so damaged,' Prescott commented, almost to himself. Then louder, 'Look at the bloody mess your lot has made of this place!'

Sally was just about to tear a strip of him when she looked at his partially hidden face. His eyes were crinkled at the edges and she knew he was smiling.

'Bloody fires,' Prescott continued, avoiding her gaze. 'If the flames don't destroy the evidence, the water does.'

Prescott scratched his head through his blue paper hood and his eyes flicked about again as he thought through everything he was seeing. 'If this is murder, we might be lookin' for someone who's savvy 'bout forensics, you know. I mean, you can't print burnt wood and you can't find shoeprints under water.'

He was suddenly distracted by the contents of the hearth. The water from the fire hose on the floor in this area of the room looked like thin black paint – a result you might expect to get after paper is burnt, creating a fine, soluble ash. Further back in the hearth, untouched by the water altogether, were the remnants of what looked like stacks of dry, charred paper. The paper was now nothing more than tiny fragments of its original form, but the volume was confusing.

Prescott picked up the longest of four fire pokers, and gently nudged the top layer of paper away in the hope of getting to some less burnt samples underneath. He tried not to damage any of the delicate paper. Eventually, he spotted a single, in-tact piece, no more than one centimetre in length, showing the instantly recognisable pale blue-green pattern from the bottom left hand corner of an old five pound note. Prescott carefully picked up this fragile piece of evidence and placed into the palm of Sally's gloved hand.

'It's cash, Sal. These stacks o' paper . . . it's all cash.'

* * *

Jack Warr was a strikingly attractive man. Thick, dark hooded brows hid the deepest brown eyes. He had a cleft chin, which showed the permanent shadow of impending stubble and, when he smiled, two long dimples appeared on either side of his mouth, running from his chin to his high, pronounced cheekbones. He had an effortlessly athletic physique that looked great in anything.

Maggie, his partner, always said it was a good job that his body was so amazing as he made no real effort with the clothes he dressed it in, but she fancied the pants off him no matter what he wore. It was those eyes that had got her in the first instance, though.

Eyebrows down, Jack's eyes would express such incredible intensity that if he told you he could take on David Haye and win, you'd believe him. Eyebrows up, he looked like a delicate, innocent soul that any woman would love to care for. This balance between man and boy was why Maggie loved Jack so much. He was her protector and her lover, her rock and her friend.

'Where's the jacket that goes with this shirt you've put out?' Jack shouted from the master bedroom. He liked to call it the 'master' bedroom, regardless of the fact that it was exactly the same size as the spare bedroom. The view over Teddington was what made it masterful, according to Jack.

Maggie didn't answer, so Jack was forced to go into the kitchen to find her. On the breakfast bar was a bowl of cereal and a cup of tea that she'd put out for him, on the back of his chair was his jacket and underneath were his shoes. Maggie's crooked smile said, 'Why do we do this every morning?'

Jack kissed and hugged her tightly. He never tired of just holding Maggie in his arms. She felt the same today as she had when they first met. Jack would maintain that Maggie's exceptional body was effortless, but she tried her very best to go to the hospital gym during every lunch break and, when Jack had the car for work, she'd leave herself enough time to walk to the hospital. For Maggie, this daily exercise was not only good for her body, but also hugely therapeutic, as it took her away from the stresses, pressures and horrors of being an F1 Doctor. Both Jack's and Maggie's jobs weren't always easy. Shift patterns and heavy workloads dictated that junk food was sometimes on the menu and, when they did get a rare day off together, they loved nothing more than going out for dinner, accompanied by casual drinking and a movie.

Maggie exercised to stay beautiful for Jack, and Jack did absolutely nothing to stay fit for Maggie. She was a health-conscious, thirty-four-year-old and he was a slobbish thirty-six-year-old. Maggie, in stark contrast to Jack's 'Heathcliff' look, had blonde hair and blue eyes. Jack adored the way she looked when she rolled out of bed in the morning, with her hair ruffled and her pale, flawless skin unhidden by make up. She was the most beautiful woman he'd ever seen, and would ever see. He had eyes for no one but her.

Maggie had just come off a night shift on the Orthopaedic Ward at the New Victoria Hospital. She was three weeks into her new rotation and, regardless of always coming home exhausted, she still got Jack ready for work before she went to bed. By the time he got home that night, she'd be gone again, so this hug had to last him at least twenty-four hours. Jack nuzzled Maggie's neck. He normally hated the way she smelt when she came home from work – the horrific combination of alcohol hand sanitizer, that chemical smell that hangs in the air in hospitals, moth balls and, occasionally, vomit – but this morning he was running late, so she'd already had time to shower and, therefore, smelt of tangerines.

Fourteen months previously, Maggie and Jack had agreed that moving from Devon to London was the right thing to do for her career. His career, in his words, wasn't as big a deal as hers. Maggie knew she wanted to be an Orthopaedic Surgeon, whereas all Jack really knew for sure was that he wanted to be able to go and watch Plymouth Argyle whenever they played at home. Jack wasn't lazy, but rather discontent. Restless. And, as he explained it, at a cross-roads.

At thirty-six, Jack should, by now, have been a Detective Inspector at least, rather than a lowly DC. When Maggie had asked Jack if they could move to London for her career, he'd said, 'Sure. Gang wrangling will be a bit like sheep wrangling, I expect. Only with knives.' Maggie had asked Jack what it was he truly wanted, and all he could come up with was 'you', which, although lovely, wasn't very helpful. Then he'd answered more seriously, 'I want that look I see in your eyes when you put that stethoscope round your neck. You're proud of what you do, Mags. You're excited. I want to feel excited.'

London was, in fact, a huge risk, both emotionally and financially, but Jack's commitment to Maggie made it the right decision. They knew no one in the South East and, although Maggie could make a lifelong friend in a supermarket line, Jack was more standoffish. He didn't care about friends – he had Maggie – but the money was a worry. They went from having both time and cash to spend at the end of the month, to being skint ships that passed in the night. And they had to plan two months in advance for any extra expenditure – for example the car's MOT. Maggie dealt with all of this, though. She was the organiser, and she was the one who never panicked when the account turned from black to red.

Jack had agreed to make the life-changing move because he'd always known that Maggie was destined for greater things, and his indecisiveness couldn't be responsible for holding her back. As it happened, Jack's current boss, DCI Simon Ridley, had heard on the grapevine of Jack's transfer and had done a little digging. Jack's reputation in Devon was as a solid foot-soldier with an exceptional eye for detail and a natural ability to talk to people, read them and work out the best way to get what he needed from them. His interview technique was greatly admired, just never pushed to its limits in the small town of Totnes. Ridley had decided to give Jack the opportunity to find his path with the Serious Crime Squad, but very quickly worked out that Jack not being stretched in his previous role was less to do with the location and more to do with Jack's own lack of ambition. However, he was diligent and got on with his work, so Ridley had kept him on . . . for now.

* * *

It was Jack's turn to have the car that morning which, as he sat in a tailback on the A3 near Battersea, he was deeply regretting. His work mobile danced on the passenger seat, pinging and vibrating away as message after message came through, some from the App version of HOLMES, as case related information was shared, and some from DCI Ridley. HOLMES was the Bible for the police force and was normally installed and issued on tablets for use in Court or on cases. But the technology was unreliable, so many officers invested in top of the range mobile phones and installed HOLMES on them instead. It was allowed – just about.

As the pinging and vibrating continued, Jack smiled and shook his head as he imagined Ridley's messages. They would be perfectly spelt and punctuated instructions for the day. Jack knew that Ridley was in meetings all morning, which was why being a little bit late was no big deal. Jack would make the time up at the end of the day anyway, seeing as Maggie would be on her next night shift and he'd be going home to a cold bed.

Ridley led a divisional team of twelve Serious Crime officers. The case that Jack was currently working on started out with one young dad, who happened to be an engineer, realising that the baby monitor in his daughter's nursery was sending a signal to three devices, rather than the two he expected. The monitor had been hacked and an unknown person or persons were watching his daughter sleep.

Once the police had the geography of the rogue signals pinned down, the legwork had begun. Hundreds of hours tracing, interviewing, ruling-in and ruling-out every known paedophile and associate in the area. Over several months, they had discovered hundreds of hacked baby monitors, all within the same fifty mile radius. They visited 756 paedophiles, their friends and their families, and they narrowed the field to thirty-two. Then to one, a Donal Sweeney, who shared a cell with a man whose never-convicted, paedophile nephew sold baby monitors to highstreet stores.

It was 8.45 by the time Jack walked down the battleship grey corridor towards CID's shared office. There was nothing remotely dynamic about this part of the station. He paused in the canteen doorway, inhaled the coffee-bean air and diverted inside.

Jack slowly worked his way through all of his text messages and emails over an espresso and a croissant dipped in honey. Jack only drank coffee at work, because Maggie hated the smell and taste of it when he kissed her, and seeing as kissing Maggie was more important than caffeine, Jack did without coffee when he was at home. But Jack needed caffeine to get him through this bloody fraud case.

The canteen was bustling with uniformed officers. Some ate heavy meals, some light breakfasts, depending on where they were in their shifts. As Jack made himself a to do list from Ridley's text messages, he giggled through his croissant, sending a fine spray of loose puff pastry across the table. Ridley had written:

Laura's post-8 p.m. report overwrites yours, rather than adds to yours from yesterday morning. Please amend in the system. Print in triplicate and leave on my desk.

Ridley was the only man in the world who texted in full sentences. Jack sat back in his chair and, wiping the stubborn, buttery crumbs from round his mouth with the back of his hand, he looked around the canteen. He could hear snippets of conversations as officers talked about the cases they were on, the arrests they'd just made, the raids they were about to make. The amount of adrenalin and testosterone flying around Jack was dizzying, and hugely disappointing, because none of it was his. Jack knew that his team would be at their desks, focussed and driven to find the dirty bastard who was watching other people's kids sleep. So why was he late and sitting by himself in the canteen? The truth was that, no matter how friendly and welcoming Ridley's team was, Jack still kept them at arm's length.

Jack had gone from being a normal sized fish in a normal sized pond, to being a very small fish in the hugest pond in the UK – the Metropolitan Police Force. And he was out of his depth. After fourteen months of working at the MET, Jack still hadn't found his calling, his passion, his heart in London and, as the months ticked by, he honestly feared that he never would.

When Jack finally walked into the Squad Room, he froze in the doorway. *Shit!* Ridley was *not* in meetings all morning and Jack being a little bit late was a *very* big deal.

Ridley didn't acknowledge Jack's presence, and no one in the team dared look away from him whilst he was talking. This was an impromptu briefing, in response to a phone call from DI Martin Prescott over in Aylesbury.

'We've just been handed a house fire, in which the charred remains of an unknown person have been discovered, together with approximately two million pounds in old money – also burnt. This is being treated as murder, arson and robbery. It's come to us because it's looking like it could be connected to one of our old cases from '95 – the biggest train robbery this country has ever seen. No one was ever arrested and thirty million plus vanished without a trace. We're heading to Aylesbury in twenty minutes.'

Then, and only then, did Ridley look at Jack. Ridley's dark eyes were a frightening combination of anger and disappointment. 'You're with me,' he said, then headed into his office and slammed the door shut.

The team shuffled uncomfortably in their seats, wanting to offer sympathy but, equally, wondering what the hell Jack thought he was playing at by being so late. As Jack bowed his head in disgrace and wondered how this day could possibly get any worse, he spotted a blob of honey sliding down the front of his trouser leg. *That's fair*, he thought.

JANE TENNISON
from the very beginning

TENNISON

HIDDEN KILLERS

GOOD FRIDAY

MURDER MILE

The groundbreaking thriller from the Queen of Crime Drama

WIDOWS

Facing life alone, they turned to crime together.

Dolly Rawlins, Linda Perelli and Shirley Miller are left devastated when their husbands are killed in a security van heist that goes disastrously wrong.

When Dolly discovers her husband's bank deposit box containing a gun, money and detailed plans for the hijack, she has three options. She could hand over the ledgers to the detective. She could hand them over to the thugs who want to take over Harry's turf. Or, she and the other widows could finish the job their husbands started.

As they rehearse the raid, the women discover that Harry's plan required four people and recruit hooker Bella O'Reilly. But only three bodies were discovered in the carnage of the original hijack – so who was the fourth man, and where is he now?

Now a major feature film

WIDOWS' REVENGE

Dolly, Linda, Shirley and Bella are back. And this time it's a fight to the finish.

Against all the odds, Dolly Rawlins and her gangland widows managed the impossible: a heist their husbands had failed to pull off – at the cost of their lives.

But though they may be in the money, they're far from easy street.

Shocked by her husband's betrayal, Dolly discovers Harry Rawlins isn't dead. He knows where the four women are and he wants them to pay. And he doesn't just mean getting his hands on the money.

The women can't keep running. They have to get Harry out of their lives for good. But can they outwit a criminal mastermind who won't hesitate to kill?

Especially when one of them has a plan of her own . . . to kill or be killed.

Available now

SHE'S OUT

After serving a lengthy sentence for the murder of her husband, Dolly Rawlins is free from prison. And she's only got one thing on her mind: the diamonds she stashed before the police caught her.

But there are people waiting for Dolly on the outside. Tough ex-prisoners who know about the diamonds, and they all want a cut.

Also waiting for Dolly is DS Mike Withey. He holds her personally responsible for the death of his sister in the diamond raid ten years earlier. And he wants her back inside.

Dolly Rawlins has other plans. But can she realise the dream that kept her going all those years in prison and avoid those who are after her?

Available now

Want to read
NEW BOOKS
before anyone else?

Like getting
FREE BOOKS?

Enjoy sharing your
OPINIONS?

Discover

READERS FIRST
Read. Love. Share.

Sign up today to win your first free book:
readersfirst.co.uk